SONOMA

By Leonard Sanders

THE HAMLET WARNING
THE HAMLET ULTIMATUM
SONOMA

SONOMA

Leonard Sanders

Delacorte Press / New York

Published by
Delacorte Press
1 Dag Hammarskjold Plaza
New York, N.Y. 10017

Lyrics from "If You Go Away" by J. Brel and Rod McKuen:
© Copyright Edward B. Marks Music Corporation. Used by permission.

Manufactured in the United States of America

First printing

Designed by Terry Antonicelli

Library of Congress Cataloging in Publication Data

Sanders, Leonard.
   Sonoma.

   I.   Title.
PS3569.A5127S6   813'.54   80–22902
ISBN 0–440–08111–4

FOR FLORENE

ACKNOWLEDGMENTS

I wish especially to thank a good friend who conceived the original story, who was unstinting of his time, interest, and expertise throughout the writing of *Sonoma*; my editor, Linda Grey, who became involved early and who offered many valuable suggestions; and my agent, Aaron Priest, who brought the three of us together and whose enthusiasm never waned.

Also, I am grateful to authors Lawrence Lee and Paul Avery, who were so gracious with their knowledge and hospitality in San Francisco; vintner John Giumarra, Jr.; and author-connoisseur Robert Lawrence Balzer for delightful insights and conversation; and the many residents of Sonoma who shared their enviable life. I hope they find room for one more winery—albeit fictional—in their midst.

PROLOGUE

THE brilliant red of the new day was breaking over the peaks of the Hualapais as Patricio Schippoletti entered Kingman. Leaving Interstate 40 as it curved eastward, he drove north two blocks on the main drag, made a U-turn, and parked his rig across from the big McDonald's. He sat for a time drinking coffee, resting, idly watching as the waitresses, gangly with adolescence, scurried to keep pace with the breakfast traffic. Their collective, cheerful frenzy brought to mind what was waiting for him back home in Sonoma. There the morning bedlam would be beginning with a still-girlish mother who could not quite cope but kept trying. Patricio smiled. He was more than content with her efforts. As a matter of fact, he was counting the hours.

The wearisome, rough roads between Bakersfield and Barstow and the long stretch of desert across to Needles were behind him. A few more miles on Interstate 40 and he would be at the cutoff for a straight shot down to Phoenix. With four or five hours of sleep, a quick turnaround, and an empty rig, he should be home by noon, day after tomorrow. He still could keep his promise to take Naomi and the boys to the Festival parade Sunday afternoon.

The thought set him in motion. He left the restaurant and walked across the street to the rig, huge and impressive in the early morning light. As always, the sight filled him with quiet pride. Silvio Moretti himself had handed Patricio the keys to the truck four years ago. Across the big trailer, in large script, was the name Moretti, along with a large replica of the winery label. An identical, smaller decal decorated the cab door.

Patricio climbed into the cab, started the engine, and cautiously pulled back onto the main drag. He made the left turn onto Interstate 40 East and began building speed for the long climb into the mountains ahead. He was attuned to the machinery. He listened carefully for any hint of trouble. The rig was running smoothly despite the heavy load. The manifest, destined for a wholesaler in Phoenix, was impressive—more than three hundred cases of varietals, along with a hundred cases of Silvio Moretti's finest vintage.

Not until he was nearing the crest of the Hualapai range a half hour later did Patricio realize that he was not alone in the cab. The first hint came with a faint rustling from the sleeper behind him. Startled, he turned to look. He got no farther than the barrel of a revolver jammed against his temple.

"Keep your eyes on the road, Patricio," a deep, raspy voice said close to his ear. "Don't try anything."

The rig was climbing the steep grade in fourth gear in low range. Automobile traffic was moving past in the left lane. Patricio could think of no covert way to signal for help. In the side mirror he saw a car slow and move into the lane behind the truck.

Patricio tried to speak. His mouth was dry. His voice was too weak for more than an inaudible croak. He tried again.

"What is this? A highjack?"

"Just keep drivin'," the voice said.

Patricio remembered Silvio Moretti's oft-repeated instructions to his drivers: "If you are highjacked, don't be a hero. Let them take the truck, whatever they want. They will be dealt with later."

At the moment, Patricio was more than willing to follow Silvio's advice.

He held the truck steady until it topped the rise. Trees, mountains were all around them. He was miles from any town, any help. He hit the splitter, gearing in preparation for the descent ahead. His mind was numb.

The pistol barrel nudged him again. "Pull off here," the voice said. "Stop on the shoulder."

Patricio braked and moved off the pavement. He eased to a stop beside the guard rail. Far below he could see the tops of trees. He remembered this stretch of road. The grade into the next canyon was the steepest on the entire run.

"Set the brake," the voice said. "Leave the motor running."

Patricio obeyed. He noticed in the mirror that the car had followed them off the road. It was now waiting behind the truck.

"Drink this," the voice said. A chunky hand shoved a bottle of gin into Patricio's chest.

Patricio's protest came from habit, without thought. "I don't drink. Bad liver. Doctor's orders."

"You've got new orders," the voice said. "Drink, or I'll blow your brains all over the windshield. I don't give a shit either way. Make up your mind. We ain't got all day."

Patricio drank. The gin was raw. He gagged. The pistol jabbed again, painfully. Patricio fought back nausea. He managed several more long swallows before his stomach rebelled. He kept control over the urge to vomit.

"That's enough," the voice said. "Now, lean forward. Put your hands on the dash."

Patricio moved to comply, but his hands never reached the panel. A blow to the base of his skull sent him to the floorboards.

Even as he fell, Patricio knew he had not been hit by the pistol but by something heavier, softer. A lead-and-leather sap, perhaps. He did not quite lose consciousness. He could smell gin, feel wetness on his chest. The remainder of the liquor had been poured over him. After a moment, as from a great distance, he heard the hiss of the air brake as it was released. The truck jerked into gear and began to move forward. Then the shift was put into neutral. The cab door slammed. The rig gathered speed.

Rolling onto his back, Patricio looked up. His vision was blurred, but he could see that no one was at the wheel. He grabbed for a handhold. His arms were like jelly. He could not make them function.

He sank back to the floorboards, helpless. Fighting for breath, he lay in paralyzed horror as the rumble of the runaway truck grew to a steady roar.

Patricio realized that he was about to die. But, strangely, the fact did not concern him as much as what he knew lay beyond his death. He was certain the highjacking and his murder were part of some larger evil. Something was terribly wrong back in Sonoma.

The thought moved him to renewed effort. Again he grabbed for the wheel and missed. He fell back onto the floorboards. The rig was still gathering speed. From the scream of the tires on the road-bed, the wind around the cab, Patricio knew that the speedometer must be nearing eighty. And then, just as he reached again and grasped the wheel, he heard another scream. Not until his lungs ran out of air did he realize that he was hearing the sound of his own voice.

BOOK 1

"Let any man who does not believe in God come to Sonoma. Let him walk the hills, feel the air, see the richness and the bountifulness of this land. . . ."

The Blessing of the Grapes,
Mission San Francisco Solano de Sonoma

CHAPTER 1

JOHNNY Moretti walked away. Homecoming. All the familiar faces, all the memories, and he walked away. He could not avoid the question.

And he did not have the answer.

He wandered deeper into the Plaza, trying to lose himself in the Festival crowd, overwhelmed by the mingled emotions that came every time he returned home to Sonoma. Giovanni Moretti, crown prince, who had become Johnny Moretti, valedictorian, class president, and football hero, who had gone out into the world, done more than he ever dreamed possible, and returned to find that all he had accomplished meant nothing. Not to those who mattered.

He was too warm in his tailored slacks and lamb suede pullover, and he felt overdressed in a sea of cutoffs, tank tops, print shirts, and walking shorts. But those who lived in Sonoma expected more of Johnny Moretti. He would not disappoint them.

Sonoma's eight-acre central Plaza, the northern terminus of the fabled, historic Camino Real, lay basking under the late September sun, its broad, sweeping lawn speckled with light filtered through a living canopy of palm, redwood, fir, eucalyptus, and an abundance of lesser trees. Carefully, Johnny searched.

To his left, a portion of the crowd had gathered to watch costumed actors prepare for the annual re-enactment of the Bear Flag Revolt. California's independence had been proclaimed at the far corner of the Plaza a century and a half ago. Now tourists were treated to a pale carbon copy each year at the Festival. Johnny moved on. He had seen it all before. Dodging the running children, he hunted through the crowd for one person—the one who had the answer.

He walked past a group of rock musicians setting up electronic gear in the amphitheater, past the Bear Flag memorial statue, past an acre or more of paintings, sculpture, and handicraft, through a carpet of families and lovers sprawled on the spacious lawn.

He was nearing the duck pond when he heard a voice behind him, calling his name. He turned.

Sophia Borneman came running across the grass, weaving through the crowd. She threw her arms around him and gave him a wet kiss on the cheek. Johnny was not in the mood for more old friends, but Sophia was special. He returned her warm hug.

She laughed and held him at arm's length for a moment. "Johnny, my God! How handsome you've grown! Look at you!"

"Fortunately you haven't changed at all," he said.

He was not being merely polite. Sophia seemed to have remained her stocky, Germanic self—friendly, outgoing, outspoken. She was not a classic beauty. But now, just short of her thirties, her wide face had assumed a healthy, mature appeal. He had always liked her. For a time, as high school classmates, they had been close friends. She was married to a Napa Valley supermarket executive, he remembered. Schmidt. Dan Schmidt. There were now two or three children. He asked about them.

"Oh, doing great," she said. She squeezed his arm and looked up at him affectionately, her soft blond hair stirring in the wind. "A big lawyer now," she said. "I see the name in the papers all the time, Giovanni Moretti, and then it hits me. My God! That's our Johnny! We've been hearing great things about you."

"Pop's propaganda," Johnny said, but Sophia's enthusiasm was contagious. She had a way of making other people feel good.

He was not even irritated when she asked the question.

"Is your father *really* selling the winery? I just can't believe it."

He shrugged. "Who knows what Pop is going to do?"

She laughed with such spontaneity that others around them turned to smile with tolerant amusement. Sophia paid no attention. "My God! There for a minute you looked just like him! And that's exactly the way he would have answered—with another question." She paused, watching his reaction. "Does it bother you, for people to say you're a lot like him?"

"No," he said. Comparisons with his father brought many emotions. Annoyance was not among them.

"It's all over Sonoma that he's selling," she said.

Johnny did not answer. He could have told her that the rumor also was all over San Francisco. He had been besieged by the press. Despite his refusal to talk, two newspaper columnists had used blind items, hinting at the impending sale of one of the biggest and best-known wineries in California.

Sophia would not give up. She studied Johnny's face. "They say Lucian Hall is already telling his friends that the deal has gone through. Dad says your father hasn't said a word. Not to anyone."

"Well, that's the way Pop is," Johnny said.

Crinkles of amusement came to the corners of Sophia's eyes, and Johnny realized that he had answered her with an evasion again.

He diverted her attention by looking over her shoulder, concentrating on the crowd. "I was supposed to meet Pop on the Plaza. Have you seen him?"

Sophia frowned in an effort to remember. "I saw him, very early, over by the wine enclosure." She glanced at her watch. "It's almost time for the Blessing of the Grapes," she said with quick emphasis. "Let's walk over to the mission."

All of Sonoma knew that the blessing would not happen without the presence of Silvio Moretti.

They strolled toward the northeast corner of the Plaza. As Sophia talked, she waved almost continuously to passing acquaintances, never taking her full attention from Johnny. It was a gift she had.

"Are you staying over for the party?"

There would be parties all over Sonoma tonight, but the party at Silvio Moretti's home would be *the* party.

"I doubt it," he said. "I just came up on business."

Sophia leaned close and whispered in his ear. "Screw business. This is Festival time! Stay over! I promise I'll save you a couple dozen dances."

"You're tempting me," he admitted. "But I've really got to get back. I have lots of work to do."

They crossed Spain Street and walked toward the roped-off area in front of Mission San Francisco Solano de Sonoma. Several hundred people were gathered at the mission bell, awaiting the blessing.

As they approached the curb, Johnny stopped and stared. Against the background of grape vines, the mission bell, the blue sky, and the red tiled roof stood a Renoir *jeune fille* come to life. She wore a hat, a small-brimmed, jaunty affair that controlled long, free-flowing brown hair.

As if she had sensed his rapt stare, she glanced in his direction. Startling pale-green eyes met his own briefly, then flicked away.

He reached for Sophia's arm. "Who is that?"

Sophia followed his gaze, then laughed. "Johnny! Stop clowning!"

"Who is she?"

Sophia studied his face. "You really don't know, do you?" She turned again toward the Renoir girl for a long moment and finally said, "I won't tell her that Johnny Moretti didn't recognize her. It would break her heart. She used to think the sun rose and set on you."

He could not believe it.

"Christina?"

Sophia was studying him again. "Christina. All grown up. Come on. I'll reintroduce you. Then I'll go home and cut my throat. I suddenly feel very superfluous."

"I can't believe it," he said again, dazed. "Christina."

He remembered her, but only vaguely. She had been a few years behind him in school—a painfully thin wisp of a girl with a face too large for her small frame. Now he could see lingering vestiges of that girl. She was still small, delicately built. But the cheekbones once too prominent had softened to give her face classic planes. The jaw line that once had seemed too pronounced now suggested a strength of character.

Christina and blond, stocky Sophia had always been so different that some people found it difficult to accept the fact that they were sisters.

"Chris, here's your childhood Prince Charming," Sophia said. "He didn't recognize you."

"No reason he should," Christina said, smiling at Johnny. "It's good to see you again." Her voice was soft, yet firm and sure.

As Johnny reached to take her hand, he noticed that her green eyes were flecked with brown. Or was it gold?

"Last I heard, you were in college," Johnny said. "What are you doing now?"

"Art museum," she said. "Boston."

The moment was awkward. Johnny could not keep from staring. Christina kept glancing away, then turning back to look up at him, the hat at a rakish tilt. He thought he glimpsed a secret amusement in those almost elusive eyes.

"Lord, it's been ten years or more," he said.

"More, probably," she said. "Neither of us seems to get back to Sonoma very often."

Sophia glanced around at the crowd. "What's happened to the ceremony? It's after eleven."

"There's been some delay," Christina said. "Father Natali and the governor came out. Then out trooped the senators and everybody else. They stood around awhile. Now they've all gone back inside."

"If anything about this Festival ever started on time, I'd be very upset," Sophia said.

"Artlessness is high art," Christina said. "That's part of the Festival's charm."

"Well, art or no art, I can't wait," Sophia said. "I've got to round up the kids. See you tonight, Johnny."

She moved away. Johnny could not resist Christina's eyes. He decided some flecks were indeed brown, some truly gold.

"Will you be home long?" he asked.

At first she did not answer. The brief silence suggested that he had intruded on delicate ground. Then she smiled. "Only a few days . . . I really don't know. I just arrived this morning."

"I live in Sausalito. Just minutes away," he explained. "I thought that if you were going to be here, I might drive up some evening and take you to dinner. We could get reacquainted. And I'd like to hear about your work. I have an interest in art."

She gave him a long, analytical look that was somehow haunted with meaning. "That would be nice—except that I probably won't be here more than a day or two."

"Look," he said on impulse. "Right now I've got to find my father. But how about taking in the party at the house tonight?"

She considered his invitation at length, concentrating so deeply that for several seconds she seemed to be in a self-imposed trance. He did not press, assuming that she was resolving complications she did not want to discuss. "I'd love to, but at the moment my plans are indefinite," she said. "Could I check with my family, and let you know?"

"By all means," Johnny said. "I wouldn't want to impose."

"As for your father," Christina added, "I think I just caught a glimpse of him over there."

Johnny turned. Silvio Moretti emerged from the crowd and came walking across First Street East toward them. He was flanked by two *paesani* Johnny remembered from his childhood. The man on Silvio's left was talking earnestly. Silvio was listening with that noncommittal expression Johnny knew so well. As they watched, Silvio glanced in their direction. For a fleeting instant Johnny saw something pass over his father's face—concern, anger, fear, irritation—something. Before he could settle upon exactly what, it was gone. Silvio stopped, shook hands with the two men in dismissal, then strode straight toward Johnny and Christina.

At seventy-four, Silvio Moretti seemed ageless. He moved with a vigor and ease a man of fifty might envy. He retained a full head of hair, now uniformly silvered. His complexion was deep olive from the many hours he spent in his fields. He inspected the vines almost daily, and supervised the cultivation and harvest. He was not especially tall—slightly under six feet—and solidly built. But the most striking thing about him, as always, was his sheer presence, a confidence and grace of movement so overpowering that crowds parted before him. As they did now. Tourists turned to stare as he crossed the street, wondering what celebrity had descended among them.

"There is something about your father that has always frightened me a little," Christina said softly. "But he is absolutely the most fascinating man I've ever met."

Johnny did not answer. He was long accustomed to his father's magnetism. Perhaps the old stories had something to do with it— stories his father had never bothered to deny.

In public Silvio seldom went beyond a handshake, but now he surprised his son with a strong Corsican embrace, and a kiss on each cheek.

"Welcome home, Johnny," he said.

He turned to Christina, taking both her hands in his. "And welcome home to you, Christina. I heard you were coming. I sent you a note. I hope you will honor us with your presence at our party tonight."

Christina smiled at him. "I hope to, thank you. But I'm uncertain about my family's plans for the evening."

"I cannot imagine your mother missing one of our parties," Silvio said. "And she brings so much life to us, I cannot think how we could give a party without her."

Christina smiled her appreciation. If she noticed that the compliment excluded her father, she gave no sign. She looked toward the mission, the waiting baskets of grapes, and changed the subject. "I don't know what's happened. The ceremony has been delayed."

"I phoned and asked them to wait," Silvio said. "There has been . . . some trouble. The blessing will begin in a moment. If you will excuse me, I'll let Father Natali know I am here."

Silvio moved through the crowd and into the mission. Johnny and Christina waited. The audience grew as word spread that the ritual was about to begin.

The slow procession emerged from the ancient doorway. First came the altar boys, in headbands and breechclouts, representing the Indian converts who had served the mission's pioneer priests. Sonoma residents in period costumes formed a tableau around the baskets of grapes to be blessed. The governor, the governor's father, the senators, the mayor of Sonoma, winemakers, and various officers of the state took places of honor behind the altar that had been erected in front of the mission bell.

Johnny's attention centered on Gregory Cavanaugh—the youngest and most unorthodox governor in California's history. Tall, blond, handsome, with a wide, open face and a beatific smile, Cavanaugh radiated irresistible warmth, and his immense popularity seemed to stem from his exceptional ability to convey his honesty and sincerity. Though Johnny liked Gregory, he did not count him among his close friends. For some reason that Johnny did not understand, a polite distance had always remained between them.

The senior Cavanaugh was another matter entirely; Johnny had known Sam Cavanaugh since childhood. Sam had been Johnny's favorite among the many professional politicians who frequently visited Silvio's private study. No matter how busy, Sam always had time for Johnny. Once, when he was four, Sam had arrived at the house with several other men and brought along a gift for Johnny —an old-fashioned wooden top. While the other men talked in another room, Sam had spent an hour playing on the floor with Johnny, showing him how to wind the string around the top, how to throw it best to make it spin.

Now Sam Cavanaugh stood close to Silvio and the Sonoma delegation of officials and winemakers. As his eyes met Johnny's, he winked. Gregory Cavanaugh stood slightly apart from the group, the hint of a smile playing at the corner of his mouth as he waited for the ceremony to begin.

Father Natali walked to the microphone.

"Is it on?" he asked. After some adjustments, an answering echo finally came from the speakers, brazenly incongruous with the archaic beauty of the rites to follow.

The priest cleared his throat and began the ceremony.

"If you are a stranger to Sonoma, the Valley of the Moon, after today I am certain you will return again and again . . . and again."

Father Natali delivered the eulogy each year, but he always managed to imbue the words with new meaning. He looked out over the crowd with impassive eyes.

"For this is a place of peace and serenity and beauty, a Garden of Eden, an oasis in our hectic world. . . ."

Johnny had heard it all many times. He leaned forward to whisper in Christina's ear. "He means we keep the roads inadequate so nobody can get here."

Christina shushed him. But she was grinning.

"And so, on behalf of the festival committee and the Mission de Sonoma, I welcome you. . . ."

"But don't stay long," Johnny whispered. "We really don't have accommodations for all of you . . ."

Christina stifled a laugh. "Hush!" she whispered.

"Let any man who does not believe in God come to Sonoma," the priest said. "Let him walk the hills, feel the air, see the richness and bountifulness of this land. Here is everlasting testimony to the existence of the Almighty. In every direction one might look there is living evidence of the master plan of the Creator. Everywhere there is the miracle and the beauty of life."

"Beautiful," Christina murmured.

As the priest talked, Johnny reveled in Christina's nearness, her flawless complexion, her delicate features, her unique allure. Throughout the rest of the ceremony she remained intent, absorbing the priest's words with complete concentration.

At last Father Natali began his benediction. "Almighty God, make bountiful this harvest. . . ."

Johnny bowed his head. He glanced up once and saw Silvio studying him with a strange look on his face.

When the ceremony was over, the crowd began to move back toward the Plaza for a concert by the valley's Dixielanders. Silvio left the group and came toward Christina and Johnny. He was uncharacteristically abrupt.

"Johnny and I must talk, Christina. May we drop you some place?"

"Thank you," Christina said. "But if you two will excuse me, I really must spend some time with my family."

"I'll call you," Johnny said.

Christina nodded, smiled as she clasped Silvio's hand, and walked away.

For a moment Silvio Moretti stood with a rare frown, watching her cross the street toward the Plaza. Johnny studied his father. Silvio seemed troubled. But before Johnny could react, Silvio put a hand on his shoulder, and the moment passed. "Come," he said. "We must hurry. Tonight we have guests. And your mother is waiting to see you. But first there is a serious matter we must discuss."

CHAPTER 2

SILVIO Moretti opened the door to the huge redwood room. Johnny crossed the pegged plank floor to the leather guest chair, battling the dark memories the paneled, book-lined room always evoked. During his childhood this room, this entire wing of the house had been off limits. His father was not to be disturbed. The room—and to some extent Silvio himself—had remained steeped in mystery. Many times through the years Johnny had been awakened late at night by the sounds of cars in the drive, and he had watched somber men file into his father's study.

Later, during his adolescence, the study had become his private hell. He had been summoned into this room time after time to face his father's stern disapproval and to endure long, puzzling, oblique lectures, filled with confusing references to Alexander the Great, the Venerable Bede, Foxe's *Book of Martyrs*, Socrates, Aristotle, Attila the Hun, Disraeli, Lucretius—names Johnny had known only vaguely. He had walked from this room finally, years ago, vowing to himself that he would never return.

Time had softened his resolve, but not the convictions behind it.

"Wine?" Silvio asked, clearing away a stack of books from his huge oak desk by the windows.

Johnny nodded, acknowledging his father's pride in experimentation. Silvio moved to the lowboy beside the wall of dark bookcases, poured the wine carefully, and returned with the glasses. He handed one to Johnny.

"Cabernet Sauvignon, seventy. Aged in Yugoslavian oak," he said. "Bottled in the summer of seventy-six. It may be our best. See what you think." He gestured a toast.

Johnny returned the gesture and sipped. The claret was rich and full-bodied. The color was deep, and the bouquet complex. With the burden of the Moretti family name Johnny had acquired some knowledge. He frequently advised friends on wine, but his father was world class.

"Smooth," Johnny said. Then, to avoid venturing a further opinion, he asked questions. For a time Silvio discussed the grape, the season, the press, acidity, salinity, and matters beyond Johnny's expertise.

After Silvio refilled the glasses, he moved to the big wing chair behind his desk. He sat and sipped the wine in silence, staring across the room toward the huge native stone fireplace nestled among the bookcases. Johnny waited. Silvio carefully placed his glass on the desk.

"I asked you here because there is a decision to be made," he said. "You may have heard something about the matter. Lucian Hall and his people have made an offer to buy the winery."

Johnny could not suppress a laugh at the understatement. "I've heard little else for a week."

"Lucian and his people have given us something to think about," Silvio said. "It's a fair offer. It deserves our attention."

Johnny sighed in exasperation. He could never get anything across to his father. "Pop, excuse me, I don't feel that this is my decision to make. I wouldn't feel right about having any voice in this."

Silvio's eyes narrowed slightly—a forewarning of his contemplative, quiet, cold anger—but his tone remained calm. "You are family. This is family business," he said in that arbitrary manner Johnny knew so well. He waved a hand in impatience. "But for the moment, let's put that argument aside. I want to know. Are you opposed?"

Johnny watched his father carefully. Silvio was full of ploys, trial balloons, conversational trapdoors. No one ever knew exactly what was in his mind.

"It doesn't matter what I think," he said. "I'm not involved—at least, not to the extent that I should take part in the decision."

"Let me put it this way, then," Silvio said. He lit a cigar and smoked for a moment. "If you were in my shoes, what would you do?"

Against his better judgment, Johnny yielded to his emotions. "You ask me. I'll tell you. If I had put my whole life into building something fine, something worthy of pride, I wouldn't sell. Not at any price."

Silvio leisurely studied the ash on his cigar before tapping it lightly into a tray. "Then you *do* have some feelings about it, all other considerations aside."

Johnny knew he had given away too much to retreat. He shrugged. "Maybe I haven't had time to absorb the idea of anyone else owning the winery," he said. "But hell, yes, I have feelings about it. In a way it would be like selling the family name. But as I said, it's not my decision."

Silvio's eyes remained impassive. "It *is* your decision," he said. "That's why I asked you here. You are a partner. You always have been."

"I don't want any part of the winery, or the sale," Johnny said. "It wouldn't be fair to Carlo. I mean what I say, Pop. I have my own career. I'm doing all right."

Silvio regarded him through a small cloud of cigar smoke. "Doing all right," he said. "You're doing all right." He worked for a moment with that thought. "I'm glad you are so proud of yourself. Maybe it means you have proved whatever it was you needed to prove to yourself."

Johnny shook his head. It was an endless argument.

"There's no harm done," Silvio went on. "You've gained some valuable experience out in the world. But Johnny, it is time you came home. There is so much to be done!"

"Goddamn it, there's no need to go through all that again,"

Johnny said. "I'm happy doing what I'm doing. It's what I *want* to do. And you have Carlo. He's happy with the winery. I never was."

"Understand me, Johnny. I am not favoring you, or speaking against Carlo." Silvio spoke slowly, choosing his words with care. "I love both my sons. You know that. But I must recognize your different capabilities. As you said, Carlo is happiest with the grapes, the press, the vats. Give him a problem with the fermentation tanks, the vines, and he is in his glory. But I must accept the fact that Carlo is . . . limited. Just as you are limited in *his* fields of interest. Carlo does not want to deal with the outside world. He has not earned the respect that is necessary to deal with other people. And that is where you are at your best. Together, you and Carlo would be a good team, Carlo running the actual operation, you behind this desk. I think in time you could earn the respect you would need among those we deal with."

Johnny tried to keep the irritation out of his voice. "Pop, I have my name on the door of one of the most prestigious law firms on the West Coast. I've just been promoted. Next week I am moving down the hall, into the executive suite. A full partner! At twenty-nine! Do you understand what that means? Yesterday, at the end of a trial, a federal judge complimented me from the bench. A federal judge! He said my final argument to the jury was the best summation he had heard in all his forty years in law."

"Don't brag, Johnny. It does not become you."

For a moment Johnny was overwhelmed by old, familiar frustrations. He could never make his father understand the way he felt about anything.

"Damn it, I'm *not* bragging. I'm just *telling* you. I'm not asking you to take pride in my accomplishments. I know that's too much to hope for. I'm only asking you to accept the fact that I find satisfaction in those accomplishments."

Silvio closed his eyes. When he opened them, they were fixed on Johnny in that heavy-lidded stare he knew so well, filled with cold appraisal, unspoken accusation. Johnny fought against his long-standing resentments. He could not afford the luxury of anger.

"So the big judge complimented you," Silvio said. "Tell me. Why do you need some judge to assess your worth for you? Come home.

Sit behind this desk. Then you can seat and unseat your own judges. Federal judges. You can tell *them* what *they're* worth."

Johnny shook his head. Silvio lived fifty years in the past. "Pop, those things just aren't done anymore. Not on that level."

"Don't tell me they're not done," Silvio said. "What you are saying is, *you* wouldn't do them. You'd rather have your name on some fucking door." He sighed. "I had hoped . . ."

He got up and walked to the window and stood for a time, looking out over Sonoma, toward the distant hills and vineyards. Then he turned and spoke slowly, in measured tones, as he studied the cigar in his hand.

"You see, Johnny, this matter does concern you, no matter what you think. This offer has a string attached. What you lawyers would call a corollary. Lucian Hall and his people have come to us saying, in effect, we will give you a fair price for your business. And, if you do not accept, then we will put you out of business."

Johnny was shocked. Hampton Industries was a respected conglomerate, an umbrella for corporations all over America, high among the *Fortune* 500, usually mentioned in the same league with Gulf & Western, IBM, Xerox. Its chairman, Lucian Hall, was featured frequently on the covers of business and news magazines. His dynamic style and innovative management attracted attention. But as far as Johnny knew, Hall's integrity had never been questioned.

He watched his father for a moment, wondering if age could have brought on a touch of paranoia.

"Did Lucian actually say that?" he asked. "If he did, it's actionable. You could take him into court. Simple extortion."

Silvio waved a hand to silence him. "Of course he did not put it into words. That's not the way these things are done. Nothing is spelled out. There is nothing you can take into court. But the message is clear. He made it plain we did not have much time to ponder our decision. Already I have delayed too long. One of our trucks was destroyed yesterday morning. A load of varietals and vintage Cabernet Sauvignon was lost. Our driver was killed."

Johnny had seen the story on page one of the *Sonoma Index-Tribune*, and he had heard talk about it in the Plaza. "Patricio Schippoletti? You think there's a connection between his wrecking his truck . . . ?"

"I have been on the phone all morning, to make certain. It was no accident. Patricio had been driving for us for years. He had never so much as scratched a fender. Patricio would not have had such an accident."

Johnny could see that Silvio had no doubts. But Patricio murdered? On orders from Lucian Hall? Johnny tried to bring his father back to reality. "What about the highway patrol? Do they call it murder?"

Silvio shrugged. "A truck runs off the road, the driver is killed. It happens every day. They do not look beyond those simple facts."

"Have you told the Arizona people what you suspect?"

"I do not need the police to tell me it was not an accident. And I do not need the police to tell me who did it." He smoked for a moment, studying Johnny. "Is that what you would do? Go to the police?"

"If I had strong suspicions, any evidence at all to offer. Yes."

"And if it was planned so carefully that nothing could be proved? And if the police could not help you? What would you do then?"

"If I really thought Lucian and his people were trying to coerce me to sell, I'd try to trap them into an admission of intent . . . some threat . . ."

"So you could take it to your courts." Silvio sighed. "No, Johnny, no. That is not their way. There will be no direct threats. Only trouble. I have just been to see Patricio's widow. Perhaps I should have waited, so I could take you with me and let you see the situation in its true light."

Johnny knew further argument would be useless. He kept silent.

"And now, if we continue to delay, something else will happen," Silvio went on. "That is the way these things work. We must make our decision. And you *are* involved. Lucian knows that you are my son. He will not ignore that fact. You have managed to walk away from decisions all your life, Johnny. You cannot walk away from this one."

Johnny refused to be cornered. "If what you say is true, I'm clearly out of my league," he said. "You're the expert in this field."

"Don't use your courtroom tactics on me," Silvio said. "You cannot disqualify yourself. This matter requires no expertise. This is a decision that must be made from personal philosophy, from emotion rather than logic. The issues are simple. The winery represents Lucian's first step in the acquisition of all our holdings. If we accept his offer, cooperate with him—surrender—we will be a family with no cares, no worries, no responsibilities other than our wealth. That is something to consider. You will have enough money to live in almost any manner you choose for the rest of your life. And your children, maybe your children's children. You cannot reject that lightly. If we refuse the offer, the strong possibility exists that we will lose all we have, perhaps be driven into debt. How do you feel about that?"

Johnny hesitated, thinking. Silvio was seventy-four. A mild stroke, with no other outward symptoms, could have brought on a trace of senility, of paranoia.

"I think you may be reading too much into it," he said cautiously.

Silvio's eyes remained impassive. "Believe me, Johnny, I know what I am saying. If we decline this offer, we can expect retaliation far more extensive than the loss of a truck and the death of a valuable man. We would be placing the winery, the vineyards, Carlo and his family, your mother, yourself in danger."

"And you."

"No. I am safe," Silvio said. "You see, they may harm everything I hold dear. But they will not harm me. There will be further demands. They will need me. That is part of the problem—something we must consider. They will want to use my . . . influence, my connections. The matter of the winery is only the first step toward taking all."

Obviously, Silvio had done much thinking about the matter, projecting an elaborate scenario. Johnny wanted to hear it all. "You mentioned alternatives," he said.

"There are two," Silvio said. "We could say no, thank you, ignore them, and be destroyed. Or . . . they also have trucks, men. They have plants . . . fields . . . vineyards . . . buildings. They have families."

Johnny was appalled, but he knew he must not let his father see that. He spoke quietly. "Pop, I'm an officer of the courts of the State of California. I'll forget what I just heard. You never said it."

Silvio's eyes narrowed into that heavy-lidded stare. "Don't you play policeman with me. I didn't *say* I would do anything. We're discussing the alternatives. This is a reply they would understand. It is worth consideration."

Silvio's deadly calm revived painful adolescent memories. Johnny found himself losing control, his voice rising. "This isn't Corsica, half a century ago! We have courts, legal protection!"

Leaning forward over his desk, Silvio spoke. His tone was low and intent. "Let me tell you something, Johnny. And don't you ever forget this. Men make their own puny little laws for the courts. Men bend those laws, break them, change them, corrupt them, turn them to their own use. But there are other laws. Basic laws. And the strongest law of all is survival. When your honor, your family, your home, your privacy, are threatened, you have to think of how you'll answer to your God. And to hell with men's chickenshit little laws."

Johnny wished he could convey to his father what he knew of precedents, the intricacies and complexities of the courts, the checks and balances of the appellate system, the marvelous, sweeping history of the law. He would never succeed. And it was his whole life.

"I'm not naive," he said. "I know that the courts are not infallible—bribery, mistakes, corruption. But our legal system is all we have. Ultimately, justice *will* prevail. We've got to believe that! Otherwise, there is no hope left for civilization."

Silvio snorted his contempt. "Justice will prevail only as long as we are men enough to make it prevail. Civilization will exist as long as there is a man who will treat other men right, and who has the balls to make everyone treat him right."

"Pop, I know what you're talking about. Forget it. You're thinking of times past. All that is dead!"

Silvio's hand slammed into the desk. "Shut up! Don't ever speak of such matters when you have no knowledge."

Johnny refused to retreat. "I've heard all those stories," he said. "I grew up with the whispering around town. You've got to face it. Times have changed. You can't depend on a bunch of old men hanging around the poker parlor."

Silvio turned his face toward the window. He was silent for a moment. "I gave you too much credit," he said. "Those men you speak of may be old. But they are men. I'm beginning to wonder if there are any other men left in the world." He turned back to Johnny. "I'm asking you. I'm begging you. Come home! If you want, we'll put your name on every fucking door in the house!"

"Pop, I want to help. But in my own way," Johnny said.

"What way would that be?"

"I do have some influence."

Silvio chuckled. "You have influence."

Stung, Johnny lashed back. "I don't give a shit what you think. There are those who think I'm a goddamn good lawyer. I'm handling a case right now that any of the senior partners would have given his eye teeth to get. The client asked for *me*! It's coming to trial. There'll be publicity, nationwide attention. If I win, I'll be one of the best-known lawyers on the West Coast. At thirty! I *do* have expertise. And I'm offering you that. If you don't want it, you can go straight to hell."

Silvio remained unmoved throughout Johnny's outburst. "Who was the client who asked for you?" he asked quietly.

Johnny could see no reason not to tell. His relationship with the client was a matter of public record. "Herbert Fraser."

"The suit involving his daughter?"

Johnny nodded.

"Why is this case so important to you?" Silvio asked. "Is *that* what you want? Publicity? Attention?"

"No matter how this case is decided, it will set legal precedents for a long time to come," Johnny said, pleased with the opportunity to explain something to his father. "It's the kind of case every lawyer dreams about."

"Very interesting," Silvio said. "But I could teach you more right here"—he pointed a forefinger at his desk—"than you'd learn in a lifetime in the courts of San Francisco. Johnny, you could do so much more here . . ."

"Pop . . ."

Silvio ignored him. "You may know your law books, your courts, but you don't know what happens among men." He tapped the desk. "This could be your real education, right here. You are too blind to see that."

Johnny was sick of it. Nothing had changed since he was in high school.

"I'm doing what I want to do," he said. "I like the life I'm living."

"I know all about the life you're living," Silvio said. "You're either out fucking everything in sight, or you're holed up like a hermit in that floating commune in Sausalito."

Silvio's summation of Johnny's leisure-hour pursuits was so accurate that it left him no room for protest. But he did not live in a commune. He at least could set his father straight on that.

"Forty percent of the people who live on the houseboats are doctors, lawyers, professional people . . ."

"Trash," Silvio said. "I know how they live." He paused. "Johnny, every man is entitled to some pleasure. But you are wasting the best years of your life. You're nearly thirty. Where is your family? Where is any evidence at all that you're accepting any responsibility for your life? For who you are? Come home! Assume your obligations!"

Johnny made one more effort toward peace. "Pop, if you're really in trouble, I want to help. But in my own way."

"Then that is no help at all." Silvio raised his hands and massaged his temples. "I'm seventy-four years old," he said. "I won't live forever. If you would come back, learn, take charge, I could die in good conscience. I only want you to accept your God-given responsibilities."

"I just don't want to manipulate people."

Silvio again gave Johnny that heavy-lidded stare. "Johnny, listen to me. There are two kinds of people in this world. Those who manipulate. And those who are manipulated. If you think about it, the choice should not be difficult to make."

Johnny gestured toward the desk. "Pop, this is the life you chose for yourself. Please don't try to make me live it. I want to live my own."

"That is a very selfish view," Silvio said. "You were born to so many blessings. You have chosen to ignore that fact. I am very disappointed in you."

Johnny put his empty wineglass on the table, rose, and walked to the door. He no longer could keep the emotion from his voice. "At least there's nothing new," he said. "No matter what I did, whatever I accomplished, you've always expected more. You've *always* been disappointed in me. That used to hurt. It really did. But you know something? I'm about to get used to it."

Silvio rose from his desk. "Johnny, even when we disagree, I can respect you for taking a stand. But you are shirking your responsibilities to me, to yourself, to your family. Am I to understand that, given the circumstances I have outlined, you would simply do nothing?"

Johnny chose his words carefully. "I think you have read too much into Lucian Hall's offer. I think there may well be some other reason for the truck wreck. Maybe it *was* an accident. I would have to be convinced otherwise."

"And if you were convinced?" Silvio insisted. "What if you found that everything I have been telling you is true, that we are being pressured to sell all we own?"

Johnny met his father's eyes. "I would see them in hell first."

Silvio smiled. "See? You have made a decision."

"Don't be too hard on your father," Anna Moretti said.

Johnny crossed the kitchen to the coffee urn and refilled his cup. "Mom, why don't you worry about his being too hard on *me*?" he asked.

Anna focused her attention on the last of the hors d'oeuvres she was preparing for the party—her own *biscotti* she would not trust to any servant. She divided the dough into small rolls. Satisfied, she placed them on a cookie sheet, wiped her hands, slid them into the oven, set the timer, and turned to Johnny.

"Try to understand him," she said.

"Is he trying to understand me?"

Anna threw up her hands. "What am I talking to? An echo? Of course your father understands you. But now he needs you. He wants you home. It's as simple as that."

She went to a cabinet, pulled out a cup, and moved to the coffee urn. Johnny waited patiently at the table.

He was furious with himself. He should not have lost his temper. His father always brought out the worst in him. Every time he faced Silvio, all his self-possession seemed to desert him. Returning home was like entering a time warp. Here nothing ever changed. Even his room was still "Johnny's room"; the rock posters and class photographs remained on the walls, his high school clothes in the closet.

Anna carried her coffee to the table and sat down with him, her hand resting briefly on his arm. The gesture brought back memories. From his earliest childhood the family had always gathered around the small table in the kitchen. Here Anna had dispensed her comfort and advice, along with her robust, savory culinary delights.

"He always makes me feel like a schoolboy," Johnny said.

Anna reached across the table and patted his hand. "Beside him, you *are* little more than a boy," she said. "Your life as a man is just beginning."

Johnny laughed. "Come on, Mom. By the time Pop was my age, he'd been on his own almost twenty years. Carlo is almost forty, and Pop still keeps him right here under his wing. He's trying to do the same with me. Why?"

Anna shrugged. "Maybe you just told me the reason. He loves his sons. He wants to protect them. He doesn't want them to go through all the terrible times he had as a child." Her hand grasped his wrist. "Johnny, for some reason, you've always seemed to feel that you have to compete with your father. I don't know why. Do you?"

"I'm not competing with him. Not in any way," Johnny protested. "The problem is that he's trying to cast me in his own mold. I don't want to follow in his footsteps. I only want to be myself."

Anna sighed. "It's a Chinese puzzle, a box within a box. Silvio tries to mold you to his own image. But because you are your father's son—so much like him—you resist."

Johnny took a deep breath and let it out slowly, bracing himself to broach a topic Anna would equate with heresy. In this house Silvio was infallible. But Johnny had to know.

"Mom, have you had any indication that Pop is becoming senile?"

Anna looked at him a moment in stunned silence before answering. "No!" she said. "Not in the least! Why do you ask?"

Johnny ignored the question and asked his own. "Don't you find him talking more and more about the old days?"

Anna considered the question. "No," she said, concerned. "But I want to know! Why do you ask? You must have a reason."

"I just thought he seems to be living more in the past."

Anna smiled uncertainly. "Silvio Moretti has always carried the
past around with him—a terrible burden. When he came to this
country, he brought a lot of Corsica with him. You know that.
There are things about him that have never changed, in the forty-
one years I've known him—things I would not want to change."

She folded her arms, leaned back in the chair, and laughed.
"Silvio changed? He shows a little age, maybe. But outside of that
he hasn't changed one iota since the first time I saw him, when he
came to our house with my father on business and stayed for dinner." She shook her head at the memory and laughed again. "Oh,
what a handsome man he was! I couldn't take my eyes off him. I
was so young. He seemed as old as my father. But such a man! He
had this splendid reserve, this quiet impact on the whole room. I
was sure he had been everywhere, seen everything. And even so, he
possessed such a fine art for seeming to want nothing so much that
evening as to be there in our home. Enjoying our food and wine,
listening to all we had to say. And I'll tell you," she went on, "I
made certain Silvio became aware of me."

Johnny had heard the story, many times. He always enjoyed the
look that came into his mother's eyes as she told it. "I doubt he
needed much encouragement," he said.

Anna slapped his hand. "Save your flattery for your own girls,"
she said. "From what I hear, some of them need it."

Johnny laughed again. The remark hit home. He doubted that
many of his girl friends would meet with his mother's approval.

"But to answer your question: Your father is in excellent health,
mentally and physically," Anna said. "I am positive of that."

"Then what about this Hampton offer?" Johnny asked. "Is it as
serious as Pop seems to think?"

"I only know that if your father says it is serious, then it is
serious," Anna said. "And if he says he needs you at home, then
you should come home."

"Mom, I can't."

She squeezed his hand. "Johnny, couldn't you, just for a little
while? A leave of absence, until all this business is settled? Then, if
you want, you could go back."

"How could I? And how could I do that to Carlo? He would
never stand for it. And why should he? He's worked at the winery

since I was in grade school. He's stuck with it through everything Pop could dish out. And now Pop wants to bring me back?"

"Have you talked to Carlo about this?" Anna asked.

"I've never seen any reason. I've never had any intention of coming back."

"Well, something can be worked out with Carlo."

Anna seemed positive, but Johnny only shook his head. "No, Mom. Nothing can be worked out with Carlo. There is no way to work anything out with Carlo. Nothing would seem fair to him, concerning me and the winery."

Anna sighed. "So much love in this house, and yet so much trouble. I don't see how it all can live under one roof." She looked at him for a moment. "Will you do something for me, Johnny, while you're here?"

"What?"

"Talk with Carlo. Tell him what is in your heart, just as you've told me. He might surprise you. He loves you. He misses his little brother. I know that for a fact. You are both fine sons. Day and night, maybe, but fine sons. Talk to him. Please."

Johnny hesitated. He did not believe a talk with his brother would accomplish anything, but he could not think of any way to say no to his mother. "I'll try," he said.

The comforting fragrance from the oven seemed suddenly oppressive, emphasized by the heavy mood hanging over the big, still kitchen.

"And Johnny," Anna added. "Think about what your father has told you. Where such things as this are concerned, I have never known him to be wrong."

CHAPTER 3

*T*HE trip home had been a mistake. Christina knew that now. Away from Sonoma, the puzzling crosscurrents in her family could be put aside, to be worried over at odd moments. She tended to forget how each real and imagined slight could be of such vital, immediate concern. Petty moment-to-moment crises had always ruled their daily lives, and now matters seemed even worse.

The chance meeting with Johnny Moretti was the only good thing that had happened since she had arrived. She was still exhilarated, light-headed from the unexpected revival of those foolish, heart-stopping, boy-crazy fancies. The years had made him even more handsome, but basically he had not changed. If things were different, Christina thought, she would have loved to explore that old, adolescent infatuation.

But the situation at home cast an undeniable pall.

"I don't know what's happening," she told Sophia. "I'm totally confused."

Sophia shrugged. "Don't worry about it. I've been trying to figure Mom and Dad out for years. If you get a clue, let me know."

They were seated in the wine enclosure, waiting—Sophia for her husband, Christina for her mother. Their table near the wooden, makeshift fence provided a view of the entrance and the sidewalk approaches. Sophia's two boys were perched at a nearby table, intent over an electronic soccer game.

Christina glanced at her watch, irritated that once again she seemed to be a burden to her family. Her mother still had twenty-five minutes to go on her shift, supervising the art bazaar at the far corner of the Plaza.

"I get such bad vibes," she said. "At times I think Mom's actually scared of him. Why doesn't she just move out?"

Sophia glanced at the children, making certain they were not listening. "I've wondered." She sipped her Fumé Blanc, frowning. "Maybe she realizes that she's all he's got. If she left, he'd be devastated." She paused, waiting until a group of tourists passed. "In some crazy way I think they really love each other."

"They have strange ways of showing it."

"Why? What's happened now?"

Christina hesitated, wondering how much to tell. She yielded to her impulse to describe the current crisis. Sophia might be able to provide some insight.

"At the moment the big issue is the party at the Morettis'. I gather that they were planning to go. But my unexpected arrival seems to have set off some argument that had been smoldering for days. Now they're not going."

Sophia frowned. "That's odd. Mom's been talking about the party for weeks. She bought a new dress."

"She claims she's changed her mind. I'm sure she wants to go. But she won't even talk about it. She lets the implication hang that it would be awkward to take me along."

Sophia put a comforting hand on Christina's arm. "That's ridiculous. You wouldn't need an invitation. Silvio and Anna would be happy to see you." A new thought struck her. "You bring anything to wear?"

"I packed an evening dress for a reception in L.A. It'll do. So that's no problem. As for the invitation, one was waiting when I arrived. I was floored. I had no idea anyone knew I was coming."

"That doesn't surprise me," Sophia said. "Silvio knows everything that happens in this town. Not a sparrow falls . . ."

Christina laughed. "Sophia! That's blasphemy."

Sophia grinned. "You can say that because you don't live here. It's true."

"Maybe so," Christina said. "Silvio himself mentioned it at the blessing. So the invitation was no fluke."

Sophia had a new thought. "Surely Mom's not concerned about your going without an escort. She's not that square."

"Again, no problem," Christina told her. "Johnny's offered to take me."

Sophia clapped her hands in easy delight. "Quick work!" Her eyes were teasing. "And how did you manage that? You must have learned some new tricks up there in Boston!"

Christina felt heat rising to her face. Sophia knew, better than anyone, the hopeless crush she'd had years ago on Johnny Moretti. Month after month, unknown to him, she had actually followed him around, doting on his effortless dignity and grace of movement, so in contrast to the other boys in school. For hours she had stood on the sidelines at football practice, watching him in scrimmage, sweeping through the line with his surprising speed, or fading back to pass with all the poise of a ballet dancer. The other players would be shouting, exchanging good-natured insults. Johnny seldom spoke. He seemed to place his total concentration on the game. Only occasionally, when the hangers-on in the stands burst into applause after some feat, would Johnny turn on one of those rare smiles that absolutely melted Christina's vulnerable adolescent heart.

What Sophia did not know was that her feelings for Johnny Moretti had lingered. She had thought of him often during the past five years. Consciously, she still tended to measure her feelings toward other men on a scale with the way she had worshipped him. She had treasured every bit of information concerning him that came her way.

Sophia was regarding her reaction with amusement and a bit of surprise.

"Look, let's don't make a big thing of it," Christina said. "Johnny is a nice, considerate person. You know that. Under the circumstances, he made a polite gesture, and I appreciate it."

"I'll bet you do," Sophia said. "What did Mom say?"

"I haven't mentioned it yet."

Sophia raised her eyebrows. "Well, if you go to the party, that may complicate your already complicated situation at home."

Christina was silent. She had been away so long that she had forgotten how much time was wasted in these myriad crises that grew out of such trivialities. She had never learned to tolerate them. She wished she had Sophia's knack for taking them in stride.

"If you were I, what would you do?" she asked.

Sophia giggled. "No contest. I would tell Mom and Dad I was going to the party with Johnny Moretti, and I might stay out till the rooster crows. They could do whatever they damned well pleased."

Margaret Borneman put the checks into her purse, closed and locked the cashbox, and waved to the art exhibits chairman to signal her departure. She was fifteen minutes late, but the delay had been unavoidable. She had been trapped by an elderly couple from San Jose, who had purchased two of her own paintings. She could not be rude.

As always, the sale of her work brought mixed feelings. She still found it immensely satisfying that anyone would want her paintings enough to spend hundreds, even thousands, of dollars. But each canvas was a milestone in a long, intensely personal process of self-discovery. She had never lost the feeling that with each painting she was selling a small part of herself to strangers.

Crossing the tree-shaded Plaza among the swarm of Festival visitors, she reflected that in this one area of her life her parents would have been proud of her. Through Christina, and to some degree Sophia, she had kept their spirit alive.

As she approached the wine enclosure, she caught sight of her daughters on the far side, under the trees. She stopped and stood for a moment, enthralled with the mood, the colors, the perfect composition.

Sophia and Christina were seated at a table near the redwood fence, their heads close together, their expressions serious. Dappled sunlight filtered down through the trees. Margaret reached for her ever-present sketch pad. It was a scene she wanted to paint.

Working rapidly, she penciled the basic lines, making extensive notes on shading, color. She would need to imbue her painting with the sense of the shimmering afternoon heat, contrasted with the calm perfection of her daughters. Sophia's golden hair was massed carelessly on her left shoulder as she leaned forward, talking. Christina, the dark, troubled beauty, was listening intently, her face framed by the jaunty hat, her lips parted slightly—a minor detail that would serve as a focal point to bring the painting to life. Beyond them, at another table, her grandsons were engrossed over a book —no, some kind of game—their blond, shaggy hair a shade lighter than Sophia's, their suntanned faces slightly darker.

But it was Christina who drew her attention—the delicate planes of her face, her rapt expression.

As she worked, she speculated on what her daughters could be discussing so seriously.

And then she knew.

Slowly, with a feeling of betrayal, she closed the sketchbook. She not only had to endure the speculation of all Sonoma on her marriage, but also that of her daughters. It was not fair.

No way existed to explain all the complexities, even if she were inclined to do so.

How could she make anyone understand that she endured Emil Borneman solely because of her overwhelming sense of responsibility? How could she make anyone realize that she had contributed, more than anyone else, toward making him what he was?

She continued to stand, watching her daughters, committing the scene to memory. Artistically and emotionally, it presented a challenge she could not resist.

Abruptly the mood, the composition, was broken as Sophia's husband Dan strolled toward the tables. The children jumped up from their game and ran to pull at his arms, begging some favor. He put a hand on each son's head and steered them toward the table where Sophia and Christina waited. Margaret tucked her sketch pad under her arm and went to join them.

Later, as she drove with Christina northward toward home through the Festival traffic, Margaret was tempted to ask what they had been talking about. But Christina seemed to be in one of those withdrawn, noncommunicative moods. She rode with her face averted, looking toward the distant vineyards, the rolling hills beyond. There was no use trying to talk to her when she was lost in daydreams. Margaret drove the narrow, crowded road effortlessly, her mind forming phrases to be used if ever she had the opportunity.

Perhaps it was hopeless. There was too much about her life that she could not tell her daughters. The rest, they would not understand. The attitudes in those days were so different. She had been born into another world.

Her daughters already had been told, many times, of her early life amidst artistic, genteel poverty. They knew hers had been a lonely life as an only child—her father an aging musician, her mother immersed in her past glories as Vienna's prima ballerina.

Margaret's father had fled Kaiser Wilhelm's conscription before World War I. Already an accomplished musician and composer, August Kretchmer believed that the life of an artist should be inviolate. After the assassination of Archduke Franz Ferdinand, he convinced the young ballerina Albertina Kriner that she should flee Austria—with him.

Throughout his seventy-two years, he had adhered to his artistic beliefs, despite his personal tragedies. Arthritis turned him from a superb violinist into a minor music professor at San Francisco City College. Changed musical tastes left his lengthy, somber compositions unpublished. Margaret had heard him say, many times, "I shall never compromise musical integrity."

Margaret was the child of her parents' later years. Albertina, already devastated mentally by what time had done to her as a dancer, was doubly bewildered by her belated motherhood. She wept often for her daughter. She was capable of doing little else.

August Kretchmer was fifty-five when Margaret was born. By then he had long ago resigned himself to a childless marriage. He and Albertina were entrenched in their habits, August with his music classes, Albertina teaching ballet. They had little room in their lives for a baby. From infancy Margaret was treated as an adult.

August found that Margaret had inherited none of his talent for music. Albertina said she lacked the rhythm for dance. But from the age of three Margaret demonstrated precocious talent in drawing. August was mollified sufficiently to joke: "At last we have a true artist in the family."

All this Christina and Sophia knew. But how could they understand the burdens of growing up with parents older than the grandparents of her classmates? Christina and Sophia had never known poverty. How could she make them understand the constant, gnawing sacrifice of patching and mending school dresses until they were threadbare, of keeping one party dress through a season, of staying home night after night because there might—just might—be an impromptu dutch treat, and her without a nickel in her purse? Could they comprehend the guilt her parents' sacrifices brought? Always, there were other children in her home, her parents' students, witnessing at first hand the Kretchmers' unadorned poverty. And added to the shame was the knowledge that all too soon she would be left alone in the world.

A few days after her high school graduation, Margaret fled to San Francisco, vowing that she would make piles of money. Never again would she need be so frugal.

But her talents were limited. She was not experienced enough to succeed as a painter, nor did she have the technique for high fashion illustration. But she was facile. She quickly developed a knack for whipping out scads of drawings for bargain basement ads— work the established commercial artists detested.

She survived.

How could she convey to Sophia and Christina the pride she felt in that modest accomplishment?

And how could she ever hope to make them understand the mores of the times, of a nineteen-year-old still a virgin in the year that Barbara Bel Geddes shocked sensibilities just by uttering the word from a Broadway stage?

It had been such an innocent world. Sophia and Christina were adept in ways she had never been.

How could she explain her complete lack of judgment in her marriage? Her experience with men had been so woefully limited.

Emil Borneman had seemed to be the answer to her every hope. He was tall, blond, and handsome, with a hint of humor in his blue eyes, a ready grin for the pleasantries of others. He was gentle, confident, full of life. He dressed well, with attention to detail. He seemed to be boiling over with grand plans. He talked enthusiastically of the money he soon would be making.

How was she to know that his self-assured manner and easy boasts hid rampant self-doubts? How could she have seen beneath the surface humor, where he harbored dark resentments against his own family, resentments so black that in time they would turn her marriage into a living hell?

His parents were German immigrants who had settled on a small acreage in northern Sonoma County. Prohibition had destroyed the market for their quality Zinfandel grapes. The farm was sold, chiefly to finance the education of the elder sons. Harold, the oldest, attended UCLA, became an engineer, won a scholarship for postgraduate work at MIT, and was frequently in the news during space shots. The middle son, Ernst, studied medicine at Johns Hopkins, specialized in surgery, and gained extensive recognition for new techniques in microsurgery. By the time Emil completed high school, the family money was gone. The older brothers had married, were busy building their own families. They did not feel compelled to sacrifice for the education of their younger brother.

Not until three years after Margaret married Emil did she learn the depth of his bitterness. He refused to attend his father's funeral. He would not speak to his brothers.

Emil spoke the language of business. Margaret had believed in him. As a salesman he was "opening up the territory" to a new line of carpeting. He talked fluently of commissions, housing starts, and retail outlets. But in his one bid for independence from his family he failed miserably. He had neither the aggressive salesman's personality nor the quiet, sincere warmth of successful salesmen in the South and West.

By the time Margaret learned of Emil's shortcomings, Sophia was on the way.

Emil's father arranged a job with Silvio Moretti, who in better times had bought the family's grapes. Emil accepted work in the vineyards, assuring Margaret that the move to Sonoma County would be temporary; soon they would be back in San Francisco. That time never came.

There was no way she could describe to Sophia and Christina the many complex, bitter disappointments in her life.

And if they could not understand these basic facts, how could they comprehend the other things?

Four miles from town the road passed through the grounds of Sonoma State School. As Margaret braked for a stoplight, six afflicted children cautiously left the curb and crossed in front of the car, holding hands. They were led by a short, stocky boy in his early teens, whose heavy brow was wrinkled with the concentration of his responsibility. Their labored, halting walk across the street brought Christina out of her reverie.

"When you were little, you always cried when you saw them," Margaret reminded her.

"I still do, inside," Christina said. The light changed. Margaret drove on through the intersection. Christina was watching the other children wandering about the grounds. "What used to bother me, I think I knew somehow that they would spend all of their lives in there."

"Well, they say they're happy," Margaret told her.

"Do 'they' really know?" Christina asked. "I would think that even the dumbest among them must sometimes wonder why he was chosen to be so afflicted."

Margaret glanced uneasily at Christina. Sometimes she worried about this dark side of her daughter's nature.

They rode in silence until the turnoff to the ranch road. Then Christina spoke, revealing what had been bothering her all the way out from town.

"You really *do* want to go to the party, don't you?"

Margaret's answer was automatic. "Christina, it's really not that important. You're home, and . . ."

"Mom, I mean this," Christina interrupted. "I wouldn't have come home if I'd known it would upset your plans. I saw Johnny Moretti at the Blessing of the Grapes. He offered to take me to the party. So that solves the problem of my being excess baggage, if that's your concern."

Margaret turned her head to hide her reaction. She waited until she was certain she could speak naturally.

"Well, if you really want to go . . ." She trailed off in indecision. Emil would be furious.

"Let's see what Daddy thinks," she added.

Although Christina now found it difficult to believe, there had been a time in her childhood when her father loved her. He had demonstrated his love in countless ways. In the deepest corners of her memory, impressions of the comfort of his arms remained, the warmth of his kisses on her neck and ears, the joy of running to him when he came home from the vineyards.

She was never certain of the exact point when everything changed. Three psychiatrists in succession had sought that moment without success. One of them had even suggested that those memories were daydreams—projections of her deep hunger for affection. But she knew otherwise.

The memories were real. She had known delicious years of total happiness. At one time her father had been loving, demonstrative, warm.

No one would ever convince her she had imagined that happening.

Nor had the psychiatrists ever found the roots of her hatred of the house in which she spent her childhood. The obsession was there, intense, undeniable.

As her mother turned off the ranch road and drove under the Moretti Vineyard sign at the head of the long driveway, Christina once again felt the oppressive sense of gloom that enveloped her each time she approached the old Victorian monstrosity.

Restored by Silvio Moretti in the early 1940s, the house was almost hidden in a small grove of redwood and eucalyptus trees, well back from the ranch road. A three-story tower and tall steeple dominated the south side. The rest of the building, for all its gingerbread, was quite ordinary. Heavy eaves, large windows, wooden pillars, and an ornate front gallery railing provided the only relief from the severe lines. A legend persisted that Robert Louis Stevenson had visited the house on his trip to the valley in 1880 and was served a glass of sherry on the gallery. Christina often wondered what he had thought of the house. Certainly he had chosen the Jacob Schram home, a few miles away, as the setting for *The Silverado Squatters*.

A row of outbuildings, scattered through the trees, housed the mechanical equipment to service Silvio Moretti's far-flung holdings. In essence the Borneman home served as headquarters for the Moretti vineyards throughout three counties. Emil maintained a small office in the corner of the largest building and, in more recent years, maintained contact with his crews by radio.

"We're late," Margaret said. "Emil's already home for lunch."

Christina caught a note of anxiety. She glanced at her mother, concerned.

Clearly, the argument over the party was a surface issue, a safe substitute for something else. Christina opened her mouth to suggest it might be better to forget the party, but before words came, she remembered Johnny Moretti, the electric moments with those brown eyes, the firm but gentle touch of his hand.

She *did* want to go to the party.

She remained silent as she followed Margaret into the house.

Emil was seated in front of the television set, reading the *Sonoma Index-Tribune*. The TV was on, the sound turned low.

He had aged since her last visit home three years ago. His once-thick blond hair, always combed straight back, had thinned to reveal pale scalp. The lines of his face had deepened. His pale blue eyes, which once held a hint of humor, were surrounded now by crow's feet and reflected only sadness. He still wore the inevitable work shirt and high-bibbed overalls, and with his aged, weathered face, resembled more and more a subject in a Grant Wood painting.

He nodded a greeting as they entered.

"I'll have lunch on the table in a minute," Margaret said, flustered. "I made a casserole. All I have to do is warm it."

"No hurry," Emil said. "We're taking the afternoon off. The men want to go to the Festival. And of course that's fine with Silvio. It doesn't matter that there's work to be done."

Christina went up to her room to change. When she returned, her mother was making trips back and forth between dining room and kitchen, carrying food, chatting through the open doors to Emil about the sale of her paintings, the crowds in town, acquaintances she had seen. Emil was listening without comment, his head back on the chair, the newspaper on his lap.

The scene was hauntingly familiar. Christina stood in the doorway for a moment, trying to determine why the atmosphere was so different.

When *had* everything changed?

She always came back to that.

"Christina? You there?" Margaret called from the kitchen. "Come on. Lunch is ready."

As they sat down at the table, Christina studied her parents.

If anything, her mother seemed younger, was even more attractive, than on her last visit.

Margaret had always placed great importance on clothing, grooming. As long as Christina could remember, her mother's bedroom had been filled with well-thumbed copies of *Vogue, Harper's Bazaar, Town and Country*. She had a flair for fashion. Given a few scarves, old skirts and blouses, and a few fragments of fabric, she could create striking, totally new costumes. She was full of energy, gregarious. All through Christina's childhood Margaret had organized groups of children for expeditions to the San Francisco Opera, museums, concerts. Christina's friends had loved her. In later years many of them told Christina that Margaret had been a tremendous influence in their lives. Christina knew they were sincere, for she had felt the effect on her own life. Margaret had deepened her awareness of beauty—of art, music, dance. Christina's own talents were limited, but before her marriage Sophia had become a pianist bordering on concert caliber.

The contrast between Emil and Margaret had always been puzzling. Christina had never known such a mismatched couple in her life.

Emil was painfully inarticulate on any subject that mattered. He disliked to leave his set routine of home and work. He was uncomfortable, awkward in the homes of others.

Now, he became aware of her attention.

"How about you?" he asked. "See anyone you knew?"

Christina smiled at him. He was making an effort. "A few. None from my age group. Most of my old friends apparently have moved away." She paused. "I did see Johnny Moretti."

He glanced at her with what she thought might be a flash of anger, but when he spoke, his voice conveyed only surprise. "Johnny? In Sonoma?" He paused for a moment, thinking. "Did he say what he's doing here?"

Vaguely disturbed at his reaction, Christina hesitated. "He said something about business."

Margaret remained atypically silent.

Emil frowned. He looked at Margaret, then turned back to Christina. "Johnny doesn't spend much time around his father now," he said. "He seldom visits home. Grown a little too big for his britches, I hear. Silvio keeps talking about bringing him back to the winery, but Johnny seems to be having too much fun playing around."

Christina stifled her impulse to jump to Johnny's defense. She had received reports vastly different concerning Johnny's life-style. "I've heard he's doing very well," she said quietly.

Margaret seemed upset. She reached for the casserole. "More macaroni?" she asked Emil.

With a wave of his hand Emil declined another serving. He also refused to be steered off the subject. He spoke in a flat, lifeless voice, with that ingrained tone of bitterness Christina remembered so well. "Johnny's had the world handed to him on a silver platter. With Silvio's money and muscle behind him, he doesn't have to worry."

Christina waited until he resumed toying with his fruit compote. She exchanged glances with her mother. She received no signal. "Johnny asked me to go to the party with him tonight."

Emil placed his napkin carefully on the table. "What did you say?"

"That I didn't know your plans. But I talked with mother. I see no reason why I can't go with Johnny. That would leave you and mother free to go . . ."

Emil turned to glare at Margaret. "No!" he said.

Margaret was sitting stiff, motionless. She faced Emil in silence.

He turned back to Christina. "You shouldn't go out with him," he said. "Johnny is too fast for you."

Christina laughed at the word. "Daddy, I've been taking care of myself for five years. I'm not exactly naive. Besides, I've known him all my life. He's always been a perfect gentleman."

"You could think of *my* feelings," he said.

"Emil!" Margaret said.

Christina stared at him, genuinely puzzled. "What do you mean?"

For a moment he seemed on the verge of lashing out at her, as he had done all through her childhood. But he hesitated. He seemed to have second thoughts. He rubbed his chin with a thumb as he searched for words. "Look, Christina, I work for the Morettis. We live in their house. Like serfs. If you go out with Johnny Moretti, it would look like you're trying to step out of place, trying to become more than you are."

Christina was frozen into stunned silence. Several seconds passed before she could speak. "Daddy, that's ridiculous! I've never felt that way about the Morettis."

"Perhaps it's time you did."

Again Christina glanced at her mother, but Margaret sat rigid, her face pale.

Christina spoke carefully. "Daddy, in the last five years I've mixed socially and professionally with people from all walks of life, some rich, some poor, some unknown, some very, very well known. I have never felt for a single moment that I was from the wrong side of the tracks."

Naked hatred blazed in her father's eyes. The words burned into her memory. "I know!" he said, raising his voice. "Just like your mother! You think you're just a little bit better than the rest of us, don't you?"

Christina did not answer. She slowly rose from her chair, placed her napkin on the table, and walked up to her room with as much dignity as she could manage.

When her mother came upstairs some time later, Christina was beyond tears. She had been lying facedown across the bed, the many uncertainties of her life sweeping through her mind.

She stirred at her mother's gentle knock.

"Johnny Moretti is on the phone," Margaret said. "What shall I tell him?"

Christina's first impulse was to send word to Johnny that she would not be able to go. But she knew that if she did, she would regret it, perhaps for the rest of her life.

If she did not go to the party with Johnny, she might never have a chance to resolve those lingering daydreams, to determine if all the heartache and sleepless nights of her adolescence had been justified.

She knew her father was wrong about Johnny and the Morettis. She resented his accusations against Johnny as much as she did those against herself.

She reached for the extension. "I'll take the call."

Margaret started to speak, then seemed to change her mind. She backed out of the room, closing the door.

Christina picked up the receiver. "The answer is yes, if you're still of mind," she said.

Johnny's voice brought immediate, warm reassurance. "Terrific. You can't know how pleased I am to hear that."

"To the contrary, I'm grateful to you," she said. "You've solved my problem of being a fifth wheel."

He was silent a moment. "Look," he said. "This is just an impulse. We've got more than five hours to kill before the party. I plan to drive back downtown and stroll around the Plaza, take in the Festival. Would you like to come?"

Christina thought of her father, waiting downstairs with his spiteful accusations, of her mother, pale and strangely disturbed.

"I would like that very much," she said.

She resisted her desire to tell him to hurry.

She did not want to stay in the house another minute.

CHAPTER 4

CARLO Moretti and Patsy Jean Litton lay writhing in her supersized waterbed, their bodies slamming together furiously in an inescapable rhythm. Carlo was drenched in sweat. The smell of sex in the small, poorly ventilated apartment was driving him into a frenzy. He struggled for a better foothold on the bed and pushed deeper into Patsy Jean, edging toward his third release in a little more than an hour. Patsy Jean had lost count. She met his renewed intensity with another spasm, arching to meet his thrusts. Then she reached behind her hip to fondle his testicles—a trick that invariably sent him over the brink.

They rolled apart, still breathing in labored gasps.

"God, Carlo, sometimes I think you're part horse," Patsy Jean said.

Carlo did not answer. Patsy Jean had a terrific body and a face that could grace a fashion magazine, but she talked too much, in that goddamn West Texas twang. At times Carlo wished she would simply shut up.

"I'll bet I carried two hundred beers out to the tables today," she said. "And you know, there's nothin' I want more right now than a good, cold beer. Isn't that funny?"

Carlo grunted and reached for a towel. He mopped the sweat from his face and hair.

"Wouldja get me one, honey?" Patsy Jean asked. "That'd be the nicest thing you could do for me, right now—get me a good, cold beer."

Using her bare hip for leverage, Carlo pushed himself off the bed. He crossed to the kitchenette and took two cans of beer from the refrigerator, pulled the tabs, and handed one to Patsy Jean.

"Thanks, hon," she said. "That's sweet. You know, I think everybody ought to have to spend some time waiting on other people. I mean, a lot of people will put a waitress down, like they're a lower class, or something. But it's good training. It teaches you to think about the other person—what the other person wants, instead of what you want all the time."

Carlo laughed. Patsy Jean looked at him suspiciously. "Are you making fun of me?" she asked.

Carlo patted her rump. "Of course not," he said. "You just have an unusual way of looking at things."

The answer did not satisfy Patsy Jean completely, but she seemed pleased.

"It's true, you know. I was really a self-centered little snot when I left home. That was one of the troubles between me and Ralph. I paid too much attention to myself, and not enough to him. I was always worrying about how my hair looked, what I had to wear. Ralph just finally got tired of it and kicked my ass out."

Carlo had heard another version, involving a tight end with the Los Angeles Rams. He offered no comment.

"Maybe things will be better with us, just because I've learned to think about other people. You know what I mean, hon?"

Carlo continued to drink his beer in silence. Patsy Jean had been talking about "us" more and more lately, despite his plain warning that his family came first. He glanced at his watch. He was due home in twenty minutes.

"I'd better shower," he said. He got up from the bed and moved toward the bathroom.

"Well, wham bam thank you ma'am!" Patsy Jean said, her voice rising in indignation. "Come back sometime, sugar. Like when you're horny again!"

Carlo sat back down on the bed. "Patsy, we're supposed to have an understanding," he said. "We've always agreed that our relationship is built on sex. Good sex. Terrific sex. You enjoy it as much as I do. You've admitted that. We've got something good going here. Why do we have to fuck it up with things we can't help?"

Patsy Jean buried her head in his shoulder. "Oh, hell, I know, Carlo." She began to cry. He held her for a time, patting her. Then she pushed away, wiped her eyes, and looked at him. "It's just that sometimes, when I'm alone, I get so goddamn blue, thinking about how you always got to go off and spend all your time with your damned family."

"Patsy, listen to me. Don't talk that way. My family is the most important thing in the world to me. I've never made any secret of that."

"I know, I know," Patsy Jean said. "But if we could just go somewhere once in a while. Like tonight. Why couldn't we pile in the car and take off for the beach, or go down somewhere around the Bay and dance awhile? No one would see us. No one would ever know."

Carlo sighed. "I've got to go to a party tonight. At Pop's house. There's no way I can duck that."

Patsy Jean sat looking at him, rhythmically tapping her empty beer can with a red fingernail.

"Okay, so you got a party to go to. What about tomorrow night? Some night next week? Can't we do it sometime?"

"Maybe," Carlo said. "I'll work on it."

He headed for the shower. Patsy Jean came and stood in the bathroom door, watching him.

"Who all is going to be at the party?" she asked.

"Mostly people in for the Festival," he told her over the sound of the water. "The governor, Sam Cavanaugh, a senator or two, a few people up from Hollywood, some of Pop's old cronies."

"I sure as hell wish I was going," Patsy Jean said. "Couldn't you sneak me in?"

Carlo laughed. "Listen, I'll keep a low profile myself around there tonight. The old man will be watching everything that moves."

He turned off the shower and stepped out onto the bathmat, reaching for a towel.

"Here, let me do that," Patsy Jean said.

Carlo stood motionless while Patsy Jean rubbed him with the towel.

"Do you think he's queer?" she asked.

"Who?" Carlo asked, startled.

"The governor," Patsy Jean said matter-of-factly. "I've heard that he's queer and is just using what's-her-name, that actress, for a cover."

Carlo laughed. "Where in hell did you hear that?"

Patsy Jean shrugged. "Oh, I've heard it several times, from different people."

"There are stories like that about a lot of famous people," Carlo pointed out. "When I was a kid, we always had a hot rumor that some actress was a lesbian, or that some big, macho actor liked to dress up in women's clothes and put on lipstick. I've always wondered where those rumors get started."

"So you think the governor's okay, huh?"

"If he's not banging that actress, he's not queer, he's crazy," Carlo said.

"I'll bet I could find out if he's a live one," Patsy Jean said.

"I have no doubt you could," Carlo said.

Patsy Jean had reached his crotch with the towel. Under her rhythmic motion, he felt himself stirring again.

Patsy Jean laughed and gave his penis a stinging slap. "No you don't! One more round with that thang today would probably kill me."

She handed him the towel and returned to the waterbed. By the time he emerged from the bathroom to dress, she had turned on the television set and was totally immersed in a game show. When he left, she hardly seemed to notice.

CHAPTER 5

CHRISTINA seemed quiet and subdued. As they drove back toward Sonoma in his Porsche, she held a handkerchief in her left hand and occasionally brought it to her face. Occupied with maneuvering on the narrow roads crowded with Festival traffic, Johnny could not be certain, but despite her stream of small talk, he thought she was fighting back tears. He took care to seem not to notice. He sensed that for the moment she might need privacy more than comfort from a comparative stranger. The thought occurred to him that he might not be the only one experiencing a difficult homecoming.

He found a parking space on the east side of the Plaza, near the Sebastiani Theatre. Arm in arm, he and Christina walked leisurely across First Street East.

A western band was swinging into "The Orange Blossom Special" as they entered the Plaza. Johnny and Christina joined the crowd in the shade of the trees and listened for a while. Then they strolled on past Grinstead Memorial Amphitheater and a performing rock band.

Christina's spirits seemed to improve. She shared her amusement over the variety of sizes and shapes among the tourists—knobby kneed men in Bermuda-length walking shorts and ankle socks, couples in matched loud shirts, oversized women in straining jeans.

They spent more than an hour wandering among the art displays on the northwest corner of the Plaza. Then, along with most of the crowd, they stood at the curb on Spain Street to watch local firemen compete with fire hoses, using an empty beer barrel as a puck. The water play drenched much of the crowd, to its collective glee. Johnny and Christina escaped with a light sprinkling, welcome in the accumulated heat of the fading day.

When they had circled the Plaza and were returning to the car, Christina pointed across the street. "Let's go over to the creamery," she said. "Please! It'll be my treat."

They crossed to the corner and entered the Old Sonoma Creamery. Beyond the delicatessen, with its smells of exotic meats and cheeses, was the ice cream parlor with the highly polished plank floors and immaculate wooden booths Johnny remembered so well. It was nearly empty. Behind the counter the attendants were busy, preparing to close. A tall blond girl of high school age came to take their order.

"Vanilla," Christina said.

"You're sure?" Johnny asked. There was a long list of flavors.

"I've always wondered why they bother to make any other kind."

"Two," Johnny told the waitress. He sat for a moment, watching Christina as she examined the signs and displays. He was certain now, from a telltale puffiness around her eyes, that she had been crying earlier.

As he watched, she seemed to retreat into herself for a time—a self-imposed trance he was coming to recognize. He waited patiently, wondering what memories the place held for her. He did not speak until the meditative glaze left her eyes, and she glanced up at him with a slightly startled smile.

"How did you ever decide to spend your time in a museum?" he asked.

"Well, why not?"

"You seem like a lively person, full of ideas. Isn't it dull?"

She made a face. There were traces of amusement at the corners of her eyes. "I hope you don't often show your ignorance in public like that."

"Well, you have to admit that museum work sounds dull. I have visions of your going around with a feather duster, tidying up a lot of old curiosities."

She laughed. "There's too much pressure to worry about a little dust. Anyhow, there's so much going on, no dust could possibly settle."

"Pressure? In a museum?"

She nodded.

"Okay, tell me. How could there be pressure in a nice, quiet, regal museum?"

The dishes of ice cream arrived. Christina ate slowly. Johnny sensed that the cold goodness would be restorative to a throat perhaps stinging a little from September sun and swallowed tears. She seemed to be savoring the nostalgia that came with the ice cream, still made pale and pure right here in Sonoma exactly as it had been made when they had to climb up on the chairs on their knees to eat from these tables.

"All right," Christina said. "I'll take you behind the big brass doors to the executive offices, for a short course in museum management."

"You have a title?"

She nodded. "Curator of Exhibitions. That automatically makes me an assistant director. Now, let's suppose I'm putting together a retrospective exhibition of the work of, say, Jackson Pollock. My staff and I will do extensive preliminary research—a job in itself. We may find that in all America there are eighty paintings I want in the show, works that best exemplify the significant points in Pollock's career. And, just for purposes of illustration, let's say you have a Jackson Pollock I want to borrow for my exhibition."

"I do have a Jackson Pollock," he told her. "And you can have it for your show. That's that."

She blinked at him. "You're kidding."

"No, I'm not," he assured her.

"*You* have a Jackson Pollock?"

"As it happens, I do. Don't you think I'm the type?"

"Frankly, no. I would have expected something more on the order of *Penthouse* centerfolds."

There was a hint of challenge in her gaze. Johnny was more puzzled than offended. "Now why did you say a thing like that?" he asked.

Christina gave him an enigmatic smile. "Oh, I have received reports on you, from time to time," she said. "Let's just say it's sometimes a smaller world than we think."

Johnny hesitated, and saw that she was amused by his indecision. Sensing a trap, he chose not to pursue it.

"My centerfolds, I don't lend," he said. "We were discussing my Jackson Pollock."

"All right. Let's suppose you are very fond of it and don't want to let it out of your sight. I would have to convince you that you must lend it for my show. So first I would ascertain where it is hanging, the importance you place on it. Is it by chance in your bedroom?"

"No."

"Where, then?"

"In my office."

"Oh, good. I mean, I was thinking of the moisture. I hear you live on a houseboat. A prominent place in your office?"

"On the wall, opposite my desk."

"Then I assume it does mean something to you, and that for the two or three months I want to borrow it, you would miss it, with the blank wall staring back at you."

"Well, I still have those centerfolds."

"Oh, hush. Now, if you were really an art connoisseur, or if you had a small art museum and the span of my show matched your busiest season, you would be very reluctant to lend it. Right?"

He thought about the blank wall. He *would* miss that painting.

"Maybe," he said.

"So what I would do, I would come to see you and convince you in some subtle way that if your painting were in my show, its value would be enhanced immeasurably, because from then on it would be considered one of Pollock's major works. I would also hint that if it were not in my show, it would for all time be considered a minor Pollock."

"I cut class a lot in law school," Johnny said, "but I think they call that extortion."

"Multiply your painting by the eighty I would need for the show, and you see what I do for a living," she said. "Six or seven major shows a year, and that's four or five hundred cases of extortion annually."

"A one-girl crime wave," Johnny said. "It must keep you busy. Who's your personal legal retainer?"

"That's just the beginning. There must be a book—an impressive art publication to record each show. I have to find an expert who can write—no small item. I have to find a prestigious, reputable publisher. Each of those eighty paintings for the show must be shipped in an individual, handsome crate. And of course insurance must be arranged on each. The insurance company may insist on a courier. Each courier must have travel accommodations, insurance ..."

"You've convinced me," Johnny said.

"I'm not finished. We have to arrange to have the right people at the opening, to get the proper attention, the so-called leading critics from the so-called right publications ..."

"Enough, enough," Johnny said. "Never again will I speak from ignorance about museum work."

Christina grinned. "Anyway, that's what I do."

"You like it?"

She seemed to consider her answer. "It's something to do. It's interesting. But I don't think I want to do it for the rest of my life."

"Good. Then you're not one of those dedicated career *persons*."

"I suppose not."

"Why don't you come back west?" Johnny asked. "Wouldn't it be better here than in Boston? I wouldn't be able to stand the winters up there."

She laughed. "Offhand, I'd say I would rather live in Boston than on a houseboat."

"Even a houseboat on a tranquil clear bay? With lots of sea life and water birds? A big roomy three-story houseboat that lets you breathe?"

"Three stories? You're joking!"

"Scout's honor."

"That I would like to see."

Johnny glanced at his watch. "We could be there and back in two hours."

Christina spooned the last of the ice cream from her dish and grinned. She looked up at him.

"I think you'd better take me home, so we can go to the party," she said.

CHAPTER 6

"CARLO was . . . unavailable," Salvatore Messino said.

Silvio grimaced. Someday Carlo would stir up serious trouble with his women. He carefully lit a cigar, taking his time. He did not want his friend Salvatore to suspect his mood. His long, exasperating talk with Johnny lingered like an ominous cloud. He could not shake a sense of foreboding.

Tonight Silvio needed a son.

Johnny chose not to fulfill his obligation.

And Carlo was out screwing.

Faithful, reliable Salvatore Messino would have to do.

Silvio and Salvatore were seated in the back of the poker parlor, in the dimly lit room that served as Salvatore's private office. The door was open, and from where he sat, Silvio could see the players at the green felt-topped tables beneath the ornate Tiffany-styled lampshades. A low murmur of voices came from the bar in the front room. Silvio found himself wishing his sons possessed the desire to share this warm camaraderie that had so enriched his own life. He turned to Salvatore.

"My Festival party comes at an unfortunate time," he said. "There are things to be done. And tonight I cannot devote the necessary attention to them."

"So you would like for me to oil and to prepare the *lupara*," Salvatore said.

He smiled to remove the bluntness of his words.

Silvio nodded, pleased. At least there were still people around him who truly understood.

It was a Corsican expression, dating back to their childhood. The *lupara* was a double barrel, sawed-off shotgun. The stock also was shortened, hollowed out for lightness and hinged for a compact bundle that easily could be concealed. The weapon was ugly and deadly, made even more awesome by the fact that it clearly was designed to be used on only one animal—man.

"I have misjudged Lucian Hall," Silvio said. "Apparently he has not risen so high that he has forgotten the past. He is pressing me sooner, and far more viciously, than I anticipated. I must give him an answer. Very soon. But there are several things I need to know before I can make a decision. There are matters that should be set in motion tonight. And I must be away from the phone for several crucial hours."

"I have nothing else to do," Messino said, smiling. "Your parties are too rich for my blood."

Silvio knew that this was not true. Salvatore's wrinkled, dark olive face retained a hint of the aristocratic bearing he remembered from their days as young men. Now in his mid-seventies, Salvatore still walked ramrod straight, proud. Yet, all through the years he had declined to attend Silvio's social functions, as if denying himself participation in a life he should have earned for himself. Silvio knew that he and Salvatore were much alike. But Salvatore lacked that essential dedication, that relentless drive necessary to build an empire of his own.

Silvio placed a business card on the desk between them.

"This man has been to see me on another matter—a problem I may be able to help him solve. He has important connections," he said. "He can put to work a Florida concern that deals in international corporate intelligence—a very specialized investigative agency. Please convey my apologies to him that I am not calling personally. Assure him that I will call later. Impress upon him the urgency. Ordinarily a report like this requires weeks. I want one in forty-eight hours. He is obligated to me. He may offer to take care of the expenses. Do not allow it. Such a request may entail unusual cost. The material may have to be obtained through unorthodox methods. Make it plain that we expect to pay whatever is necessary."

Salvatore nodded his understanding. He picked up the card. "Herbert Fraser," he said. "I have heard the name."

"My identity must be protected at all costs. The report I want consists of three parts. First, I want to know exactly what Hampton Industries hopes to gain by purchasing my winery. Is the winery the primary target—or is it my position, my influence? Second, how far are they prepared to go? We already know they are prepared to do murder. But are they prepared to incur heavy losses? Has the matter been discussed? Has money been allocated? And to whom? Third—and this is perhaps most important—what is the history of companies after they have been acquired by Hampton Industries? What has happened to the people? To the workers? To the customers? To the quality of the product?"

"A tall order," Salvatore said.

"Not for a man of proper connections," Silvio said. "And this man has those connections."

"I will convey your urgency," Salvatore said.

Silvio placed another business card on the desk.

"Call this man, offer my apologies and so forth, and tell him I will contact him personally later. Tell him I need to know much about Hampton Industries—the plants, the factories, the operations. Ask him—and this phraseology is important—ask him to determine where Hampton Industries is most vulnerable. He will know what I mean."

Salvatore nodded, still smiling. "I understand," he said. "You are cocking the *lupara*."

As Silvio entered the patio, the string ensemble were setting up their instruments and sound equipment. He stopped to talk briefly with the maestro. Silvio had hired the group on previous occasions. He was confident the quality of music would be suitable. He had gone over the selections earlier with the maestro, striking a few numbers, adding others, making certain that the maestro was familiar with the protocol for the evening.

In the house, Anna assured him that all was in readiness. The servants had arrived. No unforeseen problems had surfaced. Satisfied, Silvio hurried upstairs to dress.

For the first half hour of the party, Silvio and Anna were busy receiving guests. There were old friends to greet—some they had not seen in years. A few of the guests were business associates, peripherally a part of the wine industry, making their annual pilgrimage to the Valley of the Moon. Many were Sonoma residents, close friends whose presence was obligatory. And, shortly after eight thirty, the Sacramento-Beverly Hills entourage arrived.

The other guests formed a circle around Gregory Cavanaugh and applauded.

Silvio moved forward to greet the governor.

"Mrs. Moretti and I are most honored that you could come."

"And we're honored to be here, Mr. Moretti," the governor said.

Gregory Cavanaugh was tall, blond, and lean. His wide, open face was so devoid of guile that it seemed childlike. Only the eyes reflected his intelligence, his shrewdness. Gregory's actress friend, slim and petite, remained a pace apart, her hip-length hair sensuously following her movements. The two gubernatorial aides who had visited Silvio earlier to make arrangements stood quietly in the background.

Gregory introduced Silvio and Anna to the dozen or more young entertainers in his entourage.

Rarely had Silvio seen so much beauty assembled. Any one of the young women would have added excitement to the party. Taken together, the effect was breathtaking. The tempo of the party was interrupted for a time by their flamboyant arrival. Silvio moved among them, exchanging amenities. He then walked to the microphone on the bandstand.

His remarks were carefully planned.

All day he had been concerned that the rumors of the possible sale of the winery would cast a pall over the party. He now set out to lighten the evening.

"My friends, honored guests. Many of you with us tonight are

distinguished visitors to Sonoma, who have come to help us cele-
brate our bountiful harvest, a good vintage year. I cannot introduce
you all. But I would be remiss if I did not present some of our most
illustrious guests, beginning with our popular governor."

Cavanaugh drew more warm applause. He acknowledged the
spontaneous demonstration with a nod, his well-publicized smile
intact.

"Gregory already has announced that he will serve only two
terms as governor," Silvio added. "It is unfortunate that he plans to
end his political career so young."

The guests responded with delighted laughter and more applause. Cavanaugh's plans to run for the United States Senate were
well known.

Silvio went on down his list—the senators, the actors and entertainers—using his exceptional memory to cite the accomplishments
of each, slipping in quips and jokes that kept the guests laughing.

He concluded by inviting Gregory and his companion to open
the dance.

As the couple moved onto the floor, Sam Cavanaugh came up
behind Silvio and whispered in his ear.

"You're in good form tonight, Silvio," he said. "I hate to ask.
And I wouldn't impose on your duties as host, were it not a matter
of greatest urgency. But could Greg and I talk with you sometime
later in the evening? We'll try not to keep you long."

"Of course," Silvio said.

Anna had heard part of the exchange.

"Silvio! Surely you are not going to go off and talk business! Not
tonight!"

Silvio guided her onto the dance floor to the strains of a waltz.

"Anna," he said, "life is business, and business is life. They are
inseparable. Surely you know that by now."

He held her close, wondering what additional problems Sam
Cavanaugh and his son had brought to the Moretti family.

CHAPTER 7

FOR as long as Johnny could remember, the hillside below the family home had been planted in vines of varied origins. From the house all the way down to the flat land below, carefully tended experimental cuttings held the secrets to future Moretti vintages. It was here, back in the thirties, when most California wines sold in bulk for hardly more than Coca-Cola, that Silvio had nurtured a rare clone of Johannisberg Riesling. Here was developed the Moretti Zinfandel, a grape that produced the big, powerful, pungent wine that had become the winery's most popular label. And here, cultivated with Silvio's dedicated attention, were a few direct descendants of the first vines planted by the mission fathers in the Valley of the Moon.

During the thirties and the forties most vintners in the valley had regarded Silvio's hillside experiments as little more than a harmless hobby. Experimentation was generally considered impractical, for new vines did not produce grapes suitable for fine wine until the third year. Silvio himself never regarded a vine as mature until the tenth harvest. He sold his immature grapes to be processed in bulk under other people's labels. For his own labeling, Silvio awaited results patiently, acting on intuition and the expertise of Cal State's Viticultural College. Not until the vines had matured to his satisfaction, and he was pleased with the results of the processing, did he allow the Moretti name to be used on the products from his vineyards. In time his high standards had made the Moretti label synonymous with quality. When the wine boom started in the fifties, Silvio's proven vines were the foundation for the most successful expansion program among California's wineries. Silvio's private garden had become a legend. Tonight it served as fitting backdrop for a private party celebrating Sonoma's annual Vintage Festival.

"I'd almost forgotten what it was like from up here," Christina said. She stood looking out over the hillside vineyard, toward the lights of the town below. She was wearing a white silk chiffon evening dress that accented her narrow waist. The back was bare, and in front the shirred bodice crisscrossed, suspended like a necklace. Coral earrings, her only jewelry, softened the formality of the dress, made deeper by the olive shadows in her face. Sometimes, when she turned her green eyes to him in conversation, the little flashes of color interplayed to make him think of sea-viewing Mediterranean villages he had visited, and of the way their tinted villas looked through the sun-softened white haze.

"You should have visited more often," Johnny said.

"I was too young for your famous high school orgies," she said. "I used to come along with Mom, or Dad, on some errand or other sometimes, many years ago. But I've been gone so long, I was never invited as an adult. For me, this has always been a rather mysterious place. And fascinating."

"I wish I'd known," Johnny said. "I would have helped you solve the mystery."

"It's a wonderful party," she said. "Thank you for bringing me."

The Spanish strings lilted into "La Paloma." The patio filled with couples dancing cheek to cheek. Johnny took Christina's hand, and they stood watching.

Johnny was relieved to be away from the crowd. For more than an hour he and Christina had mingled with the guests, the two jovial senators and their serious, tense young aides, Greg Cavanaugh and his entourage, the film stars, and Silvio's friends and business associates.

He glanced at Christina. Although she was disarmingly adept at small talk, she seemed upset again. Once, earlier in the evening, while they were separated briefly, Johnny had seen her in heated argument with her mother. And now he could see her father glowering in their direction from the edge of the dance floor. As he watched, Emil said something to Margaret, and they started across the patio.

Johnny was standing with his arm encircling Christina's waist. "Here come your parents," he said.

He felt her body stiffen beneath his arm. When he turned to her, she was regarding the Bornemans' approach with undisguised dread.

"Hello, Johnny. Good to see you again," Emil Borneman said. He had aged considerably since the last time Johnny had seen him. The broad shoulders were now slightly stooped. His rotund build had settled thickly around the waist, and his pale blue eyes seemed lost in his rounded, weathered face.

Johnny disengaged his arm from Christina to shake hands. He had never fathomed Silvio's selection of dour-faced, unimaginative Emil Borneman as plant general manager. The man was totally lacking in personality.

"Good to be home," Johnny said. He glanced at Christina. "But I didn't know there would be such good company here."

"That was a pleasant surprise to us, too," Margaret Borneman said. She reached out and hugged Christina.

Margaret Borneman posed a remarkable contrast to her husband. She was still an attractive woman, with a delicate figure and well-defined features. There was something of aristocracy in her bearing. Her blue dress reflected conservative, elegant taste. She turned back to Johnny.

"I wish both of you would get home more often," she said.

Johnny smiled at her. "I can't speak for Christina, but my work keeps me busy," he said.

Christina glanced uneasily at him but did not speak. Emil Borneman had turned away from the conversation in obvious dismissal. He stood silent, his attention fully on the dancers.

"We're trying to talk Christina into staying a few days," Mrs. Borneman said to Johnny. "Maybe you can come up for dinner some evening."

Johnny had opened his mouth to accept the invitation when he saw something in Christina's eyes that stopped him. He changed his answer.

"That would be nice, except that I have a heavy schedule this week. Perhaps some other time . . ."

"We will count on it," Mrs. Borneman said. "You two have a good time."

With a grudging nod, Emil Borneman escorted his wife away. Christina watched them go.

"Sometimes I think my father is the rudest man alive," she said.

"Perhaps he's just preoccupied," Johnny said, measuring his words. "He must be a man of considerable ability. My father has always seemed to think the world of him."

Christina nodded. She was silent for a moment.

"Is your father really going to sell the winery?" she asked.

The question was so unexpected that Johnny burst into laughter. His reaction seemed to startle her, to deepen the query on her upturned face.

He explained. "All day that's been the first question everyone has asked—your sister included. I've been with you for hours, and you never bothered."

"Then I'll make up for it by asking twice. Is he?"

Johnny saw no point in evading the question. "I don't know. At this point I think it's only under consideration."

Christina watched Silvio and Anna as they danced, seeming for all the world, at that moment, the reason music was ever created. "I hope he doesn't sell," she said. "I've been around him very little, so I don't really know him. But I have the feeling he would be very unhappy without the winery. It's his life."

The number ended. Silvio said something to Anna. She nodded, then turned and walked toward the house. Silvio came across the patio toward Johnny and Christina.

"I think you're about to have the opportunity to ask the only man in town who may know the answer to that question," Johnny said.

"I wouldn't dare," Christina said under her breath as Silvio approached.

Silvio was shaking his head in mock exasperation. "I never

thought a son of mine would stand on the sidelines with a beautiful woman while there is music. I thought I raised my sons better. You have a broken leg, Johnny?"

"My fault, Mr. Moretti," Christina said. "I wanted to absorb this view from your vineyard."

Silvio turned and looked toward the lights of the town, the dark outlines of the distant hills. "I have not grown tired of it, not in more than fifty years," he said. "The vineyard was here first, you know, before the house. Everything came from this small acreage —the winery, the larger vineyards, the house. A part of the acreage, down there in the corner, once belonged to the mission fathers. Are you interested in wine, Christina?"

"As a product of Sonoma myself, Mr. Moretti. But when people learn I'm from wine country and start talking wines, I feel so ignorant. I should know more."

"I'll tell you what," Silvio said. "You come back here in the daytime, and I will take you on a tour—the vineyards, the winery, everything. Then, when you talk with your Eastern friends, you can assure them that they will never go wrong with the Moretti label."

"Oh, I already do that, Mr. Moretti."

Silvio laughed with delight. "Wonderful." The Spanish band was now into "Cielito Lindo." Silvio held out his arm to Christina. "May I have the honor, since my son is so lazy?" He glanced at Johnny. "With your permission, of course."

Silvio did not wait for a reply.

Johnny stood watching as his father and Christina danced. Silvio held her gently, moving with such enviable ease and confidence that Johnny wondered how his own dancing compared.

"A regular old roué, isn't he?" said Sophia at his elbow.

"We probably don't know the half of it," Johnny said.

Sophia snickered. "Well, he's a wonderful old man," she said. "But what I want to know is, what's with you and Christina?"

Johnny turned and looked at her. Sophia obviously was feeling her wine. Her eyes were bright, her coordination slightly off. "What do you mean?" he asked.

Sophia stared at the glass in her hand. "Oh, I just wondered what's going on," she said. "She just arrived this morning, ostensibly to see her family, and we've hardly caught a glimpse of her.

You've practically kidnapped her, hardly let her out of your sight. Not that she's put up any resistance."

"Sophia, I'm sorry," Johnny said, concerned. "I hadn't looked at it that way . . ."

She caught his arm and stopped him in midsentence. "Oh, God, me and my big mouth! I didn't mean that—not the way it sounded." She moved her hand to Johnny's face. "Look, I don't want you to get the wrong idea. If you and Christina got something going, I'd think it was the greatest thing that ever happened. I mean that, Johnny."

"Sophia," Johnny said, "Christina and I just met this afternoon for the first time since we were in high school. Let's not jump to conclusions."

"Okay, okay," Sophia said, raising a forefinger. "But I see things happening." She swayed slightly, and her hand found Johnny's shoulder for support. "That kid's really got problems," she said. "Christina and Poppa have been crosswise for years. Now it's worse instead of better. And damn it, I'm on her side. But I don't know how to make her see that."

Johnny put an arm around her. "Sophia, you've got a snootful. I hope you're not saying anything you'll regret later."

Sophia giggled. "Johnny, I'm just drunk enough to say something really important. If I don't say it now, it might never be said. And it's something I want to say." She looked up at him, frowning with intensity. "If you were my own brother, I couldn't have loved you more. You have always been so goddamned nice to me. It makes me want to bawl when I think about it. You never made fun of me, like the other kids, when I was fat, when I was wild and running around, trying to get attention. You never made me feel any the less because my father works for your father . . ."

Embarrassed, Johnny stopped her with a firm squeeze. "Good Lord, Sophia, what are you talking about? You've always been Sophia to me . . . a damn swell person."

Sophia raised her wine glass and nodded. "That's exactly what I mean." She leaned closer to his ear. "And I'm going to tell you something else, Johnny. Something that nobody knows I know. Something I'm not even supposed to know. You remember my bad eye?"

He remembered, vaguely, that there once had been something wrong with one of Sophia's eyes.

"That was a long time ago," he said.

"Bullshit. I remember it like it was yesterday. God, it was awful. I used to cry myself to sleep, every damned night. I would never be beautiful. I was the ugly little girl with the bad eye." She winced at the memory. "Kids can be so cruel. They used to gang up on me on the playground and say, 'Help, she's looking at me!' and then someone on the other side of the circle would say, 'No! She's looking at me!' "

Sophia grimaced. "And it caused trouble at home," she went on. "Poppa blamed Mom for the accident. He said it was her job to watch after us, to keep us out of the vineyards."

She described the accident. Johnny had never known the details. Playing with a group of children, she had run into the vineyards and fallen into a row of tender young plants. Splinters from a support stake had penetrated her eye, damaging the controlling muscles. Afterward the eye failed to function properly. There was no money, and Emil's insurance did not cover the expensive corrective surgery she needed.

"And you know who arranged for me to have my eye fixed?" she asked. "You know who picked up the tab?"

Johnny waited, suspecting, but not willing to guess.

Sophia nodded toward the dance floor. "Silvio Moretti," she said. "While I was in the hospital, I just happened to overhear my mother on the phone, telling him the operation was successful, thanking him, promising that she would never tell my father, or anyone, that he arranged it. Years later I found a letter from the insurance people saying they had reconsidered and would pay for the surgery. And I'll bet you can guess how that happened."

Johnny could. Such a maneuver would be nothing for Silvio. He did something similar most every day.

"Mom kept her promise. At least as far as I was concerned. She never told me. I'm still not supposed to know."

They watched Silvio and Christina dance for a moment. "You see, I know he's such a good man," Sophia said. "I think he's got this tremendous ability to love—to love everybody. It goes beyond anything most of us will ever know. He takes in so much with that love. Then he can't let go. Not of a single thing. Does that make sense?"

"It does to me," Johnny said. He had caught some of Sophia's mood. Lost in her outburst, he had continued to sip his wine unmindfully, and now the grape and such an abundance of raw adoration left the edges of his own emotions softened.

"Anyway, that's the reason I've never believed those stories about him," Sophia said.

She reached up, hugged Johnny briefly, then turned abruptly and walked unsteadily across the lawn, taking great care not to stumble.

CHAPTER 8

ANTONIO Patrucci and Umberto Vaccarelli crossed the
parking lot, headed toward the winery, listening to the faint
but insistent sounds of the party on the distant hillside.

"Silvio is really pitching a big one tonight," Umberto said.

"That's *Silvio's* problem," Antonio said. "Thank God he's the
one who's got to kiss the governor's ass. I'm really happy that's
not my line of work."

Umberto slapped him on the shoulder. "But the governor's girl
friend, that would be a different story. Ah?"

Antonio laughed. "You flatter me, Umberto. What would an old
man like me do with such a flower?"

"Tony, I know you. You would think of something," Umberto
said. "Besides, I think you have it backward. The governor is here
to kiss Silvio's ass."

They crossed the road and approached the front door of the
winery. Further up Norrbom Road, at the main warehouse, the
night foreman, Geraci, waved in welcome. Antonio waved back.
Umberto faked a quick draw of his pistol, then fanned the thumb of
his right hand, cowboy fashion.

Geraci waved a hand at them in abrupt dismissal and turned back into the warehouse. Umberto laughed.

"We should shoot off our pistols tonight, just to give Geraci a thrill," he said.

"He'd probably have a heart attack," Antonio said. "I don't think Geraci's cut out to be a gunman."

Using his master pass key, Antonio unlocked the front door of the Moretti Winery and they entered the tasting room. Antonio had thought that on this night, of all nights, he and Umberto would be alone in the building. But Frank Newton was still behind the bar. Although the winery employed a half dozen janitors, Newton complained continually about their work. He frequently came back at night, to clean behind the janitors. Tonight he was too upset to acknowledge Antonio's greeting.

"Goddamn, look at this," he said, pointing to the smooth wood of the bar. Antonio and Umberto crossed the room to look. Numerous small dents marred the polished woodwork in an area Antonio could have covered with his pocket watch.

"Know what did that?" Newton said. "Goddamn little old lady who looked like somebody's saintly great-great-grandmother. Pounded on the goddamn bar half the afternoon with the handle of her fucking umbrella. We couldn't pour the wine fast enough to suit her."

Antonio shook his head in sympathy. The winery dispensed tasting samples free to visitors as a public relations gesture. The problem was that most of the other wineries did the same. And most tourists made the circuit of all the wineries in and around Sonoma —the Sebastiani on East Fourth Street, the Buena Vista northeast of town on Old Winery Road, the Hacienda in its own scenic setting east of town, the Valley of the Moon near Glen Ellen, and Chateau St. Jean and Kenwood farther to the north. By the time they arrived at the Moretti Winery on Norrbom Road at the edge of Sonoma, some were in high spirits, demanding, even quarrelsome. Among the hundreds who came each day, there often were a few who took advantage of Silvio Moretti's generosity.

But Silvio insisted on treating all visitors courteously, no matter how rude they became. And Newton frequently found Silvio's policy difficult to practice.

"We've got one bastard that drives up here every Saturday, all the way from Oakland, just for his free glasses of wine," he said. "Now, think of what the son-of-a-bitch spends for the gas! He could stay home and buy a fucking case! But no, he'd rather come up here and sponge off complete strangers. I'll swear, I just don't understand people." He squinted across the bar at Antonio. "What the hell are you two clowns doing here this time of night?"

Antonio pointed to his pistol. "Silvio thinks we should keep a better watch on the place at night."

"Well, they sure as hell better not arm me," Newton said. "I'd probably shoot some little old lady who brought her fucking umbrella all the way from Cleveland just to pound on my bar." He shook his head in exasperation. "If you really want to know what America is all about, just ride one of those goddamned tour buses. Middle America. God love 'em."

Antonio walked away, chuckling under his breath. Newton's problems with the visiting public were a constant source of amusement for other winery employees. Unlocking the heavy plate glass doors, he led Umberto into the vastness of the winery.

Antonio had always loved the deep, rich smell that came from more than a million gallons of fermenting and aging wine. Here, in the heart of the winery, the aroma was at its best.

Antonio and Umberto patrolled through the canyons of redwood vats, the beams of their five-cell flashlights in constant movement to investigate the shadows. They circled through the building at a leisurely pace. From long habit Antonio carefully checked the temperature of each fermentation vat as they passed.

He could remember the time when the old stone building had housed the entire winery. From it the whole had grown like Topsy, each expansion made so smoothly that now few winery employees realized where one building ended and another began. High steel girders supported a metal roof that brought unity by covering all. But the point where each addition began was clear in Antonio's mind.

By the time they returned to the front of the building, Newton had completed his work and gone.

"We better check in with Geraci," Umberto said.

Antonio walked behind the bar and dialed the warehouse.

"Everything's okay here," he told Geraci.

"Still got Pistol Pete with you?"

Antonio laughed. "Umberto has found his calling."

"Don't let him shoot himself with that thing," Geraci said, breaking the connection.

For the next three hours, Antonio and Umberto continued to patrol through the building. They took long breaks for a smoke at the bar and talked of old times.

It was shortly before midnight when Antonio noticed that Number Four vat was leaking. Dark red Cabernet Sauvignon streamed into the gutter.

"Carlo and his crew started moving wine from that vat into cooperage yesterday," Umberto said. "I guess some of those knotheads got careless. Here, help me tighten this hose."

But when they looked closer, they found that the wine was not coming from a loose connection. It was flowing from somewhere beneath the vat.

"I'll take a look," Umberto said. "Maybe I can find out what happened."

He unhitched his gun belt and dropped the pistol to the concrete floor. On hands and knees he probed with his flashlight around the base, moving into the shadows.

Antonio leaned forward, straining to see the source of the leak.

He never knew exactly where the man who used the Mace was standing. The paralyzing spray hit him full in the face. He fell, his eyes, nostrils, lungs on fire, his arms and legs useless. During the few minutes he fought for breath, for life itself, he remained oblivious to what was happening around him.

By the time Antonio recovered from the effects of the spray, Umberto lay crumpled on the concrete floor, his blood mingling with the spilled wine trickling into the gutter.

Antonio's pistol was gone. His wrists were bound behind him. Two men towered over him.

"The old-timer's coming around," the big one said. "What'll we do with him?"

"Let's see if he can swim," the other said.

The big one laughed. He knelt and fitted the loop of a rope around Umberto's body. Hooking the other end to his belt, he began climbing the ladder to the top of the vat, eighteen feet above.

Antonio realized what was about to happen. He began to struggle.

"Knock it off, old man, or I'll put a bullet through you," the smaller one said.

Antonio lay on his side and watched as the two men hauled Umberto's frail body up to the scaffold, constructed as a walkway to check cap temperatures. He heard the splash as Umberto's body hit the wine deep within the vat.

"You're next, old man," the smaller man said.

The rope was lowered. Antonio struggled in vain as the smaller man knelt and tied a loop around him, then fought for breath as he was hauled upward, the rope cutting deep into his chest.

The big man dumped him on the scaffold and untied the rope. He grabbed Antonio by the arms.

"In you go," he said.

Antonio held his breath. He seemed to fall forever.

He hit the wine head first and went under. Twisting his body, kicking, he managed to return to the surface in time for a life-saving gasp of fetid air. Arching his body, pumping his legs, he kept his face above the fermenting wine, above the huge bubbles of working bacteria. A flashlight beam hit his eyes.

"Hey, Chipman! He can swim!" the big man called. The light flicked off.

Antonio looked up. The big man was framed, laughing, on the scaffold at the top of the tank, nine feet away.

The aroma was overpowering. He was already light-headed from the Mace. The wine was warm. Antonio knew that although the fermentation process had slowed on the mature wine, some bacterial activity continued, emitting carbon dioxide, keeping the enemy of wine—oxygen—at bay. He could not live long. He forced himself to take gentle, measured breaths.

Overhead the man walked away. Antonio was left in darkness.

At first he attempted to use the sides of the vat for partial support. The effort merely interfered with his swimming. Then he began moving from side to side, but the continual bumping into the redwood broke his rhythm. His edge in keeping his head above the surface was marginal, at best.

He began circling the vat, his mind racing as he tried to figure some way out. He knew that he was reaching the border of consciousness.

He bumped into Umberto's body, floating just beneath the surface. In a blinding moment of desperation Antonio knew what he had to do.

Death had saved Umberto from drowning; his lungs still retained enough air to keep the body near the surface.

By maneuvering carefully, Antonio was able to move the corpse of his old friend beneath him. Using Umberto's body as a float, Antonio managed to keep his own face above the surface of the wine. Carefully, with herculean effort, he found Umberto's face with his hands. Forcing the mouth open, he held the head against the side of the vat with one hand. With the other, he began sawing at his bonds, using Umberto's teeth.

Sobbing with frustration and fatigue, Antonio repeatedly slipped off his elusive, ghastly perch. Each time, he returned to his work, until at last the rope fell free from his wrists.

He swam away from the body. His strength was almost gone. His consciousness was fading. He began swimming around the vat, groping high on the redwood walls, seeking any irregularity that might give him foothold.

After two circuits he knew there was none.

For a few minutes then he lost his composure. He clawed at the wood, yelling, splashing. He waved his arms, stirring the air, seeking oxygen.

Exhaustion and nausea returned him to sanity.

He knew that in a few moments he would die.

There was no help within reach of his voice. He would not be missed until too late. His belt, combined with Umberto's, would not reach the top of the vat, even if he had the strength.

Reconciled to his death, Antonio rolled onto his back, floating, using only an occasional kick or flick of his hands to keep his face above the wine. A strange calm came over him.

He did not mind dying. He would have preferred proper last rites, but he had been to confession recently. He was certain that no great sin damned his soul.

He had lived a good life. His wife, his children, a few friends would miss him. But Antonio did not expect to escape the fate that befalls all men.

The only task remaining before death was to arrive at some understanding of what his life had meant—and to lament things left undone.

He had traveled from Mediterranean poverty to the kind of wealth that counted most—love, security, respect, responsibility.

One man had made that possible—his good friend Silvio Moretti.

And with that thought came his biggest regret. He wished he could tell Silvio how much their friendship had meant to him. He wished there were some way to warn Silvio that he feared these murderers intended to do Silvio himself incalculable harm.

His strength was failing now. Intoxicated by the fumes, he was nearly delirious.

And he had one final regret. He wished that Umberto had been left alive, so they could have died together—two boys from the streets of Bastia, drowning in a vat of superb wine.

A pity, Antonio thought as he slid beneath the surface.

Umberto would have roared with laughter over the humor of it.

CHAPTER 9

THROUGHOUT the evening, Sam Cavanaugh had been covertly watching Silvio's every move. Aware of the reason, Silvio adroitly kept his distance as he mingled with his guests. He waited until the party had assumed a life of its own before drifting over to the corner of the patio where Cavanaugh stood, talking with Gregory's two aides.

Silvio placed a hand gently on Cavanaugh's shoulder. "I thought I would find out what is so interesting that it keeps you off the dance floor, Sam."

Cavanaugh laughed. "Politics," he said. "What else?"

"The Bible says everything unto its season," Silvio reminded him.

"Well, politics knows no season." Cavanaugh gestured toward the party, the house. "We can't all relax and live this good life."

The two aides stood alert, listening, so alike they could have been identical twins in their three-piece pin-striped blue suits. Tom Furman was slightly taller, with horn-rims. Neil Hart wore steel-rims. The efficient, intellectual type the Cavanaughs had always treasured.

"I suppose you are right," Silvio said. "We might as well go have that talk."

"Round up Greg," Cavanaugh said to Hart.

As they crossed toward the patio entrance, Silvio paused briefly to survey the scene, to make certain the party needed no further attention at the moment. The flagstone terrace was filled with couples dancing to the haunting strains of "The Tennessee Waltz." Conversation groups had formed around the bars. At the edge of the lighted patio younger couples were drifting into the shadows. And beyond, near the experimental vineyard, Silvio could see Johnny and Christina, their heads close, deep in conversation. He watched them for a moment, concerned. Their friendship had blossomed rapidly. Too rapidly.

Silvio signaled a servant to follow him. He left the party with no qualms. He would not be missed. Anna could handle any minor problem that might arise.

He led Gregory, Sam, Furman, and Hart to his office and closed the door, shutting out the sounds of the festivities. He went to the wine rack and selected an experimental Pinot Noir blanc. The two young men sat stiffly on the big leather couch, flanking Sam. Gregory Cavanaugh took the wing chair and faced Silvio, wearing the broad effortless smile that had graced signboards and telephone poles all over California through two election campaigns.

"This must be important indeed, to lure Gregory away from that beautiful young woman," Silvio said.

Gregory laughed. His long-standing affair with the talented young actress provided endless speculation in gossip columns and national magazines.

"Maybe not as important to Greg," Cavanaugh said.

The governor seemed relaxed. But his father appeared unusually preoccupied, and impatient with the ceremonial serving of the wine. The two aides were tense.

When the wine was poured, Silvio raised his glass in toast. "To *all* the ladies," he said.

"I'll certainly drink to that," Gregory said.

Sam's appearance had changed considerably in the last few years. His bald head, long a trademark, was mottled with brown liver spots. He had added ten or fifteen pounds to his solid build, and his full, oval face was now framed by heavy jowls.

His son, by comparison, had remained remarkably fit. He turned his full smile on Silvio. The boy was certainly a charmer.

"I certainly envy you, Mr. Moretti," he said. "When I see your home, your life, I really wonder why I'm spending my time on planes, in hotels . . ."

"You are doing us invaluable service," Silvio said. "I envy you *your* life, serving the public, effecting changes. I could never be anything other than what I am—a simple farmer, a winemaker, a lover of the grape."

Sam laughed. "A fox in the vineyard is more like it."

Gregory was grinning. "We need more simple farmers like you, Mr. Moretti," he said.

Silvio dismissed the servant. As the door closed behind him, Sam glanced at his watch and turned immediately to business. "I promised not to keep you, Silvio. There is an advantage in talking with old friends. We don't have to waste time fencing. I'll get right to the point. We have heard disturbing rumors in Sacramento to the effect that we now may have a common problem—Lucian Hall."

Silvio sipped his wine for a moment, thinking. Despite this disarming approach, Sam Cavanaugh was not innocent of guile. "There is validity in the report," he said. "Hall has made an offer for the winery. At the moment, there the matter stands."

Sam was leaning forward in the chair, his wine forgotten. Gregory's famous smile was gone. Furman and Hart were hardly breathing.

"Who made the offer?" Sam asked. "Hall himself?"

Silvio nodded. "He has taken the trouble to be very persuasive. He is applying some pressure."

Sam shook his head. "That man knows no limits," he said. "He has sent word to Greg—with all the proper circumlocutions—that Greg is to take certain actions, or be ruined politically. I'm beginning to think that Lucian Hall will not stop until he owns this state—or maybe the whole country."

"Or until *he* is stopped," Silvio said.

Sam was studying Silvio with unusual intensity. "We are beginning to wonder if he *can* be stopped," he said pointedly.

Silvio took time to consider his answer. "Perhaps," he said. "Lucian is ambitious. That makes him dangerous. But it also may make him predictable."

"He is also vicious," Sam said. "He obviously believes that the end justifies the means."

Silvio gave him a rare smile. "Lucian and I will have no quarrel over philosophy, then." He turned to Gregory. "If I may ask, what is it that Lucian has demanded of you?"

Gregory frowned and glanced at his father before answering. "He wants me to veto an environmental bill, regulating harvest of redwood. It's not important in itself—the measure was designed only to mend a few deficiencies in existing legislation. I think Lucian's demand is a test—to see if I am willing to be used."

Silvio nodded. "His tactics exactly. This request would be easy to fulfill. The next would be more difficult. Have you replied to his demand?"

Gregory smiled. "I told him to go to hell."

The aides grinned.

Silvio let silence speak for a moment.

"That might not have been wise, under the circumstances," he said. "Have you considered what kind of retaliation to expect?"

Gregory shrugged. "Whisper campaigns, printed innuendo—I've been through all kinds of dirty tricks. Lucian doesn't scare me."

Silvio hesitated a moment before answering. "Gregory," he said softly, "Lucian Hall is a menace to all decent, thinking people. He represents all I see wrong in the world today. Preoccupation with profits, material things. Disdain of all human considerations. He has power. He has the cunning of a fanatic. I have a feeling about Lucian. I am deeply disturbed about him, what he might do."

"Then you do not plan to oppose him," Sam said; it was more a statement than a question.

"I have not yet made a decision," Silvio said. "The risks, the stakes must be weighed. A victory that is too costly is in itself a defeat."

Sam frowned. "I'm glad we're having this talk, Silvio," he said. "We've been friends too long not to understand and to respect each other's position. But I feel obligated to make certain you know exactly how much is at stake."

He hesitated, searching for words. Silvio knew where Sam was headed. But he wanted him to spell it out.

"I'm sure you're aware that Greg has been rising in the polls as a potential candidate for the Senate," Sam went on. "Until recently, I saw no harm in such premature exposure. It enhanced his position in Sacramento. His career could not be hurt by the attention, no matter what his future."

The lines of worry deepened on Sam's face. He studied Silvio as he spoke, measuring the effect of his words. "But in the last few weeks talk has grown far more serious," he said. "There is a large segment of the party actively seeking a standard bearer—someone who can achieve some degree of party unity. We have been approached. They think we should make our move. We *must* make a commitment. If Greg is to run in the next election, he should now be mapping strategy . . ."

Potential candidate Gregory Cavanaugh sat listening without comment. Silvio turned to him.

"Do you have the proper . . . fever for the Senate? And beyond . . . ?"

Gregory did not smile. "It's growing in me. Until the last few weeks I didn't really think about it much. The real possibility for something on the national scene was always something out in the future. But now . . ." He glanced at his father, then back at Silvio. "Yes, I want that Senate seat, whatever lies beyond. I'd like to get into it with both feet."

"How do you feel about it, Sam?" Silvio asked.

"My mind is divided," Sam said. "Naturally I'm ambitious for my son. But I wouldn't want to see him hurt. And I know he could be destroyed. Hall and his people are not alone in this. We must be careful. There are other forces that would do everything in their power to stop him."

"Are you vulnerable?" Silvio asked Gregory.

The governor spoke of himself dispassionately, even objectively, in that strange way Silvio had seen before in professional politicians. "Perhaps I'm far less vulnerable than most men in public life," he said. "I think my honesty, my sincerity are beyond question. We've been careful—my father has seen to that. I doubt they could put together a case against me—as they did on Agnew, for instance, and tried to do on Connally. I really have no apprehension in that quarter."

"I'd feel easier if he had a wife, a family," Sam said.

Gregory shook his head emphatically in disagreement but did not argue. His father had been outspoken on the point, occasionally in public.

Silvio studied Sam as father and son exchanged glances. "It sounds to me as if you've made the decision," he said.

Sam smiled. "Not really. Lord knows, the temptation is there. But we must be realistic. We must consider the obstacles. And that is why we are here. We are seeking your advice. How do you feel about it?"

Silvio was aware that Gregory was intent on his every word as he spoke to Sam. "We have worked well together for almost forty years. Your son has been a credit to you, to our continuing relationship. As we have discussed many times before, there has never been a pressing need to enter national politics in such a direct manner. What we have needed to do, we have always managed to accomplish, without risking the arena. My inclination is to continue in this manner. But," he went on with a small smile, "perhaps the time has come. I will support you."

His words eased the tension. The governor's two aides relaxed. Sam smiled and murmured his gratitude. "I've had some of those same thoughts," he added. "But I've also wondered if ambition was getting in the way of my judgment."

They spent more than half an hour mapping preliminary strategy —how to unite the various forces of the party, how to counter the money and effort Lucian Hall would contribute to Gregory's opponent. Sam dwelt at length on the dangers posed by Hall. Silvio nodded his understanding. Sam was hoping that Silvio's corporate battle would eliminate that problem. He was here to do some serious horse trading.

Young Cavanaugh put Sam's thoughts into words. As Gregory spoke, Silvio could not help but admire his adroitness, his obvious sincerity.

"Mr. Moretti, you and my father taught me everything I know about politics. I suppose what I'm here to say is that I recognize our immense debt to you. We realize that you may feel your best course is not to oppose Hall. If that is your assessment, we will of course respect and conform to your judgment. But if you should choose to oppose him, I am here to offer you whatever assistance you need.

As far as I'm concerned, the entire state administration in Sacramento is at your disposal, within the limitations of our mutual interests."

Silvio felt a rush of affection for Gregory. The offer was beautifully phrased, and generous. But he still wanted to make certain both Gregory and Sam recognized the risks.

"Gregory," he said, "Lucian Hall and I have always operated under an uneasy truce. He has not meddled in my affairs. I have taken care not to interfere in his. This offer he has made in effect ends that truce. If I oppose him, he will attempt to destroy all my connections. I will be placing you and your father in jeopardy."

"I understand that," Gregory said. "We are in this together."

Silvio nodded. "Well, you have given me much to think about," he said. "There is much to consider. And you may rest assured that whatever I decide, I will be taking all of our interests into account." He rose, signaling an end to the conference. "I will be in touch with you."

CHAPTER 10

CARLO threw a heavy arm around Johnny's shoulders. "Come on, little brother," he said. "We've got to talk. If you can tear yourself away from Emil Borneman's stunner of a daughter."

Carlo was in that rare, jovial mood beyond sobriety but short of drunkenness. Johnny hesitated, watching Christina as she moved across the dance floor.

"I seem to have lost her," he said. "Silvio's been showing her off. She's danced with Greg, both senators, and twice with that rock star. I don't know who the guy is she's dancing with now, but he looks important."

Carlo glanced at the dance floor. "Important to us," he said. "He's the head honcho at Alcoholic Beverage Control in Sacramento. Come on. Let's get out of this mess."

They walked away from the party, down into a tree-sheltered area that Silvio had landscaped and decorated with wrought-iron benches and bronze sculpture.

Carlo raised a bottle of Moretti Cabernet Sauvignon. "I brought our own," he said. "Proprietor's Reserve." He refilled Johnny's glass and eased his weight onto a bench.

"How's Gina?" Johnny asked. "I barely had a chance to say hello to her."

"Fine, fine," Carlo said absently.

"And Ariana?"

Carlo smiled. "Fine. Spends all her time these days with that damned shrunk horse."

Johnny laughed. On her third birthday Silvio had given his granddaughter a miniature Appaloosa—a full-grown stallion thirty-six inches high. The two now were almost inseparable.

The lights and sounds of the party softly penetrated the trees. Johnny and Carlo sat for a moment in a self-conscious silence. At one time, the ten-year difference in their ages had been impossible to span. Throughout Johnny's boyhood, Carlo had seemed distant, already safe in the adult world. Not until recent years had Johnny realized that his brother also had experienced problems, and had met them in his own way. Johnny had begun to see the family through Carlo's eyes.

Carlo alone had been the object of Silvio's pride, the recipient of Anna's full love and attention. Then, Johnny had changed Carlo's entire world, just by being born. Johnny had been the rebel. From an early age, he had matched Silvio's iron will with his own. But Johnny's constant battle with his father may have been easier to endure than quiet submission had been for Carlo. Johnny's rebellion won attention and concern. Carlo's obedience was taken for granted. He was the good boy. He always did what Silvio wanted.

In keeping with Silvio's expressed desire, Carlo had studied at California State's Viticultural College. Afterward, he returned home to work at the winery—as Silvio wanted. He married a fine woman of Corsican descent—and Silvio was pleased. Johnny sometimes wondered if Carlo was as happy as Silvio was with his life. But why not? Johnny liked Gina immensely. In his opinion, Carlo could not have done better. Johnny had developed an early rapport with their precocious daughter Ariana. At seven, Ariana was an ardent admirer of the dance. Once, on a whim, he had taken her to an Edward Villella performance. Her impish enthusiasm and concentrative energy fascinated him. He thoroughly enjoyed the evening. In the two years since, he had taken her to dozens of ballet performances, driving up to Sonoma to get her. Several times she had stayed overnight with him, and she constantly begged to go visit Uncle Johnny in his floating home in a bird sanctuary.

"I wish you'd bring Gina and Ariana down to Sausalito, sometime," he said. "We could take Ariana out on the Bay again."

Johnny had made many efforts to get to know his brother better, but a vague awkwardness had always remained between them.

"Well, we stay busy," Carlo said. "Gina's got so many things going, and Ariana's into all the usual kid stuff."

"You might drive down yourself sometime," Johnny said. "We could hell around a little."

Carlo laughed. "I can get drunk in Sonoma. No need to go to San Francisco for that." He reached under the bench for the bottle again. "You talk to the old man yet?"

Johnny nodded. "Another argument. The same hassle. Nothing's changed. I couldn't get anywhere with him."

"Welcome to the club," Carlo said. "He's been on a real tear the last few days."

"I can't get him to see anything from my viewpoint," Johnny said. "He makes me feel six years old."

Carlo made a face and emptied his wineglass. "You should have to put up with that every day. I'll be at the winery, or in the vineyards working with a crew, and have everything going great. Then the old man'll walk up. In five minutes, without saying more than a dozen words, he'll have everything moving off at a ninety-degree angle. Makes me look like a lump of shit standing there. Right in front of the men. I don't think he intends to do it. That's just the way he is. When he's around, he's the center of action. I've quit worrying about it. He tell you about the offer? The trouble?"

Johnny hesitated. "He told me. But I don't know what to think. Isn't Pop being overly dramatic—about Patricio? All he thinks may happen?"

"I thought so at first," Carlo said. "But let me tell you something, little brother. The old man certainly has called the shots so far. He warned me thirty minutes after the meeting with Lucian Hall that we'd have some kind of trouble."

"*Before* Patricio's wreck?"

"Days before." Carlo shrugged. "The whole thing's pretty weird. I was right there when the offer was made. To hear Lucian and the old man together, you'd think they were childhood sweethearts. Everything was polite as hell. All their fancy fencing went right over my head. I didn't suspect a thing. But they kept looking at each other as if there were some big fucking secret only the two of them knew. I think there's a lot we don't know—something to do with those old stories, maybe. I don't think Pop's telling us everything."

Johnny laughed. "Does he ever?"

Carlo nodded agreement. "Anyway, after Lucian made the offer, the old man thanked him and said the terms seemed very generous. Then he rambled around some, about how the winery was a family business, how he'd never even considered the possibility of selling. He said he'd need some time to think it over, to talk with his accountants. And that was that."

"Where was the meeting?" Johnny asked.

"Up at the house, in the office. The old man had told me to keep my mouth shut. I did. But after Lucian left, I blew off some, asked why he didn't just tell them to go to hell, right off. Pop just sat there, smoking that damned cigar, listening. The only thing he said was, 'It's a reasonable offer. It deserves our consideration.' I was plenty pissed, and I let him know it. Of course, he didn't pay any attention to me. But as I was going out the door, he told me, as casual as you please, that he would be putting two guards on each warehouse, and on all the cellars. Immediately. He told me to make certain all the burglar alarms were connected, and to call a security outfit in San Francisco to see about a closed-circuit television network. And the funny thing is, *I've* been the one worrying about security, for years. The old man never seemed to give it a second thought. We've always had tourists wandering through the place like Grand Central Station. At night we've never had anything more than a watchman or two, in case of fire."

Carlo paused a long moment and took another sip of wine. He continued in a slightly lowered voice. "Well, I did what he told me to do. Two nights later someone tried to break into the east warehouse."

Johnny was surprised. "Pop didn't mention that."

"The 'guards' the old man hired turned out to be some of his old cronies. He'd cleaned out the poker parlor. One of those old *paesani* saw the prowlers—two men. They got away. There was no good description."

"When did this happen?" Johnny asked.

Carlo paused, thinking back. "Let's see, the offer was made a week ago yesterday. The warehouse break-in was two days later. Then yesterday morning, Patricio."

"I just can't believe Lucian Hall would be connected with anything like that," Johnny said. "Good God, he's on the boards of at least six major corporations. Why would he risk it all? It doesn't make sense."

Carlo's dark eyes reflected the party lights as he studied Johnny. "Well you better start believing, little brother. Because it certainly seems to be happening."

"Do you have any solid evidence that Patricio was murdered?" Johnny asked.

"Some. But first, let's remember that the old man was saying it was murder before there was *any* evidence. All we knew was that Patricio went off the road on a steep grade the other side of Kingman. An empty gin bottle was found in the cab."

"Patricio was a fair hand with the bottle back when I knew him."

"He changed," Carlo said. "About five years ago he had a bad case of hepatitis and damned near died. It left him with a bad liver. He became quite a family man. Always worrying about leaving his wife and kids without means of support. He was really concerned about his health. Patricio hadn't touched a drop in years."

"Did the Arizona people do an autopsy?"

Carlo nodded. "The old man put the pressure on, got the report this morning. And there's a strange thing. Patricio's stomach was full of gin. But there was very little in his bloodstream—not enough to make him drunk. He had chug-a-lugged damned near enough to kill him. But he must have downed that gin less than three minutes before he went off the road."

Johnny had not believed there was even a remote possibility that Patricio had been murdered. But now he was experiencing the same suspended, breathless pause that came on those rare occasions of legal discovery, when some startling evidence or devastating prescience stirred him to know by instinct that everything fitted together.

He was beginning to accept the possibility that the driver had been killed.

"Is Pop pushing an investigation?"

Carlo grunted. "You know the old man. He thinks the police are for people without balls. When we first heard about the wreck, someone at the plant remembered that Patricio usually timed his trips for a stop at a restaurant. Pop flew a couple of *paesani* from the poker parlor over to Kingman. They checked. Two waitresses identified a photograph. Patricio was sober less than an hour before the wreck."

"I gather you think Pop is right, then."

"Let me put it this way, little brother. There sure as hell is enough to make anyone wonder."

"How do you feel about the offer?" Johnny asked.

"I'm dead set against selling," Carlo said heatedly. "I think we should have shown Lucian and his crew the door that first day. Now I wish to hell they'd just go away."

"And if they don't? If Pop is right?"

"I'd go down to the wire with them. I'm against selling under any circumstances. If we sold the winery, what in the hell would I do?"

"You'd get a considerable cash flow, Pop says."

Carlo shrugged. The wine was beginning to show in his movements now, and in his occasionally slurred words. "Who needs money? We've always had enough. God alone knows how much the old man has, stashed away here and there."

"But what if they get rough? Really rough, the way Pop thinks they will?"

Carlo's dark eyes searched Johnny's face in the half-light. "I figure I can get just as rough as anybody."

"You and Pop," Johnny said. "From the way he's talking, he's going to call out the geriatric brigade."

"That's what worries me," Carlo said. "He's batting out of his league. You'd better get your ass back up here. I need you to help me handle the old man."

"He's going to get into legal trouble if he does some of the things he's thinking about. I tried to tell him that."

"Oh, he's smart enough to stay out of trouble with the law,"

Carlo said. "It's just that those old farts around the poker parlor think they're still tough as nails. You can see it in the way they strut around like banty roosters. But when push comes to shove, it's going to take us younger studs to do the job. That's why I need you."

"What do you plan to do?" Johnny asked.

"Simply go our own way. And if anybody comes around and tries to muscle in, we'll just kick the shit out of him."

"You're talking just like Pop."

"Well, he's not the dumbest old man in the world, you know," Carlo said. "The only problem is, the times have passed him by. He's not the biggest kid on the block anymore."

"That's exactly what I tried to tell him, but for different reasons," Johnny said. "Carlo, we can let the legal system protect us. If Lucian Hall or anyone representing him makes threats, we can trap them, bring charges."

Carlo shook his head doggedly. "Hell, Lucian's got platoons of lawyers. He can take it into court and make black white, white black till doomsday. I don't want to see this thing tied up for years in a bunch of legal shit. Fuck the courts."

"It's the only way," Johnny said.

"The *only* way is to let Hall and his people know that if they mess with us, they'll wonder what the goddamn fuck hit 'em." Carlo leaned over on the back of the bench, swaying slightly. "You've always had it pretty easy, little brother. But, by God, you can't walk away from it this time. You've been at the family trough all these years without hitting a lick. It's time for you to pay your dues. You're needed. Get your ass back up here and do your part."

"It wouldn't be fair to you," Johnny said.

Carlo seemed genuinely puzzled. "What do you mean?"

"Well, good Lord, you've been working, contributing, all these years. And I've been away. I don't feel right about it, the way Pop counts me in for a full share of the profits. It's not fair to you."

"Forget the goddamn money, will you?" Carlo said, his irritation rising. "You're right about one thing. I've worked my ass off for the winery. Hell, don't think I wouldn't have liked to be out there running around, getting a little strange. But we don't just tromp grapes around here, you know. Maybe we could even use a fucking lawyer. Come back, Johnny."

"Carlo, I can't. I've got my own career."

"Career, shit! The old man has had you on his leash all along. He's just been letting you run and play. You'd better get braced. He's about to reel you in."

Carlo was drunker than Johnny realized. He knew he should not stir the old animosities between them, but he was puzzled. "What do you mean?" he asked quietly.

"That's all I'm going to say," Carlo said. "You think you're as free as a hog on ice. I'm telling you that you're not. You'll find out. You're just another puppet dancing to the old man's strings. You always have been."

Johnny fought down his anger. "Not for a long, long time, Carlo."

Carlo snickered. "There's a lot you don't know, little Johnny. There's plenty I could tell you."

"Then tell me a little of it," Johnny said. "Otherwise I might think you're full of shit."

"All right, you asked for it. Just for openers, how do you think you got into law school?"

"Simple. I applied."

But even as he said it, he was remembering that his acceptance had not been easy. His initial application had been rejected. A few days after the bad news, he had been summoned for an unusual second interview. When the eventual notification of acceptance arrived, he had dismissed the delay and confusion as so much red tape.

"The old man got you in, that's how," Carlo said. "Remember? It seems your grades during that last year of college didn't quite match your genius. For a while there, the way I heard it, you were more interested in booze, broads, and football than books. Fortunately for you, one of the old man's contacts from Prohibition days just happened to know the dean of your law school."

Johnny did not answer. He knew that Carlo spoke the truth. Yet the possibility of Silvio's interference had never before occurred to him.

"And what do you think kept you out of the draft, when other guys your age were going either to Vietnam, or Canada or Sweden? Luck? Hell, no. It was the old man. And it was the old man who landed you with that big-shot law firm," Carlo went on relentlessly.

"He's just letting you play, like a fish on a hook. He's never even considered you gone. He just says, 'Johnny's getting his education, a little experience. He'll be back.' "

Johnny was overwhelmed. He turned away, thoroughly disgusted with himself for being so naive. He no longer felt like arguing. "Look, let's drop it."

"No. We're not going to drop it." Carlo got to his feet and stood in front of Johnny, his fists clenched. "That's just the goddamned trouble. I've kept quiet too fucking long. Maybe it's time for me to play the older brother and let you know what's what. And the truth is, if all this shit comes down, like the old man thinks, it'll have to be you and me, Johnny. You and me. That's what I'm trying to get across. We'll have to fight fire with fire. And there's not much time. That's why I want to know. Right now. Can I count on you?"

Johnny rose from the bench and stepped away from Carlo. "Listen to me, Carlo," he said. "I'll do what I can. But in my own way. I'm not going to knuckle under to Pop and participate in some futile, romantic Corsican gesture out of the last century. And I'm not going to listen to you and do something rash, idiotic—and illegal."

Carlo's face was twisted into a caricature. He moved drunkenly toward Johnny, one hand out, reaching for him. "I can't believe this," he said. "Do you mean to tell me, if somebody hits you, you're too goddamn good to hit back? What are you, a fucking pansy?"

Johnny backed away. "Don't crowd me, Carlo," he said.

But Carlo was already stalking him like a boxer, bobbing and weaving. "It's coming, sure as shit," he said. "And if we don't tuck our little tails and run, little brother, we're going to have to fight. Let's see if you can."

Johnny moved away each time Carlo came too close. He put out a hand to ward him off. "Carlo, I'm trying to explain to you the way I feel. I'm a lawyer. I believe in law."

"Words," Carlo said. "Fuckin' easy way out." His face had filled with self-righteous, drunken anger. "Are you going to run, right when your family is fighting for its life?"

"Look, you're drunk," Johnny said, continuing to retreat. "We'll talk about this some other time."

"Now! We'll talk about it right now," Carlo said. "Because I've got to find out, right now. Is my little brother a quaking fucking coward? I've got to find out."

He made a jab toward Johnny's chin with his left. The punch was too light to be serious, but it was too hard to be playful. Johnny blocked it and moved away, holding his own rising anger in check.

"Carlo, I don't want to fight with you," he said. "I'm leaving."

He turned his back on his brother and started up the hill, but Carlo grabbed him by the shoulder and spun him around.

"Goddamn you, don't you walk away from me when I'm talking to you," Carlo shouted.

Johnny pushed Carlo away from him. "I'm warning you for the last time. Get out of my way."

"Or you'll what?" Carlo asked, again stepping in front of him. "Is little brother mad? Is he going to fight?"

Johnny shoved harder, intending to move Carlo firmly aside, but Carlo was off balance. He fell backward over the bench. Johnny walked by him without a word, headed for the house.

He had just reached the top of the hill and was turning toward the patio, when he heard movement behind him. Before he could react, Carlo spun him around by the shoulder and landed a solid blow to his nose.

Blinded by pain, Johnny lashed out. He connected with three hard punches before Carlo landed another to his mouth. Stunned, Johnny grappled. They fell onto the lawn. Johnny rolled on top, hammering at Carlo's face.

"Johnny!" Silvio's voice thundered near Johnny's ear.

In that sickening moment, Johnny became aware of where he was and what was happening. He was trying to move away from Carlo, when a strong hand seized his suit collar at the back of his neck and pulled him upward. He staggered to his feet.

Silvio reached down with the other hand, pulled Carlo to his feet, then held the brothers apart by their coat collars, as he would two unruly children. Johnny's nose was bleeding freely down his shirt front. Carlo's left eye was closing. His mouth was bleeding. Johnny tenderly felt his own front teeth. They were slightly loose but unbroken.

The band had stopped playing. The party guests stood at a respectful distance, watching the scene in embarrassed silence.

In the stillness, Silvio spoke in lowered tones, his words inaudible even to others standing a few feet away. "This is inexcusable! We have guests! Put your arms around each other. Laugh," he commanded them. There was a terrible intensity to his voice. "You will carry this off, or I will never speak to either of you again."

Johnny and Carlo blinked at each other. Johnny quickly saw that Silvio was showing them a way out. Maybe the only way.

He put out his hand. Carlo took it.

Their eyes met. And, with all the wine they'd had, it *was* funny— the both of them grimy, bruised, and bleeding, the startled guests, Silvio's absolute parental control over two grown men.

Johnny and Carlo threw their arms around each other and burst into genuine laughter.

The guests joined in, uneasily at first, then with contagious relief.

Within thirty minutes Johnny and Carlo's fight became a joke, the stellar event of a star-studded evening. Silvio moved through the crowd, shaking his head in good-natured exasperation over "those two sons of mine."

Anna took them into the kitchen and attempted to tend to their wounds. She threw down her cloth in disgust. "I've always told people my two boys never had a cross word," she said. "Now look at you. In front of three hundred guests!"

For Johnny, though, only one of those guests mattered. All through the rest of the evening he could not forget Christina's face, impassive and aloof, as she watched from the patio.

CHAPTER 11

SALVATORE Messino did not make his first contact until well after midnight. Despite considerable difficulty, he managed to send a message to a Pan Am flight en route from Tokyo. More than two hours later, Herbert Fraser returned Salvatore's call from Los Angeles International Airport.

Salvatore explained the situation and outlined exactly what Silvio wanted.

"Tell Silvio I'll do everything I can," Fraser said. "But I don't know if it can be done in so little time."

"A fast report is essential," Salvatore said. "Silvio asks you to take whatever measures are necessary. He was very emphatic on that."

The line was silent for a moment. "If it can be done, it'll cost plenty," Fraser said. "Probably ten times the usual rate. Some of the digging would have to be . . . unorthodox."

Salvatore did not ask Fraser to spell it out. He did not want to know. He assumed that burglary, bribery, perhaps even extortion or blackmail would be involved.

"Silvio wants you to do whatever must be done."

"I'll try," Fraser said. "But I really wonder if Silvio has thought it through—what might come down on us."

"What do you mean?"

"I happen to be in an unusual position. I see how these things work," Fraser said.

"I know." Fraser's name frequently was in the news. Although he headed his own firm, journalists usually described him as "financial adviser" to several corporations. More than one Senate investigating committee had attempted to link him to organized crime. News magazines had labeled him "the mysterious Herbert Fraser."

"Word will get back to Lucian," Fraser went on. "And Silvio will have a tiger by the tail. That son-of-a-bitch plays for keeps. God knows he has the clout. Tell Silvio to think this through very carefully."

"I will give him your message," Salvatore said.

"Another thing. If Silvio locks horns with Hall, he'll find out who his friends are."

"That might be a good thing to know," Salvatore said.

"And it might not be," Fraser said. "Lucian has won every scrap so far. You can't blame everybody for being scared shitless of him."

"I gather you don't think Silvio stands a chance."

"With Silvio, who knows? I sure as hell wouldn't bet against him," Fraser said. "I'll call you back in an hour or so."

But almost two hours passed before Salvatore's phone rang.

"I think it can be done," Fraser said. "I've made the arrangements. When can I talk to Silvio?"

"He'll call you first thing tomorrow," Salvatore said. "I'm sure he will be pleased."

"He'd better be," Fraser said. "I've just placed my ass in a sling."

The second call went easier. Reached at a phone booth on the docks in San Francisco, Bob McIntyre grasped the situation immediately.

"Forty-eight hours? I should be able to have a good scan for you by then. But let me tell you something. Getting ready to do a job might take longer. Did Silvio say anything about setting up the operation?"

"He didn't mention it," Salvatore said. "But you would be wise to be prepared. My guess is that all hell's about to break loose."

BOOK 2

"You've reopened doors that I closed a long time ago."

—Christina Borneman

CHAPTER 1

THE bodies of Antonio Patrucci and Umberto Vaccarelli lay on a tarpaulin spread between two large vats. Silvio Moretti stood at the edge of the makeshift bier, grief, anger, remorse rioting within him. And through his mingled emotions, there burned in his mind's eye a hot, flickering flame.

"The coroner gave us a preliminary report, Mr. Moretti," the police chief was saying. "Vaccarelli apparently was struck from behind and killed by the blow. They must have hauled his body up there and thrown it into the vat. But the doc said Patrucci was still alive when they dropped him in."

Silvio closed his eyes for a moment to mask his emotions, to gain a measure of relief from the grim scene. The flame continued to burn.

"Did they have any enemies you know of, Mr. Moretti?" the police chief asked. "Any trouble here at the winery?"

"No trouble," Silvio said. "You will find that Antonio and Umberto were . . . venerated . . . on these premises. The trouble came from outside of Sonoma. Of that, I assure you."

The police chief hesitated, poised on the verge of questioning

Silvio's reasoning. But he let the matter pass, at least for the moment.

"We're theorizing that they surprised the burglars. Otherwise, it seems there would have been more damage. And that seems to have been their motive. Wouldn't you say so, Mr. Moretti?"

Silvio nodded. The damage was not extensive—a few vats shattered, several thousand gallons of wine lost. But no purpose would be served by telling the police chief what had been the real target.

The burglars had done their work well.

"Maybe we'll know more after the autopsies," the police chief said. "I'll talk with you then, Mr. Moretti. At your convenience. I'll have some questions . . ."

"Of course," Silvio said, nodding his dismissal. The chief moved on to speak with his assistants while they awaited the hearse.

Across the tarpaulin from Silvio, the warehouse night foreman, Garaci, was weeping. Emil Borneman stood looking down at the bodies. His face was devoid of expression. At times Silvio envied Emil his stolid insensitivity.

Silvio encircled the makeshift bier and put an arm around Garaci's shoulders. Garaci and the two dead men had been especially close friends. Silvio felt the sobs wracking Garaci's thin frame.

"It's my fault," the night foreman said. "When they didn't check in on time, I should have come over here to see about them. But I thought . . ."

The police chief and his assistants had spread out among the winery employees, asking questions, making notes. The crowd at the scene had grown during the last few minutes. A few were still arriving for work. They stood back, shocked, unbelieving. They spoke in whispers, standing a respectful distance from the vat. Emil Borneman moved away. For the moment Silvio and Garaci were left alone with the bodies.

Silvio knelt on the bare concrete floor beside the tarpaulin to study—and to remember—the pale dead faces of his two old friends.

Umberto's face was bloated and grotesque in death, the mouth slack, the eyes staring. In startling contrast, Antonio's looked beatific, a strange laugh fixed as if in his last moments Antonio had heard the most comical thing. The effect was unsettling. Silvio had seen that same expression on Antonio's face times beyond counting during the last sixty-odd years.

They had been boy-men together, in a time when there was no childhood—the five of them, Silvio, Antonio, Umberto, Salvatore . . . Little Paulie.

With so many men dead amidst Corsica's continuous vendettas, the burdens of life came early. A boy was expected to do the work of a man, and if necessary to uphold the family honor as a man.

The memories were not pleasant. There were matters that had not been mentioned in years, even among such old friends. But those terrible days were never far from the mind. More, these two friends had known Silvio's darkest secret.

At ten years of age, as the eldest male survivor in his family, Silvio had done murder. In one night of horror he had killed not once, but three times, an act beyond the one-for-one progression of ritual vendetta. With his father's *lupara*, Silvio had paid back in that one night three generations of accumulated debts.

The audacity of the boy succeeded where the bravery of men had failed.

Silvio had found the patriarch of the Triana family asleep with a young widow. The boy Silvio had kicked the foot of the bed, waking him. Even today, sixty-four years later, he could remember vividly the stillness of the Triana house, the soft glow from a bedside lamp, the surprise on the old man's face when he saw the boy standing at his bed with the shotgun. As the old man and the woman stared, Silvio had bowed his respects to them, his elders, as he had been taught to do, then fired both barrels of the shotgun into the huge, hairy, naked chest.

He did not harm the woman. She was left as a witness. He wanted to leave no doubt as to who had avenged so many Moretti deaths.

Less than an hour later, he found the murderer of his father behind the Triana stables, shoeing a horse. For a time Silvio stood in the darkness, watching him work the horseshoe into shape. With plodding patience the huge man moved from anvil to forge and back again. Then, stepping into the light, Silvio called his name. The man turned, saw the child holding the huge weapon, and laughed. His humor vanished in the instant he saw Silvio's face. With an anguished cry, the man threw his heavy hammer, just missing Silvio's head. Silvio pulled the dual triggers. The solid loads slammed the murderer backward across the forge, where he died in the stench of his own burning flesh.

The Triana male who had killed Silvio's uncle Mario died in a neighborhood tavern. Silvio gave him only one barrel, saving the other for anyone who interfered. No one did. Silvio could still remember the sense of absolute power within the boy as he held the crowded room at bay.

Afterward, he fled into the Corsican *maquis*—the fragrant, head-high brushland where one can see and not be seen—a natural refuge that for centuries had served as sanctuary for Corsican bandits and hunted men. There he survived, stringing snares in the heavy thickets of the *maquis* to strangle the blackbirds that came to feed on the berries. For a time, he was alone, living on roots, wild apples, chestnuts, grapes, and the blackbird delicacy the Corsicans called *pâté de merle*.

It was the boy Antonio who found him, and later came regularly, bringing food and news. As time passed, Antonio, Umberto, and Salvatore took turns slipping away from the village to visit Silvio in the *maquis*. They were nimble and cunning enough to evade briefly the malevolent eyes watching them. From Antonio, Silvio learned of the death of his mother and younger brother Alberto from smallpox, no doubt aggravated by poverty and malnutrition. His youngest brother, Paolo—poor little Paulie—was left alone. It was Umberto who brought word, months later, that friends of Silvio's father had arranged for him to flee Corsica, traveling in steerage on a ship—first to Marseille, then to America. Those same friends hid and took care of Paolo—the last of the Moretti line left in Corsica —until Silvio could send for him.

And later, years later, Silvio, Antonio, Umberto, Salvatore, and Paulie pledged their lives to one another—a bond fixed forever in the heat of the flickering flame . . .

Hot tears came to Silvio's eyes as he looked at the dead faces of the friends who had shared those terrible memories, all the years of constant sacrifice.

And there, kneeling on the cement floor of his winery, Silvio took in each of his hands the hand of a dead friend, and made a vow.

CHAPTER 2

DURING his college days, and in the years since, Johnny Moretti had developed fondness for many women, deep affection for few. He had shied away from love, from any and all close attachments.

He had no illusions. He recognized as a failing his inability to establish a deep relationship. In odd moments, over a span of years, he had puzzled over the reasons. Once, in a tearful scene, an airline stewardess had accused him of fearing the closeness of love. She said he seemed to consider love a surrender of an essential part of himself—something to be resisted. To some extent he had realized that she was right. He could find no other explanation as to why, in his late twenties, he had never known total love.

The natural intimacy he felt from the first with Christina filled him with wonder. If love had nothing to do with it, why did he dote on the way she had of lowering her head, then looking up at him? Why else would he be so obsessed by her voice, her every inflection, that quizzical curve to her mouth, the way she had of going into herself in long silences? Why else, after the hundreds of women he had kissed, would a simple good-night peck linger into the next day?

But if it was love, would his shortcomings, his deeply personal deficiencies, whatever they were, prevail?

He was determined that this time he must not allow the opportunity to go by.

Sunday morning after mass, Johnny and Christina drove through the golden wooded hills north of Sonoma to the state park near Glen Ellen. Holding hands, they hiked along the tree-lined trail and stood for a long time in the awesome silence of the forest, looking down at the grave of Jack London. When they heard the voices of tourists approaching in the distance, they moved on, still without breaking their own silence, and walked down the trail to the ruins of Wolf House, now half overgrown by forest. To the east lay the Valley of the Moon, a view the *Star Rover* proclaimed to be the most beautiful on earth.

They climbed a wooden stairway to the tourist platform inside the fire-blackened stone walls.

Christina looked slowly about with detached interest. They both had been there many times before. The remains of the smoke from so long ago seemed reflected in her green eyes; they were darker in the shaded light, with a hint of circles underneath, so faint as to be barely perceptible.

He felt moved toward comment; the impulsive, disturbing words of Sophia the evening before spurred him on. "Are you tired? Maybe we could find a place to sit for a few minutes."

She gave him a grateful glance, the hint of a smile. "Oh, I guess the bedlam of trying to get away from the museum for a few days is catching up with me. I'm okay." She walked to the far edge of the platform.

He followed. "May I ask you something? If you'd rather not answer, I'll understand." He raised a hand to lighten the moment. "But I warn you, whatever you say, I won't duck off the scene."

She was looking at him with the merest stirring of curiosity and a calm that suggested only that he get on with it.

"Am I causing waves for you? At home? I get such a strong impression . . . well, what's going on?"

Christina looked away again and, amidst the ethereal surroundings of the ruins, seemed to lower her defenses for a moment.

"I had a bit of a scene with my mother over you this morning," she said, looking up at the towering ruins of a chimney. "She didn't want me to come with you today."

He would not press his advantage. He sensed it was better to turn toward lightness. "I can think of two reasons. Either it was because I'm nothing but a drunken brawler, or else *she* wants to see more of you."

"Both, maybe," Christina said. "I reasoned with her. I said I'd have two more days to spend with my family. But you and I had only today to be together."

"We'll have to do something about that," Johnny said.

"How? I have to leave Wednesday. Can you stay over through tomorrow?"

"Impossible. I'm right in the middle of final preparations for a trial. Maybe I could come up Wednesday, take you to dinner, and to the airport."

Christina shook her head. "Mother will insist on seeing me off."

He knew he could not let it end like this. "Damn it, why did you have to pick Boston? A whole continent away."

Christina looked at him for a moment. "Maybe it's better this way," she said.

Again, tourists were approaching.

Johnny did not reply.

His emotions toward her were growing too complex to express. He knew he wanted her, totally. But he also sensed that—at least at the moment—she shared his reluctance.

Returning to Sonoma, they drove to Au Relais and ordered eggs Benedict for lunch. They then walked to the Plaza, now rapidly filling with people awaiting the start of the second day of the Festival.

The mock double wedding began. Each year the ceremony was re-enacted in remembrance of the storybook marriage of the daughters of General Mariano G. Vallejo to the sons of Count Agoston Haraszthy. The general had founded Sonoma. And it was the count who had imported thousands of European vines to Sonoma and founded the modern California wine industry, before his ever-restless, adventurous spirit led him to the tropics, where he was eaten by crocodiles.

Performed in period costume in front of Mission San Francisco Solano de Sonoma, the ceremony was colorful and impressive.

Afterward, most of the crowd returned to the Plaza for a Dixieland band concert. The stores surrounding the Plaza offered window displays on historical themes, and for an hour Johnny and Christina strolled along the sidewalks, pausing occasionally to examine in detail the clothing, furniture, and art objects from the past.

As parade time neared, they drifted across the crowded Plaza to stand close by the Sonoma Hotel. Townspeople and thousands of visitors lined the tree-shaded Plaza and opposite sidewalks, awaiting the spectacle. In the distance, Johnny could hear the approaching bands.

"I've been trying to think of some way to bring up a delicate situation," he said close to Christina's ear. "I've made a date to take a young lady to a concert this afternoon. I hope the two of you will be compatible."

Christina looked up at him with a question in her eyes. But that little curve at the corner of her mouth betrayed her perception.

"Who?" she asked.

"She'll be in the parade," he said.

What the parade lacked in numbers was more than offset by timing. The procession was well spaced. Each band arrived only after at least a full block of anticipation. Each costumed horseman was allocated a generous length of the wide street for a stage. Interspersed among the bands and marching groups were the children of the Valley of the Moon. They walked, rode decorated bicycles. They dangled from a stagecoach, from carriages. There were pioneer children, Indian children, Spanish children. Some posed as grapes. All along the route the crowd applauded each "act" that passed.

"It's so corny it's good," Christina said.

Johnny pointed. "Here comes my date."

Ariana was approaching on Little Bit. She was dressed as a Spanish lady, with a mantilla, a rose in her long dark hair. Her full black skirt was strewn with red flowers. She rode the miniature Appaloosa sidesaddle, her back straight, looking neither to the left nor right. Little Bit was no less a ham, prancing along like a full-sized Arabian stallion, despite the fact that he was only thirty-six inches high. The crowd gave them genuine applause.

"That's Carlo's daughter?"

"And Little Bit," Johnny said. "She and that horse have been practically inseparable since she was three."

"Is the horse going to the concert too?"

"No, Little Bit is going home with Carlo and Gina. The concert, by the way, is by a group called Smokin'."

"Sounds wicked."

"We'll see," Johnny said. "I'm not promising anything."

Later they walked to the parking area north of the Sonoma Hotel. Carlo already had loaded Little Bit into a small trailer behind his station wagon. He was leaning against the trailer, rubbing the tiny horse's ears. His left eye was black, but some of the swelling had gone away. His lips were slightly puffed. Ariana still wore her costume. She was in the front seat of the station wagon, using the visor mirror to adjust her mantilla.

Johnny had wondered how his brother would react. He was relieved to see that Carlo was grinning. After greeting Christina, he turned to Johnny.

"I must be losing my punch. You don't look too bad."

Johnny touched his nose cautiously. "It's sore," he said. "Fortunately I only use it for breathing. How's the eye?"

Carlo shrugged. "I've got worse falling off bar stools." He glanced uncertainly at Christina, then spoke directly to Johnny. "Look," he said. "I hope you'll forget about half of what I said last night."

"About half ought to cover it for both of us," Johnny said. "Maybe the other half needed to be said."

"Maybe," Carlo said. "But we could have lived without it."

"The concert starts at four," Ariana announced through the open window of the station wagon.

Johnny glanced at his watch. "We'll make it."

"I want to sit at the front," Ariana said, stepping out and adjusting her skirts.

"All right," Johnny told her. "We'll go." He looked at Carlo. "We can talk later. But I want you to know, there are no hard feelings on my part. None at all."

"I have none," Carlo said. "I regret the whole thing. Not just because it happened in front of God and the governor and everybody, but mostly because it happened with you."

"It was my fault, more than yours," Johnny said.

"No, I was spoiling for a fight." Carlo touched his black eye. He grinned. "And I got it."

They shook hands and embraced.

Ariana, ignoring the whole scene, got her purse out of the station wagon.

"We're going to goon around and be late," she said.

Carlo kept a hand on Johnny's arm. "You better check in with the old man before you leave town," he said. He glanced at Christina, then back to Johnny. "Something . . . something else has happened."

Johnny nodded his understanding. "We'll keep in touch," he said.

As Johnny, Christina, and Ariana walked across the parking lot toward the Plaza, Christina turned and waved good-bye to Carlo, who was still standing beside the horse trailer, watching them.

"Now *that* was more like the Morettis I remembered," Christina said.

The tree-enclosed Grinstead Memorial Amphitheater on the east side of the Plaza was filling rapidly when they arrived. Ariana, gathering her long skirts with both hands, pushed her way through and found three seats down front, right beneath the stage.

Smokin' filled the air with electronic rhythm, heavily amplified, for more than an hour. From time to time Johnny glanced at Ariana. She was rapt. She often clapped her hands in a private sort of glee. It was plain to see that this child of Carlo's had a developing sense, beyond her years, for selecting what should have meaning to her, independent of the crowd. Christina sat tapping her toes to the beat. Occasionally she squeezed Johnny's hand.

After the concert they paused for a few minutes at the edge of the Plaza to watch the folk dancers before driving Ariana home.

Carlo's ranch was a little more than five miles north of town, just beyond Agua Caliente on Hooker Creek. As they wound their way through the Festival traffic on Highway 12, Ariana talked ceaselessly about the rock group, school, and her pets.

Johnny glanced at Christina, thinking she might be bored with his niece's prattle, but she was listening with the faraway expression he was coming to know.

Then Ariana fell silent. Johnny thought she at last had run out of things to say, but she seemed to be groping for words. Her struggle grew until it burst to the surface: "Uncle Johnny, would you like to see me dance?"

He knew there was much behind the question. He answered cautiously. "Sure. I have, you know." She often had demonstrated the positions and movements she had learned in class.

"No, I mean really. On stage."

"Of course," he said.

She rode for a while in silence, struggling with her problem. Johnny glanced at Christina, whose eyes met his. At last Ariana gave an exaggerated sigh.

"Well, if you just happened to find out, some way, that I was going to perform, on a real stage, do you think you could be there?"

Johnny began to see her quandary. "I might. But why in the world would I have to find out some other way?"

Ariana hesitated. "Well, Daddy said I shouldn't bother you with my recital. He said you've got more important things to do."

Sidestepping contradiction to Carlo, Johnny waited until they were past a sharp curve. "Your daddy's right, that I have a lot of things to do. But it all boils down to selecting your priorities. You know what that means, don't you?"

Ariana nodded. "Deciding what you want to do worst."

"Seeing you dance would rank right up at the top of the list. If I were to receive an invitation, I would make every effort to be there."

Ariana giggled, hugged his arm, and buried her face in his shoulder. "I'm not good, yet. But I'm getting better. You won't tell Daddy I told you?"

"I think we can work around that problem," Johnny said.

On the way back to town, Christina commented on Ariana's winsome personality. "You apparently have spent quite a bit of time with her."

Johnny told her about the ballet performances, the concerts, the weekends on his houseboat. Christina was studying him with frank concentration. "That's very generous of you," she said.

Johnny shrugged. "Not really. Selfish, maybe. Gina and Carlo seem to think I'm just being polite, tolerant of her. But I'm not. I enjoy Ariana. She's a precious, delightful kid, full of fun and ideas." He laughed. "With all she's got going, I sometimes feel she's being generous with me."

Johnny suggested they have dinner at the Capri, then drive over to El Verano and the Little Switzerland for dancing.

"I'd love to, but I can't," Christina said. "I promised Mom I'd be home for dinner. She's having some friends over . . ."

"A quick drink, then," Johnny urged.

"One, maybe."

Johnny drove to the Swiss Hotel and Grey Fox Saloon. The bar was crowded, but as they entered, one of the ice cream parlor tables was vacated.

They ordered the specialty of the bar, Bear Hair Sherry.

"I was too young to order it, before I left home," Christina said. "I missed out on a lot of things. I suppose I'm a late bloomer."

When the wine arrived, Johnny raised his glass in toast. "To us," he said.

Christina's eyes followed his raised hand. For a moment she seemed on the verge of demurral. Then they touched glasses and drank.

"When will I see you again?" Johnny asked.

"I don't know. I don't get back very often. You ever get to Boston?"

"Somehow, its charms have always escaped me," Johnny said. "I intend to make amends."

"I would be glad to see you."

"How can I hope to get to know you well, if you're so far away?"

Christina was silent for a moment. "If things are meant to be, they happen," she said. "I really believe that."

Johnny reached across the table and took her hands in his. "Christina, I can't let you just walk out of my life."

"It hadn't seemed to bother you before," she said.

"Isn't there some way I can see you again before you leave California?" he pleaded. "I have a heavy schedule through tomorrow, and Tuesday. But I could take off early Wednesday."

"I have to leave for Los Angeles Wednesday," she said. "I have an appointment with the director of the Los Angeles County Museum that afternoon. I'll be there doing research through Thursday. I'll be at the Huntington all day Friday . . ."

"When are you going back?"

Their eyes met—and lingered.

"Friday night," she said.

"If you'll come back up to San Francisco, I'll clear everything out of the way next weekend," he said. "I promise you the time of your life. Like the song says, 'I'll make you a night like no night has been, or will be again . . .' "

Christina hesitated, then shook her head. "I can't. I simply can't. I have a commitment next weekend."

"In Boston?"

She nodded.

"Is there . . . do you have someone in Boston?"

She nodded again, more slowly.

Johnny paused a moment, deciding if he should pursue it. "Serious?" he asked.

She lowered her head, reflecting, then she looked up in that special way. "Comfortable, I suppose, would be the word." She continued to look at Johnny. "We've come to depend on each other very much."

"But you want more."

"I don't know if there *is* more," she said. "Sometimes I think maybe there is. And that bothers me. But I do know this. I wouldn't want to hurt him. I think that if I did find more, he would understand, just as I would understand if he felt the need to turn to someone else."

"But you *do* feel . . . a lack?" Johnny said, yielding to his own need to know.

Christina was silent a long time before answering. "Maybe everyone feels a lack, at times. I don't know."

"Then why don't you come up next weekend? No strings attached. We won't worry about it. We'll simply have a good time. If anything is meant to happen, it'll happen."

Christina laughed, snared by her own phrase. She still hesitated. "There are other considerations," she said. "My mother is begging me to stay. I've told her I simply must go back to Boston."

"It can be our secret," he said.

Christina seemed to go into herself for a moment, thinking. Johnny waited. He was beginning to understand that she needed these contemplative moments, that she was not the surface person she at first appeared to be. She kept a lot inside herself—a reserve that to him was part of her mystery.

She became aware of his silence. She looked up at him and sighed. "I'll admit, you have a way of making Boston seem like baked beans," she said. "If you're still game next weekend, I'll come up, on one condition."

"Name it," Johnny said.

"My parents must never know. Not a word to anyone."

"I promise," Johnny said. He made no attempt to hide his elation.

After leaving Christina with her parents, Johnny drove back to the Moretti home and gathered his clothes. He searched out his mother and said good-bye. Silvio was not in his study. Johnny was on his way to his car, intending to drive to the winery to hunt his father, when Silvio's Mercedes wheeled into the drive. Johnny waited.

"I hoped you would stay over a few days, at least," Silvio said.

"I really can't," Johnny said. "There's a full day waiting for me tomorrow in the office."

"When is Christina going back?" Silvio asked.

"She'll be leaving Wednesday."

"Lovely, lovely girl," Silvio said. "And a respectable girl. She is not the kind for you to play around with, Johnny."

Johnny felt his face flush with anger. He tried to keep emotion from his voice. "Pop, you are trying to manage my career, the way I live. That's bad enough. Don't start trying to pick my women."

Silvio's eyes revealed brief amusement. "Maybe someone should," he said. He slapped Johnny affectionately on the shoulder. Johnny noticed a tenseness, a tiredness around his father's eyes.

"I will be phoning you within the next day or two," Silvio said. "When I meet with Lucian again, I want you to be here. I want to convey to him that we are acting from family solidarity."

"Pop . . ."

"No excuses," Silvio said. "Be here."

Johnny remembered Carlo's veiled message of a new development. "What's happened?"

Silvio glanced away, toward the town of Sonoma below the hill. "Antonio and Umberto have been murdered. It was done to hurt me." Silvio spoke slowly and with a deep sadness in his voice. "Two of my oldest friends, murdered because of me."

Johnny was stunned. "Murdered?"

"Antonio was still alive when he was dumped into a vat of Cabernet Sauvignon. Umberto was already dead—struck from behind. I have just been to pay my respects to some more widows. So please understand if I have little patience for your skepticism today."

Johnny remembered the two old men well. They always had been in high spirits, filled with laughter, ever ready to tease and play with the younger son of their friend Silvio Moretti. They had never Anglicized Johnny's name. Antonio and Umberto were among the few people who always called him Giovanni.

"Murdered?" Johnny said again, still trying to absorb it.

Silvio described the discovery of the bodies, the efforts of the police to reconstruct the crime. He watched Johnny's reaction closely. "You said that if they were pressuring us to sell, you would see them in hell first," Silvio concluded. "Tell me. How do you feel about it now?"

Johnny was surprised by the intensity of his own anger. Why would anyone want to kill those two amiable old men?

"I feel exactly the same," he said.

"You still think it a matter for the police?"

"More than ever."

Silvio nodded. He made no comment.

"What about you?" Johnny asked. "Does this affect your decision?"

"Of course it does," Silvio said. "I have had few days so painful in my entire life—two friends from my boyhood killed, killed because of me! I cannot help being affected. And it will not stop. What will they do next?"

"I would ask for police protection," Johnny said.

"The police can't prevent a crime," Silvio said. "You can't walk up to a policeman and say, come walk down the street with me, Mr. Policeman. I'm afraid I am going to be mugged."

"Then hire protection."

"Listen to me, Johnny. In times of trouble you want friends around you, not strangers. Friends—and family."

"Pop, I'll *try* to make it up for the meeting. But I have a very heavy week coming up. I'm still willing to help, any way I can."

Silvio looked at him for a moment before he spoke.

"Johnny, there is only one way you can help me now. Come home. Tell your partners you must take leave of absence—anything." Silvio's words seemed to come from some great, special effort, tapping some deep reserve of strength. "Come home. Be my right hand through all this. Then you can do whatever you want with your life."

Silvio turned and walked away, heading toward the house. Johnny stood watching him, marveling at his father's easy, ageless grace of movement, even in stress. He then stepped into his car, started the engine, and wheeled out of the drive, his mind consumed by a strange mixture of emotions.

Despite his deep concern, his growing fears about the Lucian Hall matter, he could not subdue his mounting exhilaration over the prospects for the weekend ahead. And he strongly suspected that Christina shared his enthusiasm.

As he drove back toward the Bay Area, he actually burst into song.

He had not felt so excited over a date in years.

CHAPTER 3

*U*NTIL that Monday afternoon, Angelina Vinza Moretti had considered herself one of the luckiest women on earth. She had never known want or adversity. The good life had been handed to her—on a golden platter.

She grew up pampered and protected, in a fabulous land of make-believe. Angelo Vinza denied his daughter nothing. Her spacious bedroom was a treasure trove of dollhouses, marionettes, puppets, music boxes. He invented elaborate games for them to play, told her spellbinding stories of princesses and princes, trees that sang lovely ballads, kings who rewarded good deeds, butterflies who lived only to bring beauty into the lives of little girls like Gina. Her mother played the piano in accompaniment to his rich baritone. By the age of ten Gina knew by heart selections from all the great operas. On Sunday mornings she raced to their bed with the comic sections, and her father would tell the stories, as she traced developments with a tiny finger. At night she usually went to sleep in his arms during the ten o'clock news. In the late afternoons she stood on the lawn, waiting for the first glimpse of his car.

The death of her father was the only tragedy Gina ever had

known. A day seldom went by, even now, when she did not think of him, his warm smile, his gentle, reassuring voice. Her visits to her mother in San Jose were painful, for they invariably wound up weeping over their memories of Angelo Vinza.

He left her principal heir to the largest cheese factory in San Jose. But almost as a last, loving gesture, he had made an even larger gift: the discovery that she still had room in her heart for another man. Gina did not learn the details until years later, in bits and pieces.

In truth, the two canny Corsican fathers had arranged a marriage.

Much later Gina had listened to the story mildly horrified, but, upon reflection, she could not be greatly surprised. Mediterranean ways ran deep. All she had known at the time was that suddenly Carlo was there in her home, equally as unaware of the circumstances, and that she was urged to be nice to him.

She needed no encouragement. With his dark good looks, his soft brown eyes and easy humor, Carlo was the most interesting and attractive man she had ever met. She was hopelessly in love with Carlo months before her father's fatal heart attack.

Nothing in her tender upbringing, or her father's plans, prepared her for Carlo's exuberant physical nature. He was a wild, impetuous lover, seducing her in the most improbable surroundings. Once, on a brief trip to Sacramento, they made love on the Capitol grounds, in the balcony of their penthouse suite hanging high over the lights of the city, on an Interstate overpass with traffic thundering beneath them. Even today Carlo was apt to render her helpless at the most inopportune moment. His ardor had not lessened with the years. He only seemed more given to moods she did not understand.

She had a perfect husband, a lovely, precious daughter, a full, happy, rewarding life.

Then this flawless world collapsed with a single telephone call that Monday afternoon.

It came at a bad time. Gina was late with the *pizzelle* she had made for the St. Francis Solono benefit auction. She still had to stop at the French bakery to pick up some rolls for dinner. The cashmere suit she had rush-ordered more than a week ago at last had arrived at the Jitterbug. She had to go by for a fitting if she expected to wear it when she spoke before the California Arts Council at its Friday luncheon in Sacramento. And Ariana had to be picked up from her ballet lesson at four.

Gina was dashing out of the house, *pizzelle* in hand, when the phone rang. With a groan of irritation she stopped, set down the swathed tray, and picked up the receiver.

"Gina?" A heavy, husky male voice.

"Yes?"

"How you doin', Gina?" the voice asked.

"Fine," Gina said, puzzled. "Who is this?"

"Doesn't matter," the voice said. "I just called to see how you're doin'. It just occurred to me that with your husband out fucking everything in town, you must be a very lonely lady. And I think you're terrific. I want to fuck you so bad I can taste if, if you know what I mean."

Gina tried to say something. She was not certain exactly what. All that emerged was a faint, strangled croak. She stood paralyzed, the mention of Carlo boiling in her mind.

The voice went on in a confident, conversational tone.

"Frankly, I think Carlo's got rocks in his head. That waitress he's fucking most of the time now doesn't hold a candle to you. Oh, Patsy Jean's good-looking. I'm not denying that. But my God, Gina. All I have to do to get a hard-on is just think about that sweet ass of yours. You know what I'd like to do to you?"

He went into specifics, calmly describing things Gina never imagined in her most erotic flights of fancy. His crude language was softened by his gentle, friendly voice. Gina clutched the phone, repelled but at the same time fascinated in a very disturbing way. All her life she had heard about obscene telephone calls.

Now she had one.

"You're sick," she said. Somewhere she had read that this was the way to handle it. Say that, then hang up.

But she could not move. Her body, her mind were numb. Nobody had told her what to do if it involved her husband.

What did all this have to do with Carlo?

"I've got to hand it to Carlo," the voice continued. "He sure can pick them. That Patsy Jean is probably a real animal in the sack. But I'll bet you and me could show them a trick or two . . ."

Gina's words came out involuntarily. She was appalled at her lack of control, even as she repeated the name. "Patsy Jean?"

"Yeah. Patsy Jean Litton. Waitress at the Valley Bar and Grill. Works seven till three, then she and Carlo go to her apartment and fuck like minks. Didn't you know that? Hell, everybody in town's laughing about it."

At last Gina moved. She slammed down the receiver and stood, trembling.

Slowly shock gave way to anger. She felt used, soiled.

She yanked up the receiver and began dialing the sheriff's office, using the emergency numbers pasted to the base of the phone, and trying to remember the name of the young deputy who had handled the case last fall when vandals spray-painted graffiti on the side of the stables. The young man had been so nice.

Halfway through the dialing, Gina stopped. She could not tell the deputy—or anyone—of those accusations against Carlo.

Gina stood, helpless, as she absorbed the knowledge that the accusations were true.

She was certain of it.

Dozens of almost unnoticed mysteries suddenly fell into place. None had been of sufficient significance to command her full attention. She had registered each almost subliminally—the faint, occasional whiff of perfume about Carlo, the isolated times he had arrived home a trifle too neat, as if he had just stepped out of the shower, the puzzling, too solicitous voices when she phoned the winery and they informed her that Carlo was out at the moment.

They knew.

Everybody knew.

Sick, Gina sank into the chair by the telephone.

She sat for a time, regaining her composure.

Anger helped.

She glanced at her watch. Almost three thirty. She picked up the phone book.

There was no Patsy Jean Litton.

Her immediate relief was quickly wiped away by the thought that a waitress probably would lead a mobile kind of life. She might not have been a resident of Sonoma long enough to be listed.

Gina called directory assistance. The operator rattled off the number. Gina held the receiver button down for a moment, thinking of a ruse.

One summer, when she had been involved in family counseling at the church, Gina had often helped parishioners in financial straits, especially young families newly arrived to work in the vineyards. She still remembered the techniques used by the bill collectors.

She dialed. A pleasant voice heavy with twang answered on the second ring.

"Miss Litton?"

"Yes. Who is it?"

"This is the retail merchants' credit bureau. I'm attempting to locate a Larry Dale Simmons. I believe he lives in your apartment complex. Do you happen to recognize the name?"

Patsy Jean immediately became helpful, solicitous. "No, hon. This here is just a crappy little garage apartment. I think the place you want is one block over, toward town."

Gina heard movement over the phone. A rustle of sheets? The creak of bedsprings?

"What hundred block would that be?" Gina asked.

"Eight hundred," Patsy Jean said. "This is nine hundred."

"I thank you very much for the information," Gina said. "You've been most helpful. I'm grateful. I'm sorry I bothered you."

"Any time, hon," Patsy Jean said. "No bother."

Gina hung up the phone and sat for a moment, still shaken. Then, abruptly, she gathered up her keys and the *pizzelle*. She almost ran to her car.

For years, she had been glad that their sprawling California ranch home was so remotely situated. But with the increasing vandalism —and now this—she was suddenly afraid to be alone.

She drove toward Sonoma, using the brakes and footfeed, squealing the tires on the turns.

In Sonoma she drove straight to the address Patsy Jean had revealed.

Carlo's station wagon was parked at the curb.

Gina drove on past. Her mind was absolutely empty. Her hands were trembling, weak. She knew that if she did not park soon, she would wreck the car.

She also knew that if she had a gun at that moment, she might do anything. She had to go somewhere with people around, someplace where sanity might return.

On impulse, she turned into the parking lot of a bar. She remained in the car for several minutes, frozen behind the wheel. At last she examined her surroundings and sighed. Her instincts had been right. She needed a drink. Badly.

She locked the car and went into the bar, carrying the *pizzelle* for the church benefit, aware despite her state of mind that it might become a shapeless, soggy mess in the heat of the car.

The bar was lined with men. Gina hesitated, then walked to a table. The bartender came to take her order.

"Double vodka martini," she said.

She placed the *pizzelle* carefully before her on the table and looked up. All along the bar the men were eyeing her. They were making an effort not to be obvious about it, and failing miserably. Gina was very aware of the hungry looks they were giving her.

And she knew that at that very moment Carlo was locked in heat with another woman.

Despite the anger, the humiliation, she could not resist curiosity.

Would Carlo be different with Patsy Jean? Was he doing the things that man had described so vividly on the phone?

Gina drank the martini quickly and ordered another. The warmth spread rapidly through her.

She turned in her chair and looked boldly at the men along the bar. Sexual appraisal could be a two-way street.

She thought again of the man on the phone.

Did all men do the things he described?

Gina felt a flush of excitement from the knowledge of her sexual power over the men at the bar. The line of male rumps kept blocking her vision. She thought of Carlo and Patsy Jean. The haunting voice from the phone continued to rumble provocative descriptions in her head.

She ordered another drink.

Maybe the man who owned that voice would wander in.

That man, or some other son-of-a-bitch.

Carlo had not been home five minutes before Ariana called. He had gone into the den and mixed a drink. He was sitting, wondering where the hell everyone was, when the phone rang. Ariana's voice conveyed her displeasure.

"Where's Momma? She was supposed to pick me up at four. And it's five!"

Carlo felt a twinge of alarm. Gina never missed appointments.

"She must be tied up somewhere. Let's give her another ten or fifteen minutes. If she doesn't show, call me back."

"Daddy, I can't goon around here all afternoon," Ariana said in disgust. "I've got schoolwork to do. And Little Bit hasn't been fed and brushed. Besides, everybody's gone. I'm here by myself. It's spooky!"

"All right, all right," Carlo said. "I'll be there to get you in a few minutes. Just sit tight."

Carlo debated what to do. One of the disadvantages of living in a small town was the fact that one could never make routine inquiries of the police. Word that Carlo Moretti was hunting for his wife would get around. On a whim, he called the winery on the remote chance Gina might have gone by his office. He reached his secretary just as she was leaving. She had not seen Gina.

The second button on the phone began flashing before Carlo hung up. He was so certain it was Ariana calling back that he did not bother with a hello.

"Yes?"

"Carlo Moretti?" a low but familiar male voice asked.

"Speaking."

"This is Joe, the manager of the Sonoma Bar. I hope I'm not doing the wrong thing. But your wife is in here, alone, and she's had a few drinks. What I'm worried about, several guys at the bar—strangers—have been giving her the eye. You know what I mean. I'm afraid there's gonna be trouble."

"My wife?" Carlo asked. What he was hearing was unbelievable. "Are you certain?"

"She's been here almost two hours." The man sounded upset. "I'd try to get her to leave, but she's in no shape to drive. And you know the fuckin' law now. If she has a wreck, it's my fault."

"I'll be right there," Carlo said.

He hung up the phone. Only then did he remember his earlier promise.

He headed for his station wagon.

Ariana would have to wait a few more minutes.

Gina was on her fifth vodka martini when Carlo walked into her vision. She had forgotten her thoughts of murder, but when she saw him, all came rushing back into her head.

"You son-of-a-bitch," she said, louder than she had intended.

Carlo attempted to put a soothing hand on her shoulder. She jerked away.

"Through with your whore already?" she asked. She knew the whole bar was listening. At the moment she did not care.

Carlo held out a hand. "Gina, come on. Let's go. Ariana is waiting for us."

Gina got to her feet and backed away from him. "I'm not going anywhere with you," she said.

Carlo kept moving toward her. She saw that she would soon be trapped against the corner booth. She tried to escape, but Carlo reached and grabbed her by the arm. Using her nails, Gina tried to reach his face. Carlo whipped her around and began moving her toward the door. Gina yelled in frustration.

At the bar, a big man in a western shirt stood up and moved in front of them.

"Where I come from, we don't manhandle women like that," he said.

"Then maybe you better go back where you came from," Carlo said. He yanked Gina toward him.

"You better get your hands off that woman, buddy," the man said.

Carlo moved Gina to one side. Off balance, she staggered against a booth.

Carlo pointed a forefinger at the man.

"Listen to me, friend, and listen well," Carlo said. "This woman is my wife. And if you don't get the fuck out of my way, you're going to be in more goddamn trouble than you ever thought possible. Understand?"

The man's eyes wavered. He glanced at Gina, then back at Carlo. He took a step backward. "I just don't like to see women treated that way," he said.

"That's your problem," Carlo said. "What I do is none of your goddamn business."

Carlo turned to Gina. "Come on," he said. "Let's go."

Gina moved back toward her table. She shook her head. She needed time to think.

"No, you go on and get Ariana," she said. "I've got my car." She sat down at the table. She almost missed the chair and had to fumble for balance. The table tipped. The bundle of *pizzelle* slid toward the edge. Gina grabbed and prevented it from falling.

Carlo did not move from the center of the floor. "You're in no condition to drive. Come on. We can send for your car."

Gina did not want to be with Carlo. She did not want to see Ariana. She wanted to be alone.

"Go on," she said.

Carlo came toward her, holding out a hand. "Gina . . ."

"Go on!" Gina shouted, struggling to her feet. "Go!"

Using both hands she whipped up the tray of *pizzelle* from the table and threw it. Carlo saw it coming. He managed to get up an arm, partially deflecting the massive tray. The whole thing seemed to explode in midair, linen tea towels, aluminum foil, and an intense shower of pastries. A sugary residue dusted down the front of Carlo's suit. Most of the pastry sailed over him and sprayed the bar.

The drinkers scrambled off the barstools, wiping their faces, hair, clothes. Then, as the humor hit them, they began laughing. Experimentally, one lifted a wedge from where it had settled in his glass. He nibbled curiously, then shoved the whole piece into his mouth.

"Man, I don't blame you," he called to Carlo. "I wouldn't let a cook like that get away."

By this time two of the men were helpfully gathering remains from the floor and awkwardly pushing them back onto the platter.

Sobered by what she had done, Gina marched past Carlo and out the door. When he came out, she was seated in the front seat of his station wagon.

He got in without comment. They drove in silence to get Ariana. The child was a little bundle of fury. She climbed into the back seat and slammed the door. "Two hours!" she said. "I've been wait-ing two hours!"

"Just calm down," Carlo said. "You're going to have to learn one of these days you can't always have your way."

Ariana sank back in her seat, subdued. Her father seldom used such words with her—and never that tone of voice.

They rode for several minutes without speaking. As they reached the outskirts of Sonoma, Ariana lowered her window.

"It smells awful in here," she said.

It was then that Gina began to cry. To her, it was like blasphemy to have left all that *pizzelle* lying back in that miserable bar. She was remembering the worn old range-top *pizzelle*-maker in the kitchen back in San Jose. She and Angelo Vinza had spent many Saturday afternoons making gorgeous *pizzelle*.

Gina could not stop her tears.

More than anything right now she needed her father.

CHAPTER 4

SILVIO and Salvatore slowed their pace. Carlo and Emil Borneman went on across the field, inspecting the vines.

The Moretti vineyards lay basking in the late September sun. Throughout the dark green expanse, occasional yellowed leaves provided a flowerlike contrast. Only an observer as experienced as Silvio Moretti would have noticed the deeper shadings in one corner, where twenty acres of choice cuttings were dying.

Carlo came striding back across the field, pounding a fist into his open palm.

"At least ten acres of Barbera gone," he said. "Another ten of Cabernet."

Emil Borneman returned and stood listening without comment. He shrugged and spread his hands in a gesture of bafflement. His broad shoulders, height, and sheer bulk made his helplessness seem even more pathetic.

"Sabotage," Carlo declared. "Has to be. Whoever did it had to know the pipe system." He glowered toward the corner of the field where the workers were gathered, waiting nervously. "I'll fire the whole goddamn bunch."

"You are not going to fire anybody," Silvio said. "Not yet."

He reached out to feel a brown leaf, drooping unnaturally below the vine. His experienced eye told him that the plant was beyond help. With the toe of his shoe he pushed away the thin layer of mulch, exposing the white crystals encrusted in the soil beneath. He explored further into the soft dirt, confirming that the brine had penetrated deep into the soil.

"Salt in the water," Silvio said to Emil. "There must be some explanation."

"The water from the well turned brackish," Emil said. "No one noticed. It's a good thing this side is on a separate line."

"Qualitative analysis of the water in that well hasn't changed one iota in ten years," Carlo said. "If there's salt in that well, it was put there."

"Maybe," Emil said. "Maybe not."

Silvio felt the dark weight of premonition. These disasters were too familiar. Old friends dead. Hundreds of vines he had cultivated for decades destroyed overnight. Lucian had used the most vicious weapon available—destruction of the things Silvio loved. Where would it stop?

"Take your men to the fringes of this poisoning," Silvio said to Emil. "There, where little water reached, push the soil back from the plants. We may save a few vines."

"That won't help the rest," Carlo said.

"Carlo, take a couple of men and pump the well," Silvio said. "Run the pipe into the drainage ditch. If the well was salted, the pump soon will bring up fresh water."

Silvio motioned to his friend Salvatore, and turned to leave the field. Carlo called after him.

"What will keep them from doing it again?"

Silvio turned back to glare at his elder son.

"I will take measures," he said.

Returning to his car, Silvio searched for the logic in the timing of the excessive actions Lucian Hall had taken. On the drive to the house, he determined the answer. Anna confirmed it for him.

"Lucian Hall phoned," she said. "He wants to meet with you tomorrow afternoon."

Silvio nodded his understanding. He motioned for Salvatore Messino to follow him into the study, closed the door behind them, then walked past his desk to stand for a moment, gazing out over Sonoma.

He was reluctant to take the next, irreversible step.

"Lucian has never forgotten Drake's Bay," he said, as much to himself as to Salvatore.

"And you still blame Lucian's father for Paulie," Salvatore said gently.

Silvio glanced at Salvatore. "Of course I do. He was there. He could have stopped it."

Salvatore nodded agreement. "I am only pointing out that this is a two-way street, old friend. And when a business deal becomes something more, something personal, logic goes out the window."

Silvio did not answer. He still could remember Paulie's innocent, untroubled face, his ready smile, his gusto for life, his eagerness to make certain he always did more than his share.

The memories were painful, even after almost a half century. Paulie had been on his way to work in the hold of a ship, unconcerned with the talk of wages and working conditions. He had not been simpleminded, as some thought, but one of God's children whose lives are uncomplicated by guile. He was hard of hearing and had difficulty with language. But Silvio knew that in many ways Paulie had been far more intelligent than anyone else suspected.

All Paulie knew that day was that it was a fine morning, and he looked forward to starting to work, pitting his strong young muscles against the cargo.

But there had been trouble on the docks; a picket line had been formed to press the workers' demands for higher wages, safer conditions. Lucian Hall's father countered with armed men—professional strikebreakers. The docks that morning were poised on the edge of violence. The battle lines had formed. As negotiator, Silvio was making one last effort to prevent bloodshed.

Paulie did not speak English. Silvio, attempting to reason with Frederick Hall, saw Paulie stride into no-man's-land, smiling in curiosity over the turmoil around him.

Silvio yelled at him, as did several of the strikers. But Paulie did not hear.

In growing horror, Silvio saw the strikebreakers raise their rifles. "Stop them!" he shouted to Frederick Hall.

"They have their orders," Hall said, turning away.

The volley did not kill Paulie instantly. Silvio reached him on the dock before he died. Paulie's look of total bewilderment was burned into his memory.

At that time, Silvio had not yet established power. Years passed before he had the opportunity to strike back. Just before the old man's death, the chance came for revenge in a way Frederick Hall would recognize.

Silvio had embarrassed the old man, cost him a fortune.

Lucian and his father had paid.

But they had not paid enough.

Silvio carefully lit a cigar while he thought about the matter, making certain he was taking the correct course. He could see no reasonable alternative.

"Lucian has gone to excessive lengths to make the situation plain," he said. "And he is pressing me for an answer. I think it is time to give him one. In kind."

He walked to the lowboy, replaced a copy of Plutarch in the bookcase, and poured two snifters of brandy produced experimentally from Moretti grapes. He handed one to Salvatore. They exchanged the gestures of a toast. Then Silvio sat down behind his desk.

"Salvatore, here is what I want you to do," he said. "Arrange a meeting for me this afternoon at the parlor." He paused for a moment. "I think this is something for the people on the docks," he said. "They are removed from us, yet we have the necessary, mutual loyalties."

Salvatore nodded. "I know who to call. But the time is short. Should I tell them what will be required?"

"I think not," Silvio said. "Tell them only that we are ready to act. They know—or suspect—what we are about to ask them to do. If they are of the caliber I believe them to be, they have already made some preparations. We will discuss the details when we meet. It will be a simple matter, but it must be done tonight, and it must be effective. I do not want to bargain tomorrow from a position of weakness."

Salvatore smiled. "This is like reliving the old days, eh, Silvio?"

Silvio sniffed the bouquet of the brandy. It was sweeter than he would have preferred.

"Unfortunately," he said. "I find myself thinking of the old days more and more."

"And now we are old," Salvatore said. "I wonder what is to happen when we are gone."

Silvio held the brandy up to the light, measuring its color. A darker product, with less sweetness, might be marketable.

He turned his attention back to Salvatore. There were few people in the world he knew better. Their friendship, begun in Corsica, had matured in the days when as boys they were doing the work of men on the docks of San Francisco.

"My sons will be here," Silvio said.

Salvatore was eloquent with his silence.

After a long pause, Silvio said, "I have made mistakes." He would not have discussed the matter with anyone else. Salvatore was the one person who understood. "One son is too rash, too impetuous. He does not have the necessary vision. The other is confused in his principles. I should have prepared them better."

Salvatore sipped his brandy. "Perhaps it requires something more," he said. "For instance, I have shared your life. I have been through the terrible times you have known. But I did not earn the respect, the position that you have been accorded. With all due respect . . ." Salvatore smiled and gestured with his snifter. "I am well-read—perhaps in some ways as well as yourself. I also worked hard. Yet, I lacked that indefinable quality that produces wealth, leadership, influence. I have been curious, Silvio. How would you define that quality?"

Silvio had given the question considerable thought. He voiced the only conclusion he had reached. "There is an innate ability in some men to bring the desires of other men into focus. It is a talent. Inherited or acquired, I do not know. It is a thing worthy of note but not especially marvelous. Just as one man can lay more bricks in a day than another."

"Do you think it is an art that has been lost in the younger generations?" Salvatore asked.

Silvio almost smiled in appreciation of Salvatore's tact. He had asked a question without asking it.

"*Lost* is not the correct word," Silvio said. "I think, for instance, that my son Johnny has this knack, this capability. But you see, his experience has been so different from our own. The word *undeveloped* might serve best. I used to think, old friend, that we were underprivileged in our youth—the privations we endured, the backbreaking work, the poverty . . ."

He paused and shook his head. There were some things he could not discuss, even with his closest friend.

"I thought I was giving my sons the best life had to offer—affluence, good schools, no worries. Now I see that in a sense it is they who have been deprived. The times of our childhood prepared us for all that was to follow. My sons, your sons, do not see the necessity for dire measures, as we do. I have tried to instill within them a feeling for the . . ."

He hesitated. The deadly secret that was ingrained in their everyday lives was rarely mentioned.

". . . a feeling for our way of life," he continued. "I have come to recognize that loyalty to our own needs is something that cannot be taught. It is something that has to be experienced. As we experienced it."

Salvatore nodded his understanding. "Perhaps there will be lessons in the events of the next few weeks."

"Perhaps," Silvio said. "And they may be valuable lessons. I too have grown soft with the times. I have been lured into thinking that our way is a thing of the past. I see now that the enemy will be with us always. He only comes in new clothing. As long as there are men who will exploit other men, the requirements will remain."

Salvatore finished his brandy, placed his glass on the table, and rose to his feet. At the door he hesitated, and turned to face Silvio. "Without our way, I would have been dead at twelve," he said. "And you would have been dead at . . . what? Ten? We owe many years of life to our way, Silvio."

"And a good life," Silvio said. "Perhaps the time has come for repayment. I am convinced that we now must revive, re-establish our way. I am certain it holds the only chance of salvation for our sons."

Silvio and Salvatore entered the poker parlor a few minutes after six in the evening. Silvio felt the familiar warmth of camaraderie he

associated with the dimly lit lounge. He knew everyone in the place
—the three grape growers deep in conversation at the bar, the five
poker players at a gaming table in the next room. Silvio waved his
greetings as he and Salvatore passed through into Salvatore's corner
office.

The two young men entered a few minutes later through the
back door, as they had been instructed. Silvio rose from his chair to
greet them. He had not met them before, but he knew them well by
reputation. He had received many reports on each.

Tom O'Brien was the one known on the docks as Tiger. Square-
built, with a thick neck and a burly, rounded head, he did not
remotely resemble a tiger. He was constructed more like a bull.
Silvio presumed that the nickname came from the tenacity evident
in his deep-set, glowering eyes. The trait was no surprise. Silvio had
known the young man's father.

Gerry Adams was lean to the point of gauntness, with long hair
and an unkempt beard. He was filled with a nervous energy that
seemed barely under control. Silvio would have been concerned
that he might be on drugs, except for irrefutable assurances from
those who knew him. The young man was reported to be extremely
ambitious, and very popular with the rank and file along the docks.
There was a belief that in time he would become a labor leader of
national rank.

Silvio took Adams's measure as they shook hands. He liked the
level intensity of the light-blue eyes.

"We have been told that you wish a job done," O'Brien said.
"We are here to . . . complete the arrangements."

Silvio nodded. He had no doubt that these two young men would
do the work. They were well-motivated. Both were ambitious, eager
to ingratiate themselves with those who now held power. No doubt
they could use the money. And an aura of accomplishment—even
if never publicly defined—would soon be attached to them.

But certain circumlocutions were in order. They were here to
"arrange" the job.

"Very well," Silvio said. "For various reasons unnecessary to
mention I find we must do something which is distasteful to me, as I
am sure it is to you. But we are men. We must do what we must do.
If you will see that this matter is taken care of, I will be most
grateful. I assure you I will never forget your kindness to me. And

if there is any trouble in the commission of the matter, I further assure you that no expense will be spared, no stone left unturned to unburden you—or anyone connected—of the responsibility. On this you have the solemn word of Silvio Moretti. If you do not accept my word, the promise is meaningless. So I must know. Do you accept my word?"

"Absolutely, Mr. Moretti," Adams said.

"Yes, sir," said O'Brien.

"Good. In return I only wish your promise that if the unforeseen should happen, I will never be connected with the matter."

"Of course, Mr. Moretti," Adams said.

"That is understood," O'Brien said. "Our position has been made very clear."

Silvio opened a map of the Bay Area and pointed to an intersection.

"There is an old warehouse at this corner, on the grounds of the Hampton Industries holdings. It is in a bad state of repair. I have taken the trouble to determine that the insurance policy on that piece of property has not been rewritten from the time when it was used for other purposes. There is no clause in the policy covering contents. If the warehouse were to burn tonight, the financial loss to Hampton Industries would be several times what I have incurred in recent weeks."

Adams glanced at the map. "We are familiar with the building, Mr. Moretti."

Silvio nodded. "I have here some photographs, so there will be no mistake," he said. "You come to me highly recommended. I will not presume to interfere with how you arrange the matter. But I would like to know how you intend for it to be done."

Adams shuffled through the photographs until he found the view he wanted.

"As you see here, Mr. Moretti, the properties are surrounded by a high chain-link fence, with Y-bars and barbed wire at the top. Difficult to climb, impossible for anyone with equipment. But this afternoon, in an accident that may have gone unnoticed, a truck turning around at this intersection backed into the fence at this corner. The resulting hole is hidden from the warehouse by stacks of wooden skids. This will allow access to the grounds."

Silvio nodded. These two young men were of the caliber he expected.

"Once inside, it is a simple matter," Adams said. "The warehouse is ancient, of pier and beam construction. The floors are wooden, and dry. If gasoline were placed along the inside of the foundations —here, here, and here—on each side, the flames would shoot right up the walls to the roof in a matter of minutes. The floor would collapse. The roof would fall, burning."

Silvio glanced at Salvatore, who gave him a brief nod, indicating that the electronic sweep device concealed in his desk detected no recording of the conversation. Neither of the young men was wired. It was a simple precaution.

"Your arrangements seem more than satisfactory," Silvio said. "You understand, of course, that the matter must be taken care of tonight. That is essential."

"Understood," Adams said. "We have only one problem." He glanced at O'Brien, then back to Silvio. "Two security guards patrol the properties. If we had more time, we could learn their schedule. As it stands, they may have to be eliminated in some manner. Do we have carte blanche to take whatever steps are necessary? It might mean more heat. We are not concerned, understand. We're ready to do whatever has to be done. But we wouldn't want to attract more attention than you wish."

Silvio hesitated. The two watchmen were from a leased service. They were not Hampton Industries employees, as he would have preferred. He understood what the young man was saying: with the two watchmen out of the way, they could work more efficiently and worry less about being caught in the act.

Silvio thought of Patricio, Antonio, Umberto.

"Do whatever you have to do," he said.

CHAPTER 5

"**I** hope you understand the importance of this case, as far as the firm is concerned," Clarence Snow said. "If Herbert Fraser is satisfied with the way we handle this, he could become one of our major clients."

"I understand," Johnny said.

In fact, he understood far more than Snow was saying. The senior partners were anxious because the case rested in the hands of the youngest member of the firm. Snow, a professional worrier, had been delegated to drop by and check Johnny's pretrial preparation.

They sat in Johnny's new office in the executive suite, on an upper floor of the Bank of America World Headquarters. Snow, lean and gaunt and troubled, massaged his bony hands as he talked. Someone once had joked that Snow was paid to nurture his ulcers. He seldom did much legal work himself. Instead, he continually worried over the cases others were taking into court, making certain of details.

"How is our case shaping up?" he asked now.

"So far, so good," Johnny said. "I've asked Mr. Fraser to visit his daughter, wired for sound. The tapes should support our contention that her personality has changed drastically. We'll have ample testimony from friends and family to the effect that before falling under the influence of the cult, she was outgoing, vivacious."

"Will the tapes be admissible?"

Johnny shrugged. "A chance we'll have to take. The courts seem to be growing more lenient. Since it's a civil case, and Mr. Fraser as a party to the taping will be able to testify as to its veracity, I believe they may be allowed."

Snow nodded in his abstract way. "What will be our basic contention?"

Johnny took a deep breath. Snow had reached the most delicate area. Johnny had spent many hours in an effort to put his client's case into proper wording. Snow's reaction would be the acid test.

"I think our best argument would be to stress the responsibility of the court—of society itself—to intervene, to recognize the girl's best interests."

Snow frowned. "In other words, to throw ourselves on the mercy of the court?"

"In a sense," Johnny admitted. "But of course I wouldn't phrase it in that fashion. I think the key word is responsibility."

"It's weak," Snow said.

"We're demanding justice, not begging for it," Johnny said. "Presented properly, I think it could be a strong argument."

Snow rubbed his bony knees, frowning. "When you come right down to it, all arguments are a plea for justice. Can't we come up with something better?"

"I've considered alternatives," Johnny said. "I think we would be in error if we attempted to attack the cult as a substandard religion. We would be into an area where established law is against us."

Snow nodded agreement.

"Since the girl is of legal age, all common custody arguments and precedents are useless. About the only other course would be to declare her *non compos mentis*. In this instance it would be difficult to prove. And it probably would work against us."

"Fraser wouldn't want to call his daughter even slightly crazy,"

Snow said. "We can't do that." He stuck his fingers beneath his vest and rubbed his troubled stomach. "We represent the aggressor in the case. Yet we are going into court with the weaker argument. I don't like it."

Johnny watched Snow's face carefully. "I think our best terminology is that Mr. Fraser's daughter, through the undue and unnatural influence of this church, has been temporarily dethroned of reason, because she is emotionally immature and susceptible. We would make it clear that we are not attacking the church or its right to exist but merely its influence in the specific instance of our client's daughter. We would not be calling the girl crazy or temporarily insane—simply the highly vulnerable victim of an unnatural influence."

"Brainwashing," Snow said.

"I think we should avoid the word," Johnny said. "It has connotations of torture, prison cells, interrogation. I think the phrases 'undue and unnatural influence,' 'susceptible,' 'emotionally immature,' and 'dethroned of reason' would be best. We could present the court with the portrait of a girl from protected, even naive circumstances, falling victim to forces beyond her ken."

Snow remained troubled. "It might work," he said. "But I still feel our position is weak."

"Fraser is scheduled to bring in the tapes this morning," Johnny said. "I'll know more after I hear them."

"Well, I'll check back with you." Snow walked to the door, paused for a moment, then turned.

"There's one thing you might bear in mind," he said. "This church will be spending a fortune for a battery of lawyers to say that this poor child, reared in the home of a profit-motivated, godless infidel, has at last found Jesus. The Holy Bible will be their brief. *We* will be portrayed as the villains in league with the devil, attempting to wrest this child out of her spiritual dedication, back to her father's materialistic world."

"If we have to, we can prove some sordid things that have occurred in that church," Johnny said. "They won't emerge lily white."

"If it comes to that, neither will we," Snow said. His next words went to the heart of the issue, to the aspect that had given Johnny so much concern. "The problem is, of course, that this is a spiritual case. A temporal court is really not the place to try it."

Herbert Fraser reacted to strange rooms like a trapped animal, nervously pacing from wall to wall, inspecting every unfamiliar object. Once this brief ceremony was over, he then took charge of the room and its contents as thoroughly as he controlled everyone and everything in his life. A big man, with coal-black hair salted sparingly with gray, bushy eyebrows, and a broad, strong face, Fraser conveyed with every movement the dynamic energy that had taken him from a southern California junkyard, where he had made a fortune while still a teenager, to corporate boardrooms and—some people said—to even more effective connections.

Johnny had seen Fraser take command of new surroundings several times during their many meetings through the last three weeks. This was Fraser's first visit to Johnny's new office. He waited while his client carefully examined the larger room, the more impressive furnishings.

"Terrific," Fraser said, walking past Johnny's desk to stand by the triangular bay window. Jutting out several feet from the side of the building, the window gave viewers the disturbing impression that the office was suspended in space, high above San Francisco. The clear day provided an uninterrupted vista from Nob Hill and the Marina to Fort Point and the Golden Gate Bridge.

Abruptly dismissing the view, Fraser glanced at the Jackson Pollock on the opposite wall, the bookcases and lowboy. He apparently recognized them as furnishings from Johnny's previous office down the hall. Satisfied, he turned and opened his briefcase.

"The tapes should be about what you want," he said, handing him a cassette. "Everything went the way we thought it would."

Johnny gestured Fraser into the wing chair beside the desk and inserted the cassette into a tape deck. He positioned the machine between them and paused.

Fraser was a difficult client, accustomed to giving orders, not taking them. Johnny was concerned about the necessity of using him as a witness. There was definite danger that Fraser would grow angry and rebellious under the restrictions of court testimony. He knew he would have to keep Fraser under a tight rein.

Now was the time to begin.

"Before we play the tape, I want you to describe for me the exact circumstances under which the recording was made."

Fraser glanced at his watch. "I've got another appointment at ten," he said.

Johnny waited for an instant before answering.

"Mr. Fraser, if we are to get your daughter back, we must prepare our case in detail. I know all of this is exasperating for a busy man. But I must impress on you that these details will determine whether we win or lose. This is an unusual case. We are going into shadow areas of law. As I've warned you, your daughter has every legal right to leave home. We must show the court that you are acting as a concerned, loving parent who has observed an abrupt, startling change in your daughter's personality. We must show that you are acting reasonably, responsibly. We must never, ever, utter one derogatory word about the church involved. All focus of our case must rest solely on what has happened to your daughter. It's a hairline, delicate difference. Do you understand what I'm saying?"

Fraser nodded impatiently. "I understand that," he said. "But I still have an appointment at ten."

Johnny gave him a poker-faced stare.

"Mr. Fraser, this case will require you to establish priorities. If it's not the most important thing in your life right now, then, frankly, there is no use in going forward with it."

Fraser glanced again at his watch. Johnny knew that he had won. "I suppose I can cancel my appointment." He looked pained.

"That may not be necessary," Johnny said. "This shouldn't take long. But it deserves your full attention. Just describe the place for me, in your own words. Tell me how she was brought in, how she looked to you, the way you both were seated throughout the taping."

Johnny reached for a yellow legal pad, uncapped a pen, and prepared to make notes. What he was about to hear would establish the foundation of Fraser's testimony.

"Let's see, I got there five minutes before two, Saturday. They'd said I'd be able to see her at two. But that preacher, this Reverend Jackson, had me taken into a waiting room. He let me cool my heels for twenty-five minutes before I was taken into his office."

"In court, you'll have to avoid derogatory, opinionated statements. Just say simply that the Reverend Mister Jackson asked to see you before you were allowed to see your daughter, and that you waited about twenty-five minutes. The jury will get the message. We must not seem, even by implication, to be criticizing Jackson or his operation. Understand?"

Fraser nodded. "Jackson talked for about fifteen minutes. I just kept quiet and listened, like you wanted. I didn't have the tape going. But I think I can remember most of it. Do you want everything he said?"

"Just give me the gist now," Johnny said. "We can go over the details later."

"Well, he said his church is rescuing dopeheads, alcoholics, runaways, people in trouble with the law, and so forth. I told him that Jenny isn't any of those. He said Jenny was 'spiritually deprived,' or else she wouldn't have come to him. I didn't argue. I let him talk for a while about different kids he said he'd rescued. He didn't call them by name. It was just 'this boy' or 'that girl.' He rambled on for a while, describing the various retreats the church operates. I gather they've got several fairly large tracts in Sonoma, Mendocino, Lake Counties. Maybe other places. Incidentally, where the hell do they get their money? I've never seen anybody around that place that looks like money."

"I don't know," Johnny said. "That might be worth looking into."

"When I asked again to see Jenny, he said, 'Of course.' I was taken into another room. I don't know what to make of this, but they've given her another name—Sister Sharon. That's what he called her. Is that important?"

"We'll make certain the jury is aware of it," Johnny said. "But there again, we're into a gray area. We could offer testimony from expert witnesses demonstrating that a new name is a psychological tool to achieve disorientation. But the defense could counter with the fact that postulants have been given new names upon their acceptance by various religions throughout the world for centuries." Johnny referred to his notes. "Please describe the room in which you met Jennifer."

Fraser frowned, remembering. "It was about twenty-two by eighteen, with a single table about twelve feet long, running lengthwise in the center of the room. Folding chairs were scattered around it, and a blackboard covered one wall. No windows. The floor was poured concrete. There were two doors, the one I used, and one at the other end, where Jenny came in."

Johnny felt a moment of elation. If Fraser's emotions could be held in check, he might make an excellent witness. He was positive, observant, and practical-minded. Such a description would make a good impression on the jury, even if the defense attempted to quibble over Fraser's estimates. They had the ring of authority.

"Was she alone?" Johnny asked.

"An older woman was with her," Fraser said. "A heavy-set woman of about thirty-five to forty. She didn't introduce herself, and I didn't ask her name. She had one hand on Jenny's elbow, and the other on her waist, walking her to the table like you would somebody who was weak and sick. When Jenny sat down, the woman walked over and stood in the corner of the room. She never said a word, all the time I was there."

"Describe Jennifer," Johnny said. "The change you saw in her."

Fraser's eyes grew troubled, and Johnny found himself hoping that this exact expression would be seen by the jury. At the moment, Fraser seemed nothing more than a worried parent. Maybe the jury would be able to see past Fraser's rough all-business facade and catch a glimpse of this human side.

"She's lost a lot of weight," he said. "Ten pounds or more. Looks bad. She's let her hair go to hell. It's stringy, dirty-looking. And she didn't have on any makeup." Fraser sat for a moment, remembering. "But the thing that got me was her eyes," he added. "They were completely lifeless. She has always had so much energy. When they brought her in she was quiet. She just sat there. She wouldn't even look at me. She just kept staring off into space, like she was in a trance." Fraser pointed to the tape deck. "You'll hear it. She kept saying the same things, over and over."

Johnny nodded. "We'll listen to it now," he said.

He turned on the machine. After a moment of tape hiss, Fraser's voice came through the small speaker. The quality of sound was good, but for a time Johnny was concerned, thinking the tie clasp microphone had not picked up Jennifer's voice. Then he realized she simply was not speaking. He could hear other small sounds in the room—the shuffle of feet, the creaking of chairs, breathing.

At last Jennifer spoke. Fraser was begging her to come home with him.

"I've had a change in values," she said. "I don't belong to that world now. I belong here. Father loves me."

As Fraser talked with her, pleaded with her, Jennifer spoke another dozen times. Each reply was rote, a repetition. The only variation was toward the end of the tape, when she said, "I don't want you to come here anymore. I'm happy here." Her frail voice came through with such strong conviction that Johnny remained a bit disturbed as he turned off the machine. He no longer was certain that the tape would work entirely to their advantage.

"I'll have the tape transcribed, and copies made," he said. "I'll want to go over it more thoroughly with you."

"What do you think about it?" Fraser demanded.

Johnny hesitated, wondering how far he should go in voicing his doubts. "You managed to get on tape exactly what we wanted," he said.

Fraser studied Johnny for a moment. "We don't have a very good case, do we?"

Johnny worded his answer carefully. "I'll be frank. No, we don't. If we were in another country, where each case is reviewed on its merits before formal filing, we probably would never get into court. But in America anybody can bring action against anyone. We are going to court. And once we're there, the way in which the case is presented will make all the difference. I still have hopes we'll succeed."

Fraser nodded, his face troubled. "There are other ways of getting her out of there, you know," he said. "I've thought about hiring some people to go right in there and take her. If I could get hold of her, I know I could talk some sense into her. And if I couldn't, I could turn her over to one of those deprogrammers."

"Then *you'd* be the defendant," Johnny pointed out. "This church has money. I'm certain they'd push prosecution. And as your lawyer, I have to warn you. You'd be in a very poor legal position. Especially if you had to hold your daughter for any length of time against her will."

"That wouldn't worry me," Fraser said. "If you want to know the truth, there's only one reason I'm trying this route first. I know

the goddamn newspapers and television would make something big
out of it. I wouldn't give a shit, myself. But my wife is dead set
against it. She says that Jenny would have to live with it the rest of
her life."

Johnny nodded his agreement.

"Maybe this is the time to say something else," Fraser added.
"I'm not a goddamn bit happy waiting on the p's and q's of the
courts. I'm willing to spend every penny I have to get my daughter
back. I'm not talking about an appeal—keeping it in the courts for
years. I'm talking about now. What I'm saying is, if you can grease
the wheels of justice in any way, just tell me when and how much."

Johnny had known this might happen. He was prepared.

"Mr. Fraser, I share your concern. And I want to help you, but if
we should do what you propose, and it were brought to light, it
would kill our case, destroy my career, and damage the reputation
of my firm." He held up a hand, palm outward, as Fraser started ·
to speak. "Understand, I'm not making a moral judgment. I'm
speaking of practical matters. Any clandestine action on our part
could wreck our case and put us in deep trouble."

Fraser frowned at Johnny for a long moment. For the first time
in their acquaintance he seemed a bit uncertain of what to say.

"Johnny, as I told your father, I want to get my daughter back,
whatever it takes, whatever I have to do. I think that's something
your father understands. I hope it's something you understand."

Johnny stared at Fraser, fighting back his anger and frustration.
He had not been aware that Fraser had talked to Silvio. He always
had known that someday those old stories about his father might
affect his professional life. But he had never dreamed that when it
happened, it would come from such an impressive source. He
waited until he had his emotions under control before replying.

"Mr. Fraser, I don't know what you've discussed with my father,
but I disassociated myself from the family business when I joined
this firm. I wasn't aware that my family name was a factor when
you asked that I handle your case. If it was, perhaps we'd best turn
the matter over to one of my partners, immediately."

Fraser seemed more puzzled than irritated. "Not unless you're
pissed off at me," he said. "Don't misunderstand me. I asked for
you because I heard, from people who should know, that you're

the sharpest guy in the business, and a real worker. Of course I was impressed by your name, your connections. Who the hell wouldn't be? I've heard nothing but good things about your father. I don't know him well. But I admire him, respect him. I know you've worked hard on my case. From talking to you I know you're a fighter, and you're on my side. I'm just laying it all out. I hope you're not pissed. If you are, I apologize."

Johnny's sudden anger was gone. "It seems I'm the one who owes an apology."

"Hell, no apologies necessary," Fraser said. "In a deal like this it's good for two guys to get to know each other. You should know the way I operate. If I'd played by the rules all my life, I wouldn't be here. I couldn't afford you as a lawyer. You're young. When you've been around as long as I have, you may see things different. And maybe I'd better tell you another thing. If this court business doesn't work, I'm ready to try something else."

"I appreciate your frankness," Johnny said. "If you wish, I'll continue to give you advice on your legal position. But I suspect we're talking about areas where I can't become involved, directly."

Fraser studied Johnny for a moment. "We'll cross that bridge if and when we come to it."

After Fraser shook hands and left the office, Johnny replayed the tape, making notes, assembling his points of argument. Then he sat at his desk for more than an hour, lost in thought, trying to fathom the hidden meanings behind Fraser's words.

Even assuming that the worst of the old stories about Silvio Moretti were true, all those things were far in the past. Johnny had heard, at various times, that his father once had dealt with Prohibition era gangsters in Chicago and the East, keeping them supplied with grapes for illegal wine; that he and Sam Cavanaugh once ran the state government in Sacramento as a private club, that in his youth he had organized the shipping and dock operations in San Francisco, that he had a hand in establishing the gambling empires in Las Vegas and Reno and the racetracks along the border, that he had lent millions to friends to help them get started in various businesses throughout the West, never charging interest, merely keeping a piece of the action.

Johnny had never doubted that the stories were true. He remembered the cars in the driveway at night, the somber men filing into Silvio's study, the mystery of the obeisance that politicians and men of power paid to Silvio.

The quiet, unassuming, gentle man tending his grapes in Sonoma once had ruled practically all commerce and government west of the Rockies. His powerful connections reached into the White House and the Congress.

That was the legend of Silvio Moretti.

He did not know the full extent of Silvio's holdings. He only knew that they were vast. And he had no doubt that Silvio still made many decisions that were merely acted out in corporate boardrooms. Johnny often had overheard his father on the phone, pulling strings with government officials, professional politicians, corporate board members, chief executive officers.

Fraser seemed to believe that those connections could be used to solve his problems.

After thinking the matter through, Johnny realized he had to consider the possibility. Herbert Fraser was a man who knew many ways to get things done. And what he did not know, he had the contacts to find out. If Fraser believed that Silvio could circumvent legal proceedings in a specific case, others—many others—must believe it too. And perhaps they were right.

Also, Johnny had to remember, Silvio himself seemed to share the belief.

CHAPTER 6

GREGORY Cavanaugh sat in the corner of the VIP Lounge at Los Angeles International, anxiously watching the doorway. His flight was only twenty minutes away. He had spent the day visiting state offices in the Los Angeles area with Tom Furman, who had just left for Washington. Neil Hart and his two assistants had driven over to San Bernardino in a rented car. They were supposed to be waiting at the airport to join Gregory for the trip back to Sacramento.

They were late.

Gregory's decision to use commercial carriers for official travel had been a highly effective political device. During his campaign for the governorship he had coined the phrase "economic rationality" to cover his disdain for the trappings of office. He had kept his word on holding down expenses. The National Guard plane normally assigned to transport the governor around the state was currently gathering dust in a hangar. Gregory seldom used the official limousine, habitually driving his own five-year-old Chevrolet. He seldom used bodyguards.

These visible facets of his administration's austerity program had one bothersome drawback: Gregory Cavanaugh did not like to be alone. He was continuously aware that he was a potential target. A retinue of aides might not offer much protection, but Gregory simply felt safer with friends around.

Growing more nervous by the minute, he left his one-suiter on a chair and walked to the doorway of the lounge. He stood watching passengers as they hurried toward the boarding gates and wondered if there could possibly have been any misunderstanding among his aides on the travel plans.

He was there in the doorway when the man found him.

"Mr. Cavanaugh?"

Gregory hesitated. He was seldom addressed as "Mr."

The man was carrying a Val-A-Pak. He held airline tickets in his other hand. An ordinary passenger. Gregory's moment of alarm vanished.

"Yes?" he said.

"A Mr. Hart is very ill in the lower lounge. They've called a doctor for him. He's been asking for you. He told me I would find you here."

Gregory thanked the man automatically, his mind racing.

A heart attack?

That was a definite possibility. Neil Hart had been working long hours lately, worrying excessively over differences between the administration and the State Senate. And Gregory had heard rumors that Neil was having marital difficulties.

Forgetting his luggage, he hurried to the escalator. It was crowded. He waited impatiently in place as he was carried to the ground floor, then dashed toward the lounge the man had indicated.

A well-dressed man with a professional appearance stood at the door to the men's restroom. Gregory had the fleeting impression of a gray three-piece suit, a gold chain across the vest, with what might be a Phi Beta Kappa key dangling.

"In here," the man said, opening the door.

Gregory did not take time to think. He assumed that the man was a doctor. He also assumed that the man would follow him into the rest room.

He was wrong on both counts. The door shut behind him with a resounding thump.

Two men were waiting in the tiled rest room. One was a giant— six feet four or five at least. The other seemed much smaller by comparison.

"Over here," the small one said, pointing beyond the urinals to an open booth.

Gregory remembered once being told that many heart attacks came while the victim was straining on the can. He hurried to the booth.

It was empty.

He was turning to demand an explanation when the giant seized him from behind.

Gregory struggled. He felt like a child in the arms of an adult. He was absolutely helpless.

"Don't fight me, and you won't get hurt," the big man said.

He lifted Gregory completely off the floor and carried him into the booth. He shifted his hold and forced Gregory's right arm back and upward. Gregory was certain the arm was on the verge of being torn from its socket. He ceased all resistance.

"Okay, little man. Do your stuff," the giant said.

The smaller man unbuckled Gregory's belt and unzipped his trousers. They fell to the floor.

Gregory tried to kick. Two things stopped him. His trousers were around his ankles. Then, as he tried to lash out, the big man pushed his arm upward another inch.

The other man yanked Gregory's shorts down, leaving him naked from the waist.

Then, incredibly, the small man was on his knees, in front of him.

Revulsed, Gregory pushed with his free hand, trying to shove the man away. The pain from his arm was excruciating. For a moment he thought he was going to faint.

"It ain't working," the small man said. He used a hand to pump experimentally at Gregory's flaccid penis.

"Fake it, then," the giant said.

The small man went back to his work. The agony, the horror seemed to last several full minutes.

The rest room door burst open. It slammed against the wall. Gregory heard a confusion of footsteps on the tile floor.

"All right. All right. Knock it off. Police," a deep bass voice boomed.

Abruptly Gregory was released. He staggered against the door of the booth for support. A badge was thrust into his range of vision.

"Sergeant Rutgers, Vice," the voice said.

"You misunderstand," Gregory said, still faint, still not comprehending what was happening. "I was attacked by these two men."

"You'll get a chance to tell your story to the judge," Rutgers said. "But be advised that I saw everything. So did Sergeant Martin here, also from L.A.P.D. Vice. And so did Reinert here, from airport security. I also have to advise you that anything you say will be used against you. Fix your goddamned pants."

Gregory understood then.

With trembling hands he pulled up his shorts and trousers as Rutgers read his rights from a printed card. Rutgers then turned to the little man.

"You're under arrest too, Herbie. Seems like you ought to know better by now. I keep telling you. The law lets you do this shit now, long as you do it in private. But you can't use the rest rooms. It's public indecency. The same law applies to straights. What if some young kid had come in here to piss?"

Sergeant Martin laughed. "That would of been fine with Herbie, I'll bet."

Herbie made no comment.

"Where's the other one?" Gregory asked Rutgers.

"What other one?"

"The big guy. The giant. The one that held me."

"I didn't see any giant. Any of you guys see a giant?"

They laughed.

Gregory shut up.

"Let's see some ID," Rutgers said.

He examined Gregory's driver's license and whistled. To Gregory's ears the feigned surprise seemed woefully unconvincing.

"Hey, we've landed a big fish," Rutgers said. "Gentlemen, meet Hizzoner the Governor, Gregory Cavanaugh."

"I told you it was him," Sergeant Martin said.

Rutgers laughed. "Tell me, Herbie. How does it feel to blow a governor?"

"Jeez, I didn't know it was the fuckin' governor," Herbie said. "He paid me fifty dollars."

He held out a bill.

Rutgers took the money. "Evidence," he said.

He pushed Gregory and Herbie up against the wall, frisked them, then put them in handcuffs.

"Come on, Herbie," he said. "Let's go down to the station so we can get you a nice cell all to yourself. We don't want you playing rotation in the holding tank again. Besides, this time you deserve special treatment. I have a feeling you're about to become famous —the newspapers, television. Maybe even the Guinness Book of Records."

"They put something in our gas tank," Neil Hart said. "We made it onto the freeway, then the car died. Right in traffic. It's a wonder we weren't killed."

"I was stupid," Gregory said. "So fucking stupid. That's what hurts, worse than anything."

"Well, they did a hell of a good job, faking you out," Hart said. "Don't worry. We'll beat them at their own game."

"I don't know how," Gregory said. "I feel so goddamned dirty. Like I've had worms crawling all over me. I've never wanted a shower worse in my life."

"Just be patient," Hart said. "You'll walk in a minute."

"I'd be better off if it was murder one. This is the end of my political career."

Hart looked at him for a moment. "Don't even say that," he said. "You just keep remembering one thing: You've got friends. And they are not going to let you down."

Ten minutes later they walked out of the police station. A battery of reporters and cameramen blocked their way, shouting a babble of questions.

Gregory paused on the steps, looked out over the crowd for a moment, then held out his hands for silence. The reporters with microphones pushed them forward in anticipation.

From long habit, Hart moved out of camera range, giving Gregory Cavanaugh center stage. He stood in wonder as Gregory, the antipolitical candidate, made an impromptu statement as eloquent as any ever conceived by a polished politician.

"I will not dignify what has happened to me today by offering a defense," he said. "However, I do wish to assure the people of California that, in time, the full truth of what occurred today will be made public. I also wish to deliver a message to a certain group of individuals who have gone to great lengths to blacken my name. The message is this: There will be a day of reckoning."

A network correspondent stepped up to Gregory's level, microphone in hand. In recognition of his senior status the other reporters remained silent.

"Governor Cavanaugh, do you believe this removes you from Senate race consideration? Is this your Chappaquiddick?"

Hart wanted desperately to signal Gregory to talk around the question, but Gregory did not hesitate.

"I hold no brief for Senator Kennedy, one way or another," he said. "As for myself, I will say this: When the truth becomes known, my position will be enhanced, not harmed. That is all I have to say. Thank you."

Hart helped Gregory push his way through to the waiting limousine Hart had hired. Gregory settled back in the seat and closed his eyes as the car headed through traffic toward the airport. Neil had managed to shift their reservations to a later flight.

Hart was replaying Gregory's remarks in his mind, evaluating the way they would sound on the evening news.

"Greg, that was fucking marvelous," he said. "If we had worked all night with a battery of speechwriters, we probably couldn't have come up with anything better."

Gregory opened his eyes. "It worked because at the moment I said it, I believed it," he said. He looked out the window and was silent for a moment.

"We can make it true," he added, almost to himself. "But we will have to move heaven and earth in the next few days."

CHAPTER 7

"*L*UCIAN Hall is behind it," Sam Cavanaugh said. "He set Greg up. There's no other explanation."

Silvio did not answer. He had reached the same conclusion, hours before. He shifted the phone to his other ear and leaned back in his chair. Again Lucian had struck where least expected.

"Tell Gregory not to worry," Silvio said. "We will find a way out of this."

"Did you see the evening news?" Sam asked.

Silvio had not. He seldom watched television.

"It was bad. The news people were actually chortling. And they interviewed that detective. Goddamned liar. But Greg made a good statement after his release. He showed class. I was really proud of him."

"He's a good boy," Silvio said. "We'll look after him."

"It's going to be rough," Sam said. "They've got four witnesses to contradict Greg's testimony. We can't let it come to trial. Yet, it's too hot for the courts to dismiss. We've got to fight it."

"Of course, of course," Silvio said.

"Already Greg's lawyers are treating it like any other case," Sam complained. "They're talking about plea bargaining! I don't want to give Lucian and those sons-a-bitches a fucking thing!"

Silvio was silent for a time as he considered the matter.

"Tell Gregory he must go on," he said finally, "business as usual. He must hold his head up, show confidence. It will be difficult. But we will need time. For the present he simply will have to endure."

"He's tough," Sam said. "He can do it."

"First we must recruit support," Silvio went on. "The initial reports will be bad. We've got to expect that. The public loves scandal. Let them have their day. Then we will come back with statements from responsible, influential people, expressing confidence in Gregory's character. That will give the public doubt—give us time to act."

They talked for more than two hours. Sam asked questions, made notes on Silvio's suggestions, but Silvio could not lift Cavanaugh's despair.

"Lucian Hall and his people think they have removed Greg from politics," he said. "Maybe they have."

"They have not." Silvio glanced at the clock. It was almost two in the morning.

"I will be meeting with Lucian later today," he informed Sam Cavanaugh. "I intend to deliver that message."

The front pages of the morning papers were filled with the story. There were pictures and interviews with the principals—even with the depraved person who claimed to have committed the perverted act.

Silvio found one consolation. The screaming headlines had shoved news of the Hampton Industries fire to the inside pages. The *San Francisco Chronicle* reported the blaze on page eighteen. Two security guards had died in the fire. Six firemen were injured.

Two photographs were used—one of the blazing building, and another of a fireman being treated for smoke inhalation.

A Hampton spokesman was quoted as saying that the old warehouse had been totally destroyed. No mention was made of the contents. The loss figures were set at a tenth of Silvio's estimates.

Silvio smiled as he read the account. Lucian was making every effort to minimize the loss.

Which meant he had been hurt.

CHAPTER 8

JOHNNY had never seen Sam Cavanaugh so nervous, so ill at ease. He kept shifting his weight in his chair. "I know you're busy," he said. "I appreciate your working me into your schedule. I suppose you've seen the papers, television."

Johnny nodded. He was uncertain of what to say. Since arriving at the office he had overheard a dozen dirty jokes told at the expense of the governor. The consensus, even in San Francisco, seemed to be that Gregory Cavanaugh's political career was over.

"I talked with your father last night, right after it happened," Sam said. "He believes we can turn this thing around. He had a number of suggestions. The first was that I come to see you, ask you to direct Greg's defense."

For a moment Johnny did not respond. He hoped his face betrayed none of the wildly conflicting emotions ignited by Sam's words. As far as he knew, this was the first case Silvio had ever sent him—the first indication Johnny had that his father even thought of him as a lawyer. The surprise was enhanced by the fact that the client was one of Silvio's closest and most influential friends, with the hottest—and apparently the most hopeless—case to come down the pike in years.

Johnny fought to keep his face expressionless. He wanted to convey the impression that his father sent him important cases every day.

"I thought Greg had counsel," he said.

"We don't like their advice," Sam said. "They're pushing us hard to make a deal—to plea bargain. Silvio suggested we bring you in, to put things on the right track."

Johnny considered the angles. His partners certainly would not relish the case. Not unless . . .

"I haven't talked to Pop," he said. "Before I say yes or no, I'll have to talk with Greg."

"Of course," Sam said. "Understand, Greg would be here himself, except that he didn't want to risk the publicity. He felt I should sound you out, see how you felt about it."

"I'd have to know more before I could venture an opinion. If you could tell me what happened—just informally, briefly."

Sam Cavanaugh described the whole incident, from the time Gregory had entered the airport lounge until he left the police station. As he talked, Johnny found himself convinced.

Gregory's story had the ring of truth.

But all solid evidence—and testimony—was against him.

"Exactly how were the vice officers able to see what was happening?" he asked.

"Greg thought it was some kind of grill, or screen—the sort of thing they usually use in that kind of situation. But I later was told that they have a one-way mirror, almost at eye level."

"In other words, they were standing only a few feet away."

"Six or eight feet, at most," Sam agreed.

Johnny tried to visualize the scene as it had happened—the three officers in a darkened room, peering through a window. Their testimony would be difficult to break—if not impossible.

"What did Pop think we could do?" he asked.

"He suggested that we get a complete background on all the officers, to begin with—every significant case they've handled, the frank opinions of fellow officers, and so forth. He thinks we may be able to find our own witnesses among airport security personnel— maybe someone who saw something unusual going on, or who knows something about the two men who led Greg into the trap. Then there is the big man—the giant, Greg calls him—who held him. Someone else may have seen him. A man of that description is memorable. Silvio suggested that you could direct the legal investigation, relying on his established contacts where necessary."

Now Johnny understood. Silvio's motivations were clear. He had sent the case to Johnny in order to lure him into Silvio's own operation.

Johnny was irritated, yet intrigued. The case had possibilities. He could not deny that he was enticed by the idea of directing such an elaborate investigation, perhaps of rescuing the reputation of a good and important man.

He made his decision, hoping he would not have cause to regret it.

"Tell Greg I'll help in any way I can. If he wants me to work behind the scenes, as silent counsel, that would be satisfactory. If he wants me to assume the position of leading counsel in the case, he'll have to make those arrangements with his present counsel."

"Of course, of course," Sam said. "I know you're busy, and I won't take any more of your time today. Greg will be pleased. We'll be in contact with you by tomorrow, at latest."

Sam was hardly out the door before Johnny picked up the phone and called his father.

"Sam Cavanaugh was here," he said.

"I hope you're taking the case," Silvio said.

"I am," Johnny said. "I'm just calling to let you know you haven't fooled me for a minute. I know you sent him to me as a step to get me behind that desk up there. It won't work."

"You do yourself and Gregory a disservice," Silvio said after a brief pause. "This matter transcends that. Sam has always thought the world of you, and Gregory deserves better legal advice and support than he is receiving. Why wouldn't we turn to you?"

"He mentioned your contacts. I'm not saying we won't need them. But I have my own."

Silvio hesitated. "This is not something we should discuss on the phone. Why don't you drive up this afternoon? It would take only a few minutes. Lucian is to arrive at three. I want you here."

"Pop, I simply can't," Johnny said. "Not this afternoon. I'm swamped. And I should get Greg's case moving."

Silvio did not respond for a moment. "All right," he said at last, "come tonight. You can give the girls in San Francisco a night of rest."

"Pop . . ."

"There are other matters to discuss."

"Pop, believe me! I can't." He spaced his next words to give them proper emphasis. "Incidentally, I read *all* of the paper this morning."

"Maybe you shouldn't be reading the paper these days if you are still having trouble with your principles. Are you still having difficulty in accepting what is happening?"

Johnny sighed in resignation.

"After what happened to Greg, I'm ready to believe anything."

Like every large legal community in the nation, the courts of Los Angeles support a number of people who defy category. Some possess rare expertise. Others do not have much talent or expertise to offer. But the court system could not function without them.

Many are former police officers, detectives, and sheriff's deputies who retired voluntarily or prematurely through changes in political fortunes. Some—those in the upper echelons—are former Special Agents of the FBI. They retain contacts and methods essential to both defense and prosecution in building a case. Others are lawyers of varying abilities and specialties, disbarred for technical reasons —or worse. A few are would-be lawyers who never quite made the grade. Sprinkled among them are those who imbue their work with a veneer of professionalism under the title "private detective" or "private investigator."

For a fee they perform the detailed legwork that a practicing attorney is simply too busy to do.

Larry Gifford was one of those men.

At one time, Gifford had served in Intelligence in the Los Angeles Police Department. When the police chief resigned, Gifford became a leading candidate for the job. He was the most popular contender from within the department. This fact was not forgotten when a new chief was brought in from outside. A few months later, under a calculated onslaught of demeaning and harassing assignments, Gifford chose early retirement. Now in his late fifties, he supplemented his pension by accepting occasional investigative work. Johnny had hired him on two cases. He liked Gifford's thor-

oughness. He also liked his direct, open manner. He reached him by
phone within an hour after talking with Silvio.

"Yes, I'm familiar with the Cavanaugh incident," Gifford said.
"In fact, I've just seen a TV interview that would gag a mule. You
have any case at all?"

"I was hoping you could tell me," Johnny said. "Do you know
either of the detectives? Rutgers? Martin?"

Gifford hesitated. "I suppose this conversation is in the context
of a privileged relationship, just you and me discussing a legal matter."

"Of course."

"Well, this is opinion, and I wouldn't want to take the stand on
it, even if I could. But by and large, detectives who work vice too
long tend to sink to a level where they're not much better than the
creeps they deal with. Rutgers and Martin could be used as text-
book examples—especially Rutgers."

"Now I'll tell *you* something in confidence," Johnny said. "Naturally we don't want to reveal the governor's defense until we have
our act together. But Gregory says they got him into the restroom
on the ruse that his aide was ill. He panicked, thinking Neil had
had a heart attack. He forgot all caution. When he walked in, a
giant of a man grabbed him from behind and held him while Herbie
did his work."

Gifford chuckled. "That's just crazy enough to be true."

"Know anything about Herbie?"

"He has a record that goes back twenty years," Gifford said.
"Most of it was in the good old days when we could bust gays just
for batting their eyelashes. As he got older, he started cruising
around high schools for chickens. He was booked a few times for
contributing to the delinquency of a minor, that sort of thing. Nothing serious. Reason I happen to know all this, he was the prime
suspect in a crime of passion a few years ago. His roommate died of
a slashed throat. Word was that the roomie was leaving Herbie for a
well-known swishy actor. But it was circumstantial. No charges
were filed."

"That case could figure in this," Johnny said. "Maybe they're
holding something on him—some evidence."

"Could be. But I doubt it."

"We've got to move fast," Johnny said. "Expense is of no concern—hire whatever help you need. We may have to put some other people on it, but I think it best to coordinate efforts down there through you."

"What exactly do you want?"

"Anything and everything," Johnny said. "For starters, we need a complete scan on Rutgers and Martin. And on Herbie. We need the physical layout of the restroom, the one-way glass setup. And I keep thinking that our break may come with the giant. Maybe you can find some leads on someone huge who's been involved in this type of thing."

"Does the governor have a good description?"

"Not detailed," Johnny said. "Six four at least, maybe taller. Dark, straight hair parted on the left, cut fairly close. Broad, swarthy face. No beard or mustache. No scars or distinguishing marks. And that's it."

"I'll get to work on it," Gifford said. He paused. "Tell the governor to hang in there," he added. "We may be able to come up with something."

CHAPTER 9

*T*HEY met at three in the afternoon, Silvio, Carlo, Lucian Hall, and two executive officers from Hampton Industries—Dax and Holson.

"My younger son, Johnny, planned to be here," Silvio said. "Unfortunately he was held up by some urgent business. He is an attorney, you know. An important case came up unexpectedly."

Lucian nodded. "He's doing very well, I understand."

"He keeps busy, his own career, family matters . . ." Silvio said.

While the houseboy served drinks and hors d'oeuvres, Silvio studied Lucian Hall.

A big man, Lucian could have stepped from the pages of his whiskey firm's advertisements offering testimonials from distinguished gentlemen. His handsome face seemed to serve mostly as a frame for his deep-set dark eyes and firm, solid jaw line. His abundant gray hair was carefully trimmed. His three-piece dark suit bore the mark of fastidious tailoring. The flawless, tanned face gave away nothing of what the man was thinking.

Silvio could not help but contrast the smooth, crafty man with the brash, impetuous youth he had known, years ago.

Lucian waited until cigars were passed and the servants had left the room. "Well, Silvio, have you had time to think over our offer?"

Silvio took his time lighting his cigar. "Yes, I have spent considerable time thinking about it," he said. "As I remarked, your offer is generous. My accountants have confirmed that fact."

He paused, letting Lucian's anticipation mount.

"The offer is attractive . . . very attractive. But . . ."

Lucian held up a hand. "Before you decide, let me make the proposal even more attractive."

Carlo moved as if to speak. Silvio fixed his eyes on his son and willed him to keep silent. Lucian edged forward slightly in his chair.

"We recognize that your principal reluctance stems from the association of the family name with the business. Of course we are buying your name and good will. We could not possibly change the name of the winery, or of its product. Therefore, here is what we are prepared to do:

"You, Silvio, will remain as head of the winery, as president and chairman of the board. We're prepared to offer you a five-year contract, at a hundred and fifty thousand per year. Carlo, if he chooses to do so, will remain as vice president in charge of production, on a five-year contract at eighty-five thousand a year, retaining his position on the board. Your son Johnny, as I understand it, is not directly involved in the winery operations. If he chooses, he also will be retained as a board member. Each board member will receive ten thousand per year, with an honorarium of two thousand per board meeting. All this would be done in an effort to continue the Moretti family association with the winery and the product, which we believe will be of benefit both to us and to you."

Silvio smoked for a moment in silence. "That is very generous," he said. "A five-year contract. What would happen at the end of five years?"

"A new contract would be negotiated, to our mutual satisfaction."

Silvio spoke quietly, in an off-hand manner, in an effort to keep Hall from suspecting that he was being drawn out. "Obviously this would be of benefit to me and to my family. But I don't understand how it would be profitable to you."

"The Moretti name," Lucian said. "You see, if you continue your association with the winery, we will be able to announce to the employees, to your customers, that there will be no change in company policies—that everything will continue as before. Less disruption that way."

"And there would be absolutely no change?" Silvio asked innocently.

"Only in a superficial way."

Silvio considered Lucian's words. Clearly, he planned to use the Moretti name as a front to mask his operations. Silvio was thankful he had spent considerable time and money on research. But he could not afford the luxury of anger.

He feigned puzzlement. "But my people would be Hampton employees, not Moretti employees?"

Lucian sensed the trap. He did not know how to evade it. "Well, yes."

"I really do not understand this," Silvio said. "Carlo does not have experience as a Hampton supervisor. Nor do I. How would we be able to implement Hampton's wishes, insofar as management is concerned?"

Lucian hesitated. "Well, ordinarily in this sort of situation we place someone in a key position, someone to coordinate operations in the field with our overall corporate structure."

"I see," Silvio said. "What, exactly, would be your man's position?"

Lucian frowned. "In this instance we probably would create a position—a spot that would carry a title. Something like executive vice president."

"Then he would be over Carlo."

Hall seemed uncomfortable. He glanced at Dax. "Only insofar as general policies are concerned."

"He would be the executive officer. Then I myself would be only a figurehead."

"Silvio, you're making too much of this," Lucian protested. "Your expertise, Carlo's expertise, are needed. We expect to make full use of your capabilities. Our man would be concerned with the talents we intend to bring to the Moretti winery—chiefly in the areas of expansion and merchandising."

"Merchandising," Silvio said.

"We'll have the Moretti label in supermarkets all over the

country—not just in the liquor stores. It's a whole new science, Silvio. Consumer surveys, marketing research. We'll bring in new talent, trained in proper business procedures. Bigger sales naturally necessitate expansion, which requires capital. We intend to pour several million dollars into growth."

"But our employees will be Hampton employees," Silvio insisted.

"Well, yes. Of course."

"With the Hampton pension plan."

Lucian hesitated again. "I'm not familiar with that aspect. You can check with our personnel director on any questions you might have."

"I have checked your performance in past acquisitions," Silvio said. "Hampton Industries maintains only the bare minimum that the government requires. Our people would suffer a considerable loss."

"Naturally we could not make exceptions for Moretti employees," Lucian said. "To do so would not be fair to our other employees."

"I'm glad to hear of your concern for fairness," Silvio said. "I assume that since our employees would be regimented to the Hampton structure, our hospitalization plan also would be phased out, to accommodate change to a lesser plan, underwritten by a Hampton subsidiary."

Lucian's dark eyes grew distant. "Silvio, I'm not familiar with these details. But as I said, we would not be able to make exceptions."

"And telephone calls through the winery switchboard would be monitored."

Lucian clearly was mystified. "Telephone calls?"

Silvio explained. "Elsewhere Hampton employees are allowed to receive a maximum of twenty-five personal telephone calls a month while at work. The switchboard is computerized, to record origin and destination of all calls. The employee is responsible for making his family and associates conform to Hampton policy. If the restricted number is exceeded, the employee is put on probation. If the number is exceeded three months out of twelve, that employee is summarily dismissed."

"That's news to me," Lucian said, glancing at Dax. "But obviously we are a business organization. I assume there have been problems concerning personal calls when the employees are supposed to be at work . . ."

"We have never had such a problem at the winery," Silvio said. "To the contrary, the dedication and concern of my fellow workers has always been an inspiration to me. I find the Hampton corporate policies demeaning. For instance, Hampton employees are warned that their desks, their files, are company property, that they must not keep personal material in them. A certain number of days of sick leave is decreed—six per annum, I think—and if that number is exceeded, the employee loses pay. In addition, the company demands a doctor's certificate in testimony that the employee is, indeed, truly sick . . ."

"Silvio, I know nothing about such things," Lucian said.

"You should," Silvio said. "Even if I were inclined to accept your offer, I could not do so in the light of what I have learned of how Hampton Industries treats its employees. Lucian, I came to America because in the old country, all around me, there was serfdom—a poverty of spirit. And now, in this country, I see in people who have contributed their lives and talents, a growing willingness to submit to the system. Corporate serfdom. The exploitation is of a different nature—and for all that even more insidious."

"Then you *are* turning us down," Lucian said.

"I have considered your offer very seriously," Silvio said. "I have gone to a great deal of trouble and expense to explore the matter thoroughly. Unfortunately, I have found a certain pattern in your conduct of affairs. You buy a company's good name, then you exploit that good name, built over the years by many conscientious people. You also exploit and cheapen reputations created through a lifetime of effort by retaining as figureheads the men who have constructed those companies. Thank you, but no thank you, Lucian. You cannot buy me. Therefore, I respectfully decline your offer."

Lucian looked at him for a moment. "I hear that in the past few days you have had an unusually bad run of luck at the winery. I was hoping that would influence you."

"The incidents have been taken into consideration," Silvio said.

"They have influenced me. But perhaps not in the way you wished."

"We also have had a serious loss," Lucian said. "Last night we had a fire that proved very costly."

"Yes. I read about it," Silvio said.

"Very costly. But fortunately Hampton Industries could endure dozens of such losses without a serious effect on our profit margin. At the moment, there is still sufficient capital that I need not reduce the amount of my offer to you. If our bad luck should continue, that might not be the case."

"That is immaterial," Silvio said. "My decision is made. It will not be reversed."

"I suspect that you will regret that decision," Lucian said. "I'm sorry. I have tried to advise you as a friend. I have negotiated to bring you the best deal I could. I hoped you would take a realistic view of the situation."

Silvio smiled. "Things are not always as they seem, Lucian." He gestured toward the morning papers, lying on his desk. "For instance, young Cavanaugh seems to be in desperate trouble. I am certain that appearances are deceiving. He will emerge from all this in far better circumstance than before."

Lucian studied Silvio for a moment, his eyes sharp with anger. Dark veins stood out on his temples, and for a moment Silvio thought he might lash out in fury. Then, with considerable effort, he brought himself under control. He rose abruptly from his chair.

"I suppose there is nothing more to say. In the light of future developments you may have occasion to change your mind. Dax will keep in touch."

"That won't be necessary," Silvio said. "I assure you. It would be a waste of time."

CHAPTER 10

MORE and more, Johnny had developed a genuine need
to be alone. He had come to value time spent with himself, and to prize the many soul-rewarding hours he
spent cloistered in his floating retreat, reading, thinking, working
in his darkroom, listening to music, watching the birds and wildlife
on the Bay.

His overwhelming desire to bring Christina into this private
world came as a surprise to him. All week, as he impatiently
awaited her arrival, his thoughts kept turning to the many facets of
his life he wanted to share with her.

This side of his nature he had never revealed to anyone.

He met Christina at San Francisco International early Saturday
morning. Not until he saw her among the disembarking passengers
did he realize that he had been afraid she would change her mind.

He gave her a long, passionate welcoming kiss. "I'm so glad
you're here," he said.

Christina clung to him for a moment. "I'm not sure I should be,"
she said. "But I really didn't lie to my mother. I told her I would be

catching a plane this morning. I just didn't tell her where it was going."

She seemed tired. As they left the airport and headed north on the Bayshore Freeway, she leaned back in the seat with her head against the rest. She turned to watch him as he maneuvered through the heavy weekend traffic.

During the drive north on 101 through San Francisco and across the Golden Gate Bridge, Christina remained silent. Occasionally she turned to watch the sailboats and fishing craft along the docks and in the Bay. North of Vista Point, Johnny took the cutoff, through Sausalito, slower but more colorful.

He wheeled into the parking area near the pier, then went to the trunk for her luggage. Christina took a few steps toward the pier, standing on tiptoe for better perspective.

"Those are houseboats?"

Johnny laughed. The size and the elaborate architecture of the houseboats always surprised those seeing them for the first time.

They walked to the pier and through the wrought iron security gate.

"Which one's yours?"

"Far end," Johnny said.

As he carried her luggage the length of the pier, Christina explored. She walked ahead, dropped behind, went from one side of the dock to the other, marveling over the imaginative architecture of the houseboats. Some of the residents were out in the sun, polishing brass, painting, or doing minor carpentry. The salt air made maintenance a continual problem.

"There are two at the end," Christina said. "Which one is yours?"

"On the right," Johnny said as they neared the house. Christina carefully stepped down the cleated gangplank and peeked through the glass doors as he carried the suitcases down and set them on the afterdeck.

Christina turned and stood for a moment, looking out across the blue waters of the Bay to the golden hills of Tiburon Peninsula. Seabirds were gathering around the distant floating log boom. Two sailboats were heeled heavily into the breeze, racing south.

"This is absolutely marvelous," Christina said. "And everything smells so good. I'll confess. I was afraid it would stink."

Johnny dug in his pocket for the keys. "I should have put your mind at ease. Everyone wonders. Yes, we have all the modern conveniences. We're connected to the city."

He slid back the glass doors and Christina entered. She walked to the middle of the living room and turned slowly, taking in the furnishings, the drawings, etchings, and photographs. She examined the kitchen, the study beyond. Then she glanced up the stairway.

"Can I prowl?"

"My house is your house," he said. "What would you like to drink?"

"Gin and tonic?"

He went into the kitchen and mixed the drinks. From above came the muted sounds of Christina sliding doors and moving from room to room. He sat and waited with the drinks until she returned. He gestured toward the couch that faced the fantail, the Bay, the hills of the distant peninsula.

"I love it," Christina said. "But I'm confused. Which bedroom is yours?"

Johnny laughed. "I move around, to fit my mood."

She seemed to think he was joking.

"I really do," he explained. "When I have to get up early, the sun comes in through the skylight in the east bedroom and wakes me. In the evening, the view from the west bedroom, with the sunset over the hills around Marin city, with the houses lighting up the slopes, is fabulous."

"And the other?"

"That's for fog. When it rolls in over the hills, it's unbelievable. If it's really thick, it plays around those big windows like something alive. It's better than anything on the late, late show." He gestured toward the Bay. "Almost every day is different out here—the sky, the water, the weather."

Christina sipped her drink and studied him. "You really do spend time here, don't you."

He nodded. "Surprised?"

"In a way. This hardly fits the superficial, playboy image."

Johnny resisted his impulse to protest. He sensed that her fencing was benevolent.

"What's on the top floor?" she asked, her eyebrows raised slightly.

"My sanctum sanctorum," he told her. "It's full of sound-proofing, the stereo system, a darkroom. I keep the door locked for the extra security because of my record albums, cameras, and darkroom equipment."

Christina understood then.

"Those pictures are yours?" she asked, rising to her feet. She went to the wall and re-examined the photographs, genuinely impressed. "Those are very good. I thought they were prints from Eliot Porter or Ansel Adams." She stepped back a pace to study one. "That pattern is fascinating. What is it?"

"Fog," Johnny said. "Through the big window up there."

"The shading, the composition, are perfect," she said. "How did you do it?"

"Three strobes outside the window as backlight," Johnny explained. "I tried for a holographic effect."

"Well you certainly got it. Have you ever exhibited these?"

Johnny laughed. "Good Lord, no. I'm just playing around with it."

At that moment, as if on cue, Johnny's cat, Don Gato, strolled into the room. He stopped and regarded the scene warily, ready to retreat if necessary, frozen in place by his cat curiosity.

"Well hello, cat," Christina said. She glanced at Johnny. "Yours?"

"Only in a manner of speaking," Johnny said. "Don Gato is—to put it mildly—rather independent. He has a private door behind that bookcase. He comes and goes as his various moods and passions move him."

Christina giggled. "I'm pleased to make your acquaintance, Don Gato." She waited, allowing the cat sufficient time to make a decision about her. He stood, nose slightly in the air, sniffing, then satisfied, he ambled on across the room. Christina knelt to scratch his ears.

"He's such a big fellow," she said. "And exotic-looking. Does he have some Siamese in his background?"

"His mother lived up the pier. He got his yellow coloring and size from her. A big Siamese was a prime suspect as the father. Don Gato has his own life, under the piers. He stays gone three, four, five days, sometimes a week. Then he comes in, demands warm milk, and sacks out for about twenty-four hours. He wakes up hungry, fills up on cat chow, then takes off again."

"Sounds like even more activity than I suspected goes on around here," Christina said, grinning.

Johnny ignored the barb. "Sometimes he needs repairs. He manages several hundred dollars a year in vet bills." He knelt beside her and ruffled Don Gato's fur. The cat rolled onto his back and fought back playfully, kicking with his hind legs, biting just short of breaking skin. "He's quite a character," Johnny explained as Don Gato performed. "Nobody owns him. Nobody tells him what to do. He lives his own life. He doesn't depend on anyone. If I'm not here when he comes around, he knows two or three other places where he can trade a few hours of quiet catship for food. If anything happened to me, he'd probably miss me, but he'd make out fine."

Christina was looking at Johnny with unveiled amusement. "You sound as if you envy his tomcat life."

Johnny shrugged. "What male wouldn't?" He pushed Don Gato away and rose to his feet. "If you'll excuse me, I'll fix him some milk."

When he returned to the living room, Christina was seated on the couch, facing the Bay. "What are those birds?" she asked, pointing.

"Mostly gulls, of various ethnic persuasions," he said. "We're in an Audubon bird sanctuary. Want to see them closer?"

He put down his drink and went into the kitchen for bread. Motioning for her to follow, he walked out onto the afterdeck and began tossing pieces of crust into the air. Within seconds dozens of the distant gulls left the water. They swooped, darted, and fought over the bread. He tossed the chunks high into the air for them to take on the wing.

"They're not that bright," Christina said. "You've done this before."

"We have a deal," Johnny told her. "As long as they perform, I won't buy a television set."

When the bread was gone, the gulls settled on the water and floated near the stern.

"You have a different kind of wild life around here than I expected," Christina said. "What else is there?"

Again Johnny ignored the teasing.

"All kinds of fish, the occasional whale, and baby seals in season," he said. He took Christina's hands in his. "What would you like to do today?"

She grinned. "I thought you had it all mapped out—'night like no other night' and all that."

"That's tonight," he said. "We've still got some morning left, and a whole afternoon. I could suggest something. But I thought I'd ask you. Isn't there something you'd like to do?"

"You'd laugh."

"Try me."

Christina sighed. "Whenever anyone learns where I grew up, he starts talking about San Francisco. I feel like an idiot. Every time we came down to San Francisco when I was a kid, either we went shopping, or to dinner, or to the theater or the opera. I've never really done all the touristy things that everyone else does. That's what I'd like to do. Really."

"You're on," Johnny said. "Let's take your things up. When you're ready, we'll do the town."

Don Gato returned to the living room and his bed by the bookcase. He made three circles in his basket, then sank into a curl, lowered his head, and closed his eyes.

Christina finished her drink and started up the stairs. "Which bedroom?" she asked.

He picked up her bags. "Pick a mood."

She laughed and raced up the steps.

He found her in the southwest bedroom—the one of glorious sunsets and brilliant, star-studded nights.

At Fisherman's Wharf they lined up with busloads of Japanese and Canadian tourists to wait for a Powell-Hyde Cable Car to Union Square. After a leisurely stroll through Chinatown they caught the cable car back to the wharf.

Johnny drove for a while over San Francisco's steepest streets, zooming up Russian Hill on Lombard, then braking and whipping through the ten famous sharp curves between Hyde and Leavenworth. He crossed Columbus to Telegraph Hill and circled up to Coit Tower. At the top they spent their pocket change on the telescopes overlooking the Bay.

On a whim, Johnny then drove Christina to the Bank of America Building and took her up to his office. In the weekend silence, without the bustle of secretaries and ringing telephones, the offices were somber and imposing. Christina lingered to admire the decor, the dark wood floor, oriental rug, and chrome-leather furniture in the reception area while Johnny walked on through and unlocked his private office.

"There's your Jackson Pollock," he said.

Christina entered his office, stopped, and gasped at the view through the angled-bay window behind Johnny's desk. She only gave the painting a brief glance.

"I'm afraid poor Jackson is upstaged," she said. She crossed to the window. "Now, if we could hang that view in the museum, we'd have something."

He walked over to stand beside her.

"Can you see your houseboat from here?" she asked.

"No, it's off to the right."

"Look, a ship is going out."

"A freighter," he said. "Container cargo."

"I would never get used to this. Your clients must be overwhelmed."

"Well, it's not always this spectacular," he told her. "Rain and smog don't do much for the view."

"And fog?"

"Ah, the fog. Every once in a while it hangs along the ground, with just the tops of buildings and bridges sticking up through it. That really gives you an other-world feeling."

She was looking up at him with her mouth set in that strange way. He pulled her to him and kissed her, first her face, then her hair, and then her mouth. Her lips were warm, alive, responsive. She met his probing tongue briefly, playfully. They kissed for several minutes before she pushed him gently away.

"I'd better look at my painting," she said.

She moved to the large canvas. Leaning over, she examined the surface texture.

"When is it dated?"

"I don't remember. I have some papers on it somewhere."

"Early fifties, I think," she said. "He introduced drip painting about forty-seven, but he really didn't work into effective fields of accents, like this, until about fifty-two or fifty-three. I think you may have one of his better paintings here. Do you know much about it?"

"I don't even know for sure if I like it," Johnny said. "I just know that, some days, it seems to show the way I feel."

Christina studied him for a moment. "I suppose you're aware that Pollock's disruptive images are believed to convey his mental stress and violence."

Teasing again—or serious? Johnny shrugged. "I'm not surprised," he said.

They drove back to the wharf for lunch at Alioto's. Afterward, they walked through Ghirardelli Square and the shops of The Cannery, pausing for a while to watch the jugglers and mime artists perform. At Pier 43, they went aboard a ferry for a tour of the harbor.

When they returned, Johnny drove north on Marina Boulevard to the Small Craft Harbor and parked.

"This is one of my favorite spots in all of San Francisco," he said.

They walked along the Promenade, watching the sailboats race offshore. The boats would tack rapidly toward the beach until the last possible moment, then jibe toward open water again. As Johnny and Christina strolled, joggers trotted past them, headed toward the southern anchorage of the Golden Gate Bridge, now outlined against the setting sun. Some of the elderly residents from the area across the boulevard had come to sit on the benches in the unseasonable warmth. Mothers kept watch as their children played along the beach.

"We're not going to miss that sunset from your special window, are we?" Christina asked.

Johnny stopped and looked at her. She met his questioning glance with a solemn, almost dreamy expression, then leaned her head on his shoulder and put her arm around his waist. He checked the position of the sun.

"We should just about make it," he said.

They returned to the car, arms entwined in an embrace. Johnny let her in from the driver's side, and she clung to him as he pulled back onto the boulevard, Highway 101, and the bridge. He cut off the expressway, geared down, and crept through the seaside traffic of Sausalito, sacrificing time to preserve the mood.

Arm in arm, they walked down the long pier to the houseboat in the gathering twilight. Clouds over Marin County were stained brilliant red from the setting sun. Gulls, stirred from their perch by a passing sailboat, circled in close to the wharf, filling the docks with their plaintive shrieks.

Don Gato was asleep, curled in his bed. Johnny and Christina went up to the west bedroom. They stood for a few minutes, sharing the gradually changing colors of sunset. Leisurely they kissed, savoring each moment. Slowly, deliberately, Johnny unbuttoned her blouse. She grinned and unbuttoned his shirt. With unhurried pleasure, he kissed her neck, shoulders, and small, firm breasts, marveling in the discovery of each perfection, each delicate, soft curve. He did not stop until the last wisp of clothing was removed.

In the twilight, arm in arm, they moved onto the bed, eager, yet caught up in the tantalizing pleasure of prolonging the inevitable. When he entered her, plunging deep, he was overwhelmed for a moment by the completeness of their unity. He paused, relishing a delicious sense of rightness, of a destiny fulfilled. Christina opened her eyes and smiled, conveying her awe in the moment. They remained motionless for a time, kissing gently, enveloped in a strange calm.

Then the passion began to build, driving them into throes of frantic effort. There was not a moment of pretense. Johnny felt Christina reaching plateau after plateau, climbing ever higher as he held himself back, finding far more joy in her gratification than in his own, until at last he could hold back no longer.

They lay for a long while, locked in each other's arms. Slowly the hills of Sausalito came alive with lights.

Entwined, they dozed for a while, awoke, made love again, then slept until midnight. They awoke famished and went downstairs to raid the refrigerator. Don Gato was gone.

In the darkened living room they watched the moon rise over

Tiburon. They made love leisurely beneath the stars on the open sundeck before returning to the bedroom and sleep.

Hours later, Christina shook Johnny awake.

"The sun's coming up," she said. "Let's try out the east bedroom."

Afterward, they lay naked to the rising sun.

"I think we cleaned out your refrigerator last night," Christina said. "What are we going to do for breakfast?"

"I have some vintage champagne stashed away," Johnny told her. "Today, I wouldn't consider anything else."

In late afternoon, coming down from a champagne high, they dressed and drove to Ondine for an early dinner of squab Montmorency.

When they returned to the houseboat, Christina was in a more serious mood.

She told him how she spent her spare time, working with a group in protest against nuclear reactors, traveling to rallies, writing letters to Washington.

"The nuclear issues are so difficult to explain," she said. "We're not against nuclear energy itself. I think the power companies could go even further with reactors, if they did it right—set aside huge nuclear parks, with on-site waste disposal, safeguards. The danger is in the way they're doing it—the absolute lies they tell. They claim one potential accident every million years, or something like that, and already we've had dozens. Several bordered on disasters. They're turning out tons and tons of radioactive waste, with no idea yet what they're going to do with it. I just don't understand how people can let them endanger our lives this way. Aren't *you* concerned?"

Johnny laughed, then realized she had misunderstood his reaction. He held up a hand to block her indignation.

"It's just that I'm way ahead of you," he explained. "Sure, I'm concerned. Deeply concerned. About a lot of things. Too many. That's my problem. There's no end to it. Take the assassination of JFK," he said. He had been eighteen at the time and deeply afflicted by the tragedy in Dallas; enough, years later, to do some research and investigating of his own. He knew the frustration of truth-seeking firsthand. "If you spent your entire life on it," he said, "and solved it, you'd still have the Robert Kennedy assassination, Martin Luther King, George Moscone, Watergate, the military-industrial alliance and Vietnam, our self-destruct economic system, capital punishment, the inequities of taxation, crime in the streets, the collapse of immigration and naturalization, busing, invasion of privacy by government and big business, the inevitable collapse of Social Security, Congressional ripoffs, the oil crises, the Middle East . . . nuclear reactors . . ."

"And whooping cranes," Christina said.

"Right! See what I mean? Pop calls me a dropout from life. But what can you do? Go crazy? In this day and time a certain amount of detachment is in itself a form of sanity."

"So you get a houseboat in a bird sanctuary and turn to photography."

"It gives me a little space to think." He was silent for a moment. "Maybe someday I will do something about those things. But I'm now convinced it will have to be done in a different way. It'll take a lot of thought, and much planning. After all, nothing anyone else has tried ever worked." He gripped her arm. "Come on upstairs. I'll show you my treasures."

Behind the locked door were treasures, indeed. Johnny had spent several thousand dollars on this room alone, soundproofing, trying various acoustical materials for proper mix. The integrated electronic equipment had been assembled over three or four years. He had never stopped to figure the total expense.

Christina was more interested in the records. She turned through the instrumentals, making appreciative sounds. Then she came to the operas.

"Oh! Beverly Sills in *Don Pasquale*! I would give an eyetooth for that."

Johnny moved past her and pulled out another album. "If you like Sills, this is my favorite—*Anna Bolena* with the London Symphony Orchestra."

They listened to records for more than an hour. Then Christina looked at her watch.

"I hate to bring this up, but I've got a plane to catch."

Johnny took both her hands in his and guided her back down the stairs to the couch in the living room. "Christina, I don't know about you. But the last twenty-four hours has convinced me that we're made for each other. I've never known anything like it in my whole life."

"It was perfect," Christina said. "I can't keep from being suspicious of anything absolutely perfect."

"It *is* perfect," he said. "I'm convinced. I can't live without you. That's how perfect I think it is."

Christina turned away. She sat for a moment, watching a sailboat move south along the distant shoreline, lost in one of her introspective silences. He waited patiently until it ended, and she looked at him again.

"It's all happened too fast," she said. "When you first came on so strong, in Sonoma, I was amused. It was a joke, in a way." She smiled at him. "I had a terrible crush on you when I was thirteen."

Johnny let doubt show on his face.

"I really did. And now I don't know how much of what I feel comes from the foolish daydreams of an adolescent girl. I'm all mixed up."

"Don't question your feelings," Johnny said.

Christina shook her head. "It isn't that simple. I thought I had found myself, come to terms with myself. And now, just in the last few days, you've changed my whole outlook . . . what I want, my whole life . . ."

"Are you talking about your career? I wouldn't want you to give up anything you felt was important."

Christina leaned her head back on the couch and looked at him. "No. I'm not talking about that. My career is important. But certainly there are things far more important. It's just that you've reopened doors that I closed a long time ago. You see, I'm so vulnerable. It's taken me a long time to get where I am, emotionally. These are things I can't talk about. Not yet. But I don't want to slide back. If I do, I might never get out of that hole again." She began to shake her head desperately. "There's so much risk for me in a situation like this."

"I'll help you," he said. "Trust me."

"I do trust you. But, Johnny, I have to be very careful. And really, I know so little about you. I've joked about it, but you do have a reputation for being very casual with women, politely keeping your distance, never making commitments."

Johnny did not bother to hide his exasperation this time. "Damn it, I want to know. Who's been spreading stories about me?"

Christina hesitated. "I can't betray confidences."

"Who?" he demanded.

"I can't name names. But I will go this far: I have a friend—someone you probably don't remember—who knew me back when I had such a terrible crush on you. She's teased me about you ever since. She's now a professional person, in the Bay Area. She has a boyfriend, who knows you, talks about you . . ."

"Don't tell me his name," Johnny warned. "Right now, I might hunt him up and kick the shit out of him."

Christina laughed. "Give him his due," she said. "He's made you sound very intriguing—moody and mysterious. Without his buildup we might not have got together. I'll admit I've found some thrill in flying close to the flame—especially since it was a delicious old flame. And now I can't keep from wondering. Why me? It's too good to be true. I can't help but feel a need for caution."

Johnny gripped her hands. "You are the first woman I've brought into this house in almost a year. You are the first woman I've wanted to spend my entire life with. I'm in love with you. Completely. Hopelessly."

She gave him a sad smile. "All my life I've waited for this to happen, and now that it has, I can't feel the joy that I should. I've had too many disappointments."

"I promise you this won't be another," Johnny said. "I want to marry you, Christina."

She frowned. "Johnny . . ."

"Will you marry me? If you will, we can work things out, I promise."

Christina looked at him for a long moment before answering. "I can't say yes right now, Johnny. But I certainly can't bring myself to say no, either, considering the way I feel. I'm an emotional wreck. You've bowled me over so completely. I need time. Let me go back to Boston and think things through."

"And talk with your friend?"

"Maybe. Does that bother you?"

"Hell, yes, it bothers me."

She gave him the wisp of a smile. "That's a very encouraging sign."

"At this point I'm grateful for *any* sign," Johnny said. "If it'll help, I'll nurture my jealousy."

Christina leaned forward and kissed him.

"Be patient with me," she said. "I have a feeling that things may work out."

After seeing Christina off at San Francisco International, Johnny returned home to find her presence lingering. Each room, each chair, each bed held memories.

Don Gato was still gone. The house seemed empty and lonesome.

He fixed himself a drink, moved a chair onto the afterdeck, and sat for a long time, watching the moon rise over the Bay. He could not imagine the reasons behind Christina's doubts, behind her reluctance toward commitment. But he sensed that in order to win her, he would have to map a strategy, conduct a carefully structured campaign.

On impulse, he went inside and ordered flowers delivered to her apartment before her arrival.

He looked at his watch.

She had only been gone two hours, and already he missed her so much he felt he would not be able to endure a week without her.

He mixed another drink and lay on the couch, watching the shimmer of moonlight on the waters of the Bay.

He was dozing when the phone rang. He picked it up on the second ring.

"Has the old man called you yet?" Carlo asked.

"No," Johnny said, groggy and tired.

"He will. The shit has really hit the fan. It seems we shipped out several hundred cases of bulk wine, labeled Proprietor's Reserve. The state liquor people are about to lower the boom on us."

Johnny sat up, fully awake. Mislabeling of wine usually resulted in heavy fines and, in some instances, a temporary suspension of license. At worst, it could mean permanent suspension.

"How in hell did that happen?" Johnny asked.

"Strangely, the same question has occurred to us," Carlo said. "You'd better get your ass back up here. Right now we could use a good lawyer."

"How's Pop taking it?"

"How do you think? I need you to help me control him. And come to think of it, I need a lawyer too. Maybe you haven't heard. Gina has filed for legal separation."

Johnny was shocked speechless for a moment. He simply could not believe it. Not Gina. There must be some mistake.

"You're kidding," he managed to say.

"I wish I were."

Johnny felt he should make some gesture. "Want me to talk to her?"

"Hell, no," Carlo said. "You'd just take her side like everybody else. At the moment I don't need anyone else to tell me what a son-of-a-bitch I am. I'm thoroughly convinced."

Silvio's phone call came a few minutes later.

"You better come up, Johnny," he said.

"Pop . . ." Johnny began.

"Don't try to dodge the issue, Johnny," Silvio said. "There's one thing you must understand. We have made our decision. We must answer for it. Now we fight for our very lives."

BOOK
3_____

"Why does love have to be such torture?"

—Christina Borneman

CHAPTER 1

SECLUDED in his apartment in Sacramento through the weekend, Gregory Cavanaugh received a running account of news breaks, gathered by Neil Hart. By Sunday evening he began to hope that matters were not as bad as they first seemed.

From around the state there came an unexpected outpouring of support. Silvio Moretti's bloc had led off the rally. By Saturday evening, newspapers and television stations were quoting a number of party officials and other influential Californians who expressed their strong confidence in Gregory Cavanaugh. Word came that piles of telegrams and letters were awaiting Monday morning delivery.

A random-sampling survey made Sunday afternoon by Gregory's aides revealed that in the legislature, where there had been early, opportunistic hints of impeachment, a hard core of Cavanaugh defense was developing.

Other favorable signs appeared. The on-camera television personnel who at first had treated the story with unconcealed glee now wore serious expressions.

The tide was turning.

Gregory was seated before the television set, watching the evening news, when Hart came in with the photograph.

He knew from the moment he saw Hart's face that they had real trouble.

Neil sank into a chair. He shook his head in desperation. Gregory saw tears in his eyes.

"Greg, goddamn it, I hate to be the one to bring you this," he said. "But somebody's got to do it. You've got to know. They've just leaked this fucking thing to the press."

Gregory suspected what the picture might show. But he was totally unprepared for the impact of the obscene, graphic detail.

In the eight-by-ten-inch glossy photograph, Gregory Cavanaugh stood in the door of the toilet, his head thrown back. He was completely naked below his suit coat and shirttail. The photograph was cropped at mid-calf. His ankles and trousers were not visible.

Herbie's face was in profile. There could be no doubt about what act he was engaged in.

Yet the worst aspect of the photograph was the expression on Gregory's face. His anguish from the excruciating pain of his twisted arm became almost a caricature of ecstasy. And even more sickening, his left hand, attempting to push Herbie's head away, seemed to be caressing the man's hair.

It was his worst moment since the event itself.

"They timed the release of this goddamned thing absolutely perfect," Hart said. "They allowed just enough time for us to rally support, then they pulled the rug out from under us again."

"Will anyone publish it?" Gregory asked. "Or use it on television?"

"We'll just have to wait and see," Hart said. "But you can bet your ass that picture is in circulation in every newsroom in the country."

Hart's habitual expression was "You can bet your sweet ass."

Gregory noted the omission.

"I just can't imagine anyone publishing it," he said.

"Newspapers have done some gross things," Hart said. "When Jayne Mansfield was killed in that wreck, someone photographed her severed head resting on the hood of her Cadillac. It was put on the national wirephoto net. Some newspapers used it, page one."

Gregory frowned. "Poor taste is one thing . . ."

He recognized the pun as he said it.

Hart, an atrocious punster, let it pass.

Gregory winced. God, was he going to be faced with this for the rest of his life?

"My contacts in the newsrooms will know before long whether they plan to use it," Hart said. "All we can do is pray it isn't as bad as it seems."

Virtually every morning newspaper and ten o'clock newscast made at least partial use of the picture. A few cropped the photograph to show only Gregory's face twisted in the throes of apparent sensual pleasure. Others chose to block out strategic portions with a black rectangle.

"Good God, that's even more obscene," Gregory said after studying the first newspapers that arrived by messenger.

Hart nodded agreement. "Wait until you read the crocodile tears they shed over having to subject their readers to such depravity in the interest of truth," he said. "They insist that the importance of the photograph makes it mandatory that they not withhold such delicious shit from their readers."

Gregory sat for a long time, looking at the photograph. Then he sighed and tossed it on the table.

"Well, let's get a copy of this thing to my lawyer," he said. "Let's see if he has any ideas."

"Which lawyer?" Hart asked.

"Johnny," Gregory said. "I think we can forget about those bastards in L.A. When they see this, they'll really fold up on us."

He sat for a moment, thinking.

"I just hope Johnny Moretti has enough of his old man in him to make a real fight out of it."

CHAPTER 2

SILVIO studied his son with concern. Carlo was showing the effects of Gina's departure. His face seemed bloated, listless. His eyes were red-rimmed. He was unable to concentrate.

Carlo's marital difficulties could not have come at a worse time. Silvio badly needed his help.

Again, he attempted to explain why they needed to proceed with caution.

"Our lawyers have been unable to ascertain exactly how much evidence the liquor control people have against us. We must know that before we can decide on a course of action. Johnny has agreed to go to Sacramento to see if Gregory can get that information for us."

"Don't we have a right to know the charges?" Carlo asked. "Why not simply demand it from them?"

"No, no. This is a matter that must be handled delicately," Silvio explained. "We must not appear concerned, or suggest in any way that we anticipate charges. And yet, we must know the seriousness of the situation. What do they have? Can we fight it in court? What will be the penalty? All this we would know in time, of course. But in order to act we must know now. Perhaps Gregory will make discreet inquiries."

"Greg's got his own troubles," Carlo pointed out.

"Gregory needs friends at the moment," Silvio said. "And we need friends. Perhaps it is to our mutual advantage to work together."

A knock sounded at the door, then Anna entered. Silvio only needed one glance to know that she was furious. He rose from his chair, alarmed at the high color in her cheeks, the tightness around her mouth.

"Mr. Dax has come to call on you," she said.

"Unannounced?" Silvio said, curious.

"Let me handle it," Carlo said, starting for the door. "He's here to twist our arm, to gloat over these charges. I'll show him what happens to people who . . ."

Silvio reached out and grabbed his elbow, stopping him. "No, no. Let's not be rash," he said. "Let's listen at least to what he has to say."

Anna did not move.

"He has shown his lack of breeding by coming unannounced," Silvio said. "Let's not reply in kind. Please show him in, Anna."

While they waited, Carlo paced the floor, fuming. "He's just lording it over us. That's what he's doing. He's just letting us know that we're supposed to kowtow when the great Lucian Hall's messenger arrives. You should let me handle this son-of-a-bitch."

Silvio was amused, but he had to keep Carlo quiet.

"Carlo, always retain your composure in situations such as this. Remember. When you speak, you're not listening. If you don't listen, you learn nothing. Let's listen to what this Mr. Dax has to say. Then we will act."

Anna brought Dax to the door. Silvio crossed the room to shake hands.

"Mr. Dax. An unexpected visit."

Without the imposing presence of Lucian Hall, Dax seemed to assume a greater air of authority. He glanced around the room without expression, ignoring Carlo's presence.

"I happened to be passing through Sonoma on business," he

said to Silvio. "Mr. Hall asked me to drop by. He thought that perhaps, with subsequent developments, you might have reconsidered his offer."

"Reconsidered?" Silvio said. "Well, yes, as a matter of fact, I have reconsidered . . ."

Carlo's mouth opened to protest. A glance from Silvio stopped him.

Dax smiled. "Wonderful," he said. "I'm glad I stopped by. Mr. Hall will be most pleased. I will instruct our attorneys to begin drawing up the papers. I'll be at the Sonoma Inn until eleven tonight, then . . ."

"I *have* reconsidered," Silvio interrupted. "Just as I reconsider all important decisions." He paused and studied Dax for a moment. "And I have determined that at no time in my life have I acted more wisely than in rejecting Lucian Hall's offer."

Carlo laughed.

Dax glared at Silvio. "Mr. Hall will not take kindly to your sense of levity, Mr. Moretti."

"Then Mr. Hall should tend to his own concerns," Silvio said.

"You could have saved yourself grievous trouble, Mr. Moretti. If you had changed your mind, accepted our offer, the liquor control charges could have been dropped. But I'm certain that when I make my report, Mr. Hall will now tell them to prosecute to the full extent of the law."

"I will not be threatened in my own home," Silvio said quietly. "Good day, Mr. Dax."

Dax started toward the door. He turned for a parting shot.

"We will not contact you again. In the future you will have to call us."

"That is the most sensible thing you've said all evening," Silvio said.

Dax slammed the door behind him.

"I don't know how you could let that son-of-a-bitch walk out that door in one piece," Carlo said.

"What would you have done?" Silvio asked.

"I would have put the bastard in a wheelchair for the rest of his life."

Silvio smiled at Carlo. "You have the passion. You only need discipline, and method."

Carlo looked at him, puzzled. Silvio picked up the phone and began dialing.

"For once," he said, "you can do something your way."

CHAPTER 3

*A*T first, the rampant hilarity in the governor's home mystified Johnny. Gregory greeted him effusively. The governor did not seem to have a care in the world. Tom Furman and Neil Hart were clowning like nightclub comedians. Gregory laughed heartily at their antics.

Within minutes, Johnny understood.

It was gallows humor—a running effort by Gregory's aides to take his mind off his troubles.

After the vast publicity over the governor's cost-cutting, the opulence of his apartment was impressive. A spacious living room and study occupied most of the lower floor of the town house. Deep-piled rugs on the polished wood floors delineated the conversation areas, furnished with chrome and leather Mies van der Rohe chairs and chrome and glass tables. Two Robert Indiana prints and a respectable Josef Albers oil decorated the walls. The study was partitioned by a bookcase wall. Johnny had heard that Gregory was a rapid reader, often completing a book at a single sitting.

Johnny endured the wit of the court jesters and waited patiently until Gregory himself turned to business.

"Well, counsel, what's the good word? By this time I figure any word at all is a good word."

"We're building a case," Johnny told him. "By taking it out of the municipal courts, appealing it direct to Los Angeles County, we'll gain a little time. Lord knows, we need it. I have to tell you, Greg. That photograph hurt. We've got to come up with something."

"Any chance of that?"

"Let's hope so," Johnny said. "If we don't hit a breakthrough right away, we should be able to obtain a stay."

Gregory frowned. "I'd hate to see that. I wish we could get this whole mess over with."

"Don't we all," Furman said.

"I meant one way or another," Gregory said. "I can't do anything until this business is resolved. Sometimes I'm tempted to pay the damned fine, just to move on to something else."

"Greg, don't even think that way," Johnny said. "A conviction—petty as it is—would be with you, the rest of your life."

"You might—in the interest of politics, of course—commit a *heterosexual* act of indecency," Hart said. "That would help us obtain a certain constituency balance."

"There goes the San Francisco vote," Furman quipped.

Johnny remained silent. The hip-politico humor did not appeal to him, even as an expediency to cheer Cavanaugh.

"We're doing all we can, Greg," Johnny said. "We have some good people on it. They're digging. As soon as I have more information, I'll feed it to you."

He paused, assessing Cavanaugh's condition. There were circles under the governor's eyes. Lines in his face had deepened. But most noticeable was the way Gregory kept his gaze on the floor. He seldom looked at anyone talking to him. Johnny watched him with concern. The psychological pressures on Greg Cavanaugh undoubtedly were devastating.

Gregory apparently had given some signal to his aides that he wished to confer with Johnny alone. Hart and Furman withdrew discreetly to the far side of the room.

Gregory sat silent for a time, his head lowered. "You know, I used to be jealous of you," he said. He did not look up.

Johnny did not know how to respond. He shook his head in disbelief. "I can't imagine any reason."

Gregory glanced across the room to where Hart, Furman, and two other aides were now talking quietly. "My father used to come home singing the praises of young Giovanni Moretti—even when you were five or six. I felt that this Giovanni Moretti was being held up to me as an example. It hurt—a kid less than half my age. But later, when you were plowing up the football fields, I saw what he meant. You have a lot of qualities I don't have, never acquired."

Johnny shrugged, embarrassed. "Well, obviously you have qualities I don't have."

Gregory nodded, his expression serious. "I'd like to think so. But the point is—and maybe I'm making it badly—my father has been after me for years to approach you about our working closer together. Of course, I knew you were involved in other things. But I want you to know that my calling on you now wasn't a matter of impulse. I've been intending to do it for years."

"Greg, this isn't necessary . . ."

"Yes, it is," Gregory said emphatically. "Maybe some of those old jealousies were there, I don't know. If so, I was wrong. I have needed you—need you now." He looked up, and his eyes met Johnny's in that sincere appeal voters knew so well. "Johnny, if I get out of this trouble, I hope you'll give serious thought to working with me. I have a good staff. But I need someone who's equipped to deal with people on his own, to handle situations I'm not able to handle, or not in a position to handle. I think we'd make a good team."

Johnny was overwhelmed. Cavanaugh's confession explained the distance he had always felt. He chose his words carefully. "I appreciate your saying that, Greg. It's a totally new thought to me. I'll certainly consider it. Of course, I'm heavily involved . . ."

Gregory nodded. "I know that. I'm talking about the future—if there is one. You know, this whole thing is such a nightmare, I keep thinking I'll wake up, and it'll be over. I've always thought that my political career would be a steady climb, as far as I wanted to go. But if we don't beat this frame-up in Los Angeles, it's all over."

"We'll win," Johnny said with a confidence he did not feel.

"We've got to do more than win," Gregory said, his smile still intact. "We've got to wipe those bastards off the map."

Johnny hated to hand him new problems. But he had promised Silvio he would take up the matter personally.

"Greg, there's something else. Pop thinks it stems from the same source as your problem. The Alcoholic Beverage Control Board is preparing charges of mislabeling against the Moretti winery."

"Shit," Gregory said, shaking his head. He ran a hand across his face. He beckoned for his aides to return. "Is this ever going to end?"

To avoid any misunderstanding, he had to make Gregory realize that he was not taking advantage of his position as the governor's legal counsel.

"Before I ask a favor, Greg, let me make this clear: Don't hesitate to say no. At this point my family only wants to explore the options. If there's any danger that we might compromise your position, let's not discuss it further. Silvio has made it plain. What you've got going is too important to risk."

Gregory laughed. "What I *had* going," he said. "Unless we turn this around, I couldn't get elected as Tijuana dog catcher."

"Let's not jump to conclusions," Hart said, approaching in time to hear the remark. "Who's the incumbent?"

Johnny refused to be sidetracked. "I mean what I said, Greg. If we can prove what really happened in Los Angeles—and I think we have a chance—I'd hate like hell for it to hit the fan later that you made an effort to influence the state's legal action against the Morettis."

Gregory studied the matter for a moment. "I see no problem," he said. "As my lawyer, you have unquestioned access to me. And it's nobody's business that we're discussing another case which—as you said—is probably closely related to my own. I can trust you. I would trust Hart and Furman with my life—in fact, I do, every day. I know that when some publisher offers them a small fortune for their memoirs, they will treat me kindly—unlike some others I could mention."

Hart laughed. "Let's get down to cases," he said. "You're using up valuable tape on my concealed recorder."

"He's kidding," Gregory said. "Actually, he has total recall. He puts everything down on paper, each night."

Johnny waited patiently. "Anyway, I do feel awkward, being here in two capacities," he said.

"No problem." Gregory explained the situation to Hart, then turned back to Johnny. "What can we do for you—and for Silvio?"

"We only want to determine the specifics of the evidence the state has—not in any effort to subvert the charges, but to determine a course of action when they become formal."

Gregory thought it through. "I see," he said. He exchanged glances with Hart and apparently found the confirmation he sought. "I find no reason why the governor's office can't make informational contact. The governor is supposed to keep himself informed as to what the hell's going on. It's no secret that our families have been allied politically for years, or that Silvio is my most important single source of support. My concern would be natural, and within the limits of propriety. Neil, why don't you call over there and see what you can find out?"

Hart moved to a phone on the far side of the room. He talked for a while in low tones, making notes. When he returned, his expression was grim.

"It doesn't look good," he said. "They have on record more than two hundred cases of mislabeled Moretti wine, at six locations, found by four inspectors on routine visits."

Gregory sighed. "That's out of my area of expertise. But that's bad, isn't it?"

"Much worse than we thought," Johnny said. "A few bottles, a case or two, could have been a mistake. But this . . ."

"I'm sorry," Gregory said. "I wish it had been better news. And if I were more firmly in the saddle at the moment . . ."

Johnny held up a hand to stop him. "No. Pop made it very plain. We are not to let you risk intervention. He said the stakes are simply too high."

Gregory nodded, accepting Silvio's opinion. "What will you do?" he asked.

"I don't know," Johnny said. "We will have to consider our options carefully and determine the best course."

Hart glanced at Furman.

"Have you noticed?" he asked. "He's beginning to sound exactly like Silvio," he said.

"There's only one thing to do, Pop," Johnny said. "Plead *nolo contendere.*"

Silvio sighed. "That is what my attorneys advise. I had hoped for something more."

Carlo was sprawled listlessly on the sofa. He looked up at Johnny. "You're going to fight Greg's charges. Why not this? Isn't it the same thing?"

Johnny shook his head. "Not at all. Greg was patently framed. There's a chance that we'll find a crack in it—a witness will recant, another witness will surface, something. But those bottles were mislabeled. The inspectors filed the reports independently and, so far as we know, honestly. There is all the difference in the world."

"Sabotage," Carlo said. "We should be able to prove that."

"We still would have only extenuating circumstances," Johnny explained. "The charges would remain valid. The bottles *were* mislabeled."

They were seated in Silvio's study—Silvio behind his desk, Carlo on the sofa, Johnny in the big leather wing chair.

Carlo seemed unusually quiet and preoccupied. Johnny attributed his mood to his separation from Gina and Ariana. Earlier, he had mentioned that Gina had taken Ariana and moved to a house in Napa. Carlo did not seem inclined to talk about it. Johnny had not pressed him.

Silvio lit one of his big cigars. "Lucian has a genuine talent for the jugular," he said. "Every single time he has hit where it hurts most. Old friends. And now, my reputation. I wish there were some way to pay the fine, accept the penalty, without damaging the reputation of the family—or of the winery."

"It's *not* the same as a guilty plea," Johnny explained. "It's just saying, yes, it happened, a mistake was made. But as responsible people, we are willing to bear the burden."

"Bullshit," Silvio said. "Ten minutes after Spiro Agnew pleaded *nolo contendere* on tax charges, the television people were on the air explaining that it was the same as a guilty plea."

"Well, they were wrong. Under the law it isn't the same at all."

"Unfortunately, the law doesn't buy Moretti wine," Silvio said. "What about the public? The man who goes into the store will remember only that the Moretti label has been misused. He will shy away from our label, and buy Mondavi, Krug, Buena Vista, Sebastiani . . ."

"Pop," Johnny said patiently. "You always tell us to examine the alternatives. Here, there is only one course to take. If we plead not guilty and go to trial, we don't have a prayer. They've got us cold. Two hundred cases in six locations, examined independently by different inspectors. Think of the publicity—new headlines every day as each inspector goes to the stand to give more damning evidence. I've got to tell you, Pop. The findings would be 'guilty as charged.' More headlines. Then we could appeal on the hope of some reversible error. More headlines. Pop, I could keep this case in the courts four or five years, maybe six or eight. But your file of news clippings would be a foot thick, and every headline would have two words in it: *Moretti* and *mislabeling*. Not even Lucian Hall could buy that much space and television time to blacken our name."

"What would the penalty be?" Silvio asked quietly.

"Probably a fine, at most a few thousand dollars, a slap on the wrist. At worst, probation."

"Probation? What if we are placed on probation, and it happens again?"

"I'd have to check precedents to be certain, but I imagine our license might be lifted, probably for a limited period."

"Or permanently," Silvio said.

"It would depend on the circumstances."

Silvio rose from his desk and walked to the window. He stood for a time, thinking, looking out over Sonoma.

"I don't like it," he said. "By pleading no contest, we are only making ourselves more vulnerable to Lucian Hall. At the moment, with a perfect record, a reputation built over many years, we could survive a single setback like this. But we have to think about the probability of Lucian making certain there *would* be a next time. We have had sabotage in the vineyards. Now in the winery. Next time, with us on probation, Lucian would have what he wants—the Moretti family out of the wine business, the winery available for a song."

"We will just have to see that there is no next time," Johnny said.

Carlo stirred. He spoke with some amusement. "And how would you do that, little brother?"

Johnny had considered the problem on his way back from Sacramento. He had an answer.

"Establish prior proof. How about a battery of sequence cameras —like they have in banks, supermarkets, public buildings? A time-registered picture every fifteen seconds or so. It would show case lot number, register the bottles going into it, document the personnel who handled each lot."

Carlo frowned, thinking. "It could be done," he said. "How much would it cost?"

"Probably less than the initial fine."

Silvio seemed dubious. "Our people would resent the cameras. I wouldn't blame them."

"Not if it were presented to them in the right way," Johnny insisted. "If they were included in the problem, they would accept the solution. If it were explained that we have been accused of mislabeling, that we know it did not happen here, that we want to protect *them* from such future accusations . . ."

"Little brother, I think you might pull your weight around here yet," Carlo said. "They probably would buy that."

"They would recognize the truth," Johnny said. "The charges are aimed at *their* professionalism. They would welcome proof."

"Still, no defense. A fine. Maybe probation," Silvio said. "I don't like the idea."

"The more you consider the alternative, the better it sounds," Johnny argued.

"I suppose so," Silvio said. He was silent for a time. "All right. We will plead *nolo contendere*." He pointed a finger at Carlo. "But no more wine leaves the premises until the cameras are installed."

Carlo walked with Johnny out to the parking area.

Johnny wanted to make some gesture toward him, express sympathy for his marital trouble. But he did not know how to put his feelings into words.

"Would you like to go somewhere and get a drink?" he asked.

"I'd better not, thanks," Carlo said. "I have some work to do tonight."

He waited until Johnny was behind the wheel of his car, then leaned over to speak through the window. "You know, the old man's way of handling things might be right," he said. "You'd better think about it, little brother."

Before Johnny could recover from his surprise, Carlo had turned and walked to his station wagon. He drove off without looking back, throwing gravel as he sped down the hill toward the street.

On the drive back to Sausalito on the narrow blacktop roads, Johnny mentally reviewed Gregory's case.

He knew he should be preparing himself for the Fraser trial, now only hours away. But the evidence against Cavanaugh puzzled him.

The case was not hopeless. The testimony of the witnesses probably could be clouded sufficiently to put the verdict into the realm of reasonable doubt, especially if Gifford's opinions could be backed with solid evidence.

The more Johnny mulled over the case, the more convinced he became that the validity of the charges rested solely on the photograph. The visual impact of the picture was sufficient to shift the scales toward conviction. Gregory's expression, his apparent caress of Herbie's head, lent support to the graphic evidence.

Yet from the very beginning there had been something about the photograph that seemed false. Johnny could not define the feeling. He kept trying to bring the vague suspicion into the grasp of logic.

By the time he reached Sausalito, he thought he had determined what seemed wrong.

The depth of field.

And the cropping of the photograph.

All the action in the picture was on the extreme left portion of the print. The entire right side was wasted space—the door, portions of the next booth.

From his own experience, Johnny knew that a photographer tends to center on the action—especially when making a hurried shot.

If the photographer had aimed at Herbie's head and Gregory's privates, much of the negative obviously had been cropped from the left side when the photograph was printed.

As soon as Johnny reached home, he went up to the third floor and his camera gear. With the photograph, a ruler, and a half dozen reference books before him, he made calculations.

When he was certain, he phoned Gifford in Los Angeles.

Gifford interrupted him immediately. "Where are you calling from?"

"Home."

"No good," the investigator said. "I hate to ask you to do this. But go to where you were the last time we talked. The phone there will ring in forty-five minutes."

He broke the connection before Johnny could speak.

Earlier in the day, on his way to Sacramento, Johnny had checked with Gifford from a phone booth just off Interstate 80 on the other side of Vallejo.

How could Gifford know that?

Forty-five minutes would be cutting it fine.

Using the Richmond-San Rafael Bridge, he reached the booth in forty minutes.

Five minutes later the phone rang.

"I just learned that my phone is hot," Gifford said. "And it stands to reason yours is no better. Phone booth to phone booth is reasonably safe."

"I'm impressed," Johnny said. "How did you know where I phoned from this morning?"

"You used your credit card," Gifford said. "And I have a friend at the phone company—an ex-cop—who was willing to spend a couple of minutes getting a readout for me in the billing office. Elementary. Other people probably have the same capability. But we're a step ahead of them, so we're probably on a safe line. The real problem is the cable-and-pair taps on my line, and no doubt on yours. They're almost impossible to locate."

Johnny was thinking of the calls he had made during the last few days—to Silvio, to Cavanaugh, to the Los Angeles lawyers.

"We could bring in the federal people," Johnny said.

"For what?" Gifford said. "Wiretapping is a crime only if you get caught. Most people don't. And these people are good. They have friends who have access to cable-and-pair information, maybe even able to do direct taps in the frame rooms at the exchange. Impossible to find, and easy to remove if anyone comes snooping around."

"Still, it's a federal rap."

Gifford laughed. "If one percent were caught, the jails would be bulging. Johnny, there are people in the exchanges who can wire you to any other phone in the city. For a cop friend, or ex-cop friend, they don't even think twice about it. But I didn't get you out to discuss the marvels of Ma Bell. I just didn't want us to be overheard."

"You come up with anything?" Johnny asked.

"Enough to give a smart lawyer a start, I think," Gifford said. "Rutgers has been on the carpet several times, and suspended several times. It's all minor stuff, but it shows what kind of guy he is. Worst item was a suspension and reduction in rank for falsifying a report in the arrest of a well-known gambler. Martin's record is not quite as bad. Worst on him is a suspension for recovering a stolen motor home, then simply forgetting to take it to the auto pound until he had taken a long vacation in it. The security guard, Reinert, has a few drunk and disorderly convictions, and one pistol toting charge that was dismissed. About the worst we can say about him is that he's completely illiterate. I have some of his daily reports. They're hilarious."

"What about Herbie?"

The line was silent a moment. "I guess you missed the evening news."

"I just got in," Johnny said.

"Herbie's dead. Beaten to death in an alley. No suspects. Police are baffled. All that shit."

"Damn," Johnny said. He slammed his palm against the side of the phone booth in frustration. "How neat. Chief witness against the governor turns up dead. God, they don't have to file charges on this one. Everyone will take it as proof that the governor has powerful friends."

"That's the implication," Gifford said. "It was the lead item on the six o'clock news. No doubt it will make the banners in the morning papers."

"Well, we haven't been to bat yet," Johnny said. "I just may have something."

He explained about the strange aspect of the photograph, as viewed from the experience of a photographer.

"If there is more to the negative than shows on the print, it would cover several degrees of field to the left—enough to take in the whole booth. If Greg's giant is in the negative, and if he's as big as Greg says, then his head and shoulders should be visible. Who was the photographer?"

"Rutgers. He used to be known around the cop shop for his collection of whore-and-client photographs. His pictures were more for sport than for evidence."

"Does he do his own darkroom work?"

"As far as I know. The kind of pictures he shot, you hardly took to the corner drugstore. And I do remember that he had a run-in over using the department's darkroom without authorization. They kicked his ass out and gave him a reprimand."

"We've got to get that negative," Johnny said.

For a moment Gifford did not respond. "This isn't my regular line of work. But I suppose we could arrange a simple bag job."

"That wouldn't help," Johnny said. "If we got the negative in a burglary, it would be tainted evidence."

"Johnny, before we do anything, we've got to know for sure it exists, and exactly what it contains. We could just open up Rutger's apartment for a quick look."

The suggestion was tempting, but he could not condone burglary. "Too risky," he said.

"I don't like the idea any better than you. But this is a high-stake game. I'll do the job myself. I wouldn't want to risk farming this one out. And I'm better than any lock-artist I know. I've caught enough of them."

"I can't go along with a break-in," Johnny insisted. "If anything happened, it'd leave us wide open."

"Then how in hell do you propose to get that negative?"

"A bench search warrant," Johnny said.

Gifford snorted. "Johnny, once you apply for that warrant, word would be all over the L.A.P.D. in five minutes. They'd have plenty of time to destroy the damned thing before the warrant was served."

Johnny did not answer. Gifford was right. But he had a deeper concern. "What worries me, they could make a new negative from the print and claim it was the original."

"You're beginning to lose me," Gifford said. "Explain it in simple terms. How do you know there's more to the negative than what we see on the print?"

"If they had used a larger lens, telescopic—one hundred eighty or two hundred millimeters or so—the depth would be more distorted. From the depth of field, I'm certain they used less than an eighty-five millimeter—probably a fifty-five. At that distance, with a normal fifty-five millimeter lens, the frame should be much wider —wide enough to show anyone standing to the left of Greg."

"Listen to me, Johnny. We might get the right judge—one who could keep it quiet until the warrant was served. And I can arrange for the right people to serve the search warrant. But we have to know exactly where that goddamn negative is, what it contains. We've got to be able to walk right to it."

"Larry, I just can't go along with burglary," Johnny said again.

"Oh, shit! Stop calling it burglary! We're not going to steal anything. If you've got a hangup on the word, let's use some semantics. I like the federal government's term, 'surreptitious entry.' I promise you, nobody's even going to know I've been there."

Johnny considered the problem at length. He concluded that Gifford was right. There was no other way. They had to know the exact location of the negative. And Gifford was an expert in these things.

"Okay," he said. "But goddamn it, be careful."

"Don't worry about me. There's one other thing. I'm not questioning your knowledge of photography. But it seems rather vague to me, in terms of a search warrant. Can you pin all of that technical jargon down to something the judge can understand?"

"To be completely convincing, I need the exact measurements of that restroom," Johnny said. "The precise distance from that one-way mirror to the door of the booth, the height of the booth partition, the width of the opening. With that information I can determine the lens used, the exact frame of the negative."

"Okay. I'll get that information," Gifford said. "I suppose you realize it'll require double fee."

"Why?" Johnny asked, not understanding.

"Your innocence is appalling," Gifford said. "A simple break-in is one thing. But for your information, wandering around the men's room at Los Angeles International with a tape measure is *really* hazardous duty."

CHAPTER 4

DAX emerged from Sonoma Mission Inn a few minutes after eleven, so angry he was beyond caution.

An hour earlier, he had told his bodyguard and chauffeur to load the luggage. But when he at last got off the phone with Lucian Hall, the suitcases and Val-A-Paks remained stacked by the door to his suite.

He stormed down the stairs and out into the parking area to find Chipman and Foster, eager to vent his bottled-up frustration on them. The cool night air, the soft moonlight filtering through the gently swaying trees assumed the aura of an hallucination compatible with his distress. Lucian Hall's scorn still burned in his ears.

"Silvio Moretti is not stupid," Hall had shouted. "You didn't have to spell it out! Silvio understands innuendo!"

Dax had tried to explain Moretti's arrogance. In doing so, he had inadvertently revealed that Silvio Moretti had made a fool of him. And that he had put the threat of the state liquor board charges into plain words.

After that Hall could not be appeased. He had shouted at Dax for almost an hour, berating Dax's judgment, his abilities, his sanity. "You get back here immediately," he had said at last. "By putting a threat into words you may have jeopardized our position."

With that, Lucian had slammed down the receiver.

And now Foster and Chipman had disappeared.

Walking out into the semidarkness, Dax could see the Hampton limousine in the drive, parked close to the highway. The dimly lit area was well screened from passing traffic by lush shrubbery. Dax moved up the hill with angry strides. As his eyes adjusted to the night, he saw movement near the car. He recognized Foster's cap, silhouetted against the night sky.

"Foster, goddamn it," Dax shouted. "I told you to see to the baggage."

Foster did not reply.

Dax was opening his mouth to repeat his order when the man turned.

The man was wearing Foster's cap and coat. But it was not Foster. Momentarily confused, Dax glanced at the car. It was definitely a Hampton limousine.

"Where's Foster?" Dax demanded.

"He's in the trunk of the car," the figure said. "But he's not to be bothered. You might say he's tied up right now."

A laugh came from the edge of the shrubbery. Dax could see another man standing in the shadows, half concealed.

Alarmed, he took a step backward, and turned to flee back toward the inn. But as he opened his mouth to shout, a hand closed over his face from behind. He was jerked off his feet. He fought. Strong hands wrestled him into the back seat of the car.

"Keep quiet, and you may live," a third voice said.

He was shoved onto the floorboard of the Cadillac. His face scraped painfully into the carpet. His wrists were pulled behind him. Handcuffs clicked. He lay helpless.

"Don't give us any trouble," someone said.

Dax remained motionless. He had no intention of giving anyone trouble.

He heard others entering the car. How many, he did not know. Doors closed. The engine started. The car circled up the drive to Sonoma Highway and turned left.

Dax moaned with terror. His awkward position and the unnatural roar of the roadbed so close to his ear gave the ride the dimensions of a nightmare. He grew certain that when they reached their destination, a bullet would be fired into his brain. The ominous silence of the men around him intensified his fear.

Several long minutes later, the car slowed. Dax was jostled as the big limousine crossed a ditch and pulled to a stop.

"Get out," one of them demanded.

His legs had turned to rubber. Completely limp, he was pulled from the car. He could not stand. He went to his knees in the dirt. He felt a vaguely familiar, clammy warmth on his legs. Someone laughed.

"He pissed his pants," a voice said.

"Please!" he heard himself begging. "Don't kill me."

"You're not worth killing," the voice said. "We only want to send your boss a message."

He was pulled to his feet and shoved across the hood of the car. Several hands grasped his head and held it firmly.

"Okay," the same voice said. "Now."

In the faint hint of moonlight Dax saw the wire snare. At first he did not understand.

And then, somehow, he did.

"No!" he screamed. "Oh, my God! No!"

"You have a consolation," the voice said. "It could be worse. Much worse. Keep that in mind."

Dax felt the snare closing on his right ear. The sound of tearing flesh was surprisingly loud. Then came the pain.

Dax screamed.

But his ordeal had just begun.

CHAPTER 5

HOWARD was at the airport when Christina arrived. His welcoming kiss seemed genuine, but she detected something different in his manner. They had spent enough time together to be aware of subtleties. Howard said nothing until they were in the Sumner Tunnel, on their way to the apartment.

"Who the hell is Johnny?" he asked, his eyes never leaving the road.

Despite her surprise, Christina felt a wave of relief. On the way back to Boston she had worried how best to tell Howard about Johnny. Her concern was wasted. Howard already knew. "Johnny's an old, old friend," she said, turning in her seat to face him. "Why do you ask?"

Howard was preoccupied for a moment with the traffic. His dark, deep-set eyes revealed nothing of his thoughts. But one hand left the wheel to brush back an errant strand of hair—always a sign he was upset. "A monster bouquet of roses came a couple of hours ago," he said. "Judging from the size, I would say Johnny is a very, very good old, old friend."

Christina carefully watched Howard, evaluating his reactions. "He is," she said softly. "Back to childhood."

He glanced at her as they emerged from the tunnel. His face revealed nothing. "I don't remember your ever mentioning him."

"No reason I should. He was in the distant past. More of a family friend."

Howard's voice was flat and lifeless. "And now he's back on the scene."

"Yes," she said.

She watched his lips for the telltale signs, but his face remained frozen. He did not speak again until they turned into the apartment parking area. After turning off the ignition, he made no move to get out of the car. "What will this do to us?" he asked.

Christina hoped he would recognize the honesty of her answer. "Howie, I simply don't know."

It was then that the tremor started in his hands. He gripped the wheel in an effort to keep her from noticing, but his arms continued to jerk uncontrollably. "You can't do this," he said. "You're not ready."

She slid across the seat and put her arms around him. "Don't," she said. "Please don't." She held him until the spasm ceased. He remained rigid, resisting. They sat motionless for several minutes. Gradually, the cold of the September night began to penetrate the car. At last, Christina relented. She put a hand on his cheek, turning his face toward her.

"Don't worry," she said. "I promise you. I won't do anything until I'm certain we're both ready."

Howard sulked in the den through the next several evenings. He arose and left for the library each morning before she was up. Twice she called him there. He refused to come to the phone. She did not know what to do. Her problem with Howard was complicated by her long, difficult hours at the museum. The research from the West Coast trip had to be evaluated in the light of the developing exhibition.

And Johnny did not help matters. He called every night, talking for an hour or more, keeping the dream alive. The apartment remained full of flowers, and each day a perfect, long-stemmed red rose arrived at the museum. For years Christina had fought to keep her private and professional lives separate, but in the glass-cage world of the museum's administrative wing, the daily visits of the florist's truck could not escape notice. She became the target of knowing smiles and not-so-veiled innuendos.

Then Howard's poetry came—long typescript letters at the office; handwritten, elaborately illustrated sheets shoved under the bedroom door. She did not need an objective opinion to know that it was the best he had ever written, even better than his prize-winning verses in the literary quarterlies. She was more than touched. She was devastated. Howard imbued his poetry with thoughts he could never speak, describing his love, her importance to him, what they meant to each other.

Christina had nowhere to turn. The pressures at the museum grew. Despite her preoccupation with her work, she could not escape the hovering knowledge that she soon must make a decision and straighten out her life. Away from work, she worried mostly about Howard, but she lived for the thrill of the nightly phone call and spent long, restless nights thinking of Johnny.

In desperation, she relented in her resolve and called Dr. Chesler for the first time in months.

When she entered the psychiatrist's office on Friday afternoon, she found him in his usual jocular mood. "Terrific eye shadow you're wearing," he said. "I would have sworn those dark smudges were real."

He had a way of keeping his therapy sessions balanced easily between light banter and serious talk. With his pixie face and wild, fluffy hair, Dr. Chesler was facile in easing painful subjects into relaxed discussion. He had a gift for proper response, for eliciting information. Within minutes, Christina was spilling out the story of her encounter with Johnny, her deep feelings about him, Howard's reaction, and her dilemma.

"I love them both, in different ways," she concluded. "I don't want to hurt either." She shook her head in exasperation. "Why does love have to be such torture?"

Dr. Chesler rhythmically tapped the knuckles of his left hand with a pencil while he contemplated her problem.

"My, my, this *is* a can of worms," he said.

He plied her with questions, making her define her emotions toward Johnny, toward Howard. He asked her about herself, her work, her feelings about the museum. They talked about her trip home, the enigma posed by her parents.

At last, the questions ceased. Dr. Chesler settled deep into his chair and tapped his knuckles through a long silence. When he spoke, all levity was gone.

"This may sound like a *non sequitur*, but it isn't. As an intern, I participated in what came to be known in my profession as the Midtown Manhattan Study. We examined a cross-section of more than sixteen hundred New York residents. It took eight years. We determined that something less than nineteen percent of those interviewed were in good mental health. On the other end of the spectrum, something less than three percent were totally incapacitated, ready for the booby-hatch." Dr. Chesler smiled. "That leaves the rest of us—more than three-fourths of the population—in a category I would call certified walking-around crazies. We're not completely well, but we're not completely sick. We can ask for advice. We can beg for help. But we can't give up. Do you understand what I'm trying to say?"

"I think so," Christina said.

"You are involved in what no doubt will be the most important decision of your life. But my ability to help you is limited. As a certified walking-around crazy, you must bear the responsibility for your actions. You can't come in here to another certified walking-around crazy and get an easy answer. I can listen, help you resolve your feelings, provide a little insight and logic, but there is too much that only you can determine for yourself. For instance, if I were to advise you to go west and marry this young man, he might be an absolute rake, for all I know. You'll have to trust your own feelings. And there's Howard. If I told you to leave him, and he did something rash—and understand I'm not implying he would— there is no way I could absolve you from a lifelong sense of guilt."

Christina was always reluctant to discuss Howard with Dr. Chesler, but now he had opened the door. "That's one thing I'm worried about," she said.

"And rightfully so," Dr. Chesler agreed. "You and Howard are locked into a complex relationship. You two will have to resolve your situation, or find your own way out of it. Basically, both of you are strong personalities. You have had to be, to assimilate and to cope with all that life has thrown at you. I have confidence in you. But it's important that you understand. You'll have to make your own decision. You're the one who will have to live with it. You also must understand that I'm not abandoning you, that I'm not copping out. When you make your decision, we can discuss it, if you want, examine it, make certain, insofar as we can, that you are doing the right thing. Do you understand all this?"

"Yes," Christina said.

"You need rest. I'll give you some pills. But don't use them as a crutch. You are being pulled apart. Get some sleep, and when you wake up fresh, tackle it. The longer you delay, the more stress."

"I understand," Christina said.

"Fine. Now, I want you to go home, lock your bedroom door, unplug the phone, and make lists, subjective—your emotions—and objective—cold, bloodless logic, for Howard, and for Johnny. Review your entire relationship with each. Then list what you can offer them, and what they can offer you. Be realistic. I suspect that by the time you've done this, you will have arrived at your decision. If you want to discuss it further, give me a ring."

She began with Howard, trying to reconcile the storm of conflicting emotions he aroused in her. She went back to the beginning.

Their relationship had started innocently, unexpectedly. Often upon leaving Dr. Chesler's office she ducked into a small delicatessen for a quick sandwich before returning to the museum. On that day, she had dawdled over coffee, thinking through the difficult session. She was jarred from her reverie as a tall, lean young man dropped awkwardly into the adjoining chair.

"Hello," he said. "You two fifteen. Me three thirty."

Christina had become adept at warding off unwanted advances. But there was something in the young man's long, sad face, his deep-set dark eyes that put her at ease, despite his soiled jeans, ragged shirt, and ancient tennis shoes.

"I beg your pardon?" she said.

He leisurely bit into his sandwich. "Chesler," he said, taking his time. "I used to wonder why on Thursdays he couldn't get his mind onto my problems as quickly as he could on other days. I knew he was thinking about his last patient. It was you. I felt you too. Your presence lingered. Then, one day when I was late, I saw you coming out the side door."

Annoyed, she turned away. She had not told anyone she was seeing a psychiatrist, and Dr. Chesler's office was designed to prevent patients from encountering each other.

"Don't worry, I'm harmless," the young man said. He continued to munch on his sandwich, talking in an off-hand, even disinterested way. "In fact, that's my basic problem. I'm probably the most innocuous individual on the face of the earth. Chesler says I let everyone feed on me without protest." He raised an elbow. "Here. Have a bite."

Despite her irritation, Christina laughed. The young man was so deadly serious. His eyes were filled with soft intelligence, and his long, solemn face seemed to hide untold suffering.

She gathered her purse in preparation for leaving.

"I wrote a poem about you," he said. He paused, spreading mustard on the other half of his sandwich. "It's in this month's *Atlantic*."

Christina hesitated on the edge of her seat. "You what?"

He gave her the wisp of his woebegone smile. "I'm a poet," he said. "Poets flash on anything that moves them. When I caught a glimpse of you that day, I wrote a poem. Right on the spot."

Christina did not believe him, but he had her off balance. "That was nice," she said.

He paused to brush crumbs from his shirt. "Next week I'll bring you a copy," he said.

That night, on a whim, Christina stopped by a newsstand and bought the magazine. She flipped through it, reading all the filler verses, and found nothing. She was certain her first impression was correct; she had met one of Dr. Chesler's most outré patients.

Fortunately, an article had caught her eye. She saved it. Two nights later, as she prepared for bed, she picked up the magazine, and there, featured in a two-page spread, was the poem. She read it with racing heart, stunned.

It was beautiful. In a few brief words he described his fleeting glimpse of the girl of his dreams, leaving a psychiatrist's office by the side door and hurrying down the hall. He saw in her angelic face, in that one glance, all the suffering and heartache of a world gone mad.

There was more—reflections and literary allusions she only half understood. But she knew the poem was exceptional; the fact that the magazine's editors had given it special treatment confirmed her belief.

And she learned his name—Howard Collins.

She did not mention the poem to Dr. Chesler the following week. After her session, she lingered over coffee in the delicatessen. Just as she was about to give up, he sauntered in, nodded, and moved to the counter to order his sandwich. He was wearing the same jeans, the same shirt and tennis shoes. As he approached, he held out a copy of the magazine.

"I've seen it," she said. "I think it's remarkably good."

He gave her his wan smile. "I'm glad you liked it. And I'm glad you've seen it. Saves me the embarrassment of watching you read it." He slid the magazine across the arm of his chair toward her. "This is an inscribed copy."

She turned to the poem. In a loose, flowing hand, he had written, "You two fifteen. Me three thirty," and his signature.

Again he talked as he devoured his sandwich. She learned that he had published other poems. He pointed to the magazine. "I got good money for that," he said. "I don't feel right about it, capitalizing on your pain. Tell you what. I'll split it with you. On a dinner. I know an Italian place with terrific food, good wine . . ."

Christina could see no harm in having dinner with him. Granted, she was slightly dismayed when he arrived in the same jeans and tennis shoes, but he seemed to be a favorite customer at the restaurant. The waiters hovered over their table. The owner came by to ascertain that everything was in order. Eventually even the chef came out of the kitchen to discuss the nuances of his dishes.

"I wrote a poem about them once," Howard explained.

Howard became a habit. He was a good companion, undemanding, sensitive to moods. He would listen for hours, giving her his full attention, expecting nothing in return. She found herself telling him things she had never told anyone.

He was eccentric. A fanatic about cleanliness, he made notable exceptions. He showered several times a day but always wore the same pair of disreputable jeans. She learned that he wore the same clothes day after day because he had no others. He did not want to be bothered with possessions. He explained that if he owned two pairs of shoes, he was continually faced with the decision of which to wear, and where to keep the other pair. As soon as Christina felt she knew him well enough, she convinced him that he owed it to himself to dress better. "Hippies went out with the sixties," she explained. When he saw that his appearance was an embarrassment to her, he bought a splendid dark gray suit, and one set of accessories. In the suit, with his tall, lanky build, and long, doleful face, he looked distinguished, Lincolnesque.

Little by little, she gathered facts about him. Not until she had known him for months did she learn that he had been in Vietnam.

"No combat," he said. "I just went around after the battles and picked up the pieces."

She did not understand.

"Graves registration," he explained. "It was their little joke. Can you think of a better Military Occupational Specialty for a brooding, contemplative poet?"

Later, he told her more. "We were the lepers over there," he said. "Untouchables. No one would talk to us. We traveled with a bale of body bags, moving around in choppers. Everyone would stand back and watch us work. It was like we were from some nether world, carrying the dead into purgatory."

He was stubborn. Although none of his several university degrees was in library science, efforts were made at the library where he had worked for the last several years to promote him into a better paying, more responsible position. He refused. He preferred to work at the checkout counter, where he could discuss books with the readers. No one at the library knew about his poetry. He would not tell them. He was obstinate on the subject; his poetry was personal.

Some nights when he came to visit Christina in her apartment, he would not leave. The first time this happened, Christina kept hinting until her patience was exhausted. "Make yourself at home, then," she told him at last. "I'm going to bed."

When she awoke the next morning, he was fixing breakfast. He had spent the night on the couch in her den. Several nights later he slept there again. The frequency increased until he was spending half his time in her apartment. Although Christina remained disturbed about the situation, there was an undeniable comfort in having him around. Technically they did not live together. He still maintained his own apartment. But more and more she took his presence for granted.

There was no sex between them. Howard was affectionate, but he remained distant. At first she was puzzled, because she never doubted his masculinity. In time his lack of aggression became a part of his comfortable nature. One night, tipsy with wine, he made a single pass at her. She was so surprised that she fended him off. He never tried again.

Not until she had known him almost a year did she learn he was impotent. The discovery came with the revelation that he had two children, a boy and a girl, six and eight.

"Nadine had good reason to leave me," he said. "You see, I tried to kill her. Three times. Chesler says I was really trying to kill my mother. But for Nadine the point was academic. She was the one who had her air supply shut off."

He seemed to hold no animosity toward his ex-wife. There was a court order barring him from seeing her or the children.

"Nadine took the kids, our house, our bank account, and my balls," he said. "The courts were probably right. I made some terrible threats. I spent a lot of time in a padded cell."

For Christina, the thought of Howard turning violent was beyond belief. He assured her it was possible. "Chesler says that I may sincerely love a woman. But I hate *women*. Deep down, I want to do violence to them."

His impotence did not seem to worry him. "Chesler's the one who has a hangup about it," he said. "I think he takes it as a personal affront that one of his patients is malfunctioning, sexually. He seems to think that if he could get my machinery working, everything would be all right. He says I'm not gay. Sometimes I think he wishes I were. At least that would be something positive. As it is, I'm nothing, a blank. I keep telling him I'm asexual. Chesler claims that's just a word, a cop-out. He says the true asexual does not exist. That's psychiatry for you."

And not until she had known him for more than a year did

Christina learn that he was rich. Money meant nothing to him. The only checks he wrote were for cash. On rare occasion he would wander by a bank and stuff his jeans with hundred dollar bills. He implied that the money came from a family trust left in his name. "At the rate I'm going, I should be able to make it last several hundred years," he said.

He never talked of his father and mother, or of his family. Christina knew absolutely nothing about them.

Dr. Chesler did not learn of their friendship for several months. When Christina accidentally revealed that they had met, he was furious. For once his professional calm failed him.

"I should refer the both of you to colleagues immediately," he said. "I wouldn't have had this happen for the world. It's unethical! What if something happened to you? I would be responsible."

Christina asked if Howard was really dangerous.

Dr. Chesler hedged. "I didn't say that. But I'm deeply concerned. The friendships you make in the outside world are your business. But when two of my patients meet here and complicate their lives, my practice, that is *my* business."

His anger cooled in time. Gradually he came to accept the situation. But he would never discuss Howard's problems with Christina, or Christina's with Howard.

Only once, long after they had met, did Dr. Chesler mention Howard to Christina. She had described some of Howard's eccentric behavior, in the context of her reactions to it.

The psychiatrist shook his head sadly. "Howard possesses an intelligence that is completely off the scale, by any yardstick. Chiefly because of that intelligence, he has made great strides. But he is still a very troubled young man."

Christina spent three long nights compiling her lists. Her outpouring of complex emotions concerning Howard filled more than forty pages in a legal-size scratch pad.

In comparison, her notes on Johnny were brief. She discovered that she knew little about him.

As Dr. Chesler predicted, her decision was made by the time she finished her lists.

She felt so strongly about it, so certain, that she did not bother to discuss it with him.

CHAPTER 6

"IT'S done," Carlo said. "He wet his pants before we did a thing to him."

From behind his desk, Silvio glanced at his eldest son. "Don't gloat, Carlo. We have committed a barbaric act. It was necessary, but it is not to be regarded with pride."

Carlo stretched to his full length on the sofa. "Well, we should have done it sooner. Maybe we wouldn't have had to put up with so much shit."

Silvio turned away and walked to the window behind his desk. He did not want Carlo to see his distaste, his disappointment.

This son remained a mystery to him. Where was his sense of identity? His dignity? What genes inspired those childish rages, that preoccupation with sensual pleasure? Where was his ambition for significant accomplishment?

In some ways Carlo seemed to be turning back into a child. After Gina left him, he had quickly fallen into a routine of coming by the house each morning for breakfast. Anna took Carlo's daily visit to the family table as a matter of course. Silvio was far less enthusiastic. There was something awry in Carlo's nature. A man should have more self-respect.

Carlo remained an emotional weakling.

And Johnny seemed overly endowed with a sense of independence.

"Are you still seeing that woman?" Silvio asked without turning from the window.

"No," Carlo said. "I promised Gina I would break it off with Patsy Jean. I meant it."

Silvio sighed. The early morning sun had just touched the distant hills, encircling Sonoma with a golden crown. In the distance the dark smudge of a grass fire marred the horizon. Again Silvio spoke to the window.

"Carlo, what do you want in life?"

Behind him there was silence. Silvio waited.

"What do you mean?" Carlo asked.

"It's a simple question—an important question. You are forty years of age, with family, position, a measure of wealth, all attained without much effort on your part. Don't you feel moved, at times, to give the world something in return?"

Again Carlo was silent. When he answered, Silvio detected an edge of anger in his voice. "I've worked damned hard—given plenty of effort—in the winery, almost twenty years," Carlo said. "I think that's a contribution."

Silvio nodded. "It is, and it is appreciated, but I am not speaking of the winery. I am speaking of yourself. You perhaps have thirty good years left. Tell me, Carlo. What do you want to do with them?"

"Work," Carlo said. "Just like I've always done."

Silvio understood. He too knew the pleasures of the warm sun in the vineyards, the rich smells, the overwhelming awareness of one's body after a day of exhausting physical work.

But there should be something more.

At no time during the hardships and difficulties of his early years had Silvio ever doubted that he would eventually achieve his goals in life, somehow.

Even now the memories were fresh. As a young man on the docks in San Francisco he had spent from twelve to fourteen hours a day at hard labor. Even so, he had managed another two or three hours of work for himself—effort that someday might remove him from the herd. Only a short time remained for rest. But always, before falling asleep on the dirty, sweat-stained mattress in his room, Silvio remained awake for at least another half-hour, creating over and over again in his mind the man he was to become.

In his mind's eye, he could see himself as he had been in those days, illiterate, still hardly more than a boy. Yet even then he had known that someday he would read all the great books. He was practically penniless, barely eking out a living at backbreaking work, but he never lost confidence that someday he would be wealthy. He was a tool of other men. But he had known that someday other men would be his tools.

He had known that in his head he carried the secrets of a skill that would make his dreams a reality.

He still remembered the exotic smells in the wine cellars of his grandfather on Corsica, and the immense pride the old man took in his art.

Silvio had listened with unwavering attention as the old man revealed the secrets of the wine. Giovanni Sebastian Moretti knew nothing of enzymes, acidity, metabolization. If he had heard the words, he would have scorned them. He knew only that wine must breathe, work, play, and sleep—all at carefully watched times and for proper durations.

Silvio could still remember the glint in the old man's dark eyes as he admonished his grandson: "Never forget this, Silvio. There is nothing in life equal to the challenge of attempting to make a truly fine wine. It is a symphony in a bottle. To create such music for the soul fills a man with great pride, yet keeps him humble, for he knows there are so very few chances given to men for such tremendous achievement."

The words lingered. Later, when Silvio came to America, he did not forget. While the other young men on the docks squandered their money on liquor and occasional women, Silvio had savored and preserved the burning in his own loins. He knew that someday he would find a woman to share his dreams.

He would be the finest vintner in America. The name of Silvio Moretti would be synonymous with fine wine. He would compose his own symphonies in bottles that bore his name.

All this he had achieved.

But for what?

The dream also included fine, obedient sons who would absorb and keep alive this passion for excellence, for achievement.

And now, in the final years of his life, this vital portion of the dream had yet to be realized.

Silvio turned from the window. Carlo was working with a pocket-sized calculator and notepad.

"Unless we get those cameras installed today, we've got a warehouse problem," Carlo said.

Silvio grunted acknowledgment. He had foreseen the difficulty. "Tell Emil to move two or three portable buildings into the space behind the main warehouse. I have been assured that the cameras will be in place tomorrow."

Carlo punched the calculator for several more seconds. The answer seemed to satisfy him. "We can just about squeak by," he said. He stuffed the gadget into his shirt pocket and reached for his jacket. "I'll be over at the crusher this morning," he said.

On impulse, Silvio put a hand on Carlo's shoulder. "Why don't you let Emil tend to that?" He gestured toward his desk. "I need you here this morning."

Carlo looked up, puzzled. "Why?" he asked.

Silvio shrugged. "There are things that must be done in connection with this Lucian Hall matter."

Carlo's face remained guarded, wary. "What things?"

Silvio thought for a moment, considering how much to reveal. "We must plan ahead, counter certain moves Lucian will make . . ."

He stopped. Carlo was studying him with a trace of a knowing smile. The silence lengthened.

"It is time you learned something of what happens here," Silvio said, gesturing toward his desk.

Carlo laughed. "Am I hearing you right? Are you offering me the job that Johnny has been turning down for five years or more?"

"I need both my sons," Silvio said.

Carlo nodded. "Carlo in the vineyards, Johnny in the office. I've heard it a thousand times. I know it by rote. Don't tell me you've changed your mind."

Silvio ignored the question. He was more concerned with a discovery. "Carlo, I never knew you resented that. I thought that with your different natures . . ."

"What's it going to be now?" Carlo interrupted. "Johnny in the vineyards, Carlo in the office?"

"Don't make light of it," Silvio said.

"I'm not." Carlo returned to the sofa, the mocking hint of a smile remaining. "Lord knows, I'm not. The thing is, I can't believe that you've given up on Johnny. Isn't this a ploy to make him want the job? If it is, I think it's the first awkward thing I have ever seen you do. Your feelings must be so strong that for once they've gotten in the way of your judgment."

Silvio sank into the chair behind his desk. He fought to keep his face expressionless. "Carlo, have you ever wondered what will happen when I am gone?"

"Of course," Carlo said. He hesitated, then spoke rapidly, as if driven by some deep-seated compulsion. "And I can tell you: I'll keep on making fine wine. Johnny will become a great lawyer, a powerful man, his own man. A separate corporation will be set up to take care of all this other stuff." He gestured toward the desk. "Mrs. Rogers will be named executive secretary, because she probably knows more than anyone about what you've been doing for the last forty years—all the deals you've made and never written down. It'll be one hell of a mess. And I doubt we will be able to get a peep out of Salvatore Messino."

Silvio felt a sharp constriction around his heart. Emily Rogers had been his secretary at the winery for thirty years, but she handled only mail and routine matters. She knew virtually nothing about his other activities. And Carlo probably was right about Salvatore.

"You apparently have done much thinking about it," Silvio said. "Am I standing in your way?"

Carlo laughed. "You always taught us to look ahead, to take the realistic view. I hope you go on another eighty years. All I've ever wanted was the winery. I've never given a shit about all the other stuff. You know that."

Silvio carefully lit a cigar. "Nor has Johnny."

"Nor has Johnny," Carlo agreed. "I think you've met your match in Johnny. I don't think he'll ever come back."

"That will leave the job open," Silvio pointed out.

Carlo smiled and shook his head. "No. Not now. Ten years ago, if you had dangled the possibility of working here with you, I probably wouldn't have been able to turn it down. I would have been miserable. I would have botched it. But I would have tried. Not now. I know myself better. And you're right. It's not my nature to pull strings with politicians, or play high-stake poker with conglomerates. But I am good at what I do—I make fine wine."

Silvio smoked his cigar for a time without speaking. In his way Carlo was sometimes surprising.

"You will get your winery," Silvio said. "And I will make an effort to keep from leaving such a . . . mess."

Carlo smiled. The trace of mockery was gone. He rose and again started toward the door, then hesitated and looked back.

"If you should see Emil before I do, tell him there's a heat problem developing in Number Five vat. We've got to watch it." Carlo paused again with his hand on the door. "And Pop, I warn you. If you *do* leave me the winery, the first thing I'm going to do is fire that worthless son-of-a-bitch."

After Carlo left, Silvio sat for several minutes, staring at the door.

Carlo would do fine with the winery. He had talent, knowledge, a feeling for the wine. There would be a problem with the business operations. But Carlo had enough basic intelligence to hire the right people.

And Carlo probably was right about Emil. The matter of Emil Borneman went back many years. Unfortunately, at the present time there was nothing Silvio could do about him.

He tapped out his cigar and placed it on an ashtray, then reached into the bottom drawer of his desk for the white telephone.

He dialed a time service in Los Angeles. A voice repeated the time, weather, temperature, and a commercial for auto loans while Silvio tested the line for a tap, using the gadget Salvatore Messino had purchased. The phone remained safe, as Silvio had expected. The special line ran to a private home more than a hundred yards away, where installation had been made under another name.

Silvio's regular office phone had been tapped for more than two months.

Using the white phone, Silvio dialed the number that connected him with a bank chairman in San Francisco. He exchanged jovial pleasantries with the man, moving toward the reason for the call.

"I understand you have under consideration a loan of some magnitude."

The chairman's hesitation was barely perceptible. "Yes. I know the one you mean. The consensus here is that it will be denied."

"I would hate to see that happen," Silvio said. "In fact, I feel so strongly about it that I will make you a deal. If the loan is defaulted, I personally will pick up the papers."

The line was silent for a few seconds. "That might be difficult to arrange," the chairman said. "Word here is that the client is overextended with his recent, rapid expansion. There have been factors to indicate that there have been some rash—even improvident—actions concerning this client."

"I know," Silvio said. "You fail to see my purpose. I *expect* the loan to be defaulted. I want the papers."

Silvio could almost hear the chairman's thoughts turning. "How would we handle it?" he asked. "The loan application fails to meet even minimum qualifications. I'm assuming, of course, that you wouldn't want your name listed as a cosigner."

"Hardly. Instead, I will assign certain certificates of deposit as collateral. I will give you a personal letter, assigning those certificates to you, to cover the loan. That should satisfy any question with the bank examiners. Your borrower is experienced in cutting corners. He knows that with the current money situation the bank is anxious to make loans. I doubt that he will suspect our trap. He already has been told by a source he trusts that your bank has a surplus available and needs to make the loan."

The chairman made several false starts before he could put his thoughts into words. "Conceivably, the loan could be made under those circumstances. But there's still a problem with the board. A loan of this size would have to be discussed . . ."

"Don't worry about the board," Silvio assured him. "The loan will be approved without discussion."

To make certain, Silvio spent the next hour on the phone, calling the other eight members of the board. Each had been handpicked by Silvio, years before, and moved onto the board in carefully orchestrated maneuvers. Each was aware that he owed his position to Silvio. But to put minds at ease, Silvio assured each member that, under the circumstances, the loan was legally proper.

In Lucian Hall's desperate quest for expansion capital he had made applications with two other banks of sufficient size to handle loans of that scope.

Silvio repeated his promise of collateral to cover those loans and conveyed to the individual members of the bank boards his wishes for prompt approval.

He then telephoned his private accountant in San Francisco and arranged the CD's, utilizing current receipts from border racetracks, Las Vegas, Reno, and from his double-blind construction firm, engaged in building more than sixteen hundred low-rent housing projects under auspices of U.S. Housing and Urban Development. Considerable money had been set aside for investment in a film, still six months away from production. That money also could be put to this short-term use.

By noon the traps were set. Lucian's own greed provided the bait.

With his calls completed, Silvio replaced the phone in his desk, locked the drawer, and drove to his office at the winery. By the time Emily Rogers returned from lunch, he had cleared the morning mail and was ready to dictate necessary correspondence. Fortunately there was little.

Problems had developed over the suspended shipments. Silvio spent another two hours on the phone, assuring distributors that the delay was only temporary.

He did not reach the poker parlor until a few minutes after six. Salvatore, always perceptive, greeted him with a measure of tolerant sympathy.

"You look as if you may have earned some of your money today," he said. "How about a good glass of wine? I have some I could recommend. Sebastiani, Mondavi, Mogen David . . ."

It was an old joke. Salvatore never tired of it. Silvio smiled and nodded agreement. "You are right, old friend. It has been a long day. And unfortunately it isn't over."

Salvatore set out a bottle of choice brandy. "I should have known. You are bringing me more work."

Silvio accepted the brandy and gestured a toast. "I am seeking advice."

Salvatore laughed. "Salvatore Messino at your service. *Con-*

sigliere of high finance. You can tell from my station in life that I have vast experience."

"Your talents are equal to this task," Silvio assured him. "Lucian Hall is so certain of success that he has forgotten caution. He is spread thin. He is robbing Peter to pay Paul. One major setback could topple his empire like a house of cards."

Salvatore looked at Silvio, his eyebrows raised in disbelief. "Are you certain? Lucian Hall? The financial wizard? The man on the cover of all the news magazines?"

Silvio nodded. "I now know his financial structure better than my own. At the moment he is riding high on his reputation. But some people are beginning to suspect, here and there. Today I set the trap. A simple push will send him tumbling into it."

"There may be a limit to simple misfortune," Salvatore said. "Even my ingenuity has been taxed . . ."

"This must be unexpected, devastating."

"We have been sufficiently imaginative, I think," Salvatore said. He raised his head and closed his eyes, as if searching for a mental list. "Sand in the crankcase of an eighty thousand dollar rig. Sugar in the gasoline supply of his trucking company. A freon leak in a storage freezer. Hundreds of thousands of dollars in meat destroyed. A sprinkler system malfunctions in a mattress factory. A three-million-dollar fire at the central warehouse of his grocery chain. An elevator cable accident in an office building—damage claims are still piling up from that one. Roaches in his bottling equipment." Salvatore shook his head, opened his eyes, and smiled. "It has been fun. But, Silvio, what can we do for an encore?"

Silvio had given the matter some thought. "There are two areas where he is most vulnerable. He recently purchased a large bakery chain—a venerable company with a long-standing reputation. He is badly underfinanced in that venture. If the bakery chain were in trouble, he would be forced to find considerable capital—and quickly."

Salvatore frowned in thought. Silvio waited until Salvatore's meditation had ended and his face had crinkled with humor.

"Sometimes I believe I have a genius for these diabolic pursuits," Salvatore said. "I have the answer. It would take a concerted effort.

A campaign. But a bakery catastrophe will be arranged. What is Lucian's other vulnerable area?"

"Accounting. He has scattered his transactions beyond the grasp of any auditing firm. He has, for instance, allocated ten to fifteen percent of the cash flow at a pharmaceutical subsidiary to nonexistent 'research and development.' Federal action to freeze those books —and those assets—at the right time will provide us with another tool."

"We will need specifics."

"I have them."

Salvatore studied Silvio for a moment. "I have one worry. You are pushing Lucian Hall into a corner. He is a dangerous man. He will retaliate with fury. There may be a simpler way. What about Lucian himself?"

Silvio sipped his brandy while he considered his reply. His reluctance to accept this simple solution was difficult to put into words.

"After all these years I would hate to have it come to that," he explained. "Certainly it would end the matter. But aside from the moral aspects, there would be other problems. He is paranoid. His home is a fortress. He moves in a bulletproofed car, accompanied by bodyguards. His office staff, his cleaning crew, his household servants, remain under constant security check. Reaching him would be difficult."

"But it remains an option."

"If necessary," Silvio said. "But I hope to withhold these drastic measures, if possible. You may hold the bakery and the pharmaceutical firm matters in readiness for the moment. I have some influence with two or three members of Lucian's board. Old favors. I may be able to give him some trouble there. Perhaps stop him."

He placed his brandy snifter on Salvatore's desk, crossed to the office door, and was preparing to say good night when he remembered.

"Lucian does need a diversion," he said. "You can start Dax on his long journey home."

CHAPTER 7

FOR the third time in an hour, Larry Gifford started the car and drove by the apartment. He was glad Rutgers had not moved. Gifford once had visited him, years ago. He was trying to recall the details.

He remembered that Rutgers had had a Colt .45 automatic for sale, and at the time Gifford had the crazy idea he would like to have a heavier automatic for rapid fire knock-down power in case he ever had to go up against a drug-crazed street punk. After seeing Rutgers's note on the dayroom bulletin board, he had phoned, gone to the apartment, inspected the gun, and over three beers, bought it for $165. Later Gifford had decided that the .45 was too much gun. He had sold it to a kid in R and I for $200.

After circling the block, he parked again and waited another twenty minutes on the dark street. During the two hours he had kept the apartment under surveillance, there had been no evidence of activity. He could see only a single light in the apartment. As he sat watching, he tried to remember the layout.

He vaguely retained the impression of four or five rooms sandwiched between an interior hall and an alley stairway.

Through discreet inquiries at the cop shop, he had learned that Rutgers now worked the second shift. He would not be off duty until eleven. Gifford also had confirmed the fact that Rutgers was still divorced from his third wife and lived alone.

Leaving his car parked in the shadows, Gifford crossed the street to a phone booth. He rang the apartment. There was no answer.

The call was a simple precaution. Sergeant Rutgers had the reputation of taking work home on occasion, even while on duty. A vice squad officer sometimes met interesting work.

Crossing the quiet street, Gifford entered the building. He stood for a moment, listening to loud voices in a ground floor apartment. Some woman was giving her man hell. Gaining a measure of confidence from the normalcy, Gifford walked softly up the stairs to the second floor. The hallway was empty. Gifford walked the length of the hall without slowing. As he passed Rutgers's door, he examined the lock arrangement.

To his surprise, there was only one lock—a simple five-pin deadbolt. Gifford had expected better—an Illinois duo, maybe, with three sets of pins that had to be picked simultaneously. Or a Medeco. Or a Miracle Magnetic.

Rutgers should know better.

Gifford stood motionless for a full minute, listening. He heard only the sounds of a television, the low murmur of voices, a toilet flush—all in other parts of the building. He heard no sound from the apartment itself. Gifford reached into the inside pocket of his coat and selected his tools.

The professional set of locksmith tools had been a gift, years ago, from a legendary thief who operated in the best homes of Beverly Hills, Malibu, and Bel Air. Eventually the thief met tragedy through his own expertise. He burgled his way right into the middle of a drug stakeout one night to the complete surprise of all concerned. A startled detective put a bullet through him. Gifford had taken the thief's lengthy confession as he lay dying, hours later in a hospital.

"You can have my stuff," the thief said. "Looks like I ain't gonna need it no more." Gifford had kept the gear, figuring that someday it might prove useful.

That day had now arrived.

Selecting a tension wrench of the correct size, Gifford carefully measured the picks with a practiced eye until he felt he had the right one.

Approaching the door cautiously, he inserted the tension wrench and used the pick to rake the pins. After five rakes—no more than three seconds—the tension wrench turned the deadbolt.

Before entering the apartment, Gifford placed an ordinary straight pin in the lock. If Sergeant Rutgers happened to drop by his apartment while on duty, his delay at the door would be enough for Gifford to scoot out the back.

Old cops are always learning new tricks.

Stepping inside, Gifford made a hurried survey of the apartment. The darkroom area had been expanded. Years ago when Gifford visited, the photographic gear had been stored in a bathroom. Now Rutgers had boarded up the kitchenette and converted it into a darkroom. The room was full of enlargers, developing tanks, print driers, and filing cabinets.

The apartment itself was a mess, with dirty clothes, empty beer bottles, full ashtrays, and TV dinner tins scattered in confusion. The bed was unmade and filthy.

After touring the apartment, Gifford concentrated on the kitchenette-darkroom. He methodically searched the filing cabinets.

The job did not take long. To his surprise, the filing system was neat and orderly. There was a large folder for each of Rutgers's wives, and another for each family member. Rutgers's famous whore-and-client photographs were arranged alphabetically under the prostitutes' working names. A few full-length portraits—some nude, some clothed—were included. Gifford could find no files for "Cavanaugh," "Gregory," or "Governor."

Nor was Herbie listed.

Using his penlight, Gifford searched the rest of the apartment. He hunted through books, under mattresses, in drawers, under drawers. He lifted the edges of the carpet and traversed the rooms. He searched the closets, the bathrooms.

He went back and spot-checked the negative files, the print files.

There did not seem to be a negative or print of Gregory Cavanaugh in the entire apartment.

Gifford looked at his watch.

He had thirty more minutes.

He went to the refrigerator, took out a beer, pulled the tab, and sat down in the living room to think.

He was certain that the negative was in the apartment, somewhere.

But where?

If Johnny Moretti were right as to its importance, Rutgers would not have entrusted the negative to anyone else.

Chances were that all the prints were made right here in this darkroom.

It was then that Gifford received his bolt of inspiration.

He rushed into the darkroom and turned on the enlarger.

The negative image of the famous photograph was reflected on the enameled white surface of the masking frame—and spilled past the masking frame, onto the surrounding tabletop.

Rutgers had not bothered to remove the film from the negative carrier of the enlarger—right where Gifford should have looked, first thing.

Dumb. Dumb.

His hands trembling, Gifford held the negative up to the light.

Johnny Moretti was right. The now-celebrated print had been made from less than a third of the negative.

Carefully, Gifford replaced the film in the enlarger.

With a felt tip pen he marked the height of the lens frame on its track. He then made four small dots on the table to mark the exact position of the masking easel.

Raising the enlarger until the entire negative was in frame on the easel, he carefully turned the focusing knob, bringing the new image into sharp detail.

The head and shoulders of a third person came into focus on Gregory's left.

Searching with his penlight, Gifford found a box of photographic paper. He sniffed at the chemicals until he determined which was the developer, the stop, the hypo. He turned off the enlarger, inserted a sheet of paper, and exposed it to the image. He plunged the paper into the developer.

Slowly, a much different photograph materialized in the solution.

Gifford waited until the image matured, then transferred it to the stop bath. Using tongs, he dropped it into the hypo to fix while he returned the enlarger and masking easel to their original positions and readjusted the focusing knob.

He switched on the light and studied the photograph.

Gregory's giant was clearly visible. The bastard was actually grinning. Gregory's right hand and wrist were jammed up almost to shoulder level.

With the full picture, the entire complexion of the situation changed. Gregory's expression became one of agony. His hand now seemed to be warding off Herbie's approach, instead of welcoming it.

Hurriedly, Gifford ran a stream of water over the photograph to wash off the hypo. There was no time to dry it properly. He carried it with him, wet.

Penlight in hand, he searched through the apartment, making certain he had left everything as he found it. He checked his watch.

Rutgers was off duty by now.

Carrying the empty beer can and the wet photograph, Gifford let himself out the front door.

He removed the straight pin from the lock and hurried down the steps. Without looking to the right or left, he walked rapidly to his car. He sat for a full minute to make certain he had not been observed.

He then drove straight to a pay phone and rang Silvio Moretti at the special number in Sonoma.

"I just scored," he said. "It's even better than Johnny thought."

"Good, good," Silvio said. He was silent for a moment. "You might wait a few days before we inform Johnny," he said. "There is something I must do first."

BOOK 4

"We are the robber barons of the twentieth century."

—Lucian Hall

CHAPTER 1

LUCIAN Hall could not contain his anger. He slammed the security report into a chair and paced his bedroom in mounting fury. Never before had his judgment been questioned by his board of directors. He had always taken whatever action he thought best, certain that the approval of his board would be a mere formality. He had built one of the nation's most dynamic conglomerates out of a staid, failing family business. He had selected his own board. He looked to them for expertise and advice—not opposition.

And now came this report from his security people. In private telephone conversations, two of his board members had expressed concern over his plan to finance further expansions. A plot was afoot to thwart action at the Monday board meeting.

Lucian picked up the bedside phone. He would be ready for them.

Punching the button that connected him with the home of his private secretary, he waited impatiently through the twenty seconds before she answered.

"Get Will Jenner up here."

"Tonight?" she asked doubtfully.

"Tonight. Have him come prepared to spend the weekend."

"Yes, sir." She no longer was surprised by late-night chores, even on a Saturday.

"Tell him to bring everything on the Moretti project, specifics on our assets, long- and short-term debt, payout, projections on revenue, tax structure vis-à-vis proposed acquisitions, anticipated effects on earnings."

"Yes, sir," she said. Security had confirmed that she always slept with a shorthand pad beside her.

"Fine. I'll send a car."

Lucian remained too agitated to return to bed with the remainder of his stack of reports.

The Moretti project was in trouble. He sensed it.

First Dax had committed a dumb, stupid breach of policy by putting a threat into words. If Silvio had taped the conversation, the mistake could be serious.

And now the Hampton Industries directors were showing the first signs of dissatisfaction. If the revolt grew to the point that the directors started looking into his recent activities, it could lead to a coup d'etat.

Lucian shed his pajamas and changed into slacks and a pullover. Jenner should arrive before midnight. They could then get to work, preparing for the board meeting.

He had labored too hard, too long, to be stopped now by a few nervous nellies.

Caution had been his father's mistake.

Frederick Hall had been too conservative, unable to see beyond the distillery he had built, its problems and profits. True, he had been a wealthy man by the standards of his day, with a huge mansion in San Francisco, a lavish summer home in Sonoma. He had survived Prohibition, thanks chiefly to a Canadian plant established years earlier. He survived the Depression. But the shortages of World War II had proved even more damaging. By the time he died, the family fortune was seriously eroded.

Within months of inheriting control, Lucian had begun his expansion, slowly at first, then more rapidly as the tax laws gave him the opportunity. Hall distillery acquired a competitor twice its size

—the venerable Hampton label. Lucian elected to use the name with the larger clout in the marketplace. The Hall monogram was retained for quality blends produced by Hampton—a device calculated to enhance the prestige of the chairman of the board.

Lucian early learned the value of financial leverage. In the early sixties he began his major expansions into other fields—a trucking firm that could deliver his merchandise cheaper, an insurance firm that could discount premiums, a grain company that could ship at a lower profit. Rapidly, his interlocking empire grew.

In the seventies expansion became his principal preoccupation. His accountants were among the first to discover that with proper manipulation the bulk of profits could be derived from tax credits. Lucian refined the art of the write-off, acquiring companies capable of showing huge book losses. In essence the government had helped Lucian Hall acquire even more wealth. His comptroller, Will Jenner, once explained it in simple terms to a puzzled board member:

"It's a sort of corporate food stamp program."

Soon the Hampton umbrella encompassed mobile home factories, fast food franchises, supermarket chains, parking garages, retail clothing outlets, office buildings, lumber mills, canneries, apartment houses.

It was a delicate balancing act. Less adept competitors became overextended, were trapped in short-term economic reversals, and went under. Lucian worked hundred-hour weeks, with no vacations, shuttling assets constantly to cover risks.

There was a price.

His wife Jana had been the first sacrifice.

"There's no use in my vegetating here," Jana said. "I would just as soon vegetate in Europe."

She was now installed in a villa on the coast of Spain. Her current trip had lasted fourteen months. She had lovers, many of them. Most were less than half her age. Lucian received reports almost daily.

And, God help him, he still loved her. He could not imagine life without her, no matter how rare her visits home.

Besides, he did not want the scandal of a divorce.

His portrait had been featured on the covers of *Time, Newsweek,*

Business Week, National Review—along with stories tracing his career. Thus far, he had managed to preserve the pretense of a happy family. No one knew that his daughter cried for days each time her name was linked with his. No one suspected that, by mutual consent, he had not communicated with his son in four years.

Time magazine had been the most snide, but every published story of his life repeated the canard that he had started his career as a bootlegger during Prohibition.

All through his professional life the story had persisted. Because of it his father had almost disowned him. His wife had never mingled in society, avoiding the certain slights and remarks. His daughter's friends never mentioned her father in her presence. His son treated him with contempt.

Silvio Moretti—and Silvio alone—was to blame.

Lucian's plan for the acquisition of Silvio's holdings went far beyond all financial considerations.

There would be deep, deep satisfaction in the payment of this old, long-overdue debt.

Will Jenner watched the girders of the Golden Gate Bridge drift by in the night. The Rolls-Royce Phantom VI purred along with regal confidence, weaving in and out of traffic. The chauffeur was alone up front, beyond the thick glass partition. The security man, Ivory, rode beside Jenner, grinning like a kid with a new toy.

"Way to go, huh?" he said.

Jenner nodded without expression, hoping to discourage Ivory. He did not succeed.

"You don't have to worry none about us getting ambushed," Ivory said. He pounded a fist against the door beside him. "This thing's lined with Kevlar, like they use in bullet-proof vests. Those windows are laminated plastic resin, with a layer of Lexgard. If somebody walked right up to the car and blasted away at us with a .44 magnum, we wouldn't have a thing to worry about."

Despite his irritation, Jenner was impressed. He had heard that Lucian Hall's personal car was a rolling tank. Ivory was full of facts.

"The fuel tank's wrapped in thirty-ply ballistic nylon. You could riddle the Michelin steel-belted radials on this thing with bullets and they'd still stay on the rims. And look here." He raised a narrow flap on the door beside him. "Gun ports. We can shoot back, and they can't shoot in." He pointed. "There's an Ingram .45 caliber machine pistol there between your legs, just in case you need it. Fully loaded. Set on cyclic. Thousand rounds a minute."

Jenner's legs jerked involuntarily. He was not comfortable around guns, or talk of guns. He glanced down. The machine pistol was in a leather holster, strapped to the seat. Jenner instinctively clutched his briefcase closer to his chest.

Ivory laughed. "There are three more of those little babies back here."

A phone buzzed. Ivory answered and began a conversation. Security seemed to be the topic. Jenner tuned out and watched the road as the big car left the main highway and began winding northward through Marin County.

In a way, he was pleased that he had been summoned to Lucian Hall's home for a weekend conference. Word would get around. His position with Hampton Industries would be enhanced. But he was worried. The detailed list of papers he had been asked to bring made plain what Lucian Hall wanted to discuss.

He would no doubt spend the weekend creating balance sheets to justify a dramatic increase in short-term debt—all for the Moretti acquisition. With projected earnings, high interest rates, and the current state of the economy, Jenner could not make such a recommendation.

Not unless Lucian Hall had more information. A good accountant develops a sensitivity to balance sheets; Jenner strongly suspected, and hoped, that he did not have the complete information on Hampton Industries.

The car slowed. A huge, well-lighted wrought-iron gate loomed ahead. The Rolls stopped. Ivory spoke softly into the phone. The gate opened.

"Smile," Ivory said. "You're on TV. That gate opens for no one who doesn't pass visual inspection."

For a short distance the road was lined with eucalyptus trees. Then the Rolls rounded a gentle curve and the house itself came into view.

In the glare of floodlights, the Hall mansion seemed enormous to

Jenner. Eight white pillars soared up three stories to support the roof over the portico. As they approached, Jenner could see that the windows of the house were covered with wrought-iron grill-work. The Rolls stopped before massive front doors.

"Don't get out yet," Ivory said.

"I beg your pardon?"

Ivory pointed. "Dobermans roam the grounds at night. They'd take your leg off. We'll wait for the handler."

Three black Dobermans trotted out of the gloom and into the glare of the portico. One stopped beneath the car window and bared his teeth at Jenner. A short, rotund man in white coveralls approached and called to the dogs. He soon had them leashed and seated in a row.

"Okay," Ivory said. "We can go in now."

Jenner stepped from the car, watching the dogs warily. They now seemed docile. The one that had bared his teeth looked away, as if embarrassed that he had almost taken a leg off the wrong person.

"I'll leave you here," Ivory said, opening the front door.

There was no butler. Instead, a uniformed guard waited at a reception desk, an incongruous affront to the ornate chandeliers, rich carpets, and dark wood paneling.

The guard looked at Jenner without expression.

"I'm William Jenner, of Hampton Industries," Jenner said with as much authority as he could muster. "Mr. Hall is expecting me."

"Yes, sir," the guard said. "Mr. Hall has been told of your arrival." He slid a sheet of paper across the desk. "If you'll just fill this out, sir."

Jenner glanced at the printed form. There were spaces for his name, time of arrival and departure, the name of the person he came to visit, the reason for his visit, and his signature.

He was tempted to hand the form back to the guard unmarked, but he did not want to make an issue of it in Lucian Hall's own home. He filled in the blanks with angry strokes that were scarcely legible.

"If it'll save time, I'll tell you. I'm not armed," he said.

"I know," the guard said. He glanced at an instrument on his desk. "I would say a half dozen keys and a small pocketknife in your left trouser pocket, about a dollar's worth of change in your right, and three or four pens in the breast pocket of your shirt." He pointed to the door and smiled. "Just like in an airport, but more accurate. If you'll just wait over there, sir, Mr. Hall himself will be with you in a moment."

Jenner waited more than twenty minutes before Lucian Hall came down the long, curving staircase. Jenner almost failed to recognize him in the casual clothing—gray slacks and a white pullover. It was the first time Jenner had seen him in other than a three-piece dark-blue pinstripe business suit.

"Will, glad you could come," Hall said. "I hope I've not inconvenienced you."

Jenner knew that Hall did not give a damn whether he was inconvenienced. "Not at all, sir," he lied. He had tickets to the Sunday 49ers game. He had promised to take his two sons.

"Good, good," Hall said. "I'll have your bag taken up. Then, if you're not too tired, we can get right to work."

He led Jenner into the library. Bookcases rose to the high ceiling. Small metal staircases gave access to a narrow balcony encircling the room. The books were in matched bindings. Hall did not allow him time to read titles.

"First, we'll want to examine our debt and payout structure," he said, gesturing Jenner toward the long library table. Jenner unlocked his briefcase and searched for the proper papers. Within thirty minutes of his arrival they were hard at work.

Hall amazed Jenner with his grasp of the Hampton financial structure. He could quote the most minute figures involving the smallest subsidiaries. Before long Jenner could see the pattern of what Hall was trying to do. He was shaving debits, bolstering assets, completely restructuring the Hampton financial picture. It was an amazing feat of legerdemain. Nothing was actually falsified, but the most damaging figures were hidden, tucked away amidst a sea of trivia. Each significant asset was spotlighted.

As an accountant with more than twenty years of experience, Jenner knew that most financial statements are works of inspired creativity, imbuing fact with a patina of misleading conclusions.

But before his eyes Lucian Hall created a masterpiece.

The Hampton structure contained a wealth of unconsolidated

finance subsidiaries. Each had borrowed heavily, with Hampton Industries providing the guarantee. The dummy subsidiary then purchased vague receivables from Hampton, for delivery at a future date. Hampton Industries got the cash, and the subsidiary got the debt, which did not show on the balance sheet.

Magic.

Other receivables had been sold to banks at a discount, without recourse. Under the rules of accounting the cash showed on the balance sheet, the debt did not. Leases on equipment and buildings had been converted to short-term, at higher cost, to minimize the obligations. Certain assets had been sold, with secret buy-back provisions, at a premium price.

Engrossed, Jenner caught the spirit of the game. He now knew that Hampton Industries was skating on thin ice. He helped Hall give that ice the appearance of bedrock.

They worked for more than three hours. Toward four in the morning, Lucian Hall leaned back in his chair and actually smiled at Jenner.

"I think that does it," he said. "Let's get some sleep, and go over it again this afternoon. Then you can work these figures into a new, concise statement."

"Yes, sir," Jenner said. "I'll get right on it, Monday morning."

Lucian Hall's smile faded. "You misunderstand, Will," he said. "This report must be ready for our directors Monday afternoon."

Awaiting arrival of two o'clock and the Hampton directors, Lucian Hall sat staring at the pictures on his desk. He never felt so alone, so abandoned, as on days when he did corporate battle.

There had been a time when his family was close, happy, loving. His son, daughter, and wife may have forgotten, but he had not. On his office desk he kept the pictures as proof—Beth as a high school senior, Nathan as a college freshman, Jana sailing a boat during their last vacation together.

The photographs were taken just before he lost contact with each. The following year, during rush week at Radcliffe, Beth was not pledged because word spread that her father was a rich bootlegger. Two months after Nathan's college yearbook portrait was made, he ran away to Paris to live with an artist, and Lucian learned for the first time that his son was a homosexual. A year after he and Jana made that vacation trip to the South Seas, she left for Europe with the first of her many gigolos.

He lived for her brief visits home. At forty-seven she was still the sexiest woman he had ever known. She denied him nothing, receiving his frantic ardor with calm amusement. The stories of her escapades, related in detail, fired his imagination, drove him to excesses that left him half out of his mind.

She was the one person in the world who could manipulate him. And she had made the most of her power.

Last night he had tried to phone her in Spain. She had not answered.

His daughter Beth had not spoken to him since the first time she failed to make the Social Register despite the impressive connections of her husband's family. He had never seen his two grandchildren.

According to detectives, Nathan was now living in Baja California with a teen-age actor of compatible sexual orientation.

Lucian sighed and rubbed his eyes. He had spent Sunday afternoon and most of the night going over the revised Hampton financial structure, making certain he had all the details committed to memory. He opened the folder and read the report once again.

Jenner's work was good. The printed statement captured the spirit of progress, expansion. Now Lucian must put it into words for the benefit of the board.

He pored over the report until his secretary alerted him. The directors had entered the building. He went into his private bath, washed his hands, and made certain that his appearance was impeccable. He then walked into the boardroom and welcomed the directors.

They had just returned from a lengthy lunch and were still jovial from cocktails and wine. Lucian moved among them, shaking hands, sharing in the banter and camaraderie. Then he escorted them to the conference table, his actions and gestures conveying the implication that, however reluctant he felt, they must get to work.

As he expected, the first portion of the meeting was routine: an examination of earnings, dividend prospects, revitalization of the trucking subsidiary, supply problems in paper products, impending legal action against a chemical plant over minor pollution. Lucian moved from item to item, guiding the directors through the discussions.

He introduced the subject of additional operating capital as if it were the least pressing part of the agenda. He merely mentioned, as if in passing, that applications for new short-term loans had been made and approved.

"The rates and payout appear satisfactory," he added. "Our finance men believe that in the light of the current money market, we were fortunate to secure the loans under these terms."

There was a moment of silence. As Lucian expected, it was broken by Talmadge Bennett, who had been the most vocal opponent of the move. As president of Wilkerson Insurance, Bennett controlled almost three percent of Hampton Industries' outstanding stock. Lucian felt certain that there was a touch of jealousy behind Bennett's stand. Bennett had been described in business publications as a financial genius, yet he always had remained in Lucian's shadow.

"Well, now, I don't know, Lucian," Bennett drawled. "The thinking over at my place is that with the current state of the economy, the prime rate and all, we should be thinking in terms of retrenchment, not expansion."

As Lucian expected, Ted Geering of Knox Air Freight spoke in support of Bennett, as if the discussion were impromptu. They did not know that Lucian had on his desk complete transcripts from hours of conversation between Geering and Bennett.

"I'm afraid I'll have to agree, Lucian," Geering said. "My people are worried about talk of recession, inflation, effects of trouble in the Middle East. Under the circumstances this looks risky to me."

"It may be a poor time to enter the wine industry," said Sylvester Griffith of Bancon. "Such a highly specialized, competitive industry. Are we prepared to take this on, Lucian?"

Griffith's remarks were unexpected. Security had not received the faintest hint of his thoughts on the subject. Lucian counted noses: three of his eight-member board already had voiced opposition. He fought an impulse to leap into a defense of his plan. He knew he must allow them to vent their feelings.

"This takes me by surprise," he lied. "Naturally, if the board considers this acquisition impractical, we will bow out immediately. At the moment nothing has gone beyond discussion—subject to your approval, of course. When the opportunity arose, I acted, assuming that I had the support of the entire board. If you do not concur . . ."

"Of course you have our support, Lucian," Bennett interrupted. "Ordinarily there would be no question in my mind about this. It just seems to me that now is a time for caution."

Geering and Griffith were nodding agreement. There was a murmur of discussion around the table. Lucian spoke quickly to regain the floor.

"Gentlemen, I think we have encountered a key issue. As I understand it, your concern is not so much the acquisition itself as our operating philosophy. From that standpoint, I think it merits our full attention." He turned to look at Bennett. "Tal, what is your principal objection?"

"Risk," Bennett said. "Plain and simple. We've got it soft and easy at the moment. But what if conditions reverse? How would we cover these short-term obligations?"

Lucian smiled. He wondered what Bennett would say if he knew some of the facts the balance sheet did not show. Or if he could see Lucian's own personal portfolio.

"That's all explained in the statement," Lucian said. "In fact, our projections for adverse circumstances perhaps overstate the case."

"I think not," Bennett said. "I see some very disturbing signs in the economy. I'm afraid we've become accustomed to abusing the principle of leverage. If we're not careful, we'll be caught short."

Lucian paused, as if in thought, waiting until he had the board's full attention.

"I agree with you to a certain extent, Tal," he said. "We do have some erratic signals for the future. But as I said a moment ago, we're faced with a policy decision. It goes beyond leverage, the state of the economy."

He rose from his chair, as if filled with a nervous energy that had to find outlet.

"I didn't build Hampton Industries blindly. I've always had a long-term plan. I studied history to learn exactly how the huge fortunes were made. I saw a pattern." Lucian enumerated the eras with his fingers. "First, the robber barons of the ninteenth century —Andrew Carnegie, John D. Rockefeller, and the exploiters, taking the raw materials out of the ground. Second, the developers, from J.P. Morgan through Henry Ford, growing up with an expanding economy. Third, in our own time, the rise of large corporations, conglomerates, still in an expanding economy. But as Tal has observed, there are signs this dynamic expansion is coming to an end. We have used up all the potential."

"Energy," Bennett said. "I've felt we should get into oil, coal, utilities . . ."

"No," Lucian said. The members of the board looked up at him in surprise. He softened his tone, as if in apology. "I happen to disagree, Tal. The future prospects of energy are *most* uncertain. Oil reserves are an unknown factor. Large portions of the world are still to be explored. Nuclear energy remains a question mark. Costs may be prohibitive. There may be sweeping discoveries next week in the use of our vast reserves of oil shale, coal. Wind turbines, solar energy from space, geothermal steam, tidal power—who knows in what direction energy will go?"

The board remained silent. Lucian turned to the easel behind him and uncovered the map Jenner had prepared.

"There is only one certainty," he said. "Land. Especially land utilized for a specific purpose. For instance, only a few areas exist in the world where precise soil conditions, climate, and altitude combine for the growing of superb wine grapes." He pointed to the map. "The portions shaded in red are the Moretti vineyards, the most choice areas of Sonoma, Mendocino, and Napa Counties. Today those vineyards are worth millions. Tomorrow they will be worth billions."

He gave the directors a few moments to study the map.

"The American market has only recently become acquainted with fine domestic wine. There is room for wide expansion in the market, with proper production, merchandising. Wine is still relatively cheap. The market will bear much higher prices on the product."

He paused for a moment, giving them time to absorb the thought.

"Tal is correct. Conglomerates to a large extent are only paper profits, created by opportunities in the tax laws. What value is there in worn-out factories? Twenty-year-old hotels? Fast-food chains, once the competition catches up? I'll tell you: They are worth the paper they can produce to raise money, and that value is declining every day."

He turned again to the map.

"We own several valuable pieces of land in this area at the moment—those shaded in blue. If you will notice in the report, those properties have appreciated to the extent that they are among our most valuable assets. This did not just happen. I guided, directed the acquisition. The land will not disappear. It is there to raise grapes, forests, grain, whatever. With control of this land we have a base for further acquisitions, using the principle of leverage as it has never been used before. A century ago the big fortunes were made in the railroads, coal, oil, steel. In this century the big fortunes will be made in the land itself. We are in the forefront of this new wave of acquisition. Gentlemen, *we* are the robber barons of the twentieth century."

Ten minutes later Lucian's on-going plan for the purchase of Moretti wineries was approved.

There were only three dissenting votes.

CHAPTER 2

JOHNNY never understood the thinking of attorneys who preferred to practice "office law." For him the opening day of a trial more than justified the many months of tedious preparation. Not even football compared for sheer excitement. Careers, issues, lives, were at stake.

As he had expected, the Fraser case attracted unusual attention.

By the time he arrived, the middle-aged groupies who doted on courtroom drama had already filled the choice seats. A half-dozen reporters crowded the small press table, apparently planning to sit through the proceedings instead of merely relying on after-the-fact interviews—the prevailing practice.

Fraser had told Johnny that he might be a few minutes late, but he and his wife were already waiting at the plaintiff's table.

Johnny noted with satisfaction that Fraser had followed his advice. Instead of the dark, imposing suits he usually wore, Fraser had chosen a soft gray flannel and conservative tie. Johnny had felt that a more subdued appearance would help to ease Fraser's dictatorial demeanor.

Mrs. Fraser seemed nervous and ill at ease. She smiled uncertainly at Johnny.

"I hope we're compatible with the decor," she said.

"Perfect," Johnny told her, taking her hand in greeting.

She was wearing a soft, matronly blue suit that complemented her still-petite attractiveness and graying hair. In many ways the antithesis of her husband, Mrs. Fraser seemed to possess considerable taste and restraint.

Johnny had spent more than six hours questioning her about Jennifer. He found her to be refreshingly open and highly intelligent. He suspected that twenty years of marriage to Herbert Fraser had destroyed much of her self-confidence.

"Jenny and her lawyers are coming in," Fraser said in a low voice. "Could we try to talk with her?"

"No," Johnny said without turning to look. "Be pleasant. Speak. But stay away from her."

Waiting until he heard the approaching footsteps, Johnny turned and greeted the defense team. Clifton Hayes, the self-styled Red-headed Wonder, nodded to Johnny and the Frasers. With the nod his tightly wound red curls danced like copper coils.

The defense also had done much sartorial preparation.

The last time Johnny had seen Fraser's daughter—in a small reception room at the church—she had been dressed in beads and a loose white robe. Her hair had been lifeless, unkempt, her face pale, sickly.

Today Jennifer wore a simple pale-yellow dress with a yoke collar that well displayed her tall, thin, aristocratic bearing. Her shoulder-length hair was well brushed and combed. She spoke to her parents, nodded to Johnny, and moved with poise and confidence to a chair Hayes was holding for her.

"She looks great," Fraser said.

"Score one for the defense," Johnny said.

A bailiff came to lean over Johnny and whisper. "Judge Parker would like to see counsel in his chambers."

Johnny and Red Hayes walked into the judge's chambers. Parker was seated behind his desk, scribbling on a legal-size document. He let his visitors stand for several seconds before he looked up, nodded, gestured for them to be seated, and returned to his scribbling. Johnny used the delay to study Judge Parker.

His round, deeply lined face was framed by a bald, sharply chiseled skull. He frowned through half-lens glasses, apparently displeased with the matter before him.

Johnny remembered Snow's last-minute warning: "He's abrupt and mean-tempered. Watch him."

Judge Parker finished his writing and looked up at Johnny. He massaged his lips before speaking.

"This is a highly unusual case you're bringing before me," he said.

Johnny could think of no answer to that. He remained silent.

"However, I see no complex issues involved," Parker continued. "We don't have a large number of witnesses. I'd like to move jury selection as rapidly as possible. I don't intend to tolerate bickering. I anticipate no more than two days of testimony, which would allow a half-day for final arguments and charge. We should be able to wrap it up this week. Does counsel have any quarrel with my timetable?"

Johnny glanced at the defense attorney, hoping Hayes would protest, but Hayes maintained his cool, aloof silence, leaving it to Johnny to antagonize the judge.

"We will be offering testimony from three psychiatrists, Your Honor," Johnny said. "I understand defense will call two psychiatrists. If their conclusions are in conflict, I can see how some time may be required for the issues to be resolved."

Judge Parker lowered his head and glowered at Johnny over the tops of his half-frames. "I do not intend to allow my court to become a debating arena for psychiatric issues. We will hear the testimony and allow the jury to decide."

Judge Parker's impatience may have impressed Hayes more than Johnny had suspected. Selection of the jury progressed rapidly—and well, in Johnny's opinion. He was attempting to place as many responsible parents on the jury as possible. Hayes used his challenges sparingly. Perhaps he knew—as did Johnny—that there were few young people waiting in the central jury room. As Johnny had anticipated, Hayes concentrated on obtaining a young jury.

Twice, in the interest of cooperation, Johnny compromised, accepting a twenty-two-year-old private secretary and a twenty-six-year-old truck driver. Both seemed reasonably mature.

By noon of the first day six jurors had been seated—two fathers, two mothers, and the two singles. After lunch Hayes began countering Johnny's strategy, using his challenges. Johnny rejected all potential jurors younger than thirty.

Shortly after two in the afternoon Judge Parker summoned counsel to the bench.

"At this rate we'll be all week just seating the jury," he said. "Let's speed it up."

"I don't know how we can," Hayes said.

"Nor I," Johnny said.

"Eventually you will have to enlarge your criteria to include intelligent jurors who might not possess your other ideal qualifications," the judge said. "I would just as soon you did it now as later."

Whether the judge's admonition had any effect on Hayes, Johnny did not know, but Hayes did not challenge the next mature woman, a mother of three, who was seated. Johnny accepted the next, a married but childless young accountant.

By four fifteen, they had seated ten jurors.

Judge Parker ignored the clock to obtain the last juror at twenty minutes after five.

That evening, exhausted, Johnny mixed a drink and pulled a chair out onto the fantail. His notes for his opening argument remained in his briefcase, untouched. He was too tired to think about it.

The sun cast long shadows across the bay, brilliantly illuminating the golden hills of Tiburon. The seabirds were gathering along the booms. Johnny was idly watching the sailboats when the phone rang behind him.

"I have an almanac," Christina said without preamble. "It lists the exact minute of sunset for each month, each day of the year, for every time zone. But it's complicated. You have to figure from the latitude and Greenwich Mean Time. How far did I miss it?"

"You are precisely on the mark. I've been watching it—alone."

"Not even Don Gato?"

"He came by a couple of days ago, stayed a few hours, and took off again. He said he missed you too."

Christina lowered her voice. "Wish I were there."

Johnny did not speak for a moment. "You could be."

The line was silent.

"I've been doing a lot of thinking," Christina said finally. "There's nothing I want more than to be with you. I know that. But I'm afraid. Before I met you, I had my head straight, perhaps for the first time in my life. I don't want to lose that."

"There's nothing to be afraid of," he told her. "We're simply two people who belong together. How could that go wrong?"

"I don't know. I just feel that it's . . . dangerous for me." Her voice trailed off.

Johnny turned and looked out the sliding glass doors. Into the silence he said, "The sun has left the hills across the bay. They're in a blue shadow. The birds are feeding. Two sailboats are steering south to get back into harbor before dark." He paused. "It's just about the exact time we reached here, that day . . ."

The line was still silent. Johnny waited.

Christina spoke hesitantly. "I've accumulated four weeks of vacation. The director has been after me to take some time off, before the busy season . . ."

Johnny found speech difficult. He had too much to say. Words were inadequate.

"Christina, please! Please come!"

Christina laughed. But there was a catch to her voice that let him know she was sharing his emotions.

"I thought I might take off for two or three weeks."

"Why not four?"

"I . . . just need enough time to be sure of myself . . . of us."

"When can I expect you?"

"Let me check with the director. We're between shows at the moment. It's a slack period. But we have a big traveling exhibition that will arrive in three weeks, and there'll be the uncrating and all that. Maybe Friday."

"Wonderful."

"And Johnny, the same restrictions apply," she said. "I don't want my parents to know I'm within a thousand miles of Sonoma."

"I hardly intended to place ads in the newspapers."

"I won't be interrupting your work, other plans . . . ?"

"Lord, no! Nothing, absolutely nothing is more important. I'm trying a tough case, but it should be over by the weekend."

He told her about the case, the problems. He led her into a description of her recent work, the success of her trip to Los Angeles.

They were about to hang up when Christina remembered.

"I meant to ask. Has your father made his decision on the winery?"

Johnny's hesitation was brief. "He's not selling."

"I'm so glad," Christina said. "I know you're not involved, directly. But I have this strong feeling that the Moretti winery ought to belong to the Morettis."

Johnny did not answer. There was no way to explain the situation.

And the fact that he no longer was uninvolved.

The courtroom was crowded. Every seat was filled, and thirty or forty spectators were standing at the back. Johnny recognized a number of attorneys who had drifted in to catch his opening argument.

For the first time, Fraser seemed apprehensive. As Johnny approached the plaintiffs' table, he rose to shake hands.

"I knew this would attract attention. But this is more than I bargained for. When we left home this morning, there were camera crews outside the gate! Isn't there some way to get into this building without running a gauntlet?"

"None that I've found," Johnny told him. "Just smile, ignore the questions, and walk right on by."

"I just want this to be over," Mrs. Fraser said.

"It'll move faster now," Johnny assured her. "The dull part is behind us."

"All rise," the bailiff said.

Judge Parker entered the room. As soon as he seated himself, he called for motions.

As Johnny expected, Hayes rose and called for dismissal.

"The charges are patently absurd," he said. "Miss Fraser is an adult under any definition of the law, free to pursue any religion she chooses, as guaranteed by the constitutions of the United States and the State of California. The law is clear, Your Honor."

Judge Parker did not hesitate. "Motion denied. The facts you cite are not challenged in the plea of the plaintiff. Rather, the plaintiff has raised other matters."

He called on Johnny to open.

"Thank you, Your Honor," Johnny said. He rose and crossed to stand by the end of the jury box. With calculation he chose his position to make the jurors turn toward him—and away from the bench. He paused for a moment, as if pondering what to say, giving the jury time to study him, to grow comfortable with him. As he spoke, he addressed each juror in turn, moving up and down the rail at the front of the box.

"We do not challenge the statement just made by the defense. Jennifer Fraser is of *legal* age. But ladies and gentlemen of the jury, you will hear evidence from qualified authority that she is not of *emotional* age, that she is highly susceptible to manipulation by others. The sole issue here is the question of the responsibility of loving parents when their child becomes a victim of her own weakness, when others take advantage of that weakness. The question of undue influence *is* a matter recognized under law. For instance, in marriage the injured party may have legal recourse for alienation of affections . . ."

"Objection!" Hayes said.

"Sustained," Judge Parker said. "Counsel please be advised that the court will instruct the jury on points of law. The counsel for the plaintiff will please confine his remarks to argument. Members of the jury will ignore the reference in their deliberations."

Johnny remained unruffled. He had made his point.

"Thank you, Your Honor," he said. He turned back to the members of the jury, allowing them to see the hint of a smile. "As the law has been defined for us by the *defense*, the constitutions of our nation and state guarantee us certain rights. But ladies and gentlemen of the jury, obviously the law is never black and white. If it were, we would not need courts, or juries. In this case it will be your duty to examine the gray area of law—as defined by the court. The sole issues here are undue influence and the continuing responsibilities of loving parents to protect their child."

He paused, allowing the jury time to absorb the argument. He lowered his voice slightly.

"We shall prove to your satisfaction that Miss Fraser did not pursue this religion of her own free will. You will hear witnesses describe how this emotionally susceptible young woman was manipulated by this organization—until she was temporarily dethroned of her reason."

Johnny turned and looked at Jennifer, giving the jurors time to study her. Flanked by Hayes and the church lawyers, she seemed pathetically frail. She wore no makeup. Under the stare of the whole courtroom she lost some of her composure. Nervously she bit her lip and glanced at her father.

Score one for the plaintiffs, Johnny thought.

He walked behind the Frasers so the jury could study her parents as he talked. "We shall demonstrate that the plaintiffs' only concern is that of a loving father and mother, concerned for their daughter, from whom they were estranged through calculated and persistent influence. We shall show that Mr. and Mrs. Fraser patiently exhausted every recourse in an effort to return their daughter to the happy, active, untroubled life she pursued before coming under the influence of this organization. We shall demonstrate that Mr. and Mrs. Fraser acted throughout from the concern, love, and compassion that would be expected of any parents whose child fell victim of such circumstances. It will be your responsibility to obtain for this young woman the emotional support and help she needs from her loving parents. You, the members of the jury, can accomplish this by carefully considering her plight, her capabilities, and the inherent responsibility of society and this court to respond to her best interests, which we shall show to be the guardianship of her concerned and able parents. Thank you."

He returned to his chair certain that he had made points with the jury.

Johnny called Dr. Samuel Saxe as the first witness, and through questioning, established Saxe's psychiatric credentials and the fact that under court auspices Saxe had subjected Jennifer to fifteen hours of psychiatric examination.

Under Johnny's detailed interrogation Saxe defined Jennifer's personality as immature, easily influenced. Dr. Saxe kept his steady, analytical gaze on Jennifer as he testified.

"She has no well defined self-image. Although she possesses an intelligence slightly above average, she lacks the self-confidence to state her own opinions. Invariably she makes references to the views of third parties as substitutes or reinforcement for her own."

Dr. Saxe remained unshaken under Hayes's cross-examination. In fact, he made a telling point when Hayes attempted to pin him down as to whether Jennifer was legally sane. Dr. Saxe's answer was immediate.

"As I'm sure you know, legal sanity is a legal definition, not a psychiatric term. It's unfortunate if this raises conflict between our professions. I am not qualified to discuss psychiatry in terms of law. I *am* qualified to give you the psychiatric answer to your question: Miss Fraser is emotionally immature to the point that she is totally dependent on others. Such individuals usually attach themselves to persons—or to institutions—as an emotional crutch."

But Hayes regained ground in the next question. "Could this excessive attachment be to the father?"

"In some instances," Saxe admitted.

Johnny had to wait until Hayes concluded his cross-examination before he could establish that Dr. Saxe did not believe Fraser was the subject of unusual attachment in Jennifer's case.

"How are we doing?" Fraser asked during the noon recess.

"This is the end of the first quarter," Johnny said. "We've scored a few points, and they've scored a few. We still have a long way to go."

Johnny's presentation progressed as planned. His other two psychiatrists bolstered Dr. Saxe's testimony, adding occasional fresh detail.

Johnny then called to the stand, in rapid succession, six young people who had been Jennifer's closest friends. Each testified that Jennifer's personality had changed abruptly, that she had "seemed like a different person" after falling under the influence of the church. Each described her former vivacious, outgoing nature, and each testified that the Jennifer they visited in the church dormitory was quiet, unresponsive, listless.

Herbert Fraser was the closing witness. Under Johnny's questioning he described his relentless efforts to find rapport with his daughter after she came under the influence of the church. He told in detail of the opposition he had received from the church officials. As Johnny expected, Fraser was a good witness. He remembered dates and specifics. The jurors seemed impressed.

But when Johnny rested his presentation on Wednesday, he cautioned the Frasers against undue optimism. "We're leading by a point or two," he said. "But it's now into the fourth quarter. And Hayes has the ball."

Snow had warned Johnny. Yet on Thursday morning he was surprised by the thoroughness of Hayes's counterattack. He had anticipated some shrewd Bible-thumping, but Hayes went further. One by one Hayes called the ministers and deacons of various fundamentalist churches to testify on the born-again aspects of religious conversion. Witness after witness—all well-dressed and impressive—used evangelical terms to describe how "accepting Jesus" altered a person's whole life. In their stated view Jennifer's dramatic change of personality—her total dedication to the church—was not unusual. In fact, it was to be expected.

There was little Johnny could do to counter Hayes's tactics. He could not risk alienating the jury by maligning the church. He could not delve into the differences among the denominations without seeming to question all religion.

But when the Reverend Mr. Jackson was called to the stand and gave a lengthy, emotional account of Jennifer's conversion to his church, Johnny applied pressure.

"How large is your congregation?"

Jackson was smooth, well-dressed, polished. "More than two thousand, counting those who permanently reside at our retreats."

"What type of people comprise your congregation?"

"Type?"

"Would you term it a good cross section of the community—doctors, lawyers, merchants . . . ?"

Jackson smiled at the jury. "Young people, mostly," he said. "More than seventy-five percent of our congregation are less than twenty-five years of age."

"What is your annual budget?"

Jackson opened his mouth to answer, but Hayes was on his feet. "Objection!"

Judge Parker summoned counsel to the bench.

"Where do you intend to go with this line of questioning?" he asked Johnny.

"Your Honor, the structure of the church, its relationship to the community are of importance if the jury is to make a decision as to Jennifer's best interests."

"And your objection?" the judge asked Hayes.

"The church is not on trial here, Your Honor. Its existence is protected by the Constitution, every concept of law."

Judge Parker frowned. He hesitated for a moment, fiddling with a scratch pad.

"Court will be in recess for fifteen minutes," he said.

Judge Parker retired to his chambers. When he returned, he did not elaborate on his decision.

"Objection sustained," he said.

The best Johnny could do in the remainder of his cross-examination was to extract from each of the religious leaders the admission that he himself led a normal life, retaining relationships with members of his family—even with those among his family, friends, and acquaintances who had not found Jesus.

Most of Johnny's own witnesses were returned to the stand. Hayes led them into testimony that, as far as they knew, Jennifer had never received religious instruction at home.

Then, on Fraser's return to the witness chair, Hayes sprang the trap. Despite Johnny's warnings, Fraser grew angry under Hayes's pointed questions and insinuations.

"I taught my daughter right from wrong," Fraser said. "She was taught moral values."

"But as a child, was she ever taken to church—exposed to any religious instruction?"

"Not . . . on a regular basis."

"At all?" Hayes demanded.

Fraser's voice was subdued. "No."

"Why not?"

"I felt she could receive adequate instruction in the home," Fraser said.

"From you?"

"From myself. From my wife."

"Do you believe in God, Mr. Fraser?"

"Objection!" Johnny said. "The personal beliefs of the witness are not at issue."

Judge Parker did not hesitate. "The objection is overruled," he said. "To the contrary, the plaintiff himself by instigating this legal action has raised the question of proper religious instruction. Exploration into the young woman's prior situation is a valid line of questioning. I will allow it. You may repeat the question."

But Johnny had bought Fraser time to phrase his answer carefully.

"I would *like* to believe," he said.

Hayes made his next question a statement. "But you do not."

"Let's say I don't know."

"Have you ever wondered about it?" Hayes asked quietly.

"Sometimes."

"But not very often?"

Fraser spoke to the jury, as Johnny had instructed him to do. "I have worked hard all of my life," he said. "I simply haven't had the time."

"You haven't had the time?" Hayes repeated, his voice heavy with sarcasm. "You have been too busy to wonder if you should establish a relationship with your Creator? To thank Him for all the material blessings He has bestowed upon you? And now you object, because your daughter has found spiritual peace?"

Fraser was losing control. He glanced at Johnny, then back at Hayes. "I don't know if there is a God," he said. "But I always figured that whether there is or not, there isn't a damned thing I could do about it."

A snicker came from the back of the courtroom. It triggered a ripple of amusement throughout the audience. Judge Parker rapped his gavel for order.

"No further questions," Hayes said.

When Fraser came back to the table, his face was tight with fury.

But Hayes had saved his best shot for last. Jennifer was called to the stand to describe her religious experience.

She spoke in a firm, strong voice. And each time she mentioned Jesus, or the church, she seemed to be making an evangelical ap-

peal direct to the jury. When Hayes ended the well-coached performance, he gave Johnny a self-satisfied smile as he returned to his
seat.

"No questions, Your Honor," Johnny said.

A ripple of surprise came from the legally oriented spectators at
the back of the room.

They knew—as did Johnny—that his refusal to cross-examine
Jennifer was a high-risk gamble.

In Johnny's office after evening recess, Snow disagreed violently
with Johnny's tactics. He insisted that Johnny should have broken
Jennifer on the stand, dramatically demonstrating her lack of emotional stability.

"I disagree," Johnny said. "Our basic contention is that the
church has used her as a pawn. We can hardly hope to win jury
sympathy by using the same tactics. We are asking society to do its
duty and protect this girl. We would be in a poor position to ask
this if *we* attacked her."

Reluctantly Snow backed down.

After closing arguments the following day, Judge Parker read his
charge to the jury.

Johnny listened carefully, trying to hear the instructions from the
viewpoint of a juror. Judge Parker gradually built to a final sen-
tence: "The jury must examine and decide on the alternatives of
leaving Jennifer Fraser in a Christian situation, or of returning her
to the atheistic parental environment in which she was reared."

The jurors received the case at two on Friday afternoon. They
were out less than an hour.

The nine-to-three split decision was to deny Fraser custody of his
daughter.

Fraser seemed to take the disappointment in stride. He walked
with Johnny to the parking lot, where they shook hands.

"We may win a reversal on appeal," Johnny said. "I'll have to
research it, but I think there were reversible errors—especially in
the charge to the jury. It almost amounted to an instructed verdict."

Fraser looked at him strangely.

"Johnny, we *will* win a reversal. That was understood."

He turned and stepped into his car. His chauffeur closed the
door.

Johnny walked to his own car, puzzling over the remark.

He went home exhausted. He knew he should be reeling from the worst defeat of his career, but he could not manage a single moment of sadness or disappointment.

In fact, he felt great.

Christina had left a message with his secretary. He was to meet her at San Francisco International at ten o'clock Saturday morning.

CHAPTER 3

GINA Moretti nervously paced the small living room, lamenting her weakness, wishing she had said no to Silvio. If she had not been feeling so discouraged at the moment he called, she might have handled it better, but her emotions were confused.

Though never expressed; her love for her father-in-law was total. His kindness, his supportive presence, had long provided her with a stability that Carlo's impulsiveness lacked. Increasingly, especially after the death of her own father, Gina had found herself turning to Silvio. She desperately wanted to see him, to share in his strength.

Nothing had worked out since her sudden move to Napa.

She had leased the furnished house and moved in a matter of hours. She had taken only bare essentials. She did not want additional burdens.

She had felt that the more quickly she acted, the less heartache there would be for everyone concerned.

But Ariana had absolutely refused to accept the fact that she had to leave her friends and activities and move to a new school. Taking

Little Bit had been out of the question. Each day Ariana left for school sniffling. She came home sniffling. At night Gina could hear her in her room, crying. She refused to eat.

And after eight days Ariana showed no sign of relenting.

Gina was emotionally exhausted. The separation had been a disaster.

One by one her women friends came, talked, and asked hesitantly if she could not forgive Carlo. To her mind there was nothing to forgive. She had thought—had been assured—that Carlo felt a certain way about her, about their life together. She simply had discovered that she had been wrong.

The friends asked what she planned to do.

For that Gina had no answer. She could not see beyond the first step—separation. The future would have to take care of itself. At the moment she was completely numb in mind and body. A healing process would have to occur before she could plan the rest of her life. She refused to talk to or have anything to do with Carlo.

She had felt that this isolation was essential to the healing process. Now she had regrets over her momentary weakness; Silvio's visit would end this vital solitude.

But she had not been able to say no to Silvio.

Although she had braced herself for his visit, she was not prepared for the emotional impact she felt as Silvio's familiar white Mercedes rolled to a stop in front of the house. She had intended to receive him calmly at the door, but when Silvio's sturdy, graceful figure started up the walk, she lost all composure. She burst out the front door and buried her face in his shoulder.

Silvio stood for a time with his arms around her, gently massaging her back.

"Ah, the pain we cause those we love, Gina," he said. He guided her toward the door. "Where's little Ariana?"

"School," Gina managed to say. She disengaged herself as they entered the door. "She . . . hasn't been adapting well to this."

"And you?"

"I'm . . . doing fine." It was the answer she gave by rote to friends.

Silvio did not reply. He stood looking at her.

Gina managed to smile. "All right. I'm in terrible shape and I know it. But Pop, I can't forgive Carlo for what he did. Please don't ask me."

"It is not my place to ask you," Silvio said. "Let us sit down and talk. These problems are as old as mankind. I have seen them in all forms, from generation to generation. They only seem new when they are happening to you."

"That doesn't make them easier."

"No. But they can be put into perspective."

He eased into the overstuffed armchair. Gina sat on the sofa, facing him.

"Pop, I'm *not* going back. I'm sorry. It's impossible. I don't want to talk about it. I know you're concerned about Carlo. I can't help it. That's the way I feel."

"Of course I am concerned about Carlo," Silvio said. "He's useless, right at a time when I need him most. But Gina, I am no less concerned about you. And little Ariana. What are you going to do here?"

"I don't know. I'm not worrying about it. Things have a way of working themselves out."

Silvio shook his head. "Nothing works itself out. We have to make our lives into what we want them to be."

"Pop, I can't forgive Carlo. Not ever," Gina said again.

"You don't *have* to forgive," Silvio said. "All you have to do is accept."

"Isn't that the same thing?"

"No. Not at all. An action can be unforgivable in itself. But we can understand—and accept—why it happened."

Gina sighed and wiped her nose with a tissue. "Carlo knew what he was doing—to himself, to me."

"Of course he did. But he didn't think of it as you think of it—and as he thinks of it now. Gina, I am going to ask you to remember what you felt in the first few hours after you learned."

Gina felt blood rise to her face. She did not answer.

"We are all subject to passions, because we are human. The more human we are, the more passion, and thank God for that. When someone we love does us an injustice, we react far more strongly—with thoughts of bodily injury, of repayment in kind, murder. Fortunately, we don't always act on those thoughts. But they are universal. Repay Carlo if you wish. Punish him. He deserves it. But do not—please do not—make Ariana and yourself pay for Carlo's mistakes."

"How could I possibly go back, after what he's done?"

Silvio leaned forward and placed a gentle hand on her cheek. "Gina, if you demand the life to which you are entitled, you can do no less. You are my daughter, just as much as Carlo is my son. I have been proud of you, always, just as I have been proud of Carlo."

Confused, overcome, Gina began to cry. Silvio waited patiently.

"Gina," he said, "don't you see that in your effort to punish Carlo, you are placing the biggest burden of punishment on yourself, and on Ariana?"

"I just don't understand how he could do it," she managed to say. "Such a cheap, tawdry thing! That waitress!"

Silvio smiled. "That in itself is indication of Carlo's casual attitude toward the affair. If he were seriously searching for substance, a competitor for you, he would have looked elsewhere."

Gina smoothed back her hair and wiped her eyes. "I just don't see how he could think that way."

"I know. But try. And I'll tell you something else. If you follow your natural inclinations, he will never treat his casual thoughts so casually again."

Gina remembered the house, the way life had been, with Ariana untroubled and happy.

The temptation was strong.

Yet . . .

"I don't see how I could go back," she said. "Life could never be the same. It just seems impossible."

"It might be easier than you suspect. Talk with Carlo. You will find him changed, and for the better. If he has to court you for a year, two years, a lifetime, it would be of benefit to you both. And Gina, this I promise you: Carlo never again will take you, or his marriage, for granted."

Gina did not know what to say. Silvio made matters seem so logical.

"I see now why they call you the old fox of Sonoma," she said, surprised at her own audacity.

Silvio smiled. Crinkles of amusement gathered at the corners of his eyes. "Is that what they say about me?"

Ariana sighted the Mercedes from two blocks away. She came running, breathless. She did not slow at the front door. Silvio barely had time to rise to his feet before she threw her arms around his waist, sobbing.

"Grandpop! Grandpop! Take me home with you! Please! Please! I hate it here!"

For a moment Silvio could not speak. He glanced at Gina. She was too upset to take charge.

Silvio sank back into his chair, still holding Ariana.

"We cannot always do what we want to do, child," he said. "You are old enough to understand that."

Gina put a hand on Ariana's head. "Ariana, please don't make things more difficult than they are." She hesitated and glanced at Silvio. "There is a possibility we may go home soon. We'll see."

Her voice broke. When she managed to speak again, it was to Silvio.

"Tell Carlo I will talk with him," she said.

CHAPTER 4

*F*ROM the moment Johnny met Christina at the airport, he could see the change in her. She was much more relaxed, almost carefree.

In the car, on their way to Sausalito, he put his arm around her and pulled her toward him. "You're looking absolutely terrific."

She snuggled against him. "The hard decisions are behind me. I'm feeling better about it."

"I hope you're referring to 'someone else.'"

Christina gave him an enigmatic glance. "In part. That wasn't easy. But it's done."

She laid her head back and closed her eyes.

Johnny kept glancing at her, savoring her beauty, her presence. "I hope this visit turns out to be permanent."

Christina did not open her eyes. But she smiled.

They spent the weekend in the houseboat, sunbathing, listening to records, moving from room to room. He suggested a trip out for dinner, but Christina did not seem inclined. He replenished his meager supply of food at a convenience store in Sausalito.

Early Monday Johnny shaved, showered, and crawled back into bed.

"I've been putting off mention of this," he said. "But I do have to make a token appearance at the office this morning."

Christina sighed. "I've only been here two days. And already the abandoned housewife syndrome."

"I would beg off," Johnny said. "But I lost an important case last week. Today I have to face my senior partners. And I have a hearing in court."

Christina snuggled against him. "Could I come watch your courtroom manner? I should know you better. I only know your bedside manner."

Johnny shook his head. "It's a corporate squabble over patent infringement. You'd be bored beyond belief. It even bores me. But if you'd like, you could drive me into town and use the car."

Christina considered, but declined. "There are about four thousand hours in your record collection I want to hear," she said.

The senior partners seemed to take the loss of the Fraser case philosophically. But Stone managed to sound a disturbing note.

"Have you discussed the appeal with Mr. Fraser?"

"Only in general terms," Johnny told him. "He's indicated he wishes to go all the way."

Stone nodded abstractedly. "Well, we'll want to put a lot of effort into it. Let's see what you can come up with."

The remark left Johnny irritated. The use of the plural and singular pronouns was loaded with meaning. "Let *us* see what *you* can come up with." Stone was re-establishing himself in the case—and in a supervisory capacity.

Johnny seethed. He did not intend to allow that to happen.

The patent infringement hearing was scheduled to begin at ten, but the judge delayed the opening and applied pressure for an out-of-court settlement. By eleven thirty Johnny, his client, and the opposition had agreed to agree. The judge delayed until two, allowing time for the minor differences to be resolved.

Johnny settled the case to his client's satisfaction—and missed lunch. He returned to the office at two thirty, intending to take care of the most urgent work, then leave early.

But the first item he saw on his desk was a call-back slip from Judge Wilkins.

Johnny was puzzled—and intrigued.

In the legal circles of northern California, Judge Wilkins was a legend—a relic of another era. During his many years in the lower courts he had never been reversed. His succinct, eloquently phrased decisions were cited in legal textbooks all over the nation. Judge Wilkins was widely considered the epitome of integrity, stature, dignity. Johnny could quote entire passages from his legal prose, but he had never met him. Judge Wilkins rarely attended social functions. He was seldom seen in public, except for his infrequent appearances on the bench in appellate court.

Johnny forgot about lunch. What could Judge Wilkins want with him?

He returned the call. After a progression of secretaries, Judge Wilkins came on the line.

"Giovanni Moretti? Young Moretti?"

The judge was shouting. Johnny assured him that he was speaking to Giovanni Moretti.

"I've been hearing good things about you, young man," the judge said, still shouting. "I thought we might have a talk."

"It would be my pleasure," Johnny said.

"Your father and I are old friends, you know. I've been keeping an eye on you. Your father has reason to be proud. You've made quite a start."

Johnny thanked him.

"Why don't you drop over by my rooms this evening? At the Pacific-Union. You know the Pacific-Union?"

Johnny assured him that he was familiar with the club. He refrained from adding that he was a member.

"We can have dinner. And talk. Seven all right?"

Johnny's hesitation was brief. He was certain Christina would understand. And he kept a dark suit in his office for emergencies. True, there was a matter of legal propriety, since Judge Wilkins might receive the Fraser case on appeal. But a certain decorum existed. Matters in litigation simply were never discussed by the principals involved.

Johnny told the judge he would be honored.

"Fine. I'll see you then."

Christina was still in a teasing mood. She pretended not to believe Johnny's excuse for working late.

"I should have known! Already I see a pattern developing. What
does she look like?"

Johnny groaned. "Well, to begin with, she's a he. And he's
bound to be knocking on the door of ninety. He's been one of my
idols ever since I went into law. I never thought I would ever have
an opportunity to meet the old gentleman, much less to break bread
with him privately. I just couldn't pass this up." He lowered his
voice. "I promise I'll make amends."

"That's better," Christina said. "Gives me something to think
about."

"I'll try not to be late."

Christina dropped her teasing tone. "Really, I don't mind. I
understand. Please don't cut your evening short on my account.
Just do me one favor."

"What?"

"Be thinking about those amends."

Johnny was confused for a moment by the small, emaciated man
who greeted him at the door. In the photographs that graced many
books in Johnny's private library, Judge Wilkins was portrayed as a
heavy-set, handsome man. Johnny was totally unprepared for the
judge's skeletal, birdlike appearance. But the handshake was firm,
and the judge walked with a confident stride as he escorted Johnny
into his living quarters.

"I hope you'll excuse my Spartan fare," he said. "After Mrs.
Wilkins passed away, I saw no purpose to keeping the house, when
my son could put it to good use."

They took facing chairs before the fireplace. While they awaited
the delivery of drinks from the club bar, Judge Wilkins made small
talk, studying Johnny with pale, filmed-over eyes.

He revealed his age as eighty-two. He seemed alert and quick-
witted. He talked briefly of Johnny's work, of his unusually fast
start in a highly competitive profession.

When the drinks came, the judge leaned back in his chair, put his feet up on the hassock, and relaxed. He smiled at Johnny.

"You remind me a great deal of your father, when he was your age," he said. "Silvio, you know, was perhaps even younger when I first knew him." He shook his head. "That was many, many years ago."

He turned to study the flames in the fireplace. He sat for a time without speaking. Johnny waited, somewhat puzzled, but curious. There was so much about his father that he did not know.

"In those years, Silvio possessed a tremendous capacity for work," the judge said. "I've never seen the like before or since. He would put in ten, twelve, fourteen hours on the docks—work that would leave most men limp. Then at night he would walk through the district, talking to people, learning, acquiring friendships, organizing the means to bring another of his friends over from the old country . . . always something afoot with Silvio."

Johnny was listening intently. The judge seemed to have forgotten he was there. For a time he gave himself completely to reminiscing.

"I was a young lawyer then, you know. Some of my clients were no better than they should be, as the expression goes. Silvio . . . performed some favors, helped me immeasurably, in circumstances that could have become a very bad situation indeed . . . an unfortunate matter that would have ruined me, ended my career. I was— am—eternally grateful to your father."

Crinkles of amusement came to the judge's pale, soft eyes. He glanced at Johnny, making certain he was listening.

"Silvio came to me for help in bringing his friends to this country. Afterward, he helped me to secure my first judicial post. He has helped me—and I have helped him—for almost six decades now. There is not a man in the world I trust more—or rely on more."

He reached out and put a frail hand on Johnny's arm.

"Your father is a most remarkable man. When I first knew him, he could not read or write. Did you know that? I think one reason he sought me out was that he knew I had the blessing of a good formal education." He explained that before the Wilkins family lost most of its inheritance in the Panic of 1907, a small portion had been set aside for the judge's education. Sobered by the new circumstances of his family, he dedicated himself to his studies. There was nothing else to depend upon, he told Johnny. He became a Rhodes scholar. Later he studied at the Sorbonne. "Silvio knew that I had been exposed to all the things he wished to acquire," he went on, and chuckled for a moment at the memory.

"Silvio, this big, practically illiterate man from the docks, dressed in rough, patched clothing, speaking broken English. He would come to me and ask, what books do I read to learn this? To learn that? He absorbed them like a desert soaking up rain. Each time we met, he would pull out a long list of words, asking me how each was pronounced. His progress was phenomenal. He forgot nothing. And later we talked—Lord, how we talked—sometimes the night through! Homer, Epictetus, Lucretius, Plato, Aristotle, Alexander, Constantine, on through Tolstoy, Dostoevsky, and the new giants of that day, Bertrand Russell, George Bernard Shaw . . ."

He glanced at Johnny and laughed.

"I prided myself as a scholar. I had been graduated with honors from the best universities. But I'll tell you one thing in confidence, Johnny Moretti. It took him ten years, but there was one man who became my equal, if not my better—a young, penniless Corsican named Silvio Moretti! He kept me on my toes!"

He fixed Johnny with a steady gaze.

"I tell you all this because I want you to understand that I know your father well, his sense of justice, his life. And why, if Silvio Moretti tells me he has an interest in the Herbert Fraser case, I listen. The matter will come before my bench on appeal. I have made certain of that. So tell me, young Giovanni Moretti. How do you feel about the case?"

Johnny hesitated, stunned, uncertain what to do. "Sir, should we be discussing it?"

Judge Wilkins shrugged. "I can think of more reasons to discuss the case than not to do so. We are two trained men, interested in justice. And to tell you the truth, I have grown impatient with convention. As I grow older, the more convinced I become that justice often needs a firm guiding hand. I followed the trial. I am familiar with the case. Tell me. Do you see honest grounds for reversal?"

Johnny frowned, as if in thought, to keep his confusion from showing. Many puzzling memories came flooding back—Silvio's quiet, persistent interest in the Fraser case; Fraser's innuendos and smug confidence every time the subject of appeal was mentioned.

The fix was in.

That, in essence, was what Judge Wilkins had just told him.

And Johnny knew that, for the first time, he was witnessing the exact way such things were done.

In any other circumstance, he would have put an end to the conversation and walked away.

But this was an unusual situation. He was talking to one of America's most revered jurists.

And he felt that Fraser *had* been treated unfairly in court. A reversal, however obtained, would be in the interest of justice.

Judge Wilkins was waiting for his answer.

"Yes, sir. There are a number of points that could merit reversal."

"What, specifically? I am interested in knowing what will be the main thrust of your appeal."

"Well, sir, I haven't yet received the transcript. I'll want to study it carefully . . ."

"Just the main points," Judge Wilkins said.

Johnny abandoned caution. In due time the judge would receive the completed appeal in writing. "Point one, the charge to the jury was in essence an instructed verdict. The judge's prejudices were evident and can be cited, word for word."

"Prejudices?"

"Yes, sir. In his charge the judge called Mr. Fraser an atheist. Mr. Fraser's testimony on the stand was that he considered himself an agnostic. Whatever the other merits of the case, I view the judge's charge as prejudicial."

"Yes," Judge Wilkins agreed. "That would make a strong basis for reversal. But there are various other aspects that might be considered."

Judge Wilkins talked for more than five minutes, citing phraseology, objections upheld or denied, minutiae of the trial Johnny had noticed only peripherally. In close examination of the transcript he probably would have found many of the items, but Judge Wilkins pinpointed several he might not have noticed.

"Of course, I will have to receive, and consider carefully, the arguments," Judge Wilkins concluded. He smiled. "But with such strong material, I would be surprised if you do not have solid grounds for a reversal on misapplication of law by the trial court."

Dinner was brought in from the club. They were served by a young waiter Johnny recognized from the club proper. He gathered from the easy rapport between the judge and waiter that the judge dined in his rooms nightly.

Under the influence of good wine, rich food, and engrossing conversation, Johnny momentarily ceased to worry about the impropriety of the visit.

"Tell me something," Judge Wilkins said as they sipped their brandy after dinner. "There was one point about the Fraser case that intrigued me. When you began your line of questioning about the financial structure of the church, did you know where you were going?"

Johnny saw no reason to hedge. Although most lawyers consider it axiomatic that an attorney should never ask a question in court unless he knows the answer, few can adhere rigidly to the belief. "No, sir," he said. "It was a fishing expedition."

Judge Wilkins laughed. "It would have been interesting to see what would have developed if Judge Parker had allowed you to continue." He toyed with his food for a moment. "I have it on good authority that the church is serving in effect as a holding company, retaining tax-free ownership of the various retreats while the value escalates."

Johnny was puzzled. "How would that work?"

"Through a loophole in the law," Judge Wilkins said. He smiled. "I have observed that whenever there is a loophole, someone will find it. A few years ago the special tax status of churches was used to obtain federal funds to build housing for the elderly, the infirm. Everyone profited—the church, the developer, the construction company, the lender, the insurance people. There was only one flaw. There was no one to live in the housing. Those subdivisions became instant ghost towns, at the expense of the taxpayer." He was silent for a moment. "In this instance the church assumes ownership, with the seller—a conglomerate—making the necessary arrangements. After several years, the church sells the land to another subsidiary of the same conglomerate, for a reasonable profit. In the meantime, the land has escalated in price and has been held in a tax-free status under all the financial relief accorded churches, and the conglomerate has had the use of the money."

Johnny wondered about Judge Wilkins's reasons for telling him this. Then he knew.

"If I had been able to develop that line of questioning, who would have been at the end of it?" he asked.

The corners of Judge Wilkins's eyes were crinkled with humor. "You've guessed," he said. "Lucian Hall."

After brandy, Judge Wilkins walked him to the door. "The next time you see Silvio, please give him a message. Tell him I said, 'I owe a cock to Asclepius.' Do you recognize the reference?"

Johnny nodded. "I believe I do, sir. Plato recorded those as the last words of Socrates. As he lay dying, Socrates suddenly remembered the debt and asked Crito if he would remember to repay it."

Judge Wilkins chuckled his delight. "I'm glad to know there still are young men who study the classics."

He held the door open for a moment. "Of course, as you no doubt have guessed, there is another, more personal meaning—one that only Silvio will understand."

On the drive home, as Johnny thought back over the long evening, he found two very disturbing facts. Silvio had used his friendship with the judge to interfere in the judicial process. And he had gone behind Johnny's back to intervene.

If his father wanted to misuse friendships, that was out of Johnny's purview. But he could not condone Silvio's meddling in his own relationship with Fraser and in his handling of the Fraser case—right or wrong.

Johnny pounded the steering wheel in frustration. It was the pattern he had seen repeated time and again.

There seemed to be no end to it.

He was nearly thirty, and still Silvio manipulated his life, just as he always had done.

By the time he reached the Golden Gate Bridge, he had arrived at a decision.

He intended to have it out with his father, once and for all.

Tomorrow, he would write Silvio a curt letter, citing chapter and verse.

From now on, Silvio could keep out of his affairs. He would make plain he meant exactly what he said.

His career was his own, win or lose.

He would no longer tolerate interference.

Christina quickly sensed Johnny's foul mood.

"I suspected from the beginning that I came at a bad time."

Johnny took her in his arms and held her. "There could *never* be a bad time, as far as you're concerned," he said. "I'm sorry. Today just went wrong. Mostly I'm irritated because these things all cropped up at once."

"Brace yourself. This may be another. Someone named Larry called from Los Angeles. You are to return his call. And he said to tell you to be careful."

"Damn," Johnny said. He glanced at his watch.

"Bad news?"

"Only that I've got to go back out for a few minutes." He hesitated, wondering how much to tell her. "This involves something that's very much in the news right now. I have to go to a public phone. This one may be tapped."

"*Now* you tell me!" Christina said. "After I've poured my heart out to you! Night after night!"

"I really don't think it's bugged," he told her. "But I have to humor people. They think I'm naive. I think they're paranoid. I settle on the side of caution."

"Can I go with you? I don't want to be left alone with a bugged phone."

They drove to a booth at the convenience store in Sausalito. Gifford answered on the first ring.

"I tried to reach you earlier. We scored. The negative—the photograph—is exactly what you thought it would be. In fact, the L.A.P.D. has made Gregory's giant. His name is Pete Rundel. He came out to Thousand Oaks as a free agent with the Dallas Cowboys a couple of years ago. He couldn't stand the two-a-days in training camp and didn't make the first cut. He moved into L.A., became a bartender here, a bouncer there. The L.A.P.D. suspected him in some strong-arm stuff. But no one ever made a case. Until now."

"He in custody?"

"Ten-four on that. And singing. I have some prints from the full negative. One is on its way to you, express. You'll get it in the morning. One went to Gregory by special messenger."

Johnny was confused.

"The search warrant has already been issued? And served?"

"I'm sorry," Gifford said. "I keep forgetting you're behind developments. I located the negative last night. Today I called your legal affiliates here to instigate the action. The rest went through like clockwork."

Johnny was elated, but he was also a bit disturbed. He had let things get badly out of hand.

"Thank God we drew a sympathetic judge," he said.

Gifford hesitated.

"No problem there," he said. "Your father took care of that. I thought you knew."

CHAPTER 5

GREGORY Cavanaugh sat with the photograph propped upright on his desk. The eight-by-ten glossy was grotesquely obscene. Gregory's long, thin, hairy legs were naked to his black socks. His trousers were a burlesque puddle across his shoes and bony ankles. The giant's bared teeth and hideous laugh were reminiscent of a still from a thirties mad-scientist monster movie.

"Beautiful," Gregory said. "Just fuckin' beautiful."

"We should make it your official photograph," Furman said. "It'd look great in the portrait gallery alongside Earl Warren, Ronald Reagan, Jerry Brown."

"We could put a caption on it," Hart said. " 'Where's the rest of me?' "

Gregory winced at Hart's wit. "Have all my steadfast friends from the Fourth Estate been summoned?"

"As many as your jubilant press secretary could round up on such short notice," Furman said. "I wish to God we had the news break on the story, but there was no way we could block developments in Los Angeles. I just talked to a source in the *Times* newsroom. There are some things you should know. Your giant has signed his statement. Internal Affairs at L.A.P.D. has announced a full investigation into the circumstances of your arrest. News bulletins are going out across the country about every fifteen minutes. And maybe it's all for the best. The groundwork is laid. One thing's for damned sure. Our illustrious governor will be the lead-off item in every P.M. newspaper, every early evening newscast . . ."

"I wish I were better prepared," Gregory said.

"Just wing it," Hart said. "Imagine you're back on the steps outside the L.A. police station. You're a natural, Greg. Speech writers only get in your way."

Unconvinced, Cavanaugh remained troubled. Finally he said, "There are some danger areas. Should I indicate I know who set the trap? I can't name names, of course. But there's a world of difference between some vague term such as 'my enemies' and 'the sponsors of my opponent' . . ."

Hart and Furman exchanged glances.

"Implication," Hart said. "That's the ticket."

Furman nodded. " 'Those who wish to turn me out of office. Those who oppose everything I wish to accomplish. Those who practice character assassination . . .' "

"Never 'opponent,' " Hart agreed. "And Greg, remember this!" He smiled grimly. "For purposes of publication you have no 'enemies.' Never, never admit you have enemies. Your opposition is merely a small, insignificant bunch of misguided assholes. And you treat them charitably because you're such a hell of a nice guy."

"All right," Gregory said. "I imply that I know more than I'm telling."

"That's the ticket," Hart said again.

"Are the copies of the photograph ready?" Gregory asked.

"We have fifty," Furman said. "Another fifty should arrive before you're through speaking."

Hart glanced at his watch. "It's time," he added. "Let's go revise the datelines on those news bulletins. In about thirty minutes they'll switch from Los Angeles to Sacramento."

To his surprise Gregory received warm applause as he entered the packed press room. He walked straight to the microphones, nodding his greetings to the senior reporters in the front rows.

"Thank you, thank you all," he said. He paused, giving the television cameramen time to adjust their minicams. He kept his face as solemn as the occasion demanded. He frowned, offering a trace of anger.

"In my last public statement, on the steps of the police station in Los Angeles, I promised the people of California that when the full facts of the charges against me were known, my position would be enhanced, not harmed. Today, I am prepared to make those facts known. At last I can tell you exactly what happened in Los Angeles International Airport."

He glanced at the reporters in the front row and waited for the pens to stop moving. Although most had tape recorders going as backup, a few were making hurried notes in order to file stories against deadlines.

"I entered the airport that afternoon with my friend and administrative aide, Tom Furman, who was en route to Washington on state business. Neil Hart, my chief of staff, was to meet me at the airport for our flight back to Sacramento . . ."

Gregory told the story in detail, describing his thoughtless panic in rushing to the lower floor, his confusion when, to his dismay, he found only strangers, not Neil Hart, in the restroom. He related the sordid acts that followed in a matter-of-fact tone, using plain words.

He had feared that there might be a few snickers, perhaps even outright laughter, over his helplessness, his humiliation. But his audience listened in empathetic silence.

"And that is exactly what happened," he concluded. "I will anticipate your first question: Why did I wait until now to tell my story? The answer is: Please consider my situation. I faced four witnesses whose accounts were in direct contradiction to my own. I had absolutely no supporting evidence. Now, thank God, I do. We were fortunate enough to secure the original negative of the photograph that received so much attention in the news media. As you will see, the uncropped photograph, made from the full negative, tells its own story."

Gregory signaled for the copies of the photograph to be distributed. He stepped back from the microphones and waited.

An excited murmur swept the room as the picture was examined. When the room quieted again, Gregory returned to the microphones.

"I understand that the, ah, gentleman on the left in the photograph has now been identified. He is in the custody of the Los Angeles Police Department."

Gregory stood for a moment, looking out over the room. He paused, then gave them his famous smile.

"I anticipated your first question," he said. "From here on you'll have to think up your own."

A dozen hands shot up. Gregory pointed to the blonde reporter from the *San Francisco Examiner.*

"Governor Cavanaugh, what action will be taken against the detectives who arrested you?"

"That is a matter for the Los Angeles Police Department," Gregory said. "I know nothing beyond the news accounts saying that an investigation will be made by the department's Internal Affairs Division. I do not feel I should comment, other than to say I will offer my full cooperation."

Gregory fielded several more questions. Then came the one he had been expecting.

"Governor Cavanaugh, obviously this was a well-planned attempt to end your political career," said the intent young man from the *Sacramento Bee.* "Do you know who instigated the effort?"

Gregory gave him the famous smile. He held it—and held it—as laughter slowly grew into a roar that filled the room.

The sound gradually died away. Gregory lowered his head, as if attempting to find the right phrase. When he looked up again, the room was hushed, expectant.

"Just let me say that there are those who consider character assassination a common political practice," he said. "Thank you."

He turned and walked rapidly toward the side door, surprised and gratified by the volume of applause. He stopped, turned, and nodded his thanks to a standing ovation, then walked abruptly from the room.

"Terrific," Furman said. "Couldn't have gone better."

"Greg, you were a full-blown triumph," Hart said. His eyes, alive with smug humor, cut toward Gregory, anticipating his reaction.

"Lord!" Gregory said, shaking his head in mock disgust at the atrocious pun.

But inside he felt great.

Everything was going to be all right again.

CHAPTER 6

ON the screen, Gregory Cavanaugh smiled, and held the smile until the sound track filled with laughter. The scene switched back to the anchorman, who made no effort to conceal his amusement.

"Turn it off," Lucian Hall said.

The screen went dark. Lucian glanced back at Dax. "What went wrong?" he asked.

"Everything," Dax said through his broken teeth, his wired jaw. He was still facing the blank television set high on the wall opposite his hospital bed. He held the remote control switch tightly in his bandaged hands.

Lucian avoided the pain of looking at Dax. A huge bandage on the right side of his head covered the wound left by the missing ear. His cast-encased legs were raised at odd angles, secured by lines and pulleys. His nose was smashed, his eyes blackened and swollen almost shut. The doctors had said that the shinbones, the kneecaps, the jaw, and the pelvis were broken. The ankles and some bones of the hands were shattered. There was only a slim chance that Dax would walk again. His three-day ride on a slow freight train must have been an indescribable agony. Dax had not been found until the boxcar was shunted into the Hampton Industries siding.

"I realize that you're in pain," Lucian said. "But I must know Silvio Moretti's exact words to you."

The reply came in grunts. "I told him. We would keep in touch. He said, don't bother. Unnecessary. Lucian will hear from me."

Lucian nodded. His question was answered. Dax himself was the message.

Moretti's audacity was beyond reason. His ingenious retaliations had been felt throughout Lucian's vast empire. Almost every hour brought new problems.

One of Lucian's most recent acquisitions—a century-old chain of bakeries—had been dealt a devastating setback. A rat had been baked into a loaf of bread. Unfortunately, the young couple who bought the loaf were activists. They promptly took the loaf to health authorities, who immediately issued an order closing the plant. The story received national attention. Overnight, sales throughout the chain had plummeted to less than ten percent of normal.

The setback was compounded by the fact that the bakery chain was underfunded. Lucian had spent a whole day assembling capital from here and there to ride out the loss.

Then a truckload of liquor had simply disappeared—along with the driver. A supermarket was robbed of Saturday receipts. A new office building, nearing completion, was found to be riddled with inferior concrete. The entire structure would have to be dismantled, at tremendous expense.

But most costly of all, the Hampton Industries computer network had suddenly gone haywire. Tapes of vital information—including customer accounts that could not be replaced—had been erased. Wrong information was rampant in the electronic files. Specialists were at a loss to explain malfunctioning on such a wide scale Business activity throughout several companies was virtually at a standstill. One savings and loan chain was so far behind in posting that all transactions had to be suspended. Rumors had been planted that the chain was in financial trouble. Customers were panicking.

Last night, Dax's chauffeur and bodyguard had walked out of the desert, weak, dehydrated, and near exhaustion. They could not give a satisfactory description of the men who left them, on foot, thirty-five miles into the Devil's Playground of San Bernardino County.

Now Silvio had somehow managed to extricate Gregory Cavanaugh from the carefully planned trap. Cavanaugh's popularity had not been dented. He still would be a leading contender for the U.S. Senate—at the expense of Lucian's own candidate.

Lucian needed a strong voice in Washington. He had plans. And Silvio's activities were placing Lucian's entire financial structure in jeopardy.

Rising from his chair, he leaned over the hospital bed. When he spoke, his voice was without emotion. But it conveyed the power of conviction.

"Dax, I can't give you much in the way of comfort, except to make this promise. Silvio Moretti will pay for what he has done to you—and to me. He will pay more than he ever imagined."

CHAPTER 7

BEFORE Gina had been home a full week, she realized that her life would never be the same again. Her anger lingered, smoldering beneath the surface. She tried. But her fury often was more than she could control.

There seemed to be no way she could regain her relaxed, comfortable relationship with Carlo. His customary self-confidence with her had vanished. He remained quiet, attentive, but wary. The change in him penetrated even Ariana's habitual self-preoccupation. Gina often noticed Ariana regarding her father as if he were a perfect stranger.

Gina was confused. In some ways she loved Carlo more than ever. He was trying. His boyish uncertainty in his new situation tugged at her heartstrings. At the same time she hated him for what he had done to her, to Ariana—to himself.

One sharp focus remained for her frustration: Her home, her life had been invaded by an outsider, a stranger. That she could not forgive nor forget.

Her rage kept building until one afternoon Gina knew that if she did not give vent to her anger, something would snap. Barely on the edge of control, she phoned Patsy Jean's apartment.

Patsy Jean answered on the second ring.

"This is Mrs. Carlo Moretti," Gina said. "I'm just calling to tell you that you had better get your fucking ass out of town, fast."

Gina had never used language like that in her life.

It was delicious.

"Now, hon, you got it all wrong," Patsy Jean said. "Me and Carlo aren't seeing each other any more. I thought you knew that."

"I don't care who you're seeing," Gina said. "I'm just telling you that if I catch you in Sonoma, I'm not responsible for what may happen."

"Hon, you don't have a thing to worry about," Patsy Jean said. "Me and Carlo were just fooling around. He loves you. He told me so, every time I saw him. There was *never* anything between us but sex. And we're not even doing that any more."

"Don't you use your filthy tongue to speak of my marriage!" Gina shouted.

Patsy Jean sighed. "Aw, hon, I'm sorry. I wish we could be friends. I really do. I just hate that it happened this way. I've always admired you. I really have. You're so pretty, and nice. And your little girl's just darlin'. Every time I'd see you, it'd make me feel so shitty, doing what I was doing."

"You should," Gina said. She was gripping the phone so hard her hand had begun to tremble. She had to reach up with the other hand to steady it. "And I'm telling you right now. If I ever catch you around my husband again, I'll kill you. So help me, I'll kill you."

The line remained silent for a moment.

"I guess if I was you, that's exactly the way I'd feel about it," Patsy Jean agreed. "And you're right. I really ought to get out of town. I've been thinking about going back to Lubbock. I've got me a job there anytime I want. That's one good thing about being a waitress, you know. You can always find a job. One's just about like another."

Gina felt more satisfaction from the call than from anything else she had done in days. The euphoria of her accomplishment lasted through the afternoon. When Carlo came home from the winery, she could not help but exult.

"I've got news for you," she told him. "Your blond whore is going back to Lubbock. You know why?"

Carlo did not answer. He waited with an odd, apprehensive grin.

"She's leaving because I called her up and told her that if she didn't get her ass out of town, I'd kill her."

Carlo stood speechless. His mouth opened, but no sound emerged.

Gina turned and headed toward the kitchen. She paused at the door.

"Dinner's almost ready," she said. "Why don't you fix us a drink, hon, while you're waitin'?"

CHAPTER 8

AT last, Johnny and his father were alone. The secretarial staff, his legal partners had long since left. The janitors had come and gone.

And now, facing his angry father, Johnny felt a small measure of triumph. For the first time in his life he seemed to have Silvio on the verge of losing his masterful self-control.

Silvio was taking care to pace his words. "Understand me, Johnny. George Wilkins and I were close friends thirty years before you were born. And just because I call on him for a favor, you think I am meddling in your affairs. It is ridiculous!"

Johnny kept his own voice unemotional, distant. "The Fraser case is mine to conduct as I see fit. When you circumvented my appeal, you compromised not only my handling of the case but also my career."

"Herbert Fraser is a valued business acquaintance," Silvio said. "He has done favors for me. I do not need your permission to return those favors."

Johnny let the silence hang. His surprise over Silvio's rare trip outside the Valley of the Moon had faded. He had not expected such a response to his letter. His anger over Silvio's curt, arrogant reply still rankled. The note now lay open on his desk:

I shall come to San Francisco to talk with you this evening. Please be in your office after five.

In keeping with Silvio's imperious way, there was no signature. Johnny leaned back at his desk and turned his swivel chair to face Silvio.

"It's the pattern, Pop," he explained. "That's what I find so disturbing. Am I to have no life of my own? You interfered with the Fraser case. You interfered with Gregory's case in L.A. . . . ."

"Johnny, I *had* to do that," Silvio interrupted. "Too much was at stake! You are still a babe in the woods. Matters like that can't be left to chance. That's stupid! You have to take hold, make things happen!"

"What you are saying is, my affairs are still your affairs."

"Johnny, I *sent* Fraser to you. I sent Gregory to you. I wanted them to have good representation. I felt you would give them that —and you did."

"But it wasn't good *enough*," Johnny said. "Is that why you thought you had to step in?"

Silvio looked at Johnny for a long moment. "All that is beside the point. I did not come here to debate the points of your childish letter."

Johnny did not respond. He sat staring at his father, waiting.

There was something different about Silvio. Johnny had never seen him so ill at ease. He rose from his chair and walked aimlessly around Johnny's office, examining the mementoes on the walls, the volumes in the bookcases. He stopped in front of the Jackson Pollock abstract and looked at it for a time, then turned slowly, head down, hesitant.

Johnny continued to wait while Silvio walked across the room to stand before him, feet spread.

"Johnny, I will ask you straight out. I demand an answer. Is Christina Borneman here, living with you?"

Johnny kept his eyes on his father, holding himself in until the initial wave of anger passed.

When he spoke, he kept emotion from his voice. "Pop, I really don't consider that any of your goddamned business."

Silvio took a step forward. He spoke with a deadly softness. "I am your father! Don't you talk to me like that! Of course it is my business. If I didn't have a reason, I wouldn't ask!"

Johnny turned Silvio's own technique on him—an oblique turn of phrase, an answer that in itself was a question.

"Why do you need to know?"

Silvio stood glaring at Johnny. Then, slowly, he nodded, as if making a concession.

"Last night Christina's mother called me. Christina has left Boston, presumably on an extended vacation, Margaret was told. No one at the museum knows where she is. Christina—and this you may not know—has been under a doctor's care. Margaret is very upset. Margaret is an old friend. I told her I would ask my son if he knew anything about Christina's whereabouts. It did not occur to me that my son would not give me a simple answer."

Johnny hesitated. Something was wrong. Why Christina's mother? Why not Emil Borneman? Why had Silvio driven to San Francisco—a trip he hated, almost never made—when a brief phone call would do?

He sensed that Silvio knew Christina was with him.

He would not box himself in by denying it, but he refused to be placed on the defensive.

"Look, Pop, Christina is twenty-six years old. She's an adult. Whatever she wants to do with her life, that's her business. Her relationship with her parents is her business. I don't see how I—or you—have any right to enter into it."

Silvio's eyes did not waver. "Is she here?"

Johnny did not want to lie, but he knew his stand was valid, and he was still trying to fathom Silvio's tactics. Whatever else, Silvio had always been fair.

"Pop, you put me in an impossible situation," he said. "If I did happen to know anything—and I'm not saying that I do—I couldn't betray Christina's confidence. Can't you see that?"

Silvio was watching Johnny's face carefully. "Then you do know. And I gather that she means a great deal to you. So I will ask you another question you may find insulting. But I have my reasons. What exactly are your intentions toward her?"

Johnny could no longer hold back his anger. He slammed the flat of his hand against his desk.

"What are you, the self-appointed moral guardian of Sonoma womanhood? Why Christina? You've never asked about any other woman I've been interested in. Does your patriarchal domain extend over your employees too? Is old Emil being doled out strong-arm protection for his daughter, instead of a raise?"

Silvio kept his voice low. "I said I have reasons for asking."

Johnny thought for a moment before replying. He certainly had no qualms about telling his father how he felt about Christina. For the last two weeks he had been bursting to tell the whole world.

"All right. I'll tell you. But for the moment, in confidence. I suppose I still have that."

"I give you my word."

"I love her. I've never felt this way about anyone before, in my whole life. I intend to marry her."

Silvio turned away. He crossed to the couch, where he stood for a time, his back to Johnny. When he spoke, his voice was low and trembling.

"You win, Johnny. I will negotiate. If you will tell me where she is, I will not tell her mother. I will not betray your confidence, Christina's confidence. I will only tell Margaret that you know, and that Christina is all right. Is that satisfactory?"

Above all else, Silvio could be trusted. Johnny did not wish Margaret to worry, to keep searching . . .

Johnny murmured agreement.

"Well?"

"She's here."

"In your houseboat?"

"Yes."

"You are lovers, then."

"What the shit is this?" Johnny shouted. Again he slammed his hand on his desk. "Do the Bornemans think I've taken advantage of their innocent daughter? Good Lord, Pop! This is the twentieth century! Wake up!"

Silvio circled Johnny's desk and walked to the window. He stood for a full minute without speaking. There was something in his stance that stopped Johnny from saying more.

"Oh, you know so much, Johnny," Silvio said. "But you really don't know anything." He turned from the window. Tears were coursing down his cheeks.

Johnny was stunned into silence.

Silvio walked toward him, arms outstretched, palms upward. "There is something I must tell you. I would rather take a knife and cut out my heart. But you have to know!"

He gestured helplessly with a hand. "You see, Margaret Borneman and I . . ."

His voice broke. Silvio took several deep breaths, and started again.

"Margaret and I . . . were once very good friends. We came together—briefly—at a time in our lives when we needed each other. We—I—made a mistake. It was a human error—an error of weakness. Perhaps it should have been rectified. But we could not bring ourselves to do it . . ."

With a rush the realization came to Johnny. In that one blinding instant he knew where Silvio's confession was headed. Many things clicked into place, things Johnny had seen but never really seen— Christina, a delicate beauty in that family of sturdy Germans, Emil Borneman's bumbling presence forever patiently tolerated by Silvio, even rewarded with position and the most lavish caretaker's home in the valley, Christina's mysterious trust fund from a distant relative that had seen her through college . . .

"Oh, my God!" Johnny said. His head was swimming. He felt faint. "Are you telling me . . . ?"

Silvio's face was filled with anguish. "You are my son," he said. "And Christina is my daughter."

With no knowledge of how he got there, Johnny suddenly was on his feet. Emotions swept through him too fast to assimilate. He felt as if he had been kicked in the stomach. He was having trouble breathing. He wanted to vomit. And when he tried to speak, his voice wouldn't work. Blinded by tears, he collided with the edge of his desk. Pain—deliciously diverting pain—shot up from his right knee.

Silvio attempted to guide him to a chair. Johnny fought him off and moved away.

At last he managed to shout out his anguish.

"How could you do this to me?"

Again Silvio gestured helplessly. "I hope that someday you will be able to forgive . . ."

Nauseated, Johnny sank into the chair behind his desk and looked at Silvio. "How could you?" he repeated. "How could you?"

Silvio wiped his face with a silk handkerchief. He walked to the couch and collapsed, leaning forward.

"If only I could make you understand how it was. At first it was only a baby on the way. An abstraction. Our decision was made on that basis. Later, as Christina grew up, into a marvelous person, I was so glad we did not have her destroyed. But now . . ."

"Who else knows?" Johnny demanded.

"No one!" Silvio said. "Absolutely no one! Margaret, me, and now, you. No one else even suspects."

"Mother?"

"She must never know!"

Johnny wiped his eyes with the heels of his hands. "How could you do this to Mom?"

"She has nothing to do with this! You leave her name out of it!"

"How can you say that?" Johnny demanded. "Of course she's involved. The insult was to her, when you went out playing around . . ."

"Shut up!" Silvio's dark eyes were furious. "Who are *you* to lecture *me* on morality? I've known your reputation—the greatest cocksman in San Francisco. A different girl every week . . ."

"That's not true . . ."

"Don't interrupt! You treat women so carelessly. You always have! Women are too easy for you . . ."

"I never got one pregnant," Johnny said.

Silvio nodded once, abruptly, as if conceding a point. "That probably speaks better of the women than it does of you. There are other ways of insulting womanhood. Let me tell you something, and you listen. I took the responsibility for my actions. I have seen to it that Christina never wanted for anything. I have paid Emil five times what he's worth, just so he could afford the standard of living I felt my daughter deserved. I made it possible for her to go to the college of her choice. And in all fairness I did the same for Sophia."

"Then there was no distant, dying aunt who left a bundle of money for their educations," Johnny said.

"There was an aunt," Silvio said. "And she was dying. But she had no money. I made an arrangement with her, in return for making her last few months more comfortable."

Johnny shook his head. He rubbed his face, trying to restore reality, sanity.

"Is there *anything* you can't arrange? Nothing you can't negotiate?" he asked Silvio. "Don't you get tired of playing God? How about doing something for me? Tell me how I can explain this to Christina."

Silvio had regained full control. He gave Johnny his poker stare. "Christina must never know."

On impulse, Johnny reached into the middle drawer of his desk, took out a folder, and slammed it on the desk between them. "I wasn't going to tell you this, but now I think I should. Christina and I were to be married a week from Saturday. Here are our blood tests, the license, reservations for our honeymoon at Tahoe. Then we were going to Europe for a couple of weeks . . ."

He raked the papers off the desk and onto the floor.

Silvio looked down at the folder. "I'm sorry," he said.

Suddenly Johnny was overwhelmed. Even the anger was gone, his fury dulled into a bone-dry ache. He had to be alone, to sort things out, to decide what to do . . .

"Get out," he said quietly to Silvio. "Just get out of my fucking life!"

Silvio looked at his son for a moment in silence. Then he nodded and turned toward the door. There he paused, his hand on the knob.

"There may be some good come of this, Johnny," he said. "Few men are brought by adverse circumstance to an understanding of who they are, forced to determine a purpose in life. It's painful, I know. It happened to me very early. I suspect it may now be happening to you."

"Good God, Pop! Spare me your lectures!"

Silvio remained in the doorway for a moment.

"I have just seen the first signs that you may be growing up," he said. "Despite all else, I am pleased by that."

Silvio left, closing the door softly behind him.

Johnny lowered his head onto the desk and wept, his shoulders heaving with great, wracking sobs.

He stayed drunk for five days. Most of that time he did not know where he was. Nor did he care. He went from bar to bar, met strange people, talked too much, and encountered unfamiliar beds. Twice someone took him home. He refused to get out of the car.

He was not yet ready to face Christina.

Early in the evening on the fifth day he awoke in a motel on Lombard. He could not remember how he got there. He staggered into the bathroom. After thirty minutes of nausea and vomiting, he went back to the rumpled bed. For more than an hour he stared at the ceiling, trying to decide what to do.

He could not tell Christina. The full truth would be devastating, perhaps tragic. He knew Christina's mind, her way of thinking. A new identity, a new father, a new family. Incest . . .

It was too much.

She simply would not be able to handle it.

There was only one thing to do. He had to face her—and lie.

For her sake, the lie had to be convincing.

Sick in mind and body, Johnny at last returned to the houseboat. He had not shaved, showered, or changed clothes for days. He was exhausted. He had fallen, somewhere, tearing the knees out of his suit. The edges of the holes were caked with dried blood from his scraped skin. His tie was gone, his shirt flapped open on his chest. He vaguely remembered that a woman in a Sausalito bar had fallen against him, ripping the buttons away.

As he opened the sliding glass door, Christina's hands flew to her mouth. "Johnny! What happened?"

He peeled off his coat and threw it into a corner. "Nothing," he said. "Nothing happened. I'm fine. Sometimes I like to drink a little."

He walked past her, heading upstairs toward a bedroom, a shower. He ripped off his shirt as he went.

Christina followed, hesitant, uncertain, her eyes wide. She reached out a hand but stopped short of touching him.

"I've been frantic," she said. "I didn't know what to do. Your office kept calling. I've never been so frightened in my life. Finally I called your father . . ."

Johnny turned to look at her. "And what did he have to say?"

Her answer was hesitant. "He told me not to worry, that you . . . had just received a terrible disappointment. And he said . . ."

"Yes?"

"He said that you were strong, that you would get over it."

Johnny laughed. Trust Silvio to include marching orders.

"What did he mean? What disappointment?" Christina asked.

Johnny could not think of an answer. He pulled his T-shirt over his head and threw it in the general direction of the clothes hamper. He started back down the stairs toward the living room with the intention of pouring a drink. Christina blocked his way.

"It's off, isn't it?"

He managed to meet her eyes. There was no use in prolonging the ordeal.

"It's off," he said.

She did not speak. Her face lost color. She did not move.

"Why?" she asked after a long silence. "I think you owe me that."

"It's just over," he said. "What you've heard about me is true. I love 'em and leave 'em. We've had our fun. Things just got too serious. I got to thinking about marriage—its limitations. I began to feel trapped. So I took off, did a little contemplative drinking. That's all there is to it. Please let me go get a drink."

Christina moved to one side. He went down to the bar, poured some bourbon over ice, and downed it. He fixed another and returned to the bedroom. Christina was sitting on the bed. She remained pale, but she was unexpectedly calm.

"I know you're lying," she said. "No one, not even the son-of-a-bitch you're trying to make me think you are, could change so completely, so fast. Something happened."

"Maybe you never knew me."

Christina pointed to the bed. "I remember what happened here. Can you look me in the eye right now and tell me we didn't have something beyond anything else you've ever known?"

He shrugged. "Okay. So you're a terrific piece of ass. Are we going to make a big deal out of it?"

She came up from the bed and slapped him, hard. Some of his

drink sloshed out onto the rug. He made no effort to defend himself.

Christina did not follow through. She backed away slowly, then fled into the bathroom and slammed the door. In a moment he heard the sounds of retching.

He went back to the bar, poured himself another drink. Then he went back up to the southwest bedroom, taking a bottle with him. It was a long wait. The sun set, the room darkened, and still he waited, drinking steadily, his emotions suspended.

At last she came into the room and flicked on the light. He squinted against the glare. She was dressed and carrying her bags. She put them on the floor by the door. Then she faced him.

"I'll survive this, because I've got to," she said. "In time I may even get over you. But there is one thing I must know. Why? Not knowing that is what may drive me crazy."

He tried to speak. His mouth would not work right. He tried again.

"I told you. The thought of marriage just began to blow my mind. The responsibility and all. The limitations. I felt trapped."

"I don't believe that. You could have chickened out before we got the license, the blood tests. I saw your eyes that day. I remember how happy you were. Your confidence in us. No one could fake that."

He shrugged. "Things build up in a man."

She studied him for a moment. "No. I can't buy that. You are your father's son. Cowardice is not your nature. I could no more expect it of you than of Silvio. Something changed your mind. What was it?"

"I came to my senses," he said. "I'm having too much fun, too good a life, to give it up."

She ignored his answer.

"I've been in that bathroom for three hours, trying to think what you could have learned about me that would have made you do this. There's nothing—not a thing—that I know of in my past that could make that much difference. You knew I've had—loved—other men. And I've made mistakes. But there's nothing in my past I couldn't share with you. If there's anything you want to know about me, just ask. I'll tell you."

"I really don't care how many men you've fucked," he said.

Her body jerked as if he had struck her.

And the reaction triggered something within him. For a moment he had trouble breathing. He fought back the sobs, but they turned into loud gasping sounds. As quick as they came, he had them under control.

But the damage was done.

Christina was staring at him with new understanding.

"Please don't lie to me anymore," she said. "You don't have to talk. Just nod yes or no. Is it something I've done?"

He shook his head no.

"Is there anything I can do about it?"

He shook his head no.

Christina came across the room and knelt down in front of him. She took his hands.

"You still love me," she said, making it more a statement than a question.

He closed his eyes and nodded yes.

She got up and walked back to the door. "You can't imagine the thoughts that have gone through my head in the last three hours. You have some pills in the bathroom—Demerol, something. I almost took them. I held your razor for an hour or more. I wanted to cut my wrists. But I sensed somehow, all along, that you were trying to protect me from something. What is it? Silvio said you had received a disappointment. What does it have to do with me?"

Johnny refused to answer.

She started crying then. "Johnny, there's nothing we couldn't face together."

He lay helplessly while she wept for several minutes.

Then a new thought came to her.

"Is it something about you?"

He did not respond, hoping she would find her way into a satisfactory explanation, but she forced an answer.

"Have you learned that you have some terrible disease, something horrible—leukemia, cancer?"

He shook his head. He could take no more. "Christina, please quit torturing me. Quit torturing yourself. There's nothing anybody can do."

She stood for a time, staring at him.

"All right," she said. "You won't tell me."

She went to the door and picked up the bags. "I have a taxi waiting."

He tried to get up to help her.

"You stay put," she said. "You're too drunk to be of any use to anybody. I'll manage."

At the door she turned and looked back.

"I hope you'll find a way to tell me," she said. "Not knowing. That's what may destroy me."

Then she was gone. Johnny waited until he heard her footsteps fade on the pier.

He turned and buried his face in the pillows.

He remained at home as long as he could—almost three hours—but it was no use.

Every room, every chair, every corner was filled with her presence. His home no longer was a refuge; it was now a repository of memories too painful to endure.

Toward midnight he put out some cat food, in case Don Gato returned, and left the house. He slipped behind the wheel of his Porsche and started driving.

He did not know where he was headed or what he was going to do.

Furthermore, he no longer cared.

CHAPTER 9

A few minutes after midnight, Carlo awoke with a strong sense of alarm. The house was silent. He lay for a time listening, certain that some unusual, loud sound had brought him from the depths of sleep.

The television set emitted static in the den. Gina had watched a late movie before coming to bed. She must have left the set turned on. Beside him he could hear her relaxed, steady breathing. From the kitchen came the soft purr of the refrigerator. There were no sounds from the road.

Carlo tried to convince himself he had been awakened by a disturbing dream. He reasoned that if any prowler were near the house, Ariana's dog would be barking his fool head off.

Feisty was small, even for a terrier, but he had awakened the whole household last fall when a carload of teen-agers had tried to spray-paint slogans on the stables.

Carlo was drifting back toward sleep when he heard the unmistakable sounds of the horses moving nervously in their stalls beyond the feedlot.

He slid his legs out of bed. He was pulling on a pair of jeans when he smelled the gasoline.

He knew instantly what was happening.

"Gina!" he yelled. "Get up! Fire!"

As he said the words, the night exploded into flames. He felt the floor beneath him slam upward as if hit by a giant hammer. He then was on his knees, groping. Foot-long fingers of flame were shooting up through broken planks in the floor. He crawled to the bedroom door. The knob was hot. He yanked the door open. The hallway was alive with flames.

Gina screamed from behind him. "Ariana!"

The room was filling with black, choking smoke. Carlo no longer could see Gina. He knew they had only seconds to get out of the house.

Confused, groping, he bumped into the big wing chair by the bed. He reached down, grasped it by the arms, raised it over his head, and threw it in the direction of the windows. Despite the roar of the flames, he heard the glass shatter.

Better oriented now, he crawled toward the bed. He felt Gina's leg brush his arm. He grabbed her, picked her up in a shoulder carry, and moved toward the windows.

He had no trouble finding the hole the chair had made. Air gusted through it in a gale, feeding the flames. Carlo put one foot on the windowsill and leaped out into the night. He landed, fell, and scrambled to his feet, still holding Gina.

She screamed in his arms as he ran away from the flames.

"Ariana! Ariana!"

Carlo stumbled. Then he was on the lawn, his head on the cool grass, fighting to get air into his lungs.

"Ariana!" Gina said beneath him. She struggled to get to her feet.

"Stay put," Carlo managed to gasp. "I'll get her."

The house was now a pyre, lighting the surrounding trees with unnatural brilliance.

He ran around toward the back. Ariana's corner room was not yet totally consumed by flame, but Carlo could not see how anyone could still be alive inside that inferno.

Still fighting for breath with half-sobs of fear, Carlo ran to his station wagon. He used the spare key under the mat to get it started. Jumping the curb, he drove across the lawn toward the north side of the house. He stopped directly under the windows to Ariana's room.

Reaching behind him, into the flatbed, he grabbed a corner of the tarpaulin kept there to haul oats and other grain for Little Bit. Wrapping the heavy canvas around him, he slid out the right-hand door. He used the front bumper as a step to climb onto the hood.

He could see nothing inside Ariana's room.

Using the palms of his hands, he punched at a screen until he had made a hole large enough to reach the hook. He tore the screen away and knocked out the window frame, then jumped into the room, falling to the floor on hands and knees.

The roar of the fire was deafening. Smoke was so thick he could not see. Groping, he found Ariana's bed.

She was not in it.

Swinging his hands in wide arcs on the floor, he found her by the door. He picked her up, ran across the room, and jumped through the window. His leap took him completely across the top of the station wagon. He fell heavily to the ground beyond, holding Ariana at arm's length, landing on his back and right shoulder.

Crawling, gasping for air, he dragged Ariana away from the fire.

Gina came running toward them. Carlo almost did not recognize her.

She was covered with black blotches. With mounting horror Carlo recognized the huge dark patches on her as charred skin. Strips of her flesh and nightgown hung loose. Most of her hair was gone.

He looked down at Ariana. She lay on the ground unmoving, lifeless.

"She's not breathing!" Gina said.

Carlo knelt over Ariana and found her mouth with his own. With a hand over her nose, he rhythmically blew air into her lungs.

"She still has a pulse," Gina said beside him. "Oh, Jesus! Blessed Mary! Please let her live!"

How long they worked over Ariana, Carlo never knew. He continued to blow air into her lungs. In tempo Gina forced it out by pressing on Ariana's chest. They worked silently. But their brief, frightened exchanges of glances spoke volumes.

At last Ariana stirred. She coughed and began fighting for breath. Then she was breathing on her own.

"She's going to be all right," Carlo said, as much to himself as to Gina.

The house was now totally engulfed in flame. Carlo reached for Gina's hand. They watched the roof collapse. A tower of sparks climbed into the night sky.

"You're burned!" Gina said, looking at his hand.

For a moment Carlo could not speak. He knew he would never forget that moment. Gina horribly burned—and worrying about him.

"I've got to get help," he said.

The station wagon was on fire. Carlo trotted across the lawn to Gina's car in the drive, thinking he might be able to jump the ignition and get it started.

He had just reached the car when he heard Gina yell.

"Carlo! The stables! Little Bit!"

Carlo turned. Sparks from the house were drifting toward the stables. The shingled roof had caught fire.

He ran back across the lawn to the feedlot. He threw open the gate and unlatched the stalls—first Little Bit, then the five quarter horses.

They thundered out into the darkness, away from the blazing buildings.

Carlo backed away to a corner of the corral and sank to the ground, exhausted. The light from the burning stables reached higher into the night.

He leaned against the corner post until he had regained his breath. He heard distant sirens.

Slowly he walked back to Gina and Ariana.

The sirens were growing louder. For a moment he saw his family through the eyes of the approaching firemen.

His jeans were in tatters. But they were the only article of clothing his family possessed. Even Gina's nightgown, Ariana's pajamas were gone. There was nothing left to cover them.

Gina was still kneeling beside Ariana. "She's breathing all right now," she said. "But she's still unconscious."

Carlo did not answer. Brain damage from lack of oxygen might be the least of her injuries. Most of her body seemed to be badly burned. Carlo knew that with burns beyond 50 or 60 percent of body surface, chances for her recovery were marginal. Infection, accumulation of bodily wastes, shock, suffering . . .

He knelt down beside Gina and took his daughter's small hand. A cold, silent rage began to build within him.

Lucian Hall would pay for what he had done to the family of Carlo Moretti.

He would pay with his fucking life.

BOOK
5

"Believe. Obey. Work."

Silvio Moretti's creed

CHAPTER 1

SILVIO stood patiently in the hallway of the hospital, waiting for the doctor to complete the examination.

From the moment Carlo phoned, Anna had been Silvio's chief concern. She had started dressing immediately. He was unable to talk her out of going to the hospital.

When she collapsed after seeing Ariana, Silvio was not surprised. She was not strong enough for the emotional shock. Anna had spent her life suffering for others. The strain of not being able to take little Ariana's pain as her own had been too much for her heart to bear.

Moving to one side of the hallway, Silvio watched the bustle of early-morning hospital traffic. The sharp antiseptic smells, the clatter of breakfast trays, the busy efficiency of the staff were unfamiliar. Silvio had never spent a day of his life in a hospital. His few visits to see others had been brief.

The door to Intensive Care swung open. Doctor Edelson paused for a moment to speak to the nurse, then came across the hall to Silvio.

"A mild coronary, apparently," he said. "We're watching her

carefully. We'll know more with another EKG in an hour or so. Right now she needs quiet, and rest."

Silvio nodded. "And my son's family?"

"Gina has third-degree burns over thirty percent of her body. Her condition is serious, but I'm hopeful. If no complications develop, she has a very good chance. Ariana's burns are more extensive—more than fifty percent of the body is involved. And I'm worried about trauma. She's in shock. But it goes beyond that. She's almost catatonic. Have there ever been any psychiatric problems with her?"

"None," Silvio said.

"Well, it's too early to tell. Her youth may help. I would feel better if she were more responsive."

"But her condition is critical?"

"There's room for hope, Mr. Moretti."

Silvio turned away for a moment to regain control of his emotions. From the first moment he saw Ariana, he had expected the worst. As had Anna.

"And Carlo?"

The doctor smiled. "The least injured, the most difficult. He has second- and third-degree burns on the hands, arms, neck, and left shoulder. He needs rest and care. But he won't stay in bed. He's been going from Gina to Ariana, back and forth."

"Is there anything we can do—any special medical attention— that could help them, or ease their suffering?"

The doctor frowned and shook his head. "Not at the moment. We're using the latest techniques. I wish there were more we could do. But this is one of those instances when we can only assist nature. You will be needed later, Mr. Moretti. I won't minimize the situation. If they survive, there is a long road ahead, painful debridement procedures, scores of skin grafts, months, maybe years of physical therapy. But for the moment we must prevent infection, regain a balance of bodily functions. This is a time of waiting. The body itself must start the healing process."

"May I see Carlo?"

Dr. Edelson smiled. He gestured toward Carlo's room.

"It would help if you'd go sit on him."

Carlo had just finished breakfast. A nurse's aide was clearing away the tray. Silvio waited until she left the room before he walked into Carlo's range of vision.

"How's Mom?" Carlo asked.

"Resting," Silvio told him. "The doctors offer hope there was no extensive damage."

Carlo punched the bed with a bandaged hand. "There seems to be no end to it." He glanced around the room, making certain they were alone. "Pop, I'm going to kill that son-of-a-bitch."

Silvio glanced at the door. "This is not the time or place to discuss such matters."

Carlo waved his bandaged hands. "I know. You'll want to study all the options. Well, excuse me, but I'm fresh out of options. If you had seen Ariana last night, lying there . . ."

Silvio patted Carlo's knee. "All right. I tend to agree with you. But such matters must be carefully considered. They require time, preparation."

"Time for something else to happen? Shit. We've waited too long, now."

"Carlo, listen to me. Always, you must act from logic, not anger."

Carlo glared at him. "Anger's good enough for me."

Silvio stood for a moment, studying his eldest son. If that temperament could be harnessed, Carlo would be a match for anyone. But the rashness . . .

"Carlo, this thing will be done correctly, or not at all," he said.

A few minutes after dawn Salvatore Messino arrived. He nodded a solemn greeting to Silvio, then focused his full attention on Carlo.

"I have taken the liberty of moving your horses over to my place," he said. "They will be safe there."

Carlo thanked him. The horses had been a minor but persistent worry—especially Little Bit.

"Also, I talked with the fire marshal. Your home and furnishings are judged a total loss. Arson will be the verdict."

"How did the sons-a-bitches do it?" Carlo asked.

"They rolled a big gasoline drum up to the back of the house. We found tracks. Possibly a heavy hand cart."

"How did they get past my dog?"

"Strychnine. Poisoned meat. We found the body by the road."

Carlo shook his head. Ariana would be devastated over the loss of Feisty.

Thank God it was not Little Bit.

"A hose was used to pump the gasoline under the house," Salvatore explained. "They put it through the crawl hole in the foundation at back. When it was ignited, it was almost the same as an explosion."

"It *was* an explosion," Carlo said.

"The floor buckled upward and shattered," Salvatore said. "That's one reason the house was engulfed in flames so rapidly."

"How come I didn't smell the gas until just before the explosion?"

"That's understandable," Salvatore said. "You had a solid, double floor. There was no direct ventilation between the crawl space and the interior of the house. The fumes had not had time to penetrate. The gasoline you smelled just before the explosion was that poured at every exit from the house. We found four empty five-gallon cans. They did not intend for you, or your family, to escape."

Carlo shook his head. At the moment he was beyond words.

Salvatore glanced at Silvio, then spoke to Carlo. "The fire marshal will be here soon to talk to you. He will be asking if you have enemies, if you have suspects, the usual questions."

"I'll tell you one thing," Carlo said. "They goddamn sure better get to those sons-a-bitches before I do."

Again Salvatore looked at Silvio.

Silvio spoke quietly. "Carlo, there is only one way to make certain you *do* get to them first. Tell the fire marshal nothing."

"What will I say?"

"For once in your life hold your temper. Tell him you do not know who set fire to your house. And that is the God's truth. You do not know who poured the gasoline, who tossed the match. That is immaterial. Let the fire marshal find the men who actually set the fire, if he can. Such hirelings are unimportant. My revenge lies elsewhere."

"*Your* revenge!" Carlo said. "Well excuse the shit out of me!"

Silvio explained patiently. "Carlo, Lucian is striking at all I hold dear—you, your family. I agree with you that this has gone far enough. I do not intend that those I love should endure more suffering because of me. I can sell the winery . . ."

"No!" Carlo said.

" . . . or I can destroy Lucian. It is as simple as that."

"If you intend to get to him first, you better get cracking," Carlo said.

He began unwrapping the bandages on his hands, tearing at them with his teeth.

Silvio seized his wrists.

"Carlo, I told you, this must be done properly. There are many things to consider." He turned to Salvatore. "What about Johnny?"

"I called his home repeatedly last night, after the fire. There was no answer. This morning I reached his associate, Mr. Snow. The law firm has not seen or heard from him in a week."

Carlo sat up abruptly. "You mean you think Lucian . . ."

"At the moment I doubt that Lucian has had anything to do with Johnny's disappearance," Silvio said. "Johnny has had a disappointment that has affected him greatly."

"But he is in danger," Salvatore said to Silvio. "There's no reason to think that Lucian will stop with Carlo and his family."

Silvio nodded. He was silent for a moment, thinking. "For what we are about to do, we need Johnny." He put a hand on Carlo's knee. "Can you travel?"

"I could use two or three hours of sleep," Carlo said. "Otherwise, I'm all right."

"Here is what we will do," Silvio said. "Salvatore, you and I will go ahead and make preparations. Carlo, I will ask the doctor to give you something for sleep. Tonight you can drive down to San Francisco and find Johnny."

"Just like that," Carlo said.

"Salvatore and I will be making inquiries," Silvio said. "We may be able to locate him."

"And it may be a fucking waste of time," Carlo said. "What makes you think he'll help us?"

"A feeling," Silvio said. "Just talk to him. Tell him exactly what has happened. Then bring him home. Bring him, even if it is at the point of a gun."

CHAPTER 2

JOHNNY was sitting in the fourth bar he had visited since dark. The woman with the Dutch bob hairdo was still with him. He had picked her up two, maybe three bars ago. She had seemed interesting. Deep brown eyes, dark soft hair, good mouth, built well, lots of humor. But as the evening and their drinking progressed, all she could talk about was her husband. Or ex-husband. She never quite defined her exact marital status, explaining only that his name was Oscar and that he could not get it up anymore without outlandish help. She seemed to relish revealing the details.

"For a while he wanted me to make it with other guys and describe everything that happened. Then he wanted me to set it up so he could watch. That's when I bugged out."

Johnny was nodding sagely, wondering how to walk away from her without unpleasantness, when he saw Carlo sitting at the bar.

For an instant, in the dim light, he was not certain. The man was dressed in beat-up jeans and an old pullover. His hands were wrapped in gauze. A large white bandage covered his neck and disappeared under the pullover. Dark bruises shadowed his right eye and cheek. Then Johnny recognized the pullover. It was his own—one he had not worn in years.

"See a ghost?" the woman asked.

"Maybe. And he looks like my brother."

Carlo glanced in Johnny's direction. Johnny raised a hand and gestured. Taking his drink from the bar, Carlo sauntered across the floor toward them.

"What the hell happened to you?" Johnny asked.

"Long story," Carlo said. "But beside you I look great." He nodded to the woman.

"Excuse me," Johnny said. "Carlo, this is . . ."

She had told him her name. But at the moment he could not remember it. She smiled at Carlo.

"Ellen will do."

"Yes, ma'am. I'll bet Ellen *would* do," Carlo said. "How are you, Ellen."

She glanced at Johnny, uncertain of Carlo's mood. She got no help from Johnny. He also was mystified.

"What brings you to town?" he asked.

"Hunting you."

"You're kidding. How did you find me?"

Carlo shrugged. "Simple. There are only two or three thousand bars in the Bay Area. Probably no more than a half-dozen have a blue Porsche parked in front. That narrows the field somewhat."

"Come on!" Johnny said, disturbed. There was an intensity, a wildness in Carlo he had never seen before.

"I had a little help from Pop's friends. They had suggestions as to where you might be. I've only been hunting two hours."

"And . . . ?"

"And I found you." Carlo turned to Ellen. "Look, lady. Do you mind if I talk with my brother alone for a minute?"

Whatever else, Johnny did not intend to be manipulated anymore—especially by his family. He reached out and took the woman's arm. "She's with me," he said to Carlo.

"Johnny, I've gone to a great deal of trouble . . ."

"To bring me a message from Pop. Right?"

Carlo glanced at the woman, then back at Johnny. "From the old man—and from me."

"Pop has nothing to say that I'm remotely interested in hearing. And anything he has to say to me can be said before my friends."

He smiled at Ellen. She smiled back.

"Don't be a horse's ass all your life," Carlo said. He reached into the pocket of his jeans, pulled out a roll of money, and peeled off a hundred dollar bill. He put the money on the table in front of Ellen.

"Good-bye, Ellen," he said. "Been nice knowing you."

Johnny rose to his feet. "Just what the goddamn hell do you think you're doing?"

With one bandaged hand, Carlo pushed him back into his chair. Johnny sat down heavily. Carlo's eyes never left Ellen.

"What do you think I am?" Ellen demanded.

"I don't know. I don't care. I only want to talk to my brother. Okay?"

Ellen snatched up her purse. "I don't have to take this."

She got up and left. Johnny made no effort to stop her. He knew he should be furious, but he felt more like laughing. Only a few minutes before he had been searching for some way to get rid of the woman. Carlo had solved his problem. And it had cost Carlo a hundred dollars. Still, he felt he should protest . . .

"Now you're insulting my women friends."

"She wasn't so insulted that she forgot to take the hundred bucks. And if you want me to take your women friends seriously, all you have to do is remember their names."

"All right, I'll ask you again. What are you doing here?"

"I'm not sure. For some reason I don't fathom, the old man thinks we can't make another move without you."

"He's got his gall. I'll say that . . ."

"Look," Carlo interrupted. "I don't know what's gone on between you and the old man. And I don't especially give a shit. I'm only here to tell you that while you've been making yourself scarce, your family has almost been destroyed."

Carlo raised a hand to stop Johnny's reaction.

"Little brother, I'm going to say what I have to say once. Then I'm going to walk right out that door." He turned and pointed. "You can go with me, or you can sit here and go to hell. Right now, that's the way I feel. I'm through fucking around with people. Including you."

This was a Carlo completely new to Johnny. "Tell me," he said.

"First, my home has been burned to the ground. My wife and daughter are in the hospital, fighting for their lives. And frankly, little brother, I don't know what the hell I'm doing here, when they need me, except that when the old man says frog, I've got this crazy fucking habit of jumping. He was worried about you. And he thought you might like to know that your mother also is in the hospital. She collapsed when she saw Ariana—a coronary. The doctors hope it's mild, but it's too early to tell."

Stunned, Johnny started to get to his feet. "Let's go," he said.

Again Carlo pushed him back into his chair.

"Wait, little brother, you'd better know exactly what's in my head." He pulled up the leg of his jeans. "Look. No socks. I don't have a pair of socks in the world. Gina's clothes, Ariana's clothes, her toys—everything's gone. Don't get me wrong. The pain, the suffering, the fact that they may not live, are enough. But the more I think about it, the thing I resent most is the fact that Lucian Hall destroyed everything personal in our lives. Everything!"

Tears came to Carlo's eyes.

"Johnny, I've had enough. I'm going to kill that son-of-a-bitch. I mean it. I'm going to lay waste."

Johnny reached out to take his arm. "Carlo . . ."

Carlo jerked his arm free. "Don't start that legal shit."

Johnny waited. He did not know what to say.

"I'm just asking one thing of you," Carlo said. "Come see Gina, Ariana, Mom. Just come look at them. Then, if you don't feel exactly the way I feel, you can go straight to hell."

"Of course I want to see them," Johnny said. "If the doctors . . ."

"Fuck the doctors. Come see them."

Johnny nodded. "All right."

"There's something else. Lucian really hit us with both barrels. There are new charges against the winery. We just heard about it late this afternoon. The state board has a witness who says he received rebates totaling more than a hundred thousand dollars from the Moretti winery during the last two years."

Johnny's mind raced ahead. "That would be the final straw," he said. "With probation pending over the mislabeling . . ."

"Right. If that witness tells his shitty story, we're out of business."

Johnny was silent for a moment, thinking. There should be some way . . .

"If it were contested, it could be kept in the courts a long time . . ."

"While we're sitting in the sewers," Carlo said. "No, Johnny. There's only one way. That lying witness won't live to see the inside of a courtroom. Not while I'm alive."

"Carlo . . ."

"Shut up," Carlo said. His eyes were wild. "Just shut the fuck up. Come to the hospital with me. Then, if you want to walk, you can walk. Okay?"

He rose and started for the door.

Johnny followed, reluctantly.

His mind was numb. Deep within him he felt a terrible premonition. Now he would have to make the decision he had been dreading all his life.

"It was little Ariana," Anna said. "The sight of that poor child lying there . . . it was just too much."

"She's going to be all right," Johnny assured her.

"No. Not ever," Anna said. "The doctors may perform a miracle. Those horrible burns may heal. But she will never be the same. Not inside. For the rest of her life she will remember."

Johnny squeezed her hand and did not answer.

Anna had been moved from Intensive Care to a private room. A special nurse sat in the corner, monitoring the oscilloscope wired to Anna's body. The heavy antiseptic smell of the hospital mingled with the fragrance of the bank of red roses Silvio had ordered. Anna seemed to be resting comfortably under mild sedation, but her normally dark complexion remained alarmingly pale.

"Johnny, you should have seen them. Gina and Ariana . . . They were charred. Tatters of skin, clothing . . . their lovely hair gone . . ."

Johnny patted her hand. "Don't think about it, Mom. They're receiving the best treatment possible. There's nothing more we can do. The important thing now is for you to rest, to get well," he said. "We worry about you. Gina knows. She is very concerned. And think of how Ariana will feel, knowing her grandmother is sick. Rest, Mom. Take care of yourself. Get well. Later they'll be needing you."

Anna smiled. She waved a hand to dismiss the subject.

"Johnny, tell me, because I want to know. What is in Carlo's mind?"

Johnny answered obliquely. "He's bearing up well, Mom."

"You know what I mean. I'm afraid he may do something foolish."

Johnny glanced at the special nurse. She seemed to be making a point of ignoring the conversation. He turned back to his mother.

"Mom, you're not supposed to worry. We'll look after Carlo."

"Have you talked to your father?"

"Not yet."

"I worry about him. The strain."

"Mom, he's a block of granite. Please! Quit worrying."

She looked at him for a moment. "I will quit worrying, Johnny, if you will promise me two things."

"All right."

"First, keep an eye on Carlo. He is too impetuous. You have your father's level head. If you are with Carlo, I won't worry."

"Okay," Johnny said.

"And second, listen to your father. These are terrible times for us. Promise me that you will listen to Silvio."

Johnny did not answer for a moment.

"Johnny! Will you?"

He smiled and patted her hand.

"Of course," he said.

Johnny pushed open the door to Gina's darkened room. The shades were drawn. In the dimness he had difficulty finding her among the array of medical support equipment. Sensing that someone was there, Gina slowly turned her head toward him. Johnny kept his face rigid to prevent her from seeing his shock.

He would not have recognized her. Her arms, shoulders, and face looked like badly molded cheese. A tent frame protected most of her body from the sheet.

Johnny retreated. Before he could close the door, she called to him. "Johnny?"

He stepped back into the room. "Gina, I just had to see you. Carlo insisted. I'll come back, when you're stronger."

Her voice came low, unnatural. "Johnny! Please! Come in."

He could see her more clearly now. An intravenous tube was fixed to her left arm. Aspiration tubes disappeared into her nose. A catheter emptied into a bottle beneath the bed. There was an overpowering stench in the room—the unmistakable smell of burned flesh.

Johnny felt his stomach constrict as he thought of the pain she must be enduring.

"You're supposed to be resting," he said.

Gina patted the bed with her free hand. "Come on over here. I feel like talking." She laughed weakly. "I'm all doped up. I'm floating. A cheap drunk. Drugs always affected me this way. I remember, when my father died, they had to give me a sedative. Instead of putting me to sleep, it gave me a high that lasted for hours."

Johnny moved closer to the bed. He saw movement across the room, over by the window. A private nurse sat there, quietly reading a magazine in the dim light. She nodded at Johnny, smiled, and pointed to her watch. She held up her hand, fingers spread, to signal five minutes. Johnny pulled a chair closer to the bed.

"Gina, can I get you anything? Do anything for you?"

"You can talk to me a little while. I mean it. I want to talk. When Carlo comes in, he looks at me and gets so angry he can't stand it. He has to leave."

She turned away. Johnny waited patiently. When she rolled her head back toward him, her eyes were wide, pleading.

"Johnny, I'm scared. Am I going to die?"

"Of course not!" Johnny said emphatically. "Don't even think like that."

She reached for his arm with her free hand. "I don't think they're telling me the truth. I remember, years ago I had a friend who was burned in a car wreck. We went to see her in the hospital. She was sitting up in bed. She made jokes, laughed with us. Three days later she was dead. They said the poisons built up in her body." Gina's voice broke. Her grip tightened on his arm. "Johnny, I think I'm burned worse . . ."

He leaned forward so she could see his face. "Gina, I won't lie to you. Of course you are badly hurt. But at this point there's no reason to think your burns will kill you. Not unless complications develop . . . and we're simply not going to let that happen. Pop has been on the phone. They're flying in a specialist from the experimental burn center at Brooke Army Medical Hospital. There have been all kinds of advances in treatment since your friend died. You'll have the best. We'll see to that!"

"If I could just be certain . . ."

"Gina, trust me," he said with more conviction than he felt. "You're going to be all right."

She did not speak for a moment. "I know it sounds selfish, worrying about myself, with Ariana, your mother . . ."

"Not at all," Johnny interrupted.

"It's just that I want to live for *them*—your mother, Silvio, Carlo, Ariana . . ." Her dark eyes narrowed with intensity.

She was becoming so upset that Johnny rose from the chair. He tried again. "Gina, you're really supposed to be resting. I'll come back later . . ."

She moved her grip to his wrist. "Johnny, please stay! I'm going crazy in here!"

He sank back into the chair.

Gina laughed softly. "It's funny, in a way. Normally I'd run if you happened to catch me if I weren't at my best. Now I look like something the cat dragged in, and I don't care."

She started crying. Johnny did not know if her tears were from pain, or frustration.

"Gina, I'm sorry this happened to you," he said.

She misunderstood. "Oh, it was my fault," she said. "Carlo got me out of the house minutes after the explosion. I don't think I was badly hurt then. But I tried to get back in through the front door, to get Ariana. I should have known Carlo was doing the right thing."

Johnny explained his meaning. "I feel that you are here, suffering, paying for the sins of the Morettis."

Gina squeezed his hand. "Johnny, I *am* a Moretti. That's something I've learned during the last few weeks. Silvio means as much to me as my own father. And what happened between Carlo and me was partly my fault. I should have made certain there was no room for another woman in his life."

"Carlo should have his ass kicked."

Gina giggled. She freed her hand to brush away the tears.

"I can tell you this, Johnny. Carlo thinks the sun rises and sets on you. He may not act like it sometimes. I don't know why."

"I'm glad you and Carlo worked things out," Johnny said. "I know how Carlo—the whole family—feels about you. We were worried about Carlo, what he would do without you."

"That's all over," Gina said. "I think we both learned from it. What I'm really worried about now is Ariana. The psychiatrist came to examine her this afternoon. I raised hell until they let me see him."

"You shouldn't be worrying about that right now."

"You know of a better time? I don't have a thing to do but lie here and think. Johnny, they're worried because she won't respond. She just lies there!"

"Gina, let's not borrow trouble. We have enough, as it is. They're doing everything possible . . ."

"But she needs us, *now!*" Gina said. "Don't you see? She needs our love—our care—now! We're talking about what she will remember the rest of her life."

Johnny nodded agreement. The doctor had called it disassociation, explaining that when the brain is overloaded, it sometimes tunes out. Ariana had been unable to face the reality of being trapped in her room. In self-defense her mind had withdrawn from the horror.

Gina's eyes were pleading with him. "But there's more to it than that," she said. "I told him my theory. I don't think he listened. Johnny, please make them understand!"

"I'll try," Johnny said. "Tell me."

"You see, this whole thing came at a very bad time for her. She's been . . . withdrawn from Carlo and me. She blamed me for the move to Napa, for leaving Carlo. All the time we were there, she actually hated me. I saw it. I felt it. For the first time in her life she couldn't have her own way. Her confidence in herself . . ." Gina's hand circled in a gesture of helplessness. "And then, when we came back, she saw the change in Carlo. For the first time, Carlo paid more attention to me than to her. That was very upsetting to her. You know how Carlo's always been with her. And now, right when she needs us most, she has this resentment . . ."

"Gina, plainly, you are worrying too much."

"It's time for worry. And for a lot of thinking. There is only one person close to Ariana, one person exempt from the whole Napa mess. You, Johnny. Will you go see her? Talk with her? See if you can get through to her?"

Johnny hesitated. "They have a no visitors sign on the door." The excuse sounded weak, even to him. He was not sure he could bear to look at her. He had always felt a special bond to Ariana. She was a dreamy-headed kid, the way he used to be, maybe still was. And he knew that before accomplishment the dream came first.

He rose, leaned over the bed, and kissed Gina gently. "All right. I'll go see her. On one condition. You'll promise to get some rest."

"I can't very well do anything else. And thank you, for the talk. I feel better. Carlo is in such a state. And I keep worrying. What is going to happen next? I'm afraid for you, for Carlo, everyone..."

"Don't think about it. All of it will be over soon."

"Johnny, they *knew* we were in that house. They knew Ariana was in her room. What kind of people would do that to a child?" She seized his wrist again.

"We can't live with it," she said. "Not another day!"

Ariana was lying on her left side, facing away from the door. Walking softly, Johnny circled to the foot of the bed. Ariana's eyes were open. She did not react as he came within her range of vision.

Johnny spoke softly. "Ariana?" He thought she might not recognize him in the sterile gown and gauze mask. "It's Johnny."

She did not respond.

Her burns were darker, more extensive than Gina's. The terrible wounds on the small, thin frame affected him far more. He had never seen anything as pathetic as her frail, ravaged body. And he recognized, in that first glance, that the doctors were offering hope only in desperation. He blinked away the tears that blurred his vision for a moment and waited until he had himself under control. Then he pulled a chair close to the bed.

"I'm going out to see Little Bit in the morning," he said conversationally. "Is there anything you want me to tell him?"

Ariana's eyes remained blank, vacant.

Her left arm was one of the few places on her body not burned. He took her hand. It lay lifeless in his own.

"I'll bet Little Bit misses you," he said. "You've got to get well. Who's going to take care of Little Bit?"

Her fixed gaze did not waver.

"And when you get well, I want you to come visit me," he said. "We'll have a great time . . ."

He kept talking—for hours. He knew that what he said was not important, but it was essential that he be with her in her suffering, that she hear the sound of his voice. As he talked, through the night, he reminisced about his houseboat, the Bay, the birds, the water, the marine life, her visits. He talked about the moonlight, the sunsets, his photography.

Each time the nurses entered to do their hurried work, he left the chair to stand by the windows until they were done. Then he returned to his monologue.

He told Ariana about his own childhood, the games he played, his treehouses, his pets, his daydreams, his friends in school, his disappointments, his discoveries, his misapprehensions about the world, his private world of make-believe . . .

He was never certain exactly when, but at some point, Ariana began listening.

For a time he hardly dared to hope that he had broken through. Gradually, the glaze disappeared from her eyes.

At last she looked at him.

He talked a while longer before he risked another direct question. He worked it in casually.

"I keep a Polaroid camera in the car," he said. "When I go out to see Little Bit tomorrow, would you like me to bring you a picture of him?"

Ariana nodded so slightly he was not entirely certain that her head moved.

He gambled on deeper response. He knew she talked to Little Bit almost incessantly.

"Is there anything you'd like me to tell him?"

For a moment he thought she was not going to answer. Then she looked at him. She spoke in a whisper.

"Tell him . . . tell him to watch out . . . for those people."

Johnny laughed, partly in relief, partly in surprise. "What people?"

"The people . . . who burned our house."

Johnny hesitated. He wondered if he should pursue the subject. He reasoned that the venting of her fears might help.

"How did you know about those people?"

Her whisper was so soft he could barely make out the words. "I heard Daddy. They tried to kill us."

"But you're safe now," Johnny said. "We're not going to let them hurt you again." A nurse entered the room, replaced the bottle over Ariana's bed, and busily set about refitting the tubes. Johnny raised Ariana's hand to his cheek. "I'll come back, when we can talk more."

Her eyes widened. "Don't go!" she pleaded. "I'm scared."

Johnny looked questioningly at the nurse. Small, trim, middle-aged, and filled with professional efficiency, she seemed to be in charge of the floor. She paused for a moment in indecision. Then she leaned over Ariana, adjusted her pillows, and motioned for Johnny to stay.

"I'll be right here," Johnny told Ariana.

He held her hand as she drifted into a deep sleep. For hours he watched her tiny chest as her breathing became more and more labored. He lost count of the times the doctors came to check her and give her medication. The nurse frequently slipped into the room to stand silently in the shadows. Once Silvio came for a few minutes, to report that Anna was resting for the moment, but that Gina was experiencing intervals of intense pain that medication could not ease. Carlo was with her.

Gradually Ariana's breathing grew huskier, more labored. Doctor Edelson's visits became more frequent. Each time he lingered longer. Once Johnny attempted to leave his chair, to give the doctor better access to the bed. Ariana's tiny hand tightened on his forefinger. The doctor motioned for him not to move.

After midnight, Ariana began moaning in her sleep and thrashing about in her suffering. Johnny rang for the nurse, who sedated her again. She quieted for a while, but when the moaning resumed, it was worse. The nurse summoned the doctor.

"Can't you ease her pain?" Johnny asked quietly.

Doctor Edelson grimaced. "I'm sorry," he said. "There are limits. I don't think she is aware now. If you would like to leave for a while . . ."

"No," Johnny said. "I'll stay."

He sat for hours, holding Ariana's hand, listening to her pitiful moans. He had never felt so helpless in his life. He watched her strength ebb relentlessly under her constant, tortured movements. Once her eyes opened, and she looked at him. She spoke in a soft, husky voice.

"Johnny. Are you coming to see me dance?"

For a moment he had no idea what was in her fevered, drugged mind. Then he remembered. "Of course," he said. "I wouldn't miss it for the world."

She smiled and was quiet for a few minutes. Then she began whimpering.

"I'm scared!" she said.

Johnny knelt on the hard tile floor and put his left arm around Ariana and her pillow, pulling her gently toward him. "I'm here, precious," he said. "I'm with you."

She quieted. The long, labored, hoarse breathing began again.

He held her for more than an hour, listening as her breath grew steadily weaker. Despite the ache from his knees, he did not shift his position. His discomfort was minute, compared with her pain. Several times her breathing stopped for the space of a few heartbeats. Each time he held his own breath, waiting until she breathed again.

And then finally the tiny chest was still.

Johnny reached for the buzzer. The nurse entered, glanced at the bed, then left quickly. The doctor returned within seconds. He listened for a moment, then slowly folded his stethoscope and returned it to the pocket of his jacket.

"I'm sorry," he said. "At least she is now beyond suffering."

Johnny eased back into the chair. Ariana's hand still rested in his, gripping his forefinger.

He waited while the nurse disconnected the tubes, the catheters. Then she gently pried his hand free of Ariana's grip and folded the arms across the tiny chest.

Slowly Johnny rose to his feet. He stood for a moment, looking down at Ariana's body, still childishly slim, yet harboring a hint of the woman that she now would never become.

In the hall, Silvio came and gave Johnny an abrupt, firm Corsican embrace. "Your mother, Carlo, Gina are all asleep, exhausted," Silvio managed to say. "Their anguish will begin soon enough. I think it best not to awaken them."

In the harsh light of the hallway, Johnny could see deep lines of fatigue in his father's face. "You should get some rest too, if you can."

Silvio nodded absently. "The doctor said her poor little lungs must have been seared. That if she had survived the burns on her body, the injuries to her lungs probably would have taken her later, with even more pain."

Down the hall, an elevator door opened. Two attendants wheeled a gurney into the corridor, then turned into the room. For a moment Johnny was overwhelmed with a need to be alone.

"I think I'll go get some air," he said.

At the nurses' station, Doctor Edelson stood facing the counter. At first Johnny thought he was making an entry in a chart, or reading something on the desk. But as he approached, Johnny could see that he was simply standing there, motionless, his shoulders slumped. Johnny did not intrude on his privacy.

As he walked out into the hospital parking lot, dawn was breaking. The morning was gray and overcast. Johnny breathed deeply of the humid air. He glanced at his watch.

He had spent more than eighteen hours in the hospital. He could still smell the burned flesh. He could still hear Ariana's moans of agony, her painful whimpering, her labored breathing. He knew he would never forget a single detail of those eighteen hours.

Carlo had been right.

He was consumed by a cold, overwhelming rage.

And it would not go away.

CHAPTER 3

CHRISTINA shoved the manuscript to one side. It was hopeless. The man knew his subject. The artistic concepts of the
Hudson River School were brilliantly grasped. But the
writing was pompous, stilted, a dry parade of facts. She could blue-
pencil the pedantic phrases, trim the long lectures. But the con-
descending tone was beyond repair.

Christina sighed and wondered what to do. A request for a revision no doubt would reduce this dean of American art critics to
apoplexy. The resulting uproar would put her job on the line and
still fail to produce a satisfactory text. Pondering the problem,
Christina was startled by a rapping on the glass wall of her office.
The research librarian, Eden Markham, was standing in the hall.
She pointed to her watch, then toward the director's office. With a
rush Christina remembered.

Staff meeting.

She gathered her notes and followed Eden, who was hurrying on
down the hall. The administration offices were hushed and empty,
evidence that the meeting already had started. Eden had been delegated to round up the stray.

By the time Christina arrived, the other members of the staff were seated in a semicircle around the desk of Director Arnold Morgan. Christina's customary chair awaited her on the far side of the room. Morgan frowned as she circled behind the other members of the staff.

"We've been waiting for a report from our curator of exhibitions," he said with mock humor. "We're wondering. Will we have a book to go with the Hudson River School exhibition?"

Christina ignored the taunting. "We have three choices," she said. "We can have a book with pretty pictures and a text no one will read. We can try to work with our temperamental author. Or we can farm out the revision job to someone who can write."

Morgan leaned back in his chair and polished his bald head with the palm of his hand. "It's that bad?"

Christina let her silence speak.

Morgan turned to smile at other members of the staff, as if including them in an unspoken joke. "And what does our curator of exhibitions suggest?"

"I would prefer to turn it over to a ghost writer."

Morgan smiled again at other members of the staff. "And who would face our esteemed author with the rewritten manuscript? You?"

The baiting was habitual with him, but for once his viciousness got through to her. "That's my job," she snapped.

Morgan blinked at her in surprise. His autocratic manner was seldom challenged by his staff. He frowned and leaned back in his chair again. "I would hate to see us make an enemy of any art critic, if we can avoid doing so—especially this one. Maybe we better think some more about this."

Talk moved on to the problem of space in the library, the carpenter's shop. No one looked at Christina. She was excluded.

She had handled it badly, and she did not know why.

Since her return from Sonoma, she had experienced more and more difficulty in concentration. At times her brain felt paralyzed. She slept little. She knew she was irritable, and she often felt tense, anxious.

She had lost both Johnny and Howard.

She had not been so alone since her first trip east, years ago.

Dr. Chesler had tried to convince her that all might be for the best.

"Obviously, this Johnny isn't wrapped too tight," he said. "Else, why would he have done these things to you? And frankly, I'm relieved that you and Howard have split. Howard's a smart boy. I think he at last realized what he was doing to you—that you two were using each other to avoid facing life. You were like two crippled children, helping each other across the street."

His metaphor was unfortunate, bringing to mind the hopeless children at Sonoma State School. But the description was apt. She worried constantly about Howard. He had disappeared. He had quit the library, moved out of his apartment, out of her life.

Nothing was left for her but the museum.

Around her discussion ranged from topic to topic. For a time the bursar complained of delays in the filing of travel expenses. The educational director proposed a greater effort to convince the schools that more in-class preparation was needed before students were brought to visit the museum. There was talk of expanding the museum publications desk to include art books not normally carried by commercial stores and the probable ill will that move would engender among community bookstores.

Eventually, in the concentric way of all their staff meetings, discussion again turned to the Hudson River School exhibition.

"It's not going to be one of our most exciting shows," Eden said.

"Why?" Morgan said. "What makes you say that?"

"Too small," she said. "Only thirty-nine paintings."

"Well, but look at the size of them!" Morgan said. "Those landscapes are huge!"

Christina was overcome by an odd sense of disassociation, as if all this were happening to someone else. "Eden's right," she heard herself say. "It's going to be a weak show."

"How come?" Morgan asked defensively.

More and more often now Christina felt that she was an observer outside of her body, a disinterested spectator watching herself perform. With this strange euphoria she considered Morgan's question.

"It lacks depth," she said.

Morgan looked at the others, his eyes wide with surprised, injured self-righteousness. "Well, the time to think about that was in the planning, before we got into it," he said. He leaned forward, his elbows on the desk, and looked at his staff, one by one. "Anybody have any suggestions?"

"What about including a few of the luminists?" someone suggested. "It's all landscape."

"What do you think, Christina?" Morgan demanded.

"It would destroy the concept of the show," she said. "What we really need is a flagship painting, something exciting—something like Church's *Icebergs*."

"Oh, fine!" Morgan said, grinning animatedly at his staff. "I'll just ring Dallas first thing in the morning and get Harry Parker on the phone. I'm sure he'll send it right up."

He received the expected laugh. The long-lost *Icebergs* had brought two and a half million dollars at auction, the highest price ever paid for any painting at that time. A large segment of Dallas probably would prefer to ship Texas Stadium to Boston on loan.

Christina was riding on a wave of calm recklessness. "It might be done," she said. "Why not a joint exhibition, home and home? Dallas may welcome a chance to place *Icebergs* in context with the entire Hudson River movement."

Morgan was quiet for a moment. "A little late for that, isn't it?"

"Might be worth a try," Christina insisted. But even as she said it, she knew the suggestion was wistful, foolish. Plans were too far advanced. The budget was frozen. All paintings for the show were on loans of limited duration; each would have to be renegotiated to extend the show for exhibition in Dallas.

Morgan frowned. "I might broach the idea with Harry . . ."

When the meeting ended, Christina was exhausted. As she returned to her office, she suddenly began to tremble. She sank into her chair and gripped the desk. She could feel herself coming apart. There was nothing she could do about it. She no longer was in control.

She saw Eden passing in the hall. Eden glanced in and hurried to her.

"Christina! What's wrong!"

"Please," Christina said. "Don't bother anyone. Just get me home."

CHAPTER 4

S ILVIO appeared to have aged ten years in two days. Seated behind his massive desk, he somehow seemed smaller, less certain of himself. He picked up a letter opener and idly tapped a palm with the blade. He fixed Johnny with that heavily-lidded stare.

"Tell me, Johnny. Are you ready to do what must be done?"

Johnny leaned back in the heavy leather wing chair and faced his father. On the sofa, Carlo raised his head in anticipation.

Johnny phrased his reply carefully.

"Depends on what you have in mind."

Silvio's gaze did not waver. "Lucian Hall has taken Ariana from us. He has caused us untold suffering. Every additional hour that Lucian lives, he is in my debt. If his lying witness lives to testify, we also have lost our winery. That is what is in my mind. I have room there for nothing else."

Johnny gestured toward the bookcases. "Pop, you've always taught us to emulate the great men. You've always held them up as an example, and I've always respected you for it. But every time you stoop to Lucian Hall's methods, you are getting down on his level. Don't you see that?"

"Survival breeds its own brand of morality," Silvio said.

Johnny rose to his feet to stand before Silvio's desk. "Pop, if Carlo goes out with a pistol and blows away that witness, the heat will land right here." He pointed to the desk. "If Lucian Hall is murdered, speculation will never stop. His death, the fire at Carlo's house, gossip about your financial battle with Hampton, everything that has happened will be linked to those old rumors about your past. Believe me, I know what I'm talking about. It'd be in the newspapers, on television for years. There'd be investigations from all levels—local, state and federal."

"Do you think I give a shit?" Carlo shouted.

Johnny ignored him and spoke to Silvio. "Pop, you always taught us to examine all the options. There are other ways to handle this."

Silvio put the letter opener back on the desk. "I'm listening."

"For one thing, you could go to the state attorney general. Give him all your facts. Demand an investigation."

Carlo laughed. "Now, *that'd* scare the shit out of Lucian."

"Lucian Hall has his own connections," Silvio said. "There would be no conclusive results."

"Then take it to the federal level. There has been talk of a U.S. Senate committee investigation into corporate practices. Use your political influence. Point the finger at Lucian."

"Pot and the kettle," Carlo said from the sofa.

Silvio glared at his elder son for a moment. He turned back to Johnny. "Carlo will never win prizes for tact, but he has a point. Lucian could make counter accusations against us."

"There is something else to consider," Johnny said. "Lucian dead might not solve all your problems. Conglomerates are modular structures. Lucian could be replaced by someone exactly like him, maybe even worse."

"It wasn't a modular executive who burned my house, killed my daughter," Carlo said. "It was Lucian Hall."

Silvio remained silent for a moment. "Johnny, if there were some way to work within the law, I would do it—for your sake, for Carlo's sake. But where has your precious law helped us? All your law can do is say, *if* we find that a crime truly has been committed, and *if* we happen to catch the offender, and *if* he happens to be convicted, then just *maybe* he will be dealt a small measure of punishment."

"Crimes *have* been committed," Johnny said. "Antonio, Umberto were adjudged homicides. That's fact."

"And where are the murderers? What chance do you see of their being convicted?"

Carlo spoke up from the couch. "I don't see any reason to argue about it. Either Johnny'll do it or he won't. If he won't, the hell with him."

Silvio sighed. "Carlo, Johnny acts from reasoning. Always you act from emotion. That is the difference between you."

"And his way takes longer."

"But it may keep him out of trouble." Silvio studied Johnny for a moment. "Tell me, Mr. Lawyer. What is justice?"

The definition that came to Johnny's mind was not from law, but from Gilbert and Sullivan.

"To make the punishment fit the crime."

"And if the law fails?"

Johnny remained silent.

Silvio nodded. "Then there is no justice. Not unless someone assumes the law's responsibilities."

Johnny knew where Silvio's argument was headed. "Through vigilante law? Pop, if history has taught us nothing else, it's that violence escalates."

"Johnny, the natural inclination of men to band together for mutual protection has a long and impressive history. Just because you are ignorant of it does not alter fact. The Camorra ruled Naples for four hundred years . . ."

Johnny gestured toward the bookcases. "Pop, I've read your books."

"Then you know that in the time of the great Cervantes the Compagnia della Garduna punished a corrupt government in a time of rampant immorality, dealt with murderers, thieves, prostitution, made the streets, highways safe again. Spain became the most powerful country in the world. The Camorra in Naples, the Mafia in Sicily. In Corsica the Unione Corse . . ."

"Pop, you're straining to find a rationalization for vigilante law. It won't work."

"Fuck Johnny," Carlo said. "I'll do it by myself."

"You cannot do it alone," Silvio said. "This is also Johnny's responsibility."

He rose from his desk and came to stand in front of Johnny. "Listen to me. There exists an exemplary code of conduct, devised by men over the centuries. Few are privileged to share this sacred brotherhood . . ."

Johnny did not answer. Silvio's eyes were begging him.

This was the moment he had known would come, someday. He recognized Silvio's argument for what it was: an invitation.

The brotherhood. Those dark rumors about Silvio were true.

He now had confirmation.

"Pop," he said quietly. "I'm not about to indulge in some out-moded, foolish, romantic gesture."

"Go look at little Ariana in her coffin," Silvio said. "Go visit Gina in her grief and pain. Look into your mother's eyes. Go out to the graves of Patricio, Umberto, Antonio. And you say what I believe is foolish?"

Behind them Carlo spoke, breaking the spell. "I don't need any goddamned rationalization. I'm doing this job for *me*. I just *feel* like doing it."

"Lucian will send me your head on a platter," Silvio said.

He spoke again to Johnny. "Listen to me. A man may subscribe to a higher code of conduct than that of the society around him. With the help of other, like-minded men, he can enforce that code."

"Romantic bullshit," Johnny said.

Silvio sighed. "If I could only make you see. When my family was destroyed by vendetta, the burden fell on me. Now the burden falls on my sons. You are better prepared. You are older. I was only ten . . ."

Johnny stared at Silvio. So, the worst of those old stories was true. "At ten? You killed, when you were ten years old?"

Silvio studied him for a moment, assessing how much to reveal. "Not once. Three times. I only tell you so you will know what kind of blood you have in your veins."

"Pop, I see the necessity of doing something. But don't *you* see?

It sometimes takes more courage to do the right thing well than to do the obvious, easy thing. Goddamn it, that's what your books are all about!"

"To hell with all this talk," Carlo said. "It's time to put up or shut up."

"For once I agree with you," Silvio said. "Johnny?"

Rising from his chair, Johnny walked past his father to the window. He stood, thinking, looking out over Sonoma, fully aware that he was making the biggest decision of his life.

From Patricio, Antonio, and Umberto to Gina and Ariana the law *had* failed them.

Neither Gregory Cavanaugh nor Fraser would have found justice but for Silvio.

He remembered Gina's words. "I am a Moretti. That is something I have learned during the last two weeks."

What did it mean to be a Moretti? That his father had killed at ten?

Was that his heritage?

Murder? The brotherhood?

Was that the only way for Giovanni Moretti? To turn against everything he believed to be good, true, just?

He remembered the words of the venerable old Judge Wilkins: "Justice often needs a firm guiding hand."

He turned from the window.

"Pop, you told me to go out into the world and get some experience. All right. I have. And I'll tell you what I've learned. Today you've got to be smarter, and tougher. Your way—the old way—won't work."

"Goddamn," Carlo exploded, but Silvio's look silenced him.

"All right," Silvio said. "Let's hear young Giovanni Moretti tell us how to be smarter and tougher."

"I think I can tell you. But first I want to know everything that has happened. If you insist on involving me in this, there can be no half measures."

Silvio hesitated only an instant. Then he described every step in the escalating battle—the offer with its veiled threat; the wiretapping and countermeasures of corporate intelligence; Patricio's death in the truck; the murders of Antonio and Umberto; the warehouse fire; the beating of Dax; the various calamities created for Lucian by Salvatore.

Johnny listened, but when Silvio had finished, he knew that something significant was still missing.

"There's more," he said. "What, exactly, is there between you and Lucian?"

Silvio frowned. He turned away. For a moment Johnny thought he would not answer, but when he spoke, his voice was heavy with emotion.

"Years ago, long before the winery existed, I worked for Lucian's father on the docks. Those were wild, tempestuous times. A strike erupted. Much ill feeling on both sides. And your Uncle Paolo—who never had an angry thought in his head, against anyone—was killed. He did not speak English. He did not even know what was happening. He was on his way to work and walked innocently into the dispute. Lucian's father gave the order for his men to fire. Little Paulie was killed, for absolutely no reason." He shook his head. "None."

He hesitated for a moment. "I bided my time, waited for an opportunity. In the last days of Prohibition I learned that Lucian Hall planned to land a shipload of liquor near Drake's Bay. You see, he was the prince of the whole family, the darling boy who could do no wrong. I arranged for the federal officers to be waiting when he touched shore with his cargo. He escaped jail, but it cost his father a fortune, and it has remained a black mark against Lucian to this day. His father never forgave him. And Lucian has never forgotten what I did to him."

Silvio sighed. The silence lengthened.

"And now you know everything," Silvio said. "So tell me. How would you be smarter and tougher?"

Johnny paused before he spoke. He would have to be certain he was covering all possibilities.

"This false witness is greedy," he began. "He's bound to be in it only for the money. Suppose I called him, as Silvio Moretti's attorney, and suggested that I might pay him considerably more money to change his story. What would be his reaction?"

Silvio considered the possibility. "He might do it," he said. "But he would be playing a dangerous game. And Lucian would only increase the sum, or apply pressure. The witness would not stay bought."

Johnny nodded agreement. "But suppose I used your tapped phone to call this witness and offered to meet him somewhere, alone. What would happen?"

Silvio's eyes widened. "As soon as Lucian Hall received the report on the telephone conversation, he would set a trap. He would have gunmen there to kill you, along with the witness. Money, evidence would be left to link you, to suggest that you and the witness killed each other in an argument over his price for silence."

"But suppose *we* set the trap. Suppose Salvatore could determine the exact layout of the rendezvous. We could have Carlo there, waiting. The trap would spring. But Carlo and I would walk away. The murder of the witness then would be laid at Lucian's feet."

Silvio considered the possibilities for a moment. "That would only be a minor inconvenience to Lucian. He would never be indicted under those circumstances."

"I agree," Johnny said. "But the witness would be eliminated, and it would point the finger away from us."

Silvio was listening. "And Lucian himself?"

Johnny took a deep breath. His plan for Lucian Hall was even more bizarre.

"I have found that Lucian is using certain churches as a tax dodge, involving a large amount of real estate. He is taking advantage of the financial benefits accorded religious groups. I don't have enough for an indictment. But with my expertise, and your connections, I could *create* sufficient evidence to get him arrested and put in jail."

Silvio gave him the wisp of a smile. "Lucian has an army of lawyers. Under the worst of circumstances, he would spend no more than a few hours in jail."

Johnny smiled back. "With your connections, one hour should be enough."

CHAPTER 5

*I*N the twilight dimness of the poker parlor, the illuminated tables and players stood out in sharp relief. It was a world that Johnny had sampled only briefly. As a cocky college freshman, he had come here several times one summer to test his new-found poker skill against the pros—Geraci, Antonio, Umberto. He had not been in the poker parlor in the years since.

Silvio led the way past the bar, the green-felt tables, nodding his greetings to acquaintances in the front rooms. Carlo followed, head down and morose. Johnny kept his eyes straight ahead, maintaining distance from men he remembered only vaguely. At the door to Salvatore Messino's private office, Silvio stepped aside to allow Carlo and Johnny to enter.

Salvatore rose from his desk and came forward to give Carlo a warm Corsican embrace and murmur condolences. He then turned to Johnny with a handshake, and a significant greeting. "It's good to see you here in these times of trouble, Giovanni."

Silvio closed the door behind him. "My sons are impatient to get started. Tell us. What have you learned?"

Salvatore motioned Johnny and Carlo to the chairs beside his desk. Silvio stood by the door, waiting.

"At last we have ascertained the name of the false witness," Salvatore said. "Eduardo Martinez. He owns a chain of liquor stores in San Diego. Fortunately he has not as yet protected himself by making a deposition."

"We've got to hit him first," Carlo said.

"There will be problems," Salvatore said. "Martinez lives in an apartment complex protected by a high wall. Security is good. His central offices are not far away, in a one-story brick building, but the area is congested during business hours. It might be better to try to set the trap elsewhere. We happen to know that he is going to the race trace in Tijuana tomorrow."

"How do you know?" Johnny asked.

Salvatore glanced at him. "A telephone conversation," he said. He handed Johnny a four-by-five inch photograph. "Here is a picture of him, made recently. He drives a new Lincoln Continental, blue with orange trim. It is his habit to visit several nightclubs after the races. Especially if he is a winner. He will be with a young woman. Sometimes when he is with a woman he goes to a motel and spends a few hours before returning. That might be a good place to arrange the rendezvous. He would be drinking, expansive . . ."

"Risky, uncertain," Silvio said. "And there would be the problem of the woman. You said there is congestion around his office by day. What would be the situation at night?"

"Perfect," Salvatore said. "But Martinez is not dumb. He might not cooperate." He smiled. "Just in case it can be arranged, I have obtained a floor plan of the building." He spread a small blueprint on his desk. "The entrance is here. Martinez has a suite of offices down the hall, in this end of the building. His private office is here, in the corner. And he has an adjoining bathroom that would serve our purpose well."

"It'll have to be his office," Carlo said. "It's perfect."

Johnny nodded. "I think if we hold out the offer of enough money, he'll go along."

"Fine," Silvio said. "What preparations have you made, old friend?"

Salvatore turned to Johnny and Carlo and handed them documents, one by one.

"Here are your driver's licenses and a selection of credit and identification cards. The driver's licenses bear your photographs, and assumed names. This identification will stand up for routine check by police or highway patrol. If the officers stop you for some reason and radio for a computer check, don't worry. The report will be satisfactory."

Johnny was curious. "How was that done?"

Salvatore gave him that appraising glance. "The gentlemen who bore these names are deceased. Neither was ever in trouble with the police."

He handed Johnny a business card. "On your arrival in San Diego go see this man. He will rent you two cars. Use the false papers. Be careful not to leave prints. When you are through with the cars, simply abandon them."

"Wear gloves while you are in the car," Silvio said.

"That would be best," Salvatore agreed. He reached into a desk drawer and pulled out two pistols. "These Colt Lawman Mark III revolvers cannot be traced. Both are chambered for the .357 magnum cartridge. They also will accept the lighter load of the .38 Special. Which cartridge would you prefer?"

"Magnum," Carlo said.

Johnny hesitated. He had not fired a pistol in years. "The thirty-eight loads, please," he said.

Salvatore put two boxes of cartridges on the desk.

"Unfortunately, Lucian Hall poses more of a problem," Salvatore said. "The man is absolutely paranoid. His house is a fortress. So are his offices. He moves from his home to his office in a bullet-proofed limousine, protected by two guards armed with machine pistols, tear gas, Mace. He is practically beyond our reach."

Silvio reached into his suit pocket and extracted a long cigar. He lit it with ceremony. "Lucian Hall has always posed a problem," he said. "Fortunately, my son Giovanni has a plan."

CHAPTER 6

JOHNNY eased the rented car into a parking space in the shadows, across from the flat, plain concrete building. The block was deserted. Ahead, a street light provided an island in the darkness.

He eased the Colt from the spring-clip shoulder holster, pushed out the cylinder, and checked the loads one last time. Earlier in the day he had dry-fired the weapon long enough to gain familiarity with it. The trigger pull was firm but not excessive. He had no concern about accuracy. The range would be short.

Easing open the car door, he stepped into the street. The pavement was dry, but a strong, damp wind came from the bay a few blocks away, rustling the trash in the gutter. He stood for a moment, carefully searching the adjoining parking lots and side streets. He saw no movement.

He could only hope that Carlo had succeeded in gaining entry.

He closed the car door and walked toward the building with firm, purposeful strides. Circling the building, he headed toward the parking lot in the rear, where he was expected to meet Martinez.

A single bulb lit the space around the back entrance. A blue Lincoln Continental, trimmed in orange, was parked near the door, at the edge of darkness. As Johnny approached, Martinez stepped from the car and walked into the glare of the light.

Johnny recognized him instantly from the photograph—the thin mustache, the dark, curly hair combed straight back, and the wide, open smile.

"Giovanni Moretti," Martinez said. His smile widened. "You walk all the way?"

For a moment Johnny did not answer, making certain no one else was waiting in the car, in the shadows.

"I parked in front," he said. "A simple precaution."

"A good idea," Martinez said. "Come on. Let's get inside."

Johnny waited as Martinez unlocked the door—a plain deadbolt with no burglar alarm. Salvatore Messino's information had been correct.

Latching the door behind them, Martinez led Johnny down a long hallway. Johnny glanced at the doors, searching for some small clue that Carlo had succeeded in breaking into the building. The offices were not of the type that would be overly concerned with security—two insurance firms, an employment agency, a speech therapist. The walls were heavily paneled, the floor well carpeted. Johnny saw no sign of Carlo's presence.

At the end of the hall, Martinez paused to open the door to his suite. The gilt sign on the door said simply:

EDUARDO MARTINEZ
INVESTMENTS, PROPERTIES

Martinez shoved open the door and turned on the lights.

He had tried. He really had, but the office decor went just a step beyond the limits of reasonable taste. The walls were too crowded with mismatched pictures. The receptionist's desk was modern and outlandishly large—too elephantine and severe. The files were a garish blue. Small tables, bookcases cluttered the room, their tops a wonderland of knickknacks and gadgets.

Four doors opened off the reception area. The floor plan on Salvatore Messino's desk was confirmed. Martinez moved toward the door marked PRIVATE. He pushed it open and turned on the light.

"Drink?" he asked.

"No, thanks," Johnny said. He took care not to glance at the closed door of the small bathroom where Carlo had planned to hide.

Martinez gestured Johnny into an armchair and moved behind his desk. His right hand flicked below the desk top briefly. Johnny was certain that from that point the conversation was recorded.

Playing for time, he waited for Martinez to open the discussion. All had gone according to plan, but the office, the building were far more isolated than they had appeared on paper. He was far deeper into the trap than they had anticipated. If Carlo had not been able to force his way into the building, Johnny would be on his own. Casually, he glanced around the office, seeking one of the signs he and Carlo had agreed upon.

He saw none.

Martinez smiled. He was smooth, a trifle too confident. "What can I do for you, Mr. Moretti?"

Johnny stared at Martinez long enough to make him uncomfortable. "You could do a great favor for me, my family, yourself," he said. "You could tell the truth to the state liquor board."

The smile faded. Johnny did not know how much of the irritation Martinez showed was affected. "Those are harsh words," Martinez said. "If I understand, you are implying that I am *not* telling the truth."

"Truth sometimes requires polish," Johnny said. "In its rough stages it may be misunderstood. We have to work with it, refine it."

Martinez hesitated. "How much are you willing to pay, if I will polish my testimony?"

Johnny gave him another stare. "I'm prepared to make it worth your while to tell the truth," he said.

"How much?"

Johnny paused, as if considering his offer. He turned his head casually and glanced at the door to the lavatory.

The sign was there.

An inch above the doorknob, Carlo had made a small mark with a pen.

Carlo was behind the door, listening, waiting.

Johnny turned back to Martinez. "I wouldn't want to disturb the competition," he said. "How much is Lucian Hall paying you?"

Martinez smiled again, but this time there was no humor behind it. "Look, let's cut the bullshit," he said. "I might cooperate with you. But on my terms. I want money. I want protection."

Johnny listened for a moment, searching for faint sounds in the silence of the building. If the trap were to succeed, the quarry should be arriving soon.

"What kind of protection?" he asked, stalling for time.

Martinez leaned forward, elbows on the desk. "Your father can put out the word. I'm not to be harmed. By anyone."

Johnny frowned, listening. From the doorway behind him came a faint sound. The brush of a shoe against carpet? The rustle of clothing? He was certain that someone was beyond the open door, listening. Martinez had not noticed.

"Martinez, I'm prepared to pay you more than Lucian Hall," Johnny said—code words to alert Carlo to be prepared for action. "One thing worries me. If you are reneging on your arrangement with him, why should I expect better treatment?"

A new voice spoke from the doorway. "Moretti's got a point there, Martinez."

Johnny did not move a muscle. Martinez swiveled in his chair to face the door. For a moment Johnny thought Martinez might reach into the desk for a gun.

"Freeze!" the voice said. "Both of you."

Johnny heard the rustle of clothing as someone entered the room behind him. He did not turn. He felt the chill of goosebumps as he awaited the bullets that would come if he had miscalculated. Blood pounded in his temples.

He forced himself to relax, to appear unconcerned.

"Foster!" Martinez said. "We were just talking . . . I haven't done anything!"

The name triggered something in Johnny's memory—Silvio's story of the beating of Dax. *Foster.* Foster and Chipman were the names of the bodyguard-chauffeurs abandoned in the desert.

He heard the movement of another person behind him.

"I'm glad we got here in time, Martinez," Foster said. "I sure wouldn't want you to do anything foolish." He paused and moved into Johnny's range of vision. "But you're dealing with the wrong Moretti. I was hoping it'd be Carlo. Chipman and I owe him. And I hear we just missed nailing him the other night."

Johnny risked looking up. To his amazement, Foster was armed with a small machine pistol—a businesslike little weapon.

Fear constricted Johnny's breathing for a moment. He had to find some way to warn Carlo that he was outgunned. Forcing himself to remain calm, he waited until he could speak casually.

"I'll tell Carlo you asked about him," he said. "But surely there wasn't any need for you to bring a machine gun along. What is that thing?"

Foster grinned. "Ingram machine pistol. Forty-five caliber. Thousand rounds a minute on cyclic." The grin widened. "Want a demonstration? On Martinez?" He pointed the gun at Martinez, whose face quickly drained of color.

Johnny turned his head slightly to make certain of the position of the second man, behind him and to the right. The man was armed only with a revolver.

It was now or never.

Johnny spoke the code words.

"I'd hate to see that happen," he said. "I was just about to make Martinez an offer. I was prepared to go as high as a half-million dollars."

On the word *million* Carlo kicked open the lavatory door. Johnny was already moving. He knew there was not enough time to go for his gun. Instead he dived for the machine pistol, pushing the barrel upward, securing a firm grip on the stock. His charge knocked Foster off balance, and they slammed into the wall. The gun fired, a short roar that filled the air with ceiling plaster and acrid cordite. Johnny brought his knee up into Foster's groin and yanked at the gun, almost bringing the weapon free, loosening Foster's finger from the trigger.

Behind him, Carlo's .357 magnum boomed in three deafening explosions. Then Carlo shouted, "Johnny! Kick loose!"

With all his strength Johnny spun, twisting the gun free, sending Foster against the wall again. Carlo's magnum boomed, but Johnny was not watching.

Martinez had emerged from behind his desk. He was bringing up a pistol, aiming at Carlo.

Without thought Johnny squeezed the trigger of the gun in his hand. The vicious little Ingram sprayed eight forty-five caliber slugs before Johnny could release the trigger. Martinez was knocked backward as forcibly as if he had been hit by a freight train. He collapsed, his chest a red mass of gore.

Johnny glanced behind him. Carlo held his pistol at his side.

Johnny and Carlo stood for a moment, breathing hard. Carlo was grinning. "You all right?" he asked.

Johnny nodded.

Carlo laughed in relief. "When you said *machine gun,* I damned near shit." He caught his breath, laughed again, and looked at the ceiling. "Christ, I thought you would *never* give the word."

Foster and Chipman were dead. Both had been hit in the center of the chest with 158-grain hollow points from Carlo's .357 magnum.

Carlo examined the bodies with satisfaction. "I'm glad to know they're the sons-a-bitches who set the fire," he said. "Makes me feel better about this. A whole lot better."

"We've got to get out of here," Johnny said to Carlo. "Give me your gun."

He took the unfired Smith & Wesson from the body of Martinez. He wiped Carlo's Colt clean of prints and pressed it into the limp hand. Then he removed his own prints from the Ingram, and returned it to Foster. Moving behind the desk, he searched until he found the tape recorder. He stripped out the cassette and put it in his pocket. He stood for a moment, checking carefully, making certain that he and Carlo were leaving nothing behind.

He handed the Smith & Wesson to Carlo. "Let's go," he said.

Carlo lingered for one last look at the Ingram. "Hey, little brother," he said. "Why don't we go after Lucian with that thing?"

Using his handkerchief, Johnny turned out the lights and closed the door.

"Don't worry," he said. "We are taking care of Lucian."

CHAPTER 7

NEVER before in his life had Lucian Hall felt so frightened, so frustrated, so helpless. "You don't understand," he told the guard. "There has been some mistake. I'm Lucian Hall. I'm not the kind of person who is arrested and put in jail."

The guard gave no sign that he had heard. He shoved Lucian through the cell door and slammed it behind him. The men in the crowded holding tank seemed to think Lucian's statement hilarious. They hooted with laughter. Lucian cringed against the bars, overwhelmed by the noise, stench, and hostility.

"Better be careful," one inmate yelled to the jailer. "You're dealin' with a real wheel."

Shaken, Lucian cautiously searched for a place to sit down. The holding tank was L-shaped, with the cell door at the smaller end. He moved to the corner of the L and examined his surroundings. Each of the nearby lower bunks was occupied by a prisoner. A few of the men were seated, but most were lying full-length on the filthy mattresses. A drunk was attempting to urinate into a seatless commode in the corner. As he staggered to keep his footing, he sprayed the concrete floor.

The mingled aromas of stale sweat, vomit, and soured urine were nauseating. Lucian was so disturbed that he spoke his thoughts aloud. "I've got to get out of here."

"Ain't we all?" said a young black in an upper bunk. "You think you got problems! Man, I got tickets to Fleetwood Mac."

Lucian pushed his way past the other prisoners. Near the end of the L he found an empty lower bunk. He spread his overcoat on the sweat-stained mattress and sat down to wait.

His lawyers should have him out within minutes.

The shock of his arrest had left him confused and disoriented. He could not understand how it had happened.

The police car had stopped his limousine within a block of his office. When the red light started flashing, his chauffeur had slowed, watching the rearview mirror.

Lucian was instantly alarmed. "Stephen, what's wrong?" he called through the intercom.

"I don't know, sir," Stephen said. "It looks like an ordinary police car. Ivory, what do you think?"

The security man was turned in his seat, his hand resting on a machine pistol. "Seems legitimate," he said. "You run a stop sign or something?"

"I don't think so," Stephen said.

"We don't want trouble with the police," Lucian said. "We better stop."

As Stephen pulled to the curb, the police car halted immediately behind, the red light still flashing. Stephen stepped from the car as the uniformed officer approached. Lucian heard the exchange clearly on the intercom.

"Mr. Lucian Hall?" the officer asked.

"This is his car."

The policeman glanced at Lucian. "Are you Lucian Hall?"

Lucian nodded through the glass partition.

"Would you step out, please. There are two officers from the state here who have business with you."

Two men in loose-fitting suits approached the car. On the sidewalk, passersby turned to stare. The heavy bulletproofed windows could not be lowered to ask the men what they wanted. Against every instinct, Lucian stepped from the car.

"Mr. Hall, I am Keith Cassidy of the State Attorney General's office. I have here a warrant for your arrest."

His mind reeling, Lucian could only stammer. "For what?"

"It's quite complicated," Cassidy said. "But basically it's for fraud."

Erratically, Lucian's main concern at that moment was to prevent his old arrest for bootlegging from being aired in the news media once again. "I demand that my lawyers be present," he said.

"You will have benefit of counsel before your arraignment," Cassidy said. "I will now inform you of your rights."

As they went through the ceremony, Lucian searched frantically for a way out. He could not risk a charge of resisting arrest; that would only complicate matters. Before the officers led him away, he turned to Ivory.

"Get on the phone. Call my secretary. Tell her to have my attorneys over there immediately."

All through the booking Lucian had expected his lawyers to arrive at any moment.

He was still waiting.

He glanced at his naked wrist before remembering that his watch had been taken from him. He had no way of knowing, but he was certain that more than an hour had elapsed since his arrest.

He could not understand why he had not been released.

His arrest might be legitimate, but men of his position simply were not treated in such high-handed fashion. Usually, even with serious charges, each step was handled on a professional level, with the opposing lawyers present.

Then, with a chill of apprehension, Lucian understood.

His lawyers probably had not been able to locate him. His arrest papers no doubt were temporarily "lost" in the files.

He could assume that Silvio Moretti had taken that precaution.

With mind-freezing certainty, Lucian knew he had been set up for execution. His murderer was now either locked in with him or soon would be coming through the cell door.

Lucian shrank against the wall and studied his fellow prisoners, wondering which one was there to kill him.

The young black? Deep scars on his cheek and forehead, a relentless scowl, and a drooping eyelid gave him more than a hint of evil. On the opposite bunk a drunk sat fiddling with a broken zipper on his jacket, mumbling to himself. Was he only pretending to be drunk? Was he the killer? Or could it be the quiet, small, bald-headed man in the upper bunk, who lay staring at the ceiling with a bemused expression?

Lucian's speculations were interrupted as the cell door opened, then slammed again. Two new prisoners entered. Lucian studied them warily.

The first was square-built, with a bull neck and rounded, close-cropped head. He walked between the bunks, looking neither to the right nor left, his deep-set eyes glowering. Behind him came a lean, gaunt young man with long hair and a scraggly beard. As they approached, the lean one kept searching around nervously, check-ing each face as they walked the length of the cell. His glance fell on Lucian—and lingered.

In panic, Lucian retreated onto the bunk. There was no place to hide. He sat hunched with his back to the wall, his feet on the edge of the mattress.

It would come soon, he reasoned. His lawyers and staff would be working desperately to find him, bringing pressure to bear. If he could only stay alive for a little while . . .

He watched the two new arrivals as they collided in their clumsy attempt to jump into upper bunks.

"You son-of-a-bitch," the bull-necked young man yelled at the gaunt one. "Keep your fuckin' feet out of my face."

He shoved the long-haired scarecrow across the aisle, into the opposite row of bunks. The scarecrow sprawled full-length on the floor, then fought his way to his feet. "Goddamn you, you ain't gonna push me around," he shouted. He aimed a blow at the square-built youth, who caught it with his shoulder.

"Go get him!" bellowed the drunk across from Lucian. "Knock the shit out of him!"

Shouts came from throughout the tank. "Fight! Fight! Give them room!" The cell turned into bedlam as the prisoners jockeyed for a view of the action.

Instinctively, Lucian knew that he himself was the real target of the melee. As the two men grappled, he moved to the edge of his bunk, facing them, ready to leap to one side if they should lunge in his direction.

Then, inexplicably, he was struck by an agonizing pain just beneath his left shoulder blade. Paralyzed, he could not breathe. Twisting, he searched feebly at his back for the source of the pain. He fumbled for several seconds. He could not reach it. His back felt strangely wet.

A few feet from him, the fight continued. Lucian tried to cry out, to attract someone's attention, but no one was turned in his direction. Slowly, he sank to the floor. The concrete was cold against his cheek. And then the lights went out.

Lucian's last moment was filled with a rush of overwhelming terror.

He was afraid of what might happen to him in the dark.

"It is done," Silvio said. He replaced the white phone in his desk drawer.

"Any complications?" Johnny asked.

Silvio rose and walked to the window. He stood looking out over Sonoma. "None," he said. "Of course, there will be investigations —the arrest, misplaced records, the other prisoners in the cell. Nothing will be found."

He glanced at Johnny.

"However, there is one more development. One that may affect our lives. Emil Borneman committed suicide. His body was found in his car, near Glen Ellen. There was a pistol beside the body. And a note. It seems that Emil was our source of sabotage—and of our leaks to Lucian Hall."

Johnny looked at his father. Silvio answered his unasked question.

"No. I had nothing to do with Emil's death. It was his own idea."

BOOK
6

*"Today you have to be smarter and tougher
. . . and more self-reliant and understanding."*

—Giovanni Moretti

CHAPTER 1

GENTLY easing the casket free from the hearse, the pall-bearers slowly carried their burden across the dry, brittle grass toward the open grave. Christina followed her mother, stepping carefully on the rough ground. Two rows of folding chairs awaited them under a wall-less tent. The sky was overcast and threatening. A gentle breeze whipped the canvas. Christina took her mother's arm as they circled the grave, now covered by her father's coffin. Garish green plastic grass provided a carpet in front of the chairs. Christina tried, but there was no way to avoid it.

Sophia had been the only one to shed tears. Margaret, with her remarkable ability to adapt to any occasion, was handling the funeral almost as a social event. Christina disapproved of her mother's manner. Yet she could not bring herself to feel sorrow for her father. She had not loved him—had, in fact, hated him at times. Now, facing his casket poised over the grave, she felt only a sad, lingering regret. She wished she could have known him better, that they could have settled their differences.

She had not wanted to come to the funeral, but somehow she had known, despite her reluctance, that she needed to close this chapter in her life.

Dr. Chesler had given her tranquilizers. She had not needed them. The long flight west, the sympathy calls at the house, the church service had been taxing, but she had borne it. And now it was almost over.

The minister who had conducted the church services took his place at the head of the casket. He motioned for the mourners to gather closer around the grave.

Christina was surprised at the number. At the church, seated in the front row, she had not been able to see much of the congregation. She had assumed that most were workers from the winery, her mother's various friends, but as she faced them across her father's grave, she recognized others—Sam Cavanaugh; Robert and Peter Mondavi; Sam and Don Sebastiani; Brother Timothy of the Christian Brothers.

Aware of her lapse of discretion, she lowered her gaze. The minister began the service. For a time she tried to concentrate on his words, but her thoughts wandered to incidents of her childhood, when her father had been a different man.

Her reverie was disturbed by the feeling that someone was staring at her. She endured the annoyance for several seconds, then glanced up in defiance.

She was so jolted that she almost spoke out.

Johnny Moretti was looking at her, his face expressionless, his eyes filled with such naked love, so much meaning, that for the moment Christina was overwhelmed. His gaze did not waver.

And suddenly, without reason, she knew more than she could understand.

Something was terribly wrong. She sensed it from the pain, the suffering she read in Johnny's eyes.

The silent, significant exchange seemed to last an eternity.

Then the spell was broken by the click of the mechanism lowering the casket into the grave.

Christina looked away, shaken. Her mother glanced at her in apprehension. Around her all was confusion. She was vaguely aware that the service had ended. Numb, she went through the formalities of receiving condolences—Brother Timothy, the Sebastianis, the Mondavis . . .

And then Silvio was there, murmuring something to her mother. Johnny stood beside him.

Silvio seemed older. She was surprised to see tears welling in his eyes. He took her hand. "I wish there were some way to make this easier for you, Christina," he said. "You have my deepest sympathy."

Christina thanked him and he moved on.

Johnny took both her hands in his and stood for several seconds, saying nothing, only looking into her eyes.

Then he gently squeezed her hands, turned, and walked away.

Christina moved through the next two hours in a daze. She kept remembering the emotion in Silvio's face, the unspoken message in Johnny's eyes.

She knew.

With disorienting speed the many mysteries of her life were answered. But with each solution came more questions, more doubts.

She waited until the guests, and Sophia and her family had gone. Her mother fixed coffee and brought it into the living room. Margaret was chatting, almost mindlessly, about her plans to move to an apartment in Sonoma and open a studio. Christina waited until the right moment.

"He wasn't my father, was he?" she asked quietly.

Margaret's face drained of color. One hand flew to her throat. The other carefully guided her coffee cup to safety. "Who . . . who told you that?" she asked, her voice trembling.

"He hated me. I hated him. You know that. There has to be an answer."

Margaret lost her composure. She seemed on the verge of tears. "Please, Christina. Not now!"

"There's no better time," Christina said. "He ruined my life! Why? The reason is so obvious. Why didn't I see it?"

Margaret took her hand. "Christina, you're upset . . ."

Christina freed herself from her mother's grip. "Look me in the eye and tell me that he was my father," she demanded.

Margaret turned away, her face buried in her hands.

Christina waited, making no move to comfort her. "Then who was it?" she asked quietly. "Who *is* my father?"

Margaret did not answer.

"Mother, tell me! Don't I, of all people, have the right to know?"

Still no answer.

"Is it common gossip in Sonoma? Is it someone so terrible, someone so low that when Johnny heard, he turned away from me?"

"No!" Margaret's cry of protest was primal. Again she reached for Christina.

Again Christina shoved her away. "Who?" she demanded.

Margaret would not answer.

But Christina knew. She spoke the name with certainty. "Silvio Moretti."

Margaret jerked erect. Her arms flailed in a helpless gesture. For a moment she could not speak. When words came, they tumbled out, defensively, frantically. "You have no reason to be ashamed! Silvio is the most magnificent man I have ever known. You can hold your head up! He loves you. He keeps up with everything you are doing. He has helped you in many, many ways. You never . . ."

Christina ceased listening. The message in Johnny's eyes now made sense.

"Then Johnny knew," she said.

"Something had to be done." Her mother stopped for a moment to dab at her eyes. "When we realized you were in San Francisco, there with him, and we didn't know what might happen, of course we had to tell him. Silvio drove down . . ."

"Oh, my God!" Christina lowered her head to the cushions of the couch, her mind a whirlwind of emotions. Scores, hundreds of innuendos, remarks, and puzzling situations were resolved. She lay for a moment, trying to absorb all she had just heard.

No wonder she had always felt such an outsider.

No wonder the Morettis had always held such fascination for her.

Without warning, anger came. She raised herself from the couch and screamed at her mother. "Why in hell didn't you tell me?"

Margaret flinched as if she had been struck. "Christina! There were so many people to consider . . ."

"And my mind, my sanity could be sacrificed! No one cared about that! And Johnny! Good God! Think of what he's been through!"

Overwhelmed, blinded by tears, she fled up the stairs to her room. She slammed the door and threw the bolt. When Margaret knocked a few minutes later, Christina refused to let her in.

She did not leave the room for two days—not until her mother brought Silvio to talk to her.

CHAPTER 2

*T*HEY met in the limestone wine cellars—vast caves lined with barrels of aging wine. The initiate was instructed to remain outside while various formalities were concluded. Silvio waited with him.

Carlo was nervous, restless. "I don't understand. Johnny went along with the other. Why won't he go all the way?"

"Johnny is a thinker," Silvio said. "He must reason things out. Give him time."

"But we ought to do it together," Carlo said. He drove his fists together. "Damn, I wish he were here."

Silvio did not answer. Carlo was right. Tonight there should be two initiates—the sons of Silvio Moretti. And the only answer Silvio had was Johnny's reply: "Pop, that is not my way."

What was Johnny's way?

Of all the men Silvio had known throughout his long life, his son Giovanni was the most complex. Stubborn, obstinate, yet capable of surprising flexibility. Idealistic almost to the point of naiveté, still he possessed that rare talent for cold, objective analysis. Gentle, sensitive, he had demonstrated as well that if the occasion warranted, he could be merciless.

Silvio sighed. There were no limits to what such a son could accomplish, given the foundation his father had built.

And that foundation had never been in better order. Once again proof had been offered that the Morettis were not to be taken lightly, by anyone. The effects of that lesson would be widely noted and long lasting.

The death of Lucian Hall in a jail cell had created a sensation in the press and on television. Thus far, the investigations had produced only increased confusion, accusations, and countercharges. The police and the news media were still attempting to put the pieces together. Now Lucian's death slowly was taking on the aura of police ineptitude. The triple slaying in San Diego was assumed to be the result of a dispute between Martinez and Lucian Hall's men, in which Martinez was foolish enough to draw his revolver in the face of a machine pistol. Silvio had no worries. All tracks were covered.

On the news of Lucian's death, Hampton Industries stock had plunged eighteen points. Through intermediaries, Silvio had bought heavily. Negotiations were now under way for Hampton Industries to trade company-owned shares to cover excessive short-term indebtedness. As yet, no one knew that Silvio held the paper. As soon as his portfolio could be consolidated, Silvio would be principal stockholder of Hampton Industries. With his existing influence on the board, the takeover soon would be only a formality.

Johnny had made it all possible.

And now Johnny refused to participate.

What could a father do with such a son?

Silvio breathed deeply of the rich aroma from the wine aging in Yugoslavian oak. He wondered how best to approach Johnny.

The situation with Christina complicated matters. He must make Johnny understand that he had always intended to do justice to her—the one serious mistake of his life.

If he only had enough time . . .

Behind him the doors opened. He turned to Carlo. "In the ceremony, show your courage. Look them in the eye. They will respect you."

Carlo was ushered in.

Silvio stood for a moment, reluctant to enter. He listened to the silence of the wine cave, alert for footsteps, hoping that at the last minute Johnny might have changed his mind.

But he knew it to be an old man's foolish hope. He was alone in the vaulted chamber.

He turned and walked on into the deepest cellar, illuminated by candles in silver holders on a long table. There he served as witness as Carlo took the oath of the brotherhood.

And when the time came, Carlo held the purple grape, the burning paper in his bare palm, and repeated the words . . .

"If I ever violate this oath, may I burn as this paper burns . . . and be crushed as this grape is crushed . . ."

Carlo held his hands without tremor as all watched the flickering flames.

CHAPTER 3

SHORTLY after dark, the phone rang. Johnny did not answer. After a dozen rings it stopped. For a while it remained silent. Then it rang again.

Johnny crossed the room, unplugged it, and returned to his chair, unwilling to accept intrusion on the serenity he had achieved during his two days of seclusion.

For hours he sat in the semidarkness of his living room, watching heavy fog play around the lights of the fantail. Don Gato lay in his bed, all four legs in the air. From time to time the big tomcat's paws jerked briefly to dreams—his only movement. Outside, rain began to fall through the fog, heightening the illusion of isolation.

Johnny had expected remorse, guilt, a multitude of emotions after his return from San Diego. Instead he felt only a constant, oppressive moral weight he knew would be with him for the remainder of his life. Silvio's long-ago lectures on the burden of responsibility for one's actions took on new and deeper meaning. He now knew what his father had endured.

But he also realized that he could not shirk from his accountability. He had done what honor—and his father—demanded. He had honored the old ways. But it was a new, rapidly changing world. One not only had to be smarter and tougher but also more self-reliant and understanding. He now knew that far more important than human life were the principles that made life worth living. He had learned that idealism alone would not suffice.

With this conviction—his freedom—he had resigned from the firm. His caseload had been reduced in anticipation of his honeymoon, so his departure was far less complicated than it might have been.

Near midnight, a faint tapping brought him from the edge of sleep. He looked up. Christina was standing on the afterdeck, huddled against the rain.

Johnny hurried to slide back the glass door. She did not move. "Johnny. Why didn't you tell me?" she asked.

He took her arm and brought her inside. She was soaked, her hair plastered against her face. He pulled her to him for a moment, then walked her toward the fire. "Let's get you warm and dry. Then we'll talk."

When he returned with towels and a robe, she had not moved. But she was trembling now, crying. "Why? Oh, why didn't you tell me?"

Gently, he slipped her raincoat from her shoulders. He blotted the rain from her hair and bundled her in the robe. Then he held her for several minutes until she quieted.

"Why?" she asked again softly.

He framed her face in his hands and looked into her eyes. "Christina, losing you was more than I could bear," he said. "I was devastated. I couldn't subject you to what I went through."

He took her to the couch and went for brandy. When he returned, she was more composed. She managed a smile. "This whole thing has been a nightmare. But you know, for the first time in my life I may get all the little pieces together. Become a whole person. I feel it."

He held her hands and nodded his understanding.

"There *are* compensations," she said. "I've lost the perfect lover. But we will always be more than brother and sister. I'll never regret that it happened."

Again he nodded understanding. Nothing would ever break the bond of their shared tragedy. Christina put it into words.

"I guess what I'm trying to say is that I now need you as much, or maybe even more than ever."

He took her into his arms and held her.

He continued to comfort her through the long night as the frustrations and fears, the suppressed anger of two decades poured out of her. He listened quietly as she told him of the puzzling incidents of her childhood, of her sense of flawed identity, of the uncanny attraction the Moretti family always held for her. She described her desperate battle to retain her sanity, the series of doctors thwarted by her meager clues.

At last, toward morning, he walked her back up the pier to her car.

Afterward, he remained awake, planning his future.

He was uncertain what lay ahead. In time, he might be able to return to his father and say, "I am ready." But that would not come until he was in a position to add, "I will do our work, but on my own terms."

He would have to find his way into this new world, where old methods no longer worked, old beliefs were no longer valid. Greater things remained to be done, and he would have to find ways to do them. He sensed that perhaps Greg Cavanaugh would be an important part of his future. Greg had that indefinable quality the media called charisma, but he needed direction, guidance, purpose. Together, he and Greg could accomplish things their fathers had never dreamed possible.

With the first hint of light in the east he made a pot of coffee and brought it back to the couch. Overnight the sky had cleared. The Bay was calm and peaceful. Quietly sipping his coffee, he watched the dawn of the new day.